Tim

Daniel A. Sheridan

Tim

ISBN: 9798352032596

Tim

FOR KATHLEEN

Tim

To My Little Doritt,

For patiently waiting all these years for me to finish my never-ending story.

With love,

Bartleby

CONTENTS

Tim - Book I: The Deerslayer

"And where, then, is your sweetheart, Deerslayer?"

"She's in the forest, Judith—hanging from the boughs of the trees, in a soft rain—in the dew on the open grass—the clouds that float about in the blue heavens—the birds that sing in the woods—the sweet springs where I slake my thirst—and in all the other glorious gifts that come from God's Providence!"

James Fenimore Cooper

Tim

FOREWORD

I first learned about Timothy H. O'Sullivan while studying the history of photography at New York University in the spring of 1989. Professor Silver clicked back and forth in a slide show comparing O'Sullivan's 1873 photograph, Ancient Ruins in the Cañon de Chelle, N.M., with Ansel Adams' view taken in 1942.

I became curious about this photographer who apprenticed for Mathew B. Brady and inspired Ansel Adams with his large-format, view camera. I then went to the Museum of Modern Art to view the photographs of O'Sullivan. At the time, I worked as a darkroom technician restoring old black and white photographs, while studying photojournalism at college.

New York University is an important place in the history of photography. This is where Brady's mentor, Samuel Morse, experimented with the new discovery he recently brought back from Paris — the Daguerreotype. His colleague, Dr. John William Draper, a chemistry professor, took one of the first known portraits with a camera on the rooftop of the university at Washington Square.

Little is known about O'Sullivan. As James D. Horan states in his biography, Timothy O'Sullivan: America's Forgotten Photographer, "There were few clues, only his name, a four-line obituary..." Though we don't know much about Tim. What remains are his photographs.

One day after class, I stood on the corner of Broadway and Tenth, the former location of one of Brady's Studios. Looking at Grace Church, I thought about O'Sullivan and his photographs. Over to the right, down the street, is The Ritz where I saw The Replacements in 1986 perform songs from their album Tim. I then decided to write a book about O'Sullivan as a young apprentice at Mathew Brady's studio and the title would be Tim...

From the outset, I must say this is a collective work. Whenever and wherever possible, I have relied on the ghosts from the past in their own words. Without them, I would not have been able to write this book. [Please see End Notes.] Among the many contributors, I wish to thank: Professor Robert Scally, the History of Ireland at NYU, Walt Whitman for his Omnibus Jaunts; P.T. Barnum for his humble Autobiography, Katy Havens for her Diary of a Little Girl in Old New York; George Townsend for taking the time to interview Mathew Brady; Gabriel Harrison for his contributions to The Photographic Art Journal; David Lear Buckman for his History of Steamboats; James David Horan for his books on Brady and O'Sullivan; and Beaumont Newhall for The Daguerreotype in America, The History of Photography, and last but not least, Timothy H. O'Sullivan.

CHAPTER 1 — STATEN ISLAND

1850

"Jeremiah! Open Up!" Margaret Brown aged about thirty dressed in her chambermaid uniform tugs on the bell-pull but hears no ring. Must be broken. She raps her knuckles upon the white wooden door. "I know you're in there. It's no use, Jeremiah. You can't hide from me." She listens for a moment. "Please, Jerry I have something very important to tell you."

From the steps of Saint Peter's Church after early morning mass, Margaret had made her way to Jeremiah T. O'Sullivan's house. Behind the church stood the Pavilion, the grand hotel on Richmond Terrace overlooking the Kill van Kull on this glorious mid-September morn. Ah, how the Kill sparkled in the sun, the sea gulls hovered in the breeze, and the cat boats bobbed in the water tethered at anchor. The fresh air snapped the clean sheets taught like land-locked sails. Last night's storm had boiled off the doldrums and the end of summer heat. For yesterday and days before, the air had hung heavy, hot and oppressive like wet laundry sagging on the line making each exertion in her work at the Pavilion all-the-more difficult.

Margaret stepped briskly along the 200-foot promenade of the grand hotel with over 300 rooms to clean and 300 chamber pots to empty, known throughout the land as the most fashionable summer retreat for the wealthy, the influential, and the famous. Beyond the Pavilion bathhouse, beyond the stones drying in the sun at low-water mark, lay the city of York surrounded by hundreds of ship masts as if faint brush strokes on canvas.

She twirled herself round one of the massive Ionic columns and thought back to last night, a night she won't soon forget, September 11, 1850 — the concert at Castle Garden to hear Jenny Lind, the Swedish Nightingale, perform at her American premiere. Miss Jenny handed out tickets to the crowd gathered at the Staten Island dock as Mr. P.T. Barnum, her manager, waited there to greet her. Mr. Genin, the hatter, had purchased the first ticket for $225. On the ferry ride over, Margaret could see the walkway lit up at night leading out from Battery Park to the little island, Castle Garden, a circular stone fort transformed into a magnificent concert hall.

Clutching their yellow tickets, ushers escorted Maggie and her friends up to the balcony lit up with yellow lamps. "Oh, how I wish we had blue tickets," said one of the girls motioning down near the stage lit in blue. The audience of 5,000 simmered with anticipation, then erupted with three cheers waving their hats and handkerchiefs as Miss Jenny approached the

1

footlights escorted by Mr. Julius Benedict who then took his seat at the piano as the Sweet Warbler sang the opening notes of Casta Diva.

At intermission, Margaret saw none other than Mrs. Mathew B. Brady standing there holding a glass of champagne milling about. She motioned her to come over as they often exchange cordial glances after mass. "Call me Julia," she insisted. She took a sip from her crystal glass. "Tell me, would your nephew, Timothy, be interested in apprenticing at my husband's daguerreotype portrait gallery?"

Out on the veranda, Margaret checked the menu behind the glass frame for the day's luncheon – stuffed egg, chicken mulligatawny, potatoes persillade, spiced watermelon, sour gherkins, crab meat salad, peach pie, and banana ice cream.

"Such lovely food in such great abundance," she thought to herself "Not just potatoes, but potatoes persillade seasoned with parsley and garlic. To think back home in Ireland, all of us sitting round the table, Mother serving us spuds with butter and nothing else. It was all she had. I do hope one of the boys sets aside an extra plate for me."

"Oh, my goodness, look at the time, I'll be needing to be at work before long." She hurried off to the sound of her boot heels clicking against the Belgian blocks paving the way along Richmond Terrace. "Good news travels fast. Good news travels fast."

Margaret continues knocking on the door. The tap-tapping of her knocking telegraphs through the door jamb past the header up the studs to the second floor of Jeremiah's bedroom with three dogs on the bed. Pepper nuzzles her head on the crest of his ankle, Rex sprawls out in the middle, while little Salty sleeps by the pillow at the head of the bed.

"Wood, wood, wood," mutters Jeremiah to his pillow. "Wooden beams, wooden floors, wooden doors. All the houses here are built entirely of wood. Back home, we'd never build a house with wood. Remember the cold earthen floor of the cottage in Kenmare, the stone walls, the thatched roof, and the smell of burning peat as you stooped low to enter."

"Why they even toss wood on the fire without so much as a care. Who would do such a thing? Burning perfectly fine wood. Back home in Ireland, we'd be out in the field, spading the turf. The peat bricks from the bog set out to dry, to keep the home fire burning." At times, for just a fleeting moment, he hesitates when tossing a log on the fire. "Someday they'll be no trees left and I'll be kicking myself for turning this to ash. But no," he tells himself, "this is America, the land of plenty."

The latch on the front door lifts from the inside. A boy about ten years old opens the door dressed in his nightshirt and bare feet rubbing his eyes in the bright morning sun.

"Good morning, Aunt Margaret."

"Good morning, Timothy. And why may I ask, are you not dressed yet?

It's nearly quarter to eight, you'll be late for school. Why were you not in attendance yesterday and all week from what I hear? Are you ill, boy!" She puts her hand to his forehead.

Tim's lips move as if to say something, but there is no response.

"Well, I have no time for your excuses, young man. Do you intend on inviting me in? Where's your hospitality?"

Aunt Margaret wipes the soles to her shoes on the rusty boot-scrape, steps into the front room off to the left, and has a look around. "A fine parlor it isn't. Though not a filthy pigsty, the room could use a good deal of scrubbing. The dull floors need waxing. The rug with all that dog hair should be taken out and given a good whack."

She sits herself down on a wooden bench seat with a rumpled cushion. "The pew at church was more comfortable. My how Father Mark Murphy looks just like his older brother, Patrick. Twins really. Remember Father Patrick saying mass day after day at Saint Peter's despite the Yellow Fever panic last summer. Black Vomit people call it. That's a more apt name to my mind than Yellow Fever. People terrified to go out. But not Father Pat, then the fever finally took hold of him. Now Father Mark is carrying on his brother's work. One brother saying mass above, the other buried under the altar below."

"Would you look at those cobwebs hanging about the walls there and all the dust clouds in the corner. The glass to the kerosene lantern is all black and the wick needs trimming. The white lace curtains are a dismal yellow. Sparkling clean windows would so brighten up the place."

And there on the opposite wall in a small wooden frame is a silhouette of her dear sister, Anne. Against an oval white background, her profile had been shadowed and traced on black paper to give a haunting likeness. Her hair pulled back tight. She had such a fine nose — those long lashes — you can almost see her eyes.

"Where is your father?"

"He's upstairs in bed."

"Oh, he is, is he? Well, would you ask him to please come down? I have something urgent to discuss with him."

"Yes, certainly Aunt Margaret."

Poor Anne at that godforsaken Quarantine Station. Those glassy eyes, lying on that bed with warm bricks at her feet, a mustard poultice applied over her stomach, delirious with the cholera. Trying to get a spoonful of castor oil in her and some pennyroyal tea, but nothing, nothing seemed to help.

Upstairs, Tim knocks, the barking dogs erupt once more, he shuts the door behind him.

"Pa, Aunt Maggie is downstairs. She wants to see you right away."

Jeremiah breathes out a soft sigh and turns over in his bed. "So, I've heard. Tell your Aunt Margaret I'll be down directly." The dogs rustle themselves out of bed and dance about the door with anxious morning bladders, the long claws of their paws clicking on the wooden floor. "And Tim, be a good lad and take the dogs out."

The three dogs bound down the stairs bouncing into each other in a stampede. They race through the parlor to the back door where they wait for Tim. Margaret makes her way to the kitchen.

"What on earth is all the commotion?" she asks as Tim lets the dogs out the back door. "Those animals should be kept where they belong. Outside."

Tim offers no response as he shuts the door and takes a seat at the kitchen table facing the black cast iron stove. Margaret sits herself down waiting in silence for Jeremiah to come downstairs.

"What, has he fallen back to bed?" she says half to herself. Just then, Jeremiah makes his grand entrance. At forty-one years, he looks old and young at the same time, grey hair going white with that school-boy face underneath the silver stubble of his unshaven face.

"Margaret. Thank you for stopping by to visit on this lovely morn." In his undershirt and suspenders, he reaches for a match on a shelf above the cast iron stove and then lights up his white clay pipe. His hair is sticking up. "I'll have a cup of tea for you shortly."

"No need to trouble yourself, Jeremiah. I have only a few matters to discuss with yourself in private and I'll be on my way."

There is an awkward pause. Margaret looks Jeremiah directly in the eye and raises her eyebrow. He returns her glare with a confused gaze. She stares hard and directs his questioning eyes towards Tim seated beside her.

"Tim, why don't you be a good lad and go out and keep an eye on the dogs while I have a word with your Aunt." The boy heads upstairs to change out of his nightshirt. "Are you sure, I couldn't interest you in a cup of tea. It would be no trouble."

"Well, all right then. If you insist, I don't mind if I do."

"I would only be too happy to oblige. How are things at the Grand Pavilion?" he asks as he busies himself lighting the stove and preparing the teapot.

"Fine, just fine. Most of the summer visitors from the Southern States have made their leave back home. They are so wealthy and so generous. And they pronounce their words ever so slowly and softly, Jerry. They don't say the word 'July' like you or I, oh no, they draw it out in a long note, Juuuuly. It is sad to see another season come to a close. Why, Mister Giuseppe Garibaldi spent the entire summer at our estate!"

"Imagine that. Mister Garibaldi at your establishment."

"That's not all. A fortnight ago, Mr. P. T. Barnum himself dined at the Pavilion then he waited at the Staten Island dock for Jenny Lind to arrive from England on board the steamship Atlantic."

"You don't say."

"Then Miss Jenny handed out complimentary tickets to her concert at Castle Garden. Me and the girls went."

"What's she like?"

"Oh, you should have seen it, Jerry. It was magical. Her singing Comin' Thro the Rye. She's an angel, a true nightingale."

"Imagine that. You and Jenny Lind fast friends. So, what do I owe the honor of your presence?" he says with a puff on his clay pipe.

"Well, Jeremiah, I promised Anne I would help look after the boys. It's just that if you must know I am deeply concerned about Timothy's future. Brother Finnerty told me Tim has not been to school these past few days."

"The boy has had a terrible cough. I'm his father. I'll have you know. I can take care of him. Don't you worry."

"Jerry, you didn't give me a chance to finish. Simmer down, simmer down. You're doing a fine job. Will you let me finish, please?"

"I'm listening."

"Well, you'll never guess who I ran into last night at Castle Garden?" She cannot bear to wait a split-second for his reply. "Why none other than Mrs. Mathew B. Brady. By the way, Father Mark Murphy has asked about you."

"Oh, he has, has he? I'm sure it's my donation he misses and not my attendance."

"Shush. Quiet." Tim comes down the stairs through the kitchen and out the back door. "Would you listen to yourself? What kind of an example are you setting for your son? Remember his brother? Father Patrick died from the Yellow Fever? He is a saint and a martyr."

"I will not be reprimanded in my own house. If you have nothing more important to say, I will take my leave and kindly show you the door."

"Please, Jerry, hear me out. That's all I ask."

"Well, have your say."

"All right then. As I was saying, I spoke to Mrs. Brady at the concert. You remember the work you did at the Brady residence?"

"Yes, the grand estate with fourteen rooms up on Grymes Hill. Cottages they call them! Remember the cottages we had back home, Maggie? Now those were cottages. My father slept all twelve children at one end and all the livestock at the other, the pigs and the cow, you didn't want to sleep at the low end."

Margaret cuts him short. "That's enough about back home."

"Do the Brady's want to settle their account? They still owe me for several days work."

"Well, that may very well be the case, but that is not the reason I came here. I came to discuss young Tim."

"Make your point woman. I am not long for this world." He stands up

5

and tends to the tea setting tray. He pours Margaret a cup and filters out the tea leaves.

"Thank you," she takes a sip, gulps, then proceeds on. "Well, Mrs. Brady would like Timothy to apprentice for her husband, Mr. Mathew B. Brady at his Daguerreotype Portrait Gallery."

"Apprentice for Mr. Mathew B. Brady, is it?" He runs his course hand through his hair and arches his shoulder back. "But, school at Saint Peter's has just begun and I had hoped he would follow in my footsteps like Thomas."

"And what? Become a carpenter?"

"What do you have against carpenters? Joseph was a carpenter."

"You needn't tell me about that, Jeremiah. The point is Timothy is not quite like Thomas."

"How do you mean?"

"You have eyes, haven't you? Thomas is big and strong and not given to foolish airs of daydreaming. You are too easy on Tim. I've seen him walking the beach, lolling in the grass, reading books, and staring out to sea when he should have been working this summer. It's not right. I'm afraid he has the touch of the poet. I have seen what the affliction did to my lay-about brother and his poor wife."

"Not right? He's just a boy yet. Summer is for children. There'll be time enough for work. He has a good head on his shoulders. He does very well with his schoolwork, except of course for arithmetic. He does get so rattled with the measurements and fractions then miss-cuts the lumber."

"But what good does it do him? How does reading and writing help him put bread on the table for a family? Do you want him to go hungry? You remember what that's like? Jerry, the boy needs a trade to make it in this world."

"Which is why I planned for him to take after me. He'll make a fine carpenter someday."

"When's the last time you had steady work?"

"The work has been slow. Very slow. But Mr. Charles Kennedy Hamilton has grand plans – a whole plot of land with 14-room cottages for all the Broadway big wigs. Hamilton Park he plans to call it."

"But what about today? You can't buy bread with empty promises. Tim will at least have steady work through the winter months. And look at you, walking round with your cracked back."

"It's true, I may not be as strong as I once was. But I am a respected carpenter who takes pride in his work."

"Jeremiah, I'm not here to debate the merits of carpentry. You'll get no argument out of me. It's a fine, fine profession. You've done very well for yourself buying this property and building this house for Anne. I'm just here to convey to you what Mrs. Brady told me and be on me way. If you want the boy to miss the opportunity of a lifetime, it will be on your conscience. I'm only trying to help."

"Well, what sort of work is it?"

"You've had your likeness taken, haven't you?"

"No actually, I've never seen the need. Tis' all vanity."

"Well, I don't know what else I can say to convince you. He'll be working for Mr. Mathew B. Brady. Does that mean anything to you?"

"I know all about Brady of Broadway and his Gallery of Illustrious Americans. Don't I read the papers?"

"Yes, so I've noticed," she says glancing at the stacks of newspapers in the kitchen. "Really Jeremiah, you should burn all of this clutter, all these papers."

"What on earth for? I've paid good money for these papers. It's like having my own library."

"Well, I think Mr. Brady would pay Timothy very handsomely at one dollar a week. Just look at the house they live in."

"Alright, I'll think it over and discuss the matter with Tim."

"That's the thing, there'll be no time to be 'thinking it over'. Mrs. Brady wants him to start first thing tomorrow. 'Have him at the Studio on Broadway tomorrow at half seven, sharp,' she said. You do know where his studio is?"

From his confused look, Margaret explains before giving him a chance to answer. "It's at 205 Broadway on the corner of Fulton Street."

"Whereabouts do you mean? It's been sometime since I've been over to York. I need my bearings."

Exasperated, Margaret explains. "Just before Saint Paul's Chapel across the street from Barnum's American Museum."

"I don't know if I want Tim working over in York. I don't like it. I don't like it one bit."

"What's not to like? He'll be working on Broadway."

"It's not right. People living on top of each other — who'll cut your throat and dump you in the Hudson as soon as look at you. It's a powder keg set to go off. You remember last year's Astor Place Riot, near thirty people killed, the seventh regiment called out. I moved here to get away from all that."

"Well, Jeremiah, like it or no, that's where the jobs are to be had, in case you haven't noticed. He won't be finding any work in sleepy Staten Island."

"I know, I know. But I'd rather he didn't leave home just yet. He's still a boy. You know the old saw, 'How do you keep the boy on the farm once he's seen Paris.' I'm afraid he won't ever come back."

"Not to worry. He'll be coming home every night on the ferry. I'll make sure of that. Don't you worry."

Jeremiah looks at her and mulls it over while rubbing the scruff of his beard. "Alright then, you've sold me on the idea, Margaret."

"Mrs. Brady will be so pleased. I've already checked the ferry schedule and The Josephine leaves at nine."

"But what about his teachers and lessons?"

"I've discussed the matter with Brother Finnerty. Take him over to York and show him the way to Brady's." She pauses a moment and reaches into her petticoat. "And take this," she says taking his hand, tucking money into his pried closed fist.

"No, Margaret, I couldn't."

"Think nothing of it. Show him a grand time. Get yourselves something at one of the eating houses. Daniel Sweeny serves up a hearty meal. And whatever you do, make sure he is at work bright and early."

"I will."

"You wouldn't want him to be late on his first day of work."

"He will be on time."

"Good. Oh yes, I nearly forgot, be sure to buy him some proper shoes, he can't be barefoot on Broadway."

Jeremiah nods.

"Then I'll be on me way."

"Don't you want to tell Tim the news?"

"Oh, goodness no! Jeremiah. It must come from you. You're his father, he listens to you."

"Well, at least stay while I tell the boy all about it."

"No, I think not. It would be better for you to tell him on your own — father to son. Please, I would only be in the way."

"Well then, I'll respect your wishes. Let me call him in before you go." Jeremiah opens the back door and sees Tim throwing a stick about the yard for the dogs to fetch. "Tim come in and say goodbye to Aunt Maggie."

As he shuts the front door afterwards, Jeremiah motions to Tim. "I need to have a word with you."

"Pa, is it about not going to school? I was not feeling well and did not wish to disturb you and Thomas — you both needed your rest."

"So, you were only concerned with our well-being. How very good of you to look after us, Timothy. Really, I don't know how to thank you. In fact, I owe you an apology, for truth be told, I thought you might have been trying to avoid your lessons."

"Oh, no Pa. I was not feeling well."

"Well, please accept my sincerest apology for thinking that."

"Yes, Pa."

"Good then, I just wanted to make sure you realized this." There is a momentary awkward pause. Thinking the discussion has ended Tim gets up from the kitchen table and starts to leave. His father puts his big paw on the boy's shoulder and sits him back down. "You'll leave, when I say you can leave, and not a moment before."

"Yes, Pa."

His father gets up and pours himself and his son a cup of tea. "Here you go, Tim," he says as he places the tea on the table. "Now then, you remember over the summer that nice lady, Mrs. Brady, when you helped Tom and I build that cottage on Grymes Hill."

"She gave us each a bottle of Sands Sarsaparilla. It purifies the blood. Very kind."

"Yes, that's right, that's right. Well, the thing is I've arranged for you to apprentice at Mr. Brady's shop. What do you think of that?"

Tim does not respond. The silence is broken by the sound of the dogs barking outside. He gets up and lets them inside. They bump into each other looking for a pat on the head, a possible table scrap, and then take their place underneath the table.

"So, Tim won't that be grand."

"But what about school?"

"You've had enough of school. You start tomorrow."

"Tomorrow?"

"Yes, bright and early."

"For how long?"

"Well, you'll apprentice for four or five years, then become a journeyman for another five, and then after that, who knows with a little luck, you'll become a full-fledged master of your trade and one day own your very own shop. Won't that be grand?"

"For the rest of my life until I die?"

"Tim, don't make it sound like a death sentence. I'm not sending you up the River."

"But you told me I'd be working with you and Thomas soon as I finished my schooling."

"Well, I've changed my mind. It's for your own good, Tim. You'll be working in a nice fancy establishment on Broadway. You won't have to burden yourself lugging heavy lumber or falling off ladders or gashing yourself with the teeth of the saw. You'll become a fine gentleman."

"But I like working with you and Thomas."

"There's no two ways about it. That's final. I've made my decision."

Rather than look his father in the eye, Tim looks down at the oak grain of the kitchen table and does not respond.

"Well, if it isn't Mr. Rip Van Winkle awoken from his twenty-year slumber!" says his father as Thomas makes his grand entrance. The sixteen-year-old with sandy-blond hair looking a little worse for the wear takes a seat at the kitchen table.

"What's all this talk? I hear my name being bandied about. It had all better be good," says Thomas.

"And what time did you get in from playing nine pins with the boys last night may I ask?"

"Must have been just after you went to bed."

"Well if you say so, Rip," says his father half-mockingly. He quotes in his deep narrator voice from the oft-told bedtime story. "The strange man with a keg of liquor – the mountain ravine – The wild retreat among the rocks – the woe-begone party at nine pins – the flagon…"

As if on cue, Timothy and Thomas join in chorus, "Oh! That flagon! That wicked flagon!"

"All right lads, no time to dally. Tim and I are taking the nine o'clock ferry."

"Where are ye headed?" asked Thomas.

"Why, over to York of course."

"Why on earth would ye want to go there? Nothing but cutthroats and pickpockets."

"Never-you-mind, Thomas. We haven't time to waste. Quick as you can, Timothy."

CHAPTER 2 — FULTON'S FERRY

1850

Stepping up with his bare feet between the white wooden rungs, Tim holds onto the railing to watch the commotion of locomotion about the ferry at New Brighton landing. Deckhands ready at the gates motion the passengers to hurry aboard. Ladies holding their parasols in the morning sun glide magically along the gangplank in hoopskirts hiding their perambulation. Gentlemen in waistcoats hasten their stride.

A sleek black carriage trots past the teamster pulling hard on the harness to his wagon loaded down with steam trunks from guests at the Pavilion. The horse will not budge. She's a lot like me, thinks Tim looking at the horse, not wanting to get onboard.

Just then the piercing whistle grabs him by the back of his neck in an iron vise. He turns himself round in deafening confusion looking up at the brass steam whistle belting out. The smokestack towers above the pilot house, he sees the captain in his white cap and black coat, then just below, set against the white wood, the black sign in gold painted letters, The Josephine.

"There you are Tim," says his father releasing his grip with his left holding a small paper bag in his right. "I've been looking all over for you. Reach in for some roasted peanuts." In between mouthfuls, Jeremiah offers up commentary on the unfolding scene before them. "Ah, she's a stubborn dray. He'd better whisper sweet nothings in her ear if he hopes to get her on board." The foot passengers funnel to the left and right down the cattle chutes while the horse and carriages head straight to the main deck, big as a wide-open barn.

"What's a dray, Pa?"

Stooping down to the boy's eye level, "A dray is a work horse. Why, just look at her, Tim." Her sooty coat of charcoal grey looks as though she's been rolling around in the ash heap. "Look at those hindquarters. Massive flanks, well-muscled, sure footed, legs thick as marble columns. She's a heavy horse bred for hard work I'll wager she's 17 hands high, a Percheron probably by the looks of her. She has the power of Samson in her."

Jeremiah extends his arm, pointing, calling attention, the fabric from his coat ruffles in Tim's ear while whiskers bristle his cheek. "Now look at that Hackney pulling that fancy Phaeton." The open black carriage, lightly sprung, immense wheels, pencil-thin spokes pulled by a reddish-brown horse with white markings. "A gentlemen's horse for gentlemen work. See how sleek his legs are. That Hackney is 14 hands, if that. Ah, look now, the teamster has given the old girl some striped candy." Stretching her neck for a bite, a tentative step, then another and the horse pulls the wagon aboard.

The final whistle blows and the gate swings closed at the ferry dock — Fulton's Floating Bridge, they call it, an ingenious design, set upon a pontoon rising with the tide to meet the stationary pier. With the chug of steam, the churn of water, the frothy swirl of foam, the ferry begins to lunge forward. Giant water buckets with holes cushion the banged-up pier from the impact of repeated ferry blows.

Tim stands quietly transfixed by the wake pulling him away from the one place he remembers calling home. "I've never seen the pier from this far away," says Tim thinking back to his summer days of jumping off the dock and swimming in the Kill van Kull. Barefoot all summer long, September is the time for getting shoes.

New Brighton Landing fades further and further from view as they pass by the Pavilion on Richmond Terrace giving way to a broad panorama of Staten Island.

Off to the left, at the tip of the island, are some brick buildings on a hill with a long pier extending out to a T-shaped dock with ferry boats lashed.

"What's that over there?"

"Oh, that." Jeremiah pauses hoping Tim asks no more questions about that place. "That is the Quarantine Station." Too young to remember. "No sense in looking to stern, Tim. Let's head to the bow."

With the headwind and sun on their face, the Josephine takes them past Robbins Reef Lighthouse off Constable Hook, in the distance lies Upper New York Bay. A side-wheeler under a full head of steam passes by. As she turns and heads off into the distance, Tim can see paddlewheels on both sides and two great smokestacks billowing smoke. The ship's name, Thomas Hunt, painted on the stern, underneath in smaller letters, Perth Amboy, NJ.

A boy comes by distributing hand-bills. "Savannah Route!" he hollers out. "Montgomery, Mobile, Memphis, and New Orleans!" He forces one into Jeremiah's hand. He looks it over. "Cabin Passage to Savannah $15, Steerage $6. Baggage! Baggage! Baggage! Checked to All Points Free of Charge!" All the summer folk from the Southern States are headed home just as Maggie said. Funny, he muses, how they come here to make their summer escape while the locals head up the River to the Catskills.

Tim tugs on his father's sleeve. "Pa, I have one question. Do you know where the paddlewheel might be?"

"Well, it must be around here somewhere. Have a look around and report back."

Tim heads off to explore the ship. Making his way through the summer visitors milling about, he comes back with a dejected look on his face.

Neither stern nor sidewheel to be found.

"No luck, eh?"

With Tim in tow, Jeremiah approaches a deck-hand push-brooming a pile of hay and horse manure over the side.

"That's a fair question," the old codger whistles S's between the gap in his teeth. "Look over yonder at our sister ship, Samson, making the return voyage from York." He leans upon the broom dressed in his sailor button-breaches.

"Two hulls joined together with the engine and paddlewheel in the center. The wheel is thus protected from all the dockings we do and the ice flows in winter." He pauses, chewing on some straw.

"A ferryboat is a vessel like no other. No fore, no aft, both ends with a rudder, so she never has to turn about. In the days before Fulton, we had a team of six horses walking round in a circle to turn the capstan. You've heard of Fulton's Folly, the Clermont, but did you know, it was Mr. Fulton who also invented the first steam ferry, The Jersey, back in 1812."

"Why, that's where we're headed. Fulton Street. When do we dock on the other side?"

"Owing to wind and tide, we'll be at the foot of Whitehall Street before the clock strikes half."

"Thank you kindly," says Jeremiah as the old hand gets back to work.

Turning to his son, "It is a wondrous age we live in, Timmy my boy. Steamboats and locomotives. When I was your age, we didn't have such contraptions. Now, so you won't forget the corner of Mr. Brady's establishment on Broadway, think of Mr. Fulton's steamship invention. Alright then?"

"Yes, Pa. Fulton Street. I'll remember."

Jeremiah and Tim stand together at the railing in silence listening to the wind and waves against the flat-bottomed ferry as it paddles along drawing them closer and closer to the isle of Manhattan. A deep trough sprays them gently about the face.

Over to York, says Tim to himself. I've never been 'Over to York' that I can recall. The street I live on, York Avenue, this is where it leads. What is so special about this place? They pronounce York with such reverence like the word 'church'. That time in the classroom when Brother Finnerty asked for a show of hands. 'Who here has been over to York?' Not a soul raised their hand except for one. 'Only Francis!' Brother said with a sigh.

Francis was our hero. Not for going over to York, but for the treasure he brought back on the eve of the Fourth. We had all gathered around him and that bright red paper box. Hadfield's Fireworks Depot, No. 47 Maiden Lane, read the top filled with crackers, torpedoes and joss-sticks.

What fun we had. We battled all day long just like Napoleon and Lord Wellington at Waterloo. Artillery, prepare to fire, went the command. Fire!

The hiss of lit fuses, thunderbolt explosions, and the lingering fog of black powder. In my haste, I threw away the matchstick and held onto the cracker. Eardrums clanging, my hand whacked hard as hammer to anvil. The fellows, oh how they laughed. "Toss, the cracker Timmy, not the match!" they kept repeating. Lucky, I didn't lose my thumb at that. You can't very well hold a hammer without a thumb.

Tim marvels at the movement of his thumb, reaching out, making a pincer grasp in the breeze.

"Grabbing at the wind, are you?" smiles his father. "Try as you may, you can never catch her. The wind is a vixen. You need a sail like that periauger to grab hold of her." He points to the small vessel common about New York Harbor loaded down with an oxen team and barrels of goods, low to the water, deckhands at the oars, sails holding taut with the wind.

The steam whistle signals an immense black clipper ship with three masts reaching high into the sky. Tim looks to the distance and sees sailing ships of every kind: square-riggers, schooners, cutters and small dinghies plying their way, slowly dodging the steamships and tugboats.

To the right, docked along the wharves of the East River, a forest of ship masts stretches far as the eye can see. To the left, the circular fort on its own little island connected to Battery Park by a long footbridge. That must be Castle Garden, thinks Tim.

The whistle blows again. The passengers gather about the gate in anticipation. Dead ahead lay South Ferry with slips for Jersey, Staten Island, and Brooklyn. The Josephine takes the middle slip and begins to back-pedal. Two wooden piers extend out like welcoming arms ready to stop a charging toddler with a mother's embrace.

"Move back," shout the deckhands. "Move back!"

CHAPTER 3 — THE OMNIBUS

1850

As the passengers disembark, Tim turns around to look for his Pa, but a heavy boot stomps down on his toe, and the crush of the crowd pushes him forward, flowing with the river of people out to the wide-open expanse of paving stones at Whitehall Street. Hot on the soles of his feet, he heads for the cool shade standing beneath a tree by Battery Park. Four girls in summer white dresses spread out like picnic-blankets sit on the grass.

He looks for his father among the rows upon rows of omnibuses. Horse and driver stand ready to all parts of the city. Knickerbocker Stage Co., reads one, painted on the side Broadway, Bleecker Street, Eighth Avenue & 23rd Street — off kilter in elegant cursive, Sixpence on the Avenue. On the center panel is an oval painting of an elderly woman with a refined nose, the Lady Washington. Tim sees other omnibuses: The Dolly Madison, the Benjamin Franklin, and the Alexander Hamilton.

"Polish your shoes, young gentleman sir? Sixpence for a shine!" asks one of the boot-blacks lugging a box of shoe-shine supplies.

"No, thank you," says Tim lifting his foot. "See, I am not wearing any shoes."

Another boot-black comes by and elbows his friend with a wink. "For an extra penny, I'll blacken between your toes," he laughs as Tim runs away.

A hawker standing by his pushcart captures Tim's attention.

"Get your guidebook here. Don't find yourself lost without one!" He picks up a copy of The Stranger's Handbook for the City of New York, What to See and How to See It. There is an image of a great stone fortress on the cover with the words Croton Reservoir beneath. He puts it back down and looks up.

Tim stares with wonder at a hand-tinted lithograph entitled Souvenir of New York. Before him a hawk-eye view of Manhattan Isle looking down from way up high. Look at all the ship masts and rigging surrounding the island. He takes a step closer and marvels at the attention to detail. Each city street meandering this way and that, the buildings painstakingly etched, the church steeples, the parks with sprinkling fountains, the sidewalks with people…. Taking another step closer, a faint whisper of ink at the bottom piques his interest, Drawn from nature & on stone J. Bornet.

"Timothy! Thank goodness I found you! I thought I lost you forever. Then where would I be?" He kneels down to give the boy a hug. "Hold on to me coat and never let go," he whispers in his ear, "never let go the coat."

"Yes, Pa."

"Quick now, we must catch the omnibus, there are only a few seats left."

Tim stands in place holding firm, stubborn as an anchor. His father looks round. "What is it lad, we haven't time for nonsense."

He points in silence up to the lithograph.

"Alright then. Alright."

Over at the omnibus, Jeremiah opens the back door. Gentlemen crowded shoulder to shoulder turn their heads with perturbed glares as if he just opened the privy door without knocking. Ladies in their long flowing dresses sit contentedly on the red velvet cushions. Not a seat to be had.

"Ye can ride up top with me," says a voice from behind. Turning around, they are greeted by the omnibus driver tipping his stovepipe hat. Dressed in a long frock coat faded by the sun, weathered by the rain, buttons big as silver dollar coins, stamped with the words Knickerbocker Stage Co. encircling an omnibus pulled by two horses. One button, dangling by just a thread, strains to contain the big belly protruding outward. "Best seat in the house," he entreats holding out the palm of his hand. "That'll be sixpence each, one shilling if you please."

Jeremiah pauses to consider the fare, second-guessing himself as the driver stashes the twelve and a half cents in his pocket. They follow him round the great big wagon wheels. A stagger to his gait, one leg shorter than the other, a three-inch platform nailed to the bottom of the driver's right boot. "Clamber up top whilst I tend to the boys." After checking the harness and patting down the horses, Ginger and Nut, he heaves himself up and sits himself down compressing Tim in the middle with his soft belly girth. Jeremiah extends his arm around Tim's shoulder giving the boy some breathing room. "Fine weather we're having."

"Like a breath of Catskill Mountain air." He grabs hold the reins, sparking the whip, barking out, "Heave Hoh, Ginger! Heave Hoh, Nut!" As the omnibus lumbers along, his voice changes cadence back to a soft conversational tone. "The name is Cornelius."

"I'm Jeremiah T. O'Sullivan and this here is my son, Timothy."

"Pleased to meet ye. Where's your hat, boy? Did it blow off on the ferry?"

"The lad is always losing hat after hat running around," explains Jeremiah.

"You don't want the sun beating down on your head making you senseless."

Freckles on his face, streaks of blond in his brown hair, Tim reaches in his pocket and unfolds his Souvenir of New York upon his lap.

"What have we here? Do you aim to be my navigator?" Cornelius says with a hearty laugh.

"Sir, do you know where we are?"

"I should hope so and don't be calling me, 'Sir', Cornelius will do just fine. Well now, let's have a look see," says he, stretching his arm back and forth until the lithograph comes into focus. "Aye, here's the North River and over here is the East. See here, amongst this clump of trees, this is Battery Park, that's where we are, we're headed along State Street."

"But, isn't this the Hudson River?"

"Well, if you aim to be navigator on my ship, you'll refer to it by its proper name, the North River. No self-respecting navigator calls it the Hudson, only when you get above Yonkers, clear all the way to Albany."

At the corner of Bridge and State Street, a man holds his walking cane up high. "Halt Boys! Halt!" shouts Cornelius. A rider hops off, a rider climbs aboard. A hand reaches up through a hole in the roof at the rear of his seat and coins drop into the sixpence trap. He repeats the command, "Heave Hoh, Ginger! Heave Hoh, Nut"

"May I ask why so many ships are anchored about the East River?"

"This is the Dry Dock District. That's where all the shipyards are lad. From Pike Street all the way up to Thirteenth Street — thousands upon thousands of workmen building ships bound for Boston, California, Liverpool, the Far East, and Australia. Why, the William H. Brown Shipyard recently launched The Arctic — 3500 tons, a length of 295 feet with water wheels 35 feet in diameter if you can believe it!"

Cornelius turns his attention back to the lithograph. Surrounding the center panorama of Manhattan, there are smaller images of various buildings and churches on all sides. He points to the frames along the top. "This here's South Ferry where you landed, Castle Garden is just over there. You can see it just barely through the trees." Tim leans forward to see round the big belly. A lady in her bonnet and a gentleman with a straw hat, stroll arm in arm in the shade of the trees by the fence of the public walk. The covered footbridge extends 200 feet out in the harbor. There is a gated entrance with the letters chiseled in granite, Castle Garden. Tim compares it to the lithograph then looks again. Strange, somehow it doesn't look quite the same.

"Lean back, lad before my elbow cracks your skull." He tugs left on the reins to veer out of the way of a red wagon stacked high with wooden barrels pulled by two gigantic Shire horses passing close by on the right. "Steam Ale." Jeremiah reads the elaborate black letters on the side, "The New York Steam Brewery, 15 Downing Street, New York, between Bleecker & Bedford." He reads further, "Brewers of Superior Ales, Ambers and Porters by the new process of Steam."

Jeremiah interjects, "Tim, stop asking so many questions and let the good man attend to his work."

"Now, now, it is quite alright. No harm in asking questions. I can assure you."

"Well then, thank you for showing the boy the ropes. I'll tell you, a tankard of ale from that wagon would whet my thirst!"

"I could go for a barrel myself when this day is done." He turns to Tim. "Recognize this one?" he quizzes with his finger tapping at the upper right corner.

Tim notices the small print. "It says Croton Reservoir."

"So, you can read?"

"And write too." Tim says with a hint of pride. "Is this a fortress?"

"No, lad! What did you just get off the boat!" he says with a laugh. "Why, yes you did indeed. This is where they collect all the drinking water. It's the most popular of tourist attractions."

"Are there no wells around here?"

"The wells are poisoned with cholera. Never drink from the well. Five thousand perished during the outbreak last year." Cornelius breathes a sigh of relief. "Thank goodness for the Croton. I can recall the Croton Water Celebration back in '42. The procession was seven miles long, two miles of firemen and their steam engines, you should have seen it. Now that's a profession in great demand. Become a plumber or a pipefitter. I should have listened to my mother instead of battling the elements from this perch." He holds the reins with his left and draws Tim's attention to the lithograph. "See this?"

"High Bridge," the boy reads.

"Now then, High Bridge is not merely a bridge, but a great aqueduct bringing pure mountain water across the Harlem River..." his voice trails off as he points back to the upper right corner with a thud finishing his sentence, "right here to the Croton. Workmen finished building High Bridge two years ago. It is a sight to behold. Great stone arches crossing the Harlem River."

"Will we pass by it?"

"Not on the Knickerbocker Line. But you'll see most of the sites on this here Souvenir of New York. We're fast approaching Bowling Green."

Cornelius halts the omnibus in his usual spot along the shade of the trees by the black wrought iron fence. "Wait here while I let some of the passengers off." Tim feels the morning chill as the warmth of Cornelius leaves his side. The bench seat teeters up at the great weight that has been lifted.

"Bowling Green!" he announces opening the rear door to assist the ladies off. "Do be sure to stop at the Atlantic Garden for your morning tea. Tell them Cornelius sent ye."

Over the fence, at the center of the small park, the soft mist from the fountain shooting water straight up in the air. "We'll be here just a minute, lads," he shouts up, leaning his shorter leg on the fence, looking up and down the sidewalk for potential fares.

From across the street, holding a mug of coffee, a man with slicked back hair in a long white apron makes his way over to Cornelius.

"Here you go, Old Elephant, compliments of the house."

Cornelius takes the mug and unfolds the linen wrapping a few scones. "Thank you, Samuel. Now that's the stuff," he says after a gulp.

"Look down yonder, Tim — that building standing on the corner. That is the Washington Headquarters Hotel, Number One Broadway — the beginning and the end of the most famous street in all the world."

The square building four stories tall bustles with activity as coachmen unload passengers and guests climb the curved staircase. "Some still call it the Old Kennedy House — it was owned by Captain Archibald Kennedy of the Royal Navy — built back in 1760 with bricks imported all the way from Holland. General Washington made his headquarters there for a time during the War for Independence. If you go inside to the north room, they preserved the very furniture the good General sat upon and the desk where he made his plans." Tim imagines a feather quill in hand scratching away by candlelight.

From up high the omnibus, the boy sees projectile spittle of scones punctuating off with every consonant Cornelius pronounces. "Across the street is Number Nine Broadway, the Atlantic Garden. In the time of Revolution, that was known as Burns' Coffee House where the Liberty Boys would hold their meetings."

Tim looks across Broadway. Nestled tightly between tall buildings on either side, the Atlantic Garden looks strangely out of place, the short one in formation, the odd man out, only three stories tall, a cedar shingle roof with a large chimney in the center. Missing shutters here and there, the stucco chipped away to reveal the red brick underneath, the old-fashioned windowpanes, thick and blurry, like looking through the bottom of a bottle. Tim sees a Liberty Boy raise a pewter mug. The large black lanterns dangle above, the menu board on the sidewalk sits next to a strange contraption — a short hitching post of some sort.

"What's that thing over there, Cornelius?"

"What now? I'm trying to tell you about the Liberty Boys! Were you not paying attention?"

"Don't interrupt," says his father.

"But I'd like to know, Pa."

"You, mean the Johnny Pump, have you never seen one of those over in Staten Island? When the fire alarm rings and the Johnnies come charging down the street with their fire engines blazing in full glory, they hook the fire hose up and have water straight from the Croton. Now, can I finish my story?"

"Yes, you may," Tim says with a wink.

Cornelius takes another gulp, dunks the raisin scone and points through the wrought iron fence at the fountain. "Long before that water fountain, there was a statue of King George the T'urd sitting on his horse, gilded in glimmering gold, the supreme ruler of the British Empire and all her colonies. Do you know what happened at the reading of the Declaration of Independence in July of 1776?"

"No," say Jeremiah and Tim in unison.

"The Liberty Boys toppled that statue attaching ropes and pulling with all their might. Then they snapped off the royal figureheads to this very fence." Cornelius walks along the black painted fence, running his hand along the rungs with pointy spikes at the very top. "One pike, two pike, three pike, four...," he hums half to himself. He stops at the twelfth, stout and square, and points to the flat broken top. "See right here? This is where they broke the figureheads off. And do you know what they did with these symbols of tyranny?"

"No," say Jeremiah and Tim again in unison.

"The Sons of Liberty sent all that precious lead up to Litchfield, Connecticut, to the home of Oliver Wolcott. His wife and daughters melted King George and his horse down into 42,000 musket balls for the patriots to use against the lobster-backs."

"Now where'd you take your history lessons, Cornelius?" asks Jeremiah.

"Why, the ale house of course." Cornelius drains the last bit of coffee from his mug and sets it down on the granite curb by the bottom of the fence. "Aye! We must be on our way!" Quick as Saint Nick, he climbs up top. "Heave Hoh, Boys! Blast me forgetfulness where are ye headed?"

Tim blurts out before his father, "Number 205 Broadway at the corner of Fulton Street."

"Now that's what I like to hear, a man sure of his destination. You'd be surprised at how many people wander about aimless in this life, not even knowing the name of the street they tread upon. So, you're going to Brady's to have your likeness taken — father and son. How very nice. You know, there are other establishments that don't charge Broadway prices and it looks as though you could use a pair of shoes... and don't be forgetting a proper hat! That's the same way I stepped off the boat. No shoes, no hat."

"I'll be getting the boy some shoes," Jeremiah pauses, "And a hat, don't you worry. Summer has but ended and his feet do grow like spuds. No sooner do I buy a pair then his toe breaks through the leather."

"Don't I know it, don't I know it," repeats Cornelius. "I have seven of my own."

"Can you recommend a shop? As you so deftly advised, I don't wish to be robbed blind paying Broadway prices."

"I know just the place for shoes — A.T. Stewart's just behind City Hall. Then you can stop by Genin the Hatter, next door to Barnum's."

The omnibus lumbers along to the sound of wagon wheels turning and horseshoes clopping upon the Belgian blocks. Bowling Green tapers in like a bottleneck with Broadway stretching far as the eye can see, the many rooftops of omnibuses before them like stepping-stones with the spire of Trinity Church in the distance.

"What a commanding view you have from way up here!" remarks Jeremiah.

"Sometimes I fancy myself a king upon his throne with all my subjects down below. This is my fiefdom and I the ruler."

"Cornelius, where is Mr. Brady's shop?"

"See, Tim, we're right here at Steven's House, Number 21 Broadway," he says walking his finger up Broadway on the Souvenir of New York. "This is Trinity Church. There is the Park and City Hall. Brady's is on the corner of Fulton Street, t'urd door south of Saint Paul's. Take a look at the small painting at the bottom."

Tim reads aloud, "Halls of Justice, The Tombs."

"No," Cornelius snaps. "Not the Tombs, you don't want to find yourself there — not ever. The one next to it."

Tim tries again, "Barnum's Museum and Astor House."

"That's it. Brady's is right across from Barnum's."

"Pa, can we visit the American Museum?" asks Tim. "Francis told me all about the Witch of Staten Island at Barnum's. Please Pa, it won't be out of the way."

"We'll see, lad. We'll see."

Cornelius turns to Jeremiah, "Now, you're sure I couldn't point you in the direction of another gallery. Rufus Anson only charges two shillings for a sitting, while Brady will set you back two dollars or as much as five dollars."

"See, here's the thing," says Jeremiah. "We'll not be sitting for our likeness or any such foolishness. Young Tim starts his apprenticeship tomorrow morning at Mr. Brady's."

"Good for you, lad," slapping his back repeating. "Good for you!"

The horses slow their pace. "Look yonder Tim at Bunker's Mansion House — Number 39 Broadway. That is where George Washington lived as president long before Washington City ever existed on a map. Imagine him strolling up Broadway on a Sunday with Martha in his arm to Saint Paul's Chapel. Did you know back in the day, York was the capital of these United States?"

"No, I did not," admits Jeremiah. "You do have a wealth of knowledge."

"Wealth of knowledge? Me? I am but a pauper. When you've been up and down these roads as many times as I've been, you can't but help pick up a thing or two along the way. I love this old town... the very stones of her street. Well, maybe not the cobblestones blast them, they rattle me ivories to the very nerve, I am so glad to see them replaced with the Belgian blocks."

Tim keeps his attention focused on the lithograph of Manhattan. "Now then navigator, if you keep your nose buried in that map of yours, you'll never find your way. Head up. Keep a sharp eye out for your landmarks."

Tim looks up. Leaning back, his gaze is drawn up and up, higher and higher and higher to the tippity-top of the spire of Trinity Church, the tallest structure in all the land. At the corner of Wall Street, the omnibus pulls to the side. "Seventy-nine Broadway, Trinity Church! Custom House!" he shouts out and then draws out the notes to a crescendo, "Merchant's Exchange!"

As the curbside traders make their exit, Cornelius elbows Tim in the side. "Close your mouth lad, unless you enjoy pigeon poop for breakfast." Jeremiah laughs a hearty laugh.

"For a shilling, you can climb all 308 steps of the steeple — standing 284 feet tall. There are resting places along the way. I could never make the climb with this limp of mine, but I'm told the view is heavenly..."

He loses his train of thought to the competing shouts of newsboys on the corner. "Get your Herald here! California admitted to the Union!" Another hollers louder, "President Millard Fillmore signs Fugitive Slave Act! Read all about it in The Tribune!"

Bringing Tim back down to earth, he points across the street at the graveyard, "There you'll find the final resting place of Alexander Hamilton and Robert Fulton, God, rest their souls... and don't forget Captain Lawrence. Do you know his famous last words, Timmy-my-boy?"

Tim shakes his head.

"Don't Give up the Ship!"

All along the fence, Tim sees the bootblacks plying their trade, young boys just about his age lugging wooden boxes with boot-rests, grimy faces and dirty hands, shining the shoes of bankers and brokers. A short newsboy, no older than eight, arm outstretched with The New York Sun, bumped and jostled by hurrying passersby, holds his ground, "Jenny Lind Tells All... All for a Penny, And Only in The SUN!"

"Shouldn't those boys be in school?" asks Tim.

"They have to work," says his father. "That's the way of the world."

"The boy's right, the bootblacks and newsboys should be in school and out playing games," counters Cornelius, "look at them all, the orphans of Broadway, many of them have no place to call home, except newspaper row."

"What's that building way down the street there?"

"You mean the one that looks like a Greek temple. That is number 28 Wall Street, the Custom House – built in 1830 with marble from the quarries of Tuckahoe."

"Tuckahoe?" Tim repeats, "Where's that?"

"Oh, way up north in County Westchester."

As they pass by the Trinity office building at the corner of Thames Street, Tim begins to notice the varying shades of granite grey, red brick, marble white, brownstone, and sandstone — some buildings with cast iron Corinthian columns painted black, others with Doric columns painted white.

"Old Elephant!" shouts a driver waving his hat on an approaching omnibus, southbound on Broadway. He reels up the reins at 147 Broadway on the corner of Liberty Street at the American Telegraph Company building. Kipp & Brown, 9th Avenue Hudson & Canal reads the side panel.

"Yellow Joe! How goes the battle?" responds Cornelius.

"Madness up Broadway, I tell ya. Stark raving madness! I barely made it through."

"Isn't it always."

"Bust me knuckles, this is different, Old Elephant. I've not seen such crowds in all me years. There's a great ruckus at Barnum's – he's set a stage out on the corner of Ann Street to hold a ticket auction for Miss Jenny's concerts. Jenny Lind Mania they're calling it. If you have any sense, you'll heed my warning and take the back way up Nassau Street." He hesitates a split-second searching for an exaggeration, eyes darting, tongue curling vowels formulate in his mouth. Tim watches the Adam's apple move up and down his long, scrawny neck. "I'll wager me mother, you'll not make it. This is ten times worse than the Astor Place Riot."

"Come now, Yellow Joe. You know very well that collateral does not hold water, never did to the best of your knowledge. Make an honest bet."

"Alright then, two rounds at Daniel Sweeny's."

"Consider it won. I shall not be thwarted."

"Be on the lookout, the fare inspectors are out and about," warns Yellow Joe. He suspiciously eyes Jeremiah and Tim up and down. "I hear tell of these Benedict Arnolds dragging a child along to aide in their subterfuge."

Just then, the impatient tap-tapping of a cane on the roof comes from down below. The two drivers pretend not to hear.

"Keep your head, Old Elephant. Something tells me I'll be finding you in the Tombs."

"Who me? I'll muddle through, Yellow Joe. Not to worry."

The tap-tapping grows louder and louder.

A voice snaps, "Driver, do not tarry!"

"Oh, my, you captured a live one. Like I've been saying, we need iron bars, not curtains and glass windows to contain these wild beasts. He'll be demanding his sixpence before long," he remarks over the banging from below. "Listen, will you be at the concert on Friday? Patsey Dee was asking for you."

The pounding roof rattles the windows.

"Rest assured I'll be there."

Yellow Joe holds his stovepipe hat over his heart while the omnibus rolls away. "Parting is such sweet sorrow..."

In the distance he hears, "Bring Young Elephant."

"I will," Cornelius shouts backward.

After a time, Tim asks, "Why does he call you Old Elephant?"

"Tim, stop asking so many impertinent questions."

"T'is nothing," he says to Jeremiah then to the boy, "That is my cognomen. I'm told I have a gallant physique from the stern. Amongst us drivers, my bosom friends, we have these endearing names. There's Broadway Jack, Dressmaker, Balky Bill, and Pop Rice. They call my brother Young Elephant."

"Can I call you, Old Elephant?"

"Why, yes you may," he says with a wink. "In fact, you just did."

"Will you be seeing Jenny Lind then?"

"Oh, no. Not I. The boys are holding a benefit concert at the Broadway Theatre for the Kipp and Brown Stage Line whose stables burned to the ground. It was a sad loss of fine horses trapped in the blaze. Nothing against Miss Jenny, but I am wise to Barnum and his humbugs."

At the corner of Cortlandt Street, Cornelius stops the stage with a shout, "Maiden Lane!"

"Old Elephant, how come the sign on that building says Cortlandt Street?"

"Cortlandt is to the west of Broadway whilst Maiden Lane meanders her merry way down to the East River."

Recognizing the sound of the street name from the fireworks box, Tim asks, "Say now, do you know of a Hadfield's shop on Maiden Lane?"

"Oh, sure lad, this is the Toy District – up and down Maiden Lane you'll find toy stores on either side of the street: Hadfields, Althof and Bergmann, Peter Tiers, Strasburger and Nuhn. All the fancy goods you can think of... tin soldiers, toy horses and spinning tops from the best toy makers in the world."

"Jossticks and crackers?"

"Oh yes, all the jossticks and crackers you please."

Tim's imagination runs wild and his restless limbs struggle to get free.

"Come on, Pa, let's get off here!"

"No, son."

A couple strolls up Maiden Lane, a little girl lags behind pushing a china doll in a toy carriage.

"Please, Pa."

"No, I said. We haven't the time or the money."

Old Elephant puts his hand on the boy's shoulder and sits him back down. "Now that's a good boy. Heed your father."

As they approach John Street, Old Elephant stands up tall looking further up the 'Way. "Well, I'll be...Yellow Joe was right. Hold tight to your hats, boys, looks like we're headed for some rough seas," he commands then pauses to make an aside, "well, all except you Tim, you have no hat!" He laughs and sits his big belly back down.

CHAPTER 4 — BROADWAY & FULTON

1850

The omnibus slows as it approaches 187 Broadway not far from the corner of Dey Street. "Keep your chin up, lad. We'll be approaching Brady's shop before you know it."

"Where then?"

"You tell me, you're the navigator," counters Old Elephant.

His father pipes in, "Please, stow that map away."

The boy reluctantly folds the lithograph and puts it in his coat pocket. Up and down the 'Way, Tim notices the sidewalk awnings in various stages of undress, wrapped tight in a blanket roll or stretched out all the way to the curb supported by poles tall as the street-lamps.

He looks to his left at J.C. Booth & Co. No. 187. Behind the window, a neatly arranged display of shirts, gloves, suspenders, and cane umbrellas. To the side, a sign leads his eye up to the second story, Miniature & Jewel Case Manufactory.

"I don't see it, Old Elephant."

"You will, soon enough."

Tim looks to his left, then to his right, then back again. He sees the hand sign pointing up the stairs, the words Portrait Gallery, No. 189 Broadway. "There it is! I found it!" he shouts out triumphantly.

"No, you haven't. Take another look. That is Jeremiah Gurney's Portrait Studio. Nice try though. Keep looking."

Tim turns to the right. A broad canvas sheet ripples large black letters in the breeze, Edward Fox, Tailoring Establishment, No. 202 Broadway.

"That's not it, where can it be?" he says to himself. His head begins to swirl looking this way, an' that way, an' this way, an' that... Earle's Carpet Warehouse. He follows the telegraph wires to the next building. Lanphier the Tailor, Warnock the Hatter. "No, that isn't it." The telegraph pole guides his gaze back down to street level — standing all alone — a short hitching post with a wrought iron ring leaving a rusty stain on the chiseled granite.

"Old Elephant, I can't locate Brady's shop anywhere."

"Keep looking, Lad."

Up ahead, an ice wagon stops suddenly in the middle of the road. Old Elephant pulls back on the reins shouting, "Whoa now, Ginger! Whoa there, Nut!" The iceman comes around to the back and opens the black door with white painted letters, Knickerbocker Ice Co., 190 West Street. He pulls back the leather curtain trapping in the cold air. Block set upon block covered in a thick coat of sawdust.

"You there," hollers Old Elephant, "Yes you, my good man, you can't be blocking Broadway. I have passengers with places to be. Make way like a good fellow!"

Taking a moment to mop his brow with his pocket kerchief, the iceman grabs hold of a dripping block with the claws of an iron clamp. He turns his back then disappears down the stairs of the gaping hole in the sidewalk into the darkness.

"Turn your back on Cornelius Ryan!" he says out loud. The color in Old Elephant's face gets flushed with anger, leaning forward, shouting down the stairs. "Did you not hear me! See here! I was talking to you. I have passengers with places to be! You're blocking Broadway! Clear the 'Way!" He repeats again, "Clear the 'Way!" There is a long pause. "Don't make me come down there!"

Tim thinks better than to pester Old Elephant in his agitated state. He scans the street again. Smith's Segar Store stands at the corner of Fulton and Broadway. Next door is Genin the Hatter, Prepare for a Rainy Day, cautions the sign. Everyone has a proper hat except for me... women in their bonnets, newsboys in their caps. "Where's your hat, lad?" jars in his ear. From his head to his toes, he burns with shame — no shoes, no hat, and out of place on Broadway.

Drowning out Old Elephant's shouts, a bass drum thumps inside Tim's chest, brass trumpets and trombones blast in his ear, a snare drum taps on his skull, cymbals crash chaotically overhead, a tin whistle pierces the air, and down below on the sidewalk, the din of the crowd mixes with muffled shouts.

"What on God's good green earth is that racket?" shouts Jeremiah.

"That my friend is the cacophony of Barnum's Band." Old Elephant points up. On the third story, a wrought iron balcony wraps around the building, letters the size of casement windows painted along the side: A-M-E-R-I-C-A-N double-space M-U-S-E-U-M. In between each window, oval paintings of exotic creatures: a serpent, a giraffe, an elephant, and a zebra.

Tim looks up on the balcony at the band with their bright red uniforms and gold piping, cheeks puff into the tuba, white gloves clasp cymbals, the long brass arm of the trombone slides back and forth.

Jeremiah covers his ears. "Dying pigs strike better chords. They are butchering God Save the Queen. Have they no mercy?"

"That melody is more properly called My Country 'Tis of Thee."

"Well, I wish they would stop."

As they pass the corner of Ann Street, Tim reads the continuation of window sized letters along the facade — B-A-R-N-U-M'-S then he mentally completes the thought, Barnum's American Museum. Draping the building, a canvas sheet three stories tall, features a painting of Jenny Lind with her out-stretched arm and a nightingale perched on her hand reminding him of Saint Francis of Assisi.

The omnibus comes to a dead halt. The narrow canyons of Broadway open wide with Chatham Row jutting off at a sharp angle to the right creating the town trapezoid known simply as The Park. In the far distance City Hall, the great water fountain sprays taller than all the treetops. Before them, a crowd thick as a wheat field, nothing but hat-tops and bonnets all turned in the same direction. Up high on a lamp post, a boy clutches tightly, legs wrapped around. A man raps his cane upon the wooden stage with one hand shouting into the megaphone with the other.

"Walk up ladies and gentlemen and see the greatest wonder of the age — the real Swedish nightingale, the only specimen in the country!"

All of Old Elephant's shouts go unheard, absorbed by the crowd, drowned out by the band. He singles out a young fellow with a stove pipe hat tipped to the side. He belts out his familiar refrain. "I'm talking to you. You can't be blocking Broadway. I have passengers with places to be! Make way, my good man. Make way!" Eyes meeting eyes, pupils staring into pupils, hands in his pockets, the tough puffs on his tight-clenched segar and turns about face joining the rest of the crowd.

"Did ye see that? Turned his back on me. A Bowery Boy no doubt! Oh, what a fine mess I've gotten us into. I should've listened to Yellow Joe." Exasperated, he hands Jeremiah the reins.

"Here take this," he mutters. "Mother was right, I am hog-headed with tiny pig ears that don't know how to listen. Never have, never will."

Down on the ground, Old Elephant wades through the crowd pushing people out of the way, tugging hard on the jittery horses, inching his way, muddling through, one step at a time, person by person. Some step out of the way, others hold their ground, Old Elephant thrusts his stiff arm to clear the way.

Turning heads, angry expressions, upset jeers, a man pushes back, a circle forms around Old Elephant, from behind, another kicks the back of his leg, his knee buckles to the ground, a walking cane whacks his faded blue coat hard as a beaten rug with thuds of dust puffing from his broad shoulder-back.

Tim looks down at his hands and finds himself holding the reins. The circle closes tighter, a kidney punch lands with all its might. Old Elephant's hat topples off with a sidewinder to the head, disappearing from view he sinks into the kicking crowd.

Just then, a blurring motion from the corner of his eye — a rolled-up sleeve grabs a shoulder and cracks the circle, tearing it open. Then that familiar fist starts hammering away. That's me Pa', he says to himself. Hold steady with the left, double-tap with the right, then drive her home, he'd whisper to me. WHAM! He sees his father grab another by the cravat, double-tap then pound the nail home.

"Behind you, Pa! Behind you!" Jeremiah turns himself round, "Hit me when I'm not looking!" He grabs the thrusting cane and rips it away, making a broad sweeping motion, widening the circle, tapping the paving stones for added measure. "Stand clear!" he repeats, "STAND CLEAR!"

Stooping down low he wraps Old Elephant's arm round his shoulder and heaves up with all his might to get him on his feet again. The horses rear up on their hind quarters, kicking at the air with their front legs, magically parting the crowd as Moses the Red Sea.

"Hold tight to the reins, Timmy!" Old Elephant shouts. He reaches for the harness and tries to settle down the horses. "I'm alright boys! They didn't hurt me at all," soothing them with a pat. "God bless you, Ginger and Nut. Ole Cornelius is just fine, just fine and dandy. Don't you boys worry about me."

"Follow the flagstones," he says leaning hard on Jeremiah as they plow through the thinning crowd. "It will take us to the Park… head for the fountain." The smooth walkway leads across the bumpy expanse of stones at the wide intersection of Chatham Row, Ann Street, and Broadway.

Parked by the cool shade of the trees and the mist of the fountain, Old Elephant staggers with his newly acquired cane, a gift from Jeremiah, to the back of the omnibus to let the passengers off. He musters the breath to call out, "Astor House, Saint Paul's Chapel. American Museum." Nearly all the passengers disembark, then he adds definitively, "Last stop!"

"What's the meaning of this?" shouts the lone passenger still sitting in the back of the omnibus. "I have an appointment to keep with Doctor John Moffat."

"You'll find the good doctor on the corner of Anthony Street."

"But that is a good eight blocks away!"

"Beg your pardon sir, I called 'Last Stop'. I'm master of this omnibus. The horses need their rest. They are in a most excited state and I don't want them hoofing a poor little flower girl. Here's your sixpence… Take a saunter up Broadway, the best show in the world, free to all. You will thank me later. If you pass Leonard Street, turn back, you've gone too far."

He clicks the back door closed and hangs his trusty "Off-Doody" sign.

"Let's take a breather, boys, over by that weeping willow. It is ever so peaceful there…"

Tim climbs down from his perch and runs through the gate of the Park to catch up to Old Elephant who is leaning hard on his father. He notices the boot with the wooden extension dragging along. He eavesdrops on their shoulder-to-shoulder banter.

"I had them in the palm of me hand. You had no right to interfere."

"So, you were playing possum then? That was the plan?"

"Every fighter has a plan until they get punched in the face."

"A fighter? I mistook you for a helpless babe in a cradle."

"I was merely catching me breath. I could've taken them all with one fist. Believe you me."

"It boils me blood to see a pack of wolves set upon one. They're brave as a group, but single one out and off they go yelping away!"

"Jeremiah, I have you to thank for winning me wager with Yellow Joe not to mention saving me hide."

"Speak not another word of it."

"You and Timothy must join us for midday supper at Daniel Sweeny's House of Refreshment. He serves a hearty meal. Number 11 Ann Street, just opposite Barnum's. You can't miss it."

"That is a most kind offer."

"Set me down on that bench overlooking the fountain pool," he says then whispers close to Jeremiah's ear, "Have Tim go back to the coach and fetch my pail. The horses are frothy with thirst and I feel a tad seasick."

As the lad walks twenty paces away, he heaves up in a gushing torrent of vomit splattering the pavement and Jeremiah's boots. He retches again. Raisins from the scones float this way an' that way. "Get it out," says Jeremiah with a pat upon the back.

Tim returns with the pail.

"Tend to the horses, lad. Go to the fountain."

"What's happened to Old Elephant then?"

Doubled over, waiting for another tremor. "He'll be fine. Now when you're done with the horses, you can bring us a pail of water."

Returning from the fountain, Tim looks at Old Elephant's uncovered head and thinks better than to ask 'Where's your hat?' at a time like this. His black curly hair is matted down about the crown, he steps closer, thick dark blood oozes from a gash.

"Pa, he's bleeding."

"I'll be fine. It's just a scratch," he says sitting upright, dabbing his kerchief in the bucket then to the back of his head. A refreshing breeze catches the drooping branches of the weeping willow. He dips the ladle in the bucket and takes a sip of water. "Over there, that majestic tree looks like Venus beside a pool with her long golden hair shimmering down. I can see her fingertips trailing daintily in the water..."

"That knock on the head has made you punch drunk. Is that water or whiskey you're sipping?" asks Jeremiah.

Paying him no mind, Old Elephant continues right on. "Look over yonder, Tim. That is the world-famous Astor House. That is what all of the other hotels in this city aspire to be. They say you have not really lived, until you have 'Put up at the Astor.' The softest eider down pillows you could ever lay your head upon. Why, Andrew Jackson and Sam Houston spent the night there, as did Charles Dickens. The list goes on and on. Three hundred and forty rooms, constructed with granite all the way from the quarries of Quincy, Massachusetts. Inside you will find a courtyard complete with the finest restaurant, a garden with trees and even a fountain."

"They put a fountain inside a house?" asks Tim. "Whose house did you say that was?"

"John Jacob Astor, the richest man in all the land. Well, he was until he passed to his own reward two years ago. The Herald published his entire will. He was worth $20 million dollars if you can believe it. He left four hundred thousand dollars to build the Astor Library, fifty thousand to the little town of Waldorf, his place of birth in Germany, the rest to his family, but not a blessed penny to me. I was much aggrieved at the reading of the will. Well then, navigator, let's have a look at that map of yours."

Tim unfolds his Souvenir of New York upon his lap.

"See here," he says pointing to the image of Astor House opposite the Park then tracing an imaginary line up Broadway. "This is where the Astor Opera House is located all the way up at Astor Place... Dis-Astor Place is what most folk call it now on account of that dreadful riot last year. Near thirty souls perished, the Seventh Regiment called out. Luckily, John Jacob Astor did not live to see what happened to his precious Opera House. There's talk of shuttering the doors for good. And it but recently opened a few years ago... Aye, but the place is cursed. There has not been another performance there since that tragic event. Some say it will be forever known as the Massacre Opera House."

"Did he ever ride on your omnibus?"

"John Jacob on the Lady Washington? Perish the thought, Tim. He had his own coach with a fine team of horses and not one driver, but two. I saw him one day swathed in rich furs, with a great ermine cap on his head and a dozen servants besides, all tending to his every need."

"Old Elephant, what is a hermes cap?"

"The ermine is a weasel with the softest pelt you could ever touch. That is how John Jacob Astor earned his fortune in the fur trade. He barely spoke the King's English when he arrived. He headed up the North River and into the wilderness with little more than a pack on his back. He paddled his canoe up Lake George then sailed up Lake Champlain to bargain with the Indians and voyageurs.

"In all his dealings, he surrendered precious little and demanded dearly in return. He opened his little shop selling furs and amassing his riches with the China Trade. One day, he vowed to himself that he would someday build the grandest house on all of Broadway. Behold the Astor House."

"Well, I like our house in New Brighton much better," says Tim. "I wouldn't want to live in a granite house. There are too many rooms.

Whoever heard of a house with 340 rooms?"

Old Elephant laughs while his father slaps him hard on the back.

"Now haven't you forgotten something, Tim?"

"What, my hat?"

"No, and it's not your shoes either. Think, lad, think."

With no response other than Tim's blank expression, Old Elephant continues, "Well, you're certainly not the first navigator who missed his mark."

"Oh, yes… Mr. Brady's shop."

"Oh yes, indeed. I don't know how you could have missed it. Look beyond to the Astor House, over there is Saint Paul's Chapel, standing between Vesey and Fulton Street. The building next to it is Brady's."

"Where???"

"Oh, it's no use. Are you in need of a spyglass?"

"Tim has the eyes of a falcon, don't you, lad?" Jeremiah says in his defense.

"I still can't make it out."

"Bat eyes is more like it! You're hopeless! You'd fly into the side of a barn," says Old Elephant. "Look up high, higher still. See the number 205?"

Tim reads out, "E. Anthony, Engravings, Dagger Materials."

"No, No, No… that is word is not dagger. That is Daguerrean."

His father tries to soothe Tim, pointing his long arm, guiding his gaze. "Look just below. See that big black sign with the white letters?"

"Oh, I see now… Brady's Gallery of Daguerreotypes."

"Land Ho! Columbus, you discovered America!"

Tim continues reading, "Ah, there's yet another sign. Brady's Daguerrean Miniature Gallery. How could I have missed it?"

"Don't be so hard on yourself, Tim," says his Pa. "The eyes play tricks on us from time to time, letting us see what they want us to see."

"Your father is right. Answer me this, you've heard the expression 'Plain as the nose on your face.' But, have you ever seen your nose?"

Tim furrows his brow and strains his eyes together.

"Hey now, stop that, you'll wind up as cross-eyed as James Gordon Bennett." Before Tim can ask who, Old Elephant explains, "He is none other than the editor of the New York Herald."

After an awkward pause, forgetting the point he was trying to make, Old Elephant slaps his knee. "Alrighty then, the picnic in the Park is hereby declared over. Let's be on our way and get ye to Stewart's. Collect the pail, like a good boy."

No sooner does he stand, then he crumbles back down. "Whoa, there," he calls after Jeremiah and Tim. "I haven't got my sea legs yet. Those boot-kicks to the head have addled me brain. Lend us a shoulder then?"

Back at the omnibus, Old Elephant takes down his off-doody sign and assists the ladies coming from the Astor House up the little back steps. "To the Marble Palace," command their attending gentlemen one after the other, almost without exception. "To the Marble Palace it tis," he repeats.

Back on top, he takes a deep breath and a sip from his pewter flask. "Ah, that's better now. The bed spins have abated. Finish her off," he says reaching round Tim with a flask-tap on Jeremiah's shoulder. "Fresh air, paying passengers, and the world at my command in these here reins. Yah Now! Boys! Yah!"

As the omnibus heads north alongside the Park, the long row of trees stretches far in the distance, all the tension and congestion blows way with the breeze and the rustle of leaves. There are no more cross streets to contend with, no more delivery drivers blocking the way, no hotels and restaurants to stop at, no tailors and hatters, just tree after shady tree.

"This is my favorite stretch of Broadway," says Old Elephant. "This is my Gulf Stream. No headwinds bearing down on ye, just smooth sailing from here. See how Ginger and Nut are happy at ease, trotting along with no yank on the reins. I'll tell you something, a little bit of the Garden of Eden is on the other side of that high iron railing."

Tim sees a black squirrel scamper on the grass stopping for a minute to pick up an acorn topped with a brown cap.

"Now in the time of British Rule, the Park was called the Commons," he hears Old Elephant say. "On that ground, the Liberty Boys heaved up a pole, tall as a ship mast, only to see the British soldiers tear her down. Now do you know what word was written at the very top of that pole?"

"No..." says Tim with his father in anticipation of the answer.

"The word 'Liberty' is all. But the Boys set that Liberty Pole back up in defiance only to see it tore down time and time again." After a long pause, changing to a more light-hearted tone, he adds, "We'll be at the Marble Palace before ye can whistle Yankee Doodle Dandy."

"Is that the Marble Palace over there?"

"Oh no, that is City Hall." Old Elephant reaches in his pocket and takes out a small black handbook and gives it to Tim.

"What's this? Your daily missal?" he asks.

"Not quite."

Tim reads the title page, "Price Ten Cents. Norton's Hand-Book of New York City containing 44 engravings of the most celebrated public buildings in the city."

"Turn to page three."

"The City Hall," he reads aloud in a hesitant voice, "is one of the most prominent buildings in New York standing near the center of the Park."

"Skip down a bit..."

"The fronts and ends are of marble from Stockbridge, Massachusetts, but the back is constructed of free-stone. At the time it was built, marble was expensive, and it was determined to finish the back with cheaper stone. It was maintained that the population would never, to any extent, settle above Chambers Street, and therefore the rear of the hall would rarely be seen."

"That bit always makes me laugh. Fine reading, now turn to page 22."

Tim flips to the dog-eared page. "On the corner of Broadway and Chambers street, the site in former times of the Washington Hotel, stands Stewart's Marble Palace, the largest dry goods store in the world."

"Don't just read about it. Why don't you take a look for yourself," says Old Elephant.

Tim puts the handbook down and looks up at the immense structure before him. "Notice the Corinthian columns and the light cream Tuckahoe marble. The building is five stories tall and takes up the entire block to Reade Street. Construction finished only two years ago."

Tim reads the black letters on the building, A.T. Stewart & Company. "Now, Mr. Alexander T. Stewart is the richest merchant in all the world, second only to the Astor's. He opened his first dry goods store in 1823 or thereabouts after arriving from Belfast."

Across the 'Way, a great commotion, a huge crowd gathered pointing up at the building, a woman appears at the window and waves a gloved hand. The crowd erupts into cheers.

"Old Elephant what is going on over there?"

"Oh, that," he waves his dismissive hand, "that is Jenny Lind of course. She is staying at the Irving House over there. Crowds of twenty thousand were there when the Atlantic docked at Canal Street. Welcome to America! Welcome Jenny Lind! Read the triumphal arches. One zealous spectator fell into the river. Two hundred musicians and three hundred firemen in their red shirts bearing torches escorted her to the Irving House in Mr. Barnum's carriage."

The crowd roars again as Miss Jenny drops one of her handkerchiefs. The blue and yellow Swedish flag hung in her honor flutters with the wind.

"Now, getting back to the Marble Palace, inside you'll find an immense hall 80 feet high and 100 feet long lined with full length mirrors, the hall of mirrors they call it. All the merchandise you can imagine from every corner of the world worth an estimated $10 million. There are some 350 clerks attending to your every want and need. Oh goodness me, that reminds me, I must assist the ladies off... they come from all over the country to see the latest fashions at the Marble Palace. Last year, Mr. Stewart chartered a ship to send provisions for the relief of the people suffering from the famine back in Ireland."

"God bless him," says Jeremiah.

With the crowd rushing back and forth, some holding parcels, Tim notices an elderly woman sitting with a shawl wrapped about her wearing dark spectacles seated at a table selling apples. Her sad quiet expression brightens with an approaching customer then dims as they pass away.

"Come down from there, lad!" shouts Old Elephant. "This is your destination. Remember?"

Down at street level, Tim gets jostled by the stream of shoppers as he makes his way to Old Elephant holding out his handbook.

"It's yours to keep, Timothy," he stoops down low, "There's a map in the back to help you find your way. And don't you worry about Apple Annie, I see the way you look at her. Have no pity on her. Mr. Stewart sees to it that none of his doormen run her off. She's there every day. He takes good care of her." He whispers in his ear, "Just so you know, she's not really blind. It's all part of her act."

"How's your head holding up, Old Elephant?"

"Fine, just fine," he says shaking Jeremiah's hand. "We'll save you and Tim a seat at Daniel Sweeny's then. Let's say half past one as the bell rings at Saint Paul's."

Tim runs up and gives Old Elephant a hug.

"Hey, what's this now? I've been beaten to the ground one too many times this day. Off with ye! And get yourself a proper hat and some shoes!"

CHAPTER 5 — BARNUM'S AMERICAN MUSEUM

1850

"Pa, can I please take these off?"

"Absolutely not!"

"But I am suffocating. I can't hardly breathe with these on!"

"You'll get used to it, once the leather breaks in."

Staggering awkwardly, the stiff leather boots dig into his calf with a chaffing rub every step of the way, walking block after block since leaving Stewart's heading back down Broadway, passing Chambers, Warren, and Murray. Constricted and trapped his feet struggle to break out and breathe.

"Well, can I at least loosen the laces? I can't move me ankles."

"Fine then."

Tim sits down on the high granite curbstone at the corner of Park Place at 231 Broadway outside William T. Jennings Clothing Store. Next door is Meade Brothers Daguerreotype Gallery at 233 Broadway.

He looks at the paving stones wet with horse urine, brush strokes from the street sweepers, straw poking out of the clumps of horse manure. He breathes in deeply the earthly odor trying to flush out all the perfumes and stifling soap smells at Stewart's Department Store. He takes another breath and holds it in, like trying to rinse out a bad taste in his mouth.

Jeremiah walks over to Tim still sitting at the curb fiddling with his laces. He kneels down. "C'mon then, Tim. Have you forgotten how to tie? Say not another word about them boots and I'll take you to Barnum's."

"You mean it?"

From the the Astor House, they pause to take in the commanding view of Barnum's American Museum — painted gleaming white, taking up the entire corner of Broadway and Ann Street, the bright red letters trimmed in blue. Tim notices how the proper distance puts things in perspective.

"Look on the rooftop, Pa, near the flagpole with the Stars and Stripes, there looks to be a lighthouse up there. What is that curious little shed doing up on the roof?" wonders Tim. "It must be an outhouse." Two words are painted in big black letters, one on top of the other: Camera, then on the next line, Obscura.

Pulling at them with sights and sounds, reeling them in, the swirling music, the gravitating crowds, while the hawker beckons.

"Step right up ladies and gentlemen. See Titania the Queen of the Fairies, only 24 inches high. Feast your eyes on the Feejee Mermaid, the mariner legend come to life captured by Mr. Barnum in all her mystery."

He points with his cane at the poster of the beautiful, bare-breasted mermaids swimming in the ocean. "That alone, my good friends, is worth the price of admission."

He thumps his cane as an exclamation point. "See the club which killed Captain Cook. This and 5,000 curiosities await you! You shan't be disappointed. All courtesy of Phineas T. Barnum, the Napoleon of his profession, untiring in his efforts, who hath spared no expense in procuring these specimens from every continent under the sun for the edification of his fellow American compatriots."

Jeremiah steps up to the ticket window.

"A ticket for me and my son, please."

"Alrighty, that'll be one bit for the boy and two bits for yourself."

As Jeremiah counts out the 12½ cents for the boy and two bits for himself, Tim tugs on his coat, "Pa, what's this 'bit' the man asked for?"

"Goodness lad, you need to understand your coinage if you hope to work for Mr. Brady. Hold out your hand."

Half expecting a rap with a ruler, he clenches his eyes and feels coins drop onto the palm of his hand.

"Open your eyes. Now, what have you got there?"

"Two pennies, a dime, and a ha'penny.

"Twelve and a half cents?"

"Good Tim! There you hold one bit in the palm of your hand."

"So, a shilling is the same as a bit?"

"That's it. Now here's another bit. What does that equal?"

"Twenty-five cents?"

"Right again!" He drops a quarter on top, slightly tarnished, dated 1839, Miss Liberty seated beside a shield. "Now, by what other name do they give a quarter?"

"Two bits."

"And, how many bits to a dollar?"

"Eight."

"There's hope for you yet, Timmy me boy."

"Get your Barnum Guidebook here!" Tim sees a little boy, loaded down with a stack of pamphlets, muscling through the crowd shouting, "Discover all the hidden treasures in America's Museum. All for a shilling! A keepsake to treasure for years to come!"

What a big voice for such a little boy. Tim looks at the kindly face of the man on the front cover. Barnum's American Museum Illustrated. There is a little boy bursting through the page running wild in a dream-cloud of imagination past an elephant with ivory tusks. Up at the top it reads, "Price 12½ cents." A shilling is one bit, he says to himself.

"Pa, can I get Barnum's program, please Pa?"

"You have money in your hand, haven't you?"

With that Tim runs off through the tall swaying crowd after the boy. "Hey," he yells after Tim holding his program. "You gave me an extra ha' penny." Before Tim can say thank you, the boy disappears into the thicket of dresses and long coats.

Tim looks down at the copper half-cent coin. A lady with braided hair and the word Liberty on her headband, the year is 1834. That was six years before I was born. He counts the stars surrounding her, seven and six make thirteen. He flips the coin and stands there looking at it. "Half cent," he sees, surrounded by laurels and United States of America.

"Tim-Oh-Thee!"

Oh, that's not a happy pronunciation. He hears his name again.

"Here I am, Pa! Over here!" In an instant, he sees four shades of emotion flash one after the other on his father's face. First, his worried look changes to relief then to a frown about to utter a cautionary word, but he stops himself and grins his "who the devil cares" expression.

He grabs Tim by the hand. "C'mon then. Let's see Mr. Barnum's Curiosities."

Through the grand entrance of Barnum's American Museum, they step past a row of gas burners casting a subdued, yellow light. By the flickering light they walk into a parlor of wax figures with the busts of Benjamin Franklin, Lafayette, Andrew Jackson, and names he doesn't quite recognize: Cicero, Socrates and Homer.

"Are they real, Pa? Did Barnum cut their heads off, drain the blood and guts, and stuff them full of saw dust?"

"Goodness no! Timothy, where'd you get a notion like that? Those are wax figures with glass eyes and horse-hair."

Following the crowd, they ascend the grand staircase, on the landing before them, a life-size oil painting of Jenny Lind. "Take home a likeness of the Swedish Nightingale," reads the sign behind a glass counter-top on the second floor. A busy clerk, a line of customers. "Hurry, while supplies last! Copies of a Superior Daguerreotype of Jenny Lind for Sale. Daguerrian Portrait by Mr. Jeremiah Gurney. $3.00."

Hanging on the opposite wall, Tim sees an American flag, torn and faded with thirteen stars. The placard reads, "This is the flag General Washington ordered to be raised at The Battery on the 25th of November, 1783 at the Evacuation of New York by the British troops. This same flag was again hoisted on October 19, 1847 at the laying of the cornerstone to the Washington Monument."

Further on they pass through the picture gallery: Daniel Boone, Henry Clay, James Madison, Dolly Madison, and John Scudder, the founder of the American Museum.

In the adjoining room, a display of the clothes that General Tom Thumb wore when he visited Queen Victoria. Tim looks closely at a daguerreotype of the little fellow only 38 inches high, standing on a table, leaning his hand on Mr. Barnum.

"Pa, come have a look at General Tom Thumb!" he shouts across the room. Look at Tom Thumb standing proud, hand on his hip, with his little cap tipped to the side. Stamped on the bottom, Daguerreotype by Samuel Root.

"So that's what the little General looks like."

"Do you think we'll get to see him? Oh my, what's that over there?"

Tim rushes over to see a grotesquely withered arm and sun-bleached hand hanging on the wall. This fragment of humanity once belonged to that most notorious pirate, Tom Trouble, reads the accompanying placard. His body was nailed to a plank and left to rot at the entrance to the harbor at Saint Thomas for all to see.

"Did you ever hear of the notorious pirate, Tom Trouble, Pa?"

"No, I can't say that I have."

A great crowd is gathered below the sign for the Feejee Mermaid. Waiting patiently with his father, Tim hopes to finally catch a glimpse of the beautiful, bare-breasted Feejee Mermaid. As the long line inches forward, Tim begins to notice unhappy faces in the crowd as they turn away from the front near the red velvet rope.

There is the same sour expression on everyone's face, young and old — a grimace etched with disgust in their grin and a foul stench in their nostrils. Getting up on his tippy toes, peering over shoulders, there on the display, his eyes suddenly see a grotesque monkey's head with a shriveled expression attached to the body of a dead fish. A squeamish feeling comes over Tim. His father pulls him away.

"That is no mermaid! I can tell you that," says Jeremiah, "We have been had by Mr. Barnum, Tim!"

This way to Niagara Falls, reads a big hand sign with a pointing finger to a room with a miniature model of the horseshoe falls with running water tumbling over the precipice. Before his father can catch up to him, Tim darts off to the Cosmoramic Room – a circular room, he stands in the center with the crowds and looks in all directions at the city of Paris with the palace and garden of Versailles painted far as the eye can see.

Quick on his heels, his father catches up with Tim as he enters the Magic Lantern Room taking a seat in the darkened theatre as the operator projects images of the Rock of Gibraltar, the Acropolis, the city of Athens, the Roman Coliseum, and the island of Malta.

Coming out of the theatre, Tim skips past the animal displays of elephants, zebras, and giraffes.

This way to the Witch of Staten Island, points the sign. There before him, a gruesome wax figure horror scene, an old woman hunched over, wearing a tattered shawl, smiling a sinister, Hansel and Gretel witch's grin, and holding a bloody axe.

Tim shudders at the scene before him – the life-like wax figure hacking a mother and child, broken bones and shattered skulls with a burning house in the painted background.

The story board tells the tale: Polly Bodine murdered her brother's wife Emeline Housman and their infant daughter Ann Eliza on Christmas Night, 1843, then to hide her despicable deed she set fire to the house on Richmond Terrace, Staten Island.

Tim stares closely. "I can see her breathing Pa! Her eyes twitched!"

"Come now, Tim. I think you've seen enough of Mr. Barnum's curiosities."

"Pa, do you think she was hung for what she did?"

"No, she was acquitted."

"What's that mean?"

"She was declared not guilty." His voice trails off trying to change the topic. "Let's follow the sign upstairs to the third floor and see what this Lecture Room is all about."

As they take a seat in the crowded theatre, the gas lamps flicker once, then gradually darken. The magic lantern lights up and displays a scene of domestic bliss, drawn by George Cruikshank, — food on the table, children playing by a warm fire, a kitten toying with a dog's tail, and the father raises a glass with one hand while holding a bottle of spirits with the other. Look at the tall grandfather clock and there's a silhouette on the wall. The image suddenly disappears.

The magic lantern clicks and the second slide appears – this time things don't look so happy – the fire has gone out, the cat is up on the table licking at an empty plate while the father sits slumped in his chair with a frown on his face.

Tim feels an elbow to his side and a whisper from his Pa just like he does at church. "What do you say we clear out of here and get some ice cream? I saw a sign."

Nearing the exit, an usher holding a dark lantern advises them to sit back down. "You don't want to miss a performance of The Drunkard by the playwright William H. Smith? Do you?" He pauses a moment grabbing a sheet of paper at the table, holding out a fountain pen. "Here then, be a good man and sign the pledge."

"I should have known better than to go into a Lecture Room," mutters Jeremiah.

He hears over his shoulder, "C'mon back and sign the pledge. C'mon then. Do it for the little one."

Jeremiah tugs tightly to Tim's hand quickening their pace.

Up on the rooftop garden, there is a cool refreshing breeze, Barnum's bright red flag flaps high above beside the Stars and Stripes. In between a spoonful of ice cream, they walk over to the glass enclosed parapet, the lighthouse – Barnum's celebrated Drummond Light which can be seen for a mile up Broadway.

"Look at the line of people waiting to get in that shed over there, Pa. Let's go over there."

"What is it now, a line for the privy?"

"No, Pa, it says Camera Obscura."

After waiting patiently in line, they enter the crowded dark room to see an image shining down on a round table before them.

"Oh my, look at that, you can see Saint Paul's Chapel," remarks a voice from the shadows. "How is it possible? Where is it coming from?" says one with wonder. A cynical deep voice, "Oh, it's just another of Barnum's humbugs like the Feejee Mermaid. He cannot fool me."

A man holds out his hand breaking the beam of light. "It is no humbug. This is a law of nature known from the time of the Greeks. See now, look up at the small opening in the roof."

The chins lift up to look at the ray of light from a small aperture in the ceiling through a convex lens and a mirror reflecting the image down onto the viewing table.

Outside, squinting their eyes adjusting to the bright sunshine, Tim stands at the railing next to his father pointing down to the city five stories below. Just like in the Souvenir of New York, a hawk-eye view, rooftop chimneys with trails of smoke, a woman hanging laundry on the line, ship masts in the distance. "Look, Pa, you can see for miles and miles. There's the fountain in The Park, over there's City Hall, there's the Astor House."

"Not so close to the edge, Tim."

"Pa, look at the steeple of Saint Paul's. There's Mr. Brady's Gallery of Daguerreotypes. Why are there so many skylights on his roof? His whole rooftop is made of glass shingles."

"Perhaps Mr. Brady built a greenhouse of some sort to grow flowers."

"Pa, can we go have our likeness taken together? It'll be grand. I'll stand beside you like Tom Thumb."

Jeremiah points to the clock of Saint Paul's and kneels down. "Tim, I'm sorry but we haven't the time. Remember, we must meet Old Elephant for midday supper."

CHAPTER 6 — THE EATING HOUSE

1850

This way to egress, reads the sign pointing down the dimly lit stairwell. They descend landing after landing, then open a door leading out to a narrow brick alleyway. Spun around, not sure where they are, they wander around the corner to Fulton Street.

"Well, Timothy we couldn't have planned it any better. Right there is Smith's Segar Store. Wait here while I get a pouch of tobacco for me pipe."

Tim looks across the 'Way at E. Anthony's Daguerreotype Supplies Shop, there's a black hand sign with white letters pointing up the stairs to Brady's Gallery. He stops himself while his father lights his clay pipe with a double-puff. "What do you say we see about getting you a proper hat at Mr. Genin's? Now let's make haste, we don't want to keep Old Elephant in wait."

Inside the haberdashery, shelf upon shelf of wooden hat molds. Hats, hundreds of hats to choose from, floor after floor, display after display, hats, canes, walking sticks, umbrellas. How about that cap, Tim? Perfectly fine wool cap. Sailor's caps, captain's caps, straw hats, top hats, stovepipe hats.

Mr. Genin approaches. "May I be of assistance? I can see you're having some difficulty. Deciding on a hat is at times bewildering from our extensive line of hats. You must realize that a hat is not merely an article of clothing to protect your head from the sun, the snow, the cold, the wind, and rain. Oh no, on the contrary, a proper hat is most often the first thing one notices about you.

"The hat is your calling card, I always say. It identifies you just as surely as Mr. Doggett's Directory of New York City lists your occupation next to your name and address. One glance at your hat and the public knows in an instant whether you are a fur-trapper or a mariner, a lamplighter or a policeman, a stevedore, an admiral, or the mayor of New York."

Mr. Genin continues, "In selecting a hat, the first question I begin with is what is your trade? Oh, a hat for the boy, I see we have school-boy hats, straw hats, wool caps, newsboy caps, messenger boy hats. I see... Mr. Brady is it? Well, well, Mr. Brady is an artiste, most highly respected in his field as a daguerreotyper. I have a few suggestions. I see, that's not to your liking. You don't prefer this one either. This is one is not for you. Well then, may I ask what style of hat you had in mind?"

Tim tugs on his father's coat. "Pa, tell him I want a cap like Tom

Thumb."

"Oh, the Little General is it?" says Mr. Genin. "Let me check our inventory. The navy-blue wool cap, gold braid, narrow leather brim polished to a high gloss in the military style? Is this what you had in mind?"

"That's it!" Tim snatches it with excitement and pulls it down over his head standing in front of the looking glass.

"Oh, would you look at yourself," says his father stooping down to his eye level pointing into the mirror. "That suits you fine."

Tim pulls the cap over his left eye just like Tom Thumb. Perhaps, Tom and I will become best of friends. He will see me on Broadway and admire my cap and say he has one just the same. Then he will tell me all about his trip to meet Queen Victoria and his travels of the world with Mr. Barnum.

"The hat makes the man, that's what I always say. A fine choice."

"We'll take it."

Stepping smartly on Broadway outside of Genin's, Tim looks again across the 'Way and tries one last time. "Pa, could we please go to Mr. Brady's to have our likeness taken. It will be ever so grand with my new cap standing next to you. Please, Pa."

"Now, Timothy, we haven't the time for sentimentality. Listen to the bells chiming half past. Quickly now, we mustn't keep Old Elephant in wait."

Round the corner of Broadway, to the cool shade of the side street in the shadow of Barnum's tall overpowering building, sits the little building nestled there with the gold letters against the black sign, Daniel Sweeny's House of Refreshments, No. 11 Ann Street, New York.

"Walk right in, Sir. Table for two, Sir? Meeting Old Elephant is it? Right this way, gentlemen. He's been expecting you."

My, what a mess on the floor. There's sawdust everywhere you look sprinkled underneath the tables, like footprints in the sand showing the pegs of the floorboards, clumps of wet sawdust. There's more sawdust here than at the lumberyard.

"Over here!" They see a hand raised among rows of long bench seats, packed tight as a church pew, shoulder to shoulder, glasses clinking, tables set out, no white tablecloths to muffle the sound of plate, knife, fork, and spoon to wood.

"Take a seat, sir. Be with you in-a-minute, sir."

"Would you look at my little navigator! I didn't hardly recognize you in your hat." Old Elephant musters a stiff salute.

Taken aback by his bruised face more pronounced since he last saw him, the white of his right eye filled with cherry red blood, it is painful to look at.

He grabs the boy by the back of the neck pulling him close like his talks with Ginger and Nut to hear his whisper, "Hey now, don't look at me as though you've seen an apparition. I'm quite fine. Never been better. Let's have a look at your new boots."

Releasing his grasp, standing up, raising his voice to a horse command, "Jeremiah, say hello to Broadway Jack, Pop Rice and Balky Bill. This here is me brother James - Young Elephant and you know Yellow Joe."

Suspicious squinting eyes, "I'm wise to you Mistah Inspector. The boys and I are taking our much-deserved afternoon respite waiting for the evening tide of passengers to commence."

"Yellow Joe, he is no inspector. I can attest to that. Jeremiah saved me hide in the altercation outside of Barnum's. If it were not for him, I would not be sitting here before ye."

Black vest, white shirt, black pants, white apron. "What can I get you and your friends, Old Elephant?"

"Good day, Nathaniel. Porters all around courtesy of Yellow Joe."

A gentleman from the next table shouts over. "Waiter! Oh, waiter! Ohhh, Wayyy-terrr!"

"Coming, sir. Be-with-you-in-a-minute, sir." Turning his attention back to Old Elephant, "Now, how about the lad?"

"Oh, yes, we mustn't forget, Tim. A cool cup of Croton for the boy, thank ye kindly, Nat!"

"Waiter!! Where is my porterhouse steak?"

"Coming, sir."

"Well, has the cow been slaughtered or is it still out to pasture? I have been waiting here for over a month it seems."

"Ready-in-a-minute, sir. Coming directly, sir."

"Where did he disappear to? Oh, waiter! Waiter!"

"Here Jeremiah, you and Tim take a gander at the menu."

"See here, Old Elephant. What are these abbreviations all about? Is d. for dollar?" asks Jeremiah in a hush. "I haven't the coin."

"Goodness, no! D. is for sixpence and S. is for shilling. Small plate – sixpence, large plate – shilling. Say you want roast poultry and sirloin steak that would be one shilling sixpence or 18 pence. See?"

Nathaniel returns balancing a tray of pewter mugs setting them gently down gently as a sleeping babe in the crib.

A table behind, all the men are wearing bright red shirts discussing the great fire in Brooklyn at Kelsey's Alley – twenty buildings destroyed, 200 families put out. Tim tugs on Old Elephant's sleeve. "See now, those are the firefighters at that table. Over there are the poets of the press traipsing in from newspaper row on Nassau Street – that's Horace Greeley, editor of the Tribune with one of his knights of the pen, George G. Foster. You get all kinds at Daniel Sweeny's."

Tim overhears jumbled conversations: So that's what all the thunder was about! A hundred-gun salute! I thought the British Navy were firing broadsides in New York Harbor again.

Did you hear John A. Post fell into the North River at the foot of Vesey Street on Saturday night? It doesn't surprise me, the Tribune said he was intoxicated. Lucky for him he was rescued by officers of the third ward. Unlike that poor unfortunate man of the Hudson River Railroad – run over by the 7 o'clock morning train south of the sawmill near Yonkers.

Now what did you say was the cause of the celebration? I see... passage of the bill that adds California to these United States. George, Mister Ross stopped by to make a call, he was most aggrieved that we misprinted his address. Yes, the one who manufacturers the Jenny Lind canes. His address is 57 Reade Street, not 47. He vociferously insisted that the correction appear on page one, top of the fold. Oh yes, I am quite sure James Gordon put him up to it, but we have no choice...

Tim's eavesdropping ears get suddenly and rudely interrupted with a loud slap on Old Elephant's back.

"WALTER!" he shouts, "My, you are a sight for sore eyes!"

Standing before them, is a man holding a glass-bottomed pewter mug.

"It looks as though you are the one with the sore eye, Old Elephant, not I. Are you quite alright? Can I help you home to your mother?"

"Don't you worry about me, Walt. I've never been better. You should see the sorry state of the other fella. Tell me, how goes it? Where have you been? I so miss our many exhilarating night-times."

"I'm fine. Couldn't be better. I've left the print work for good. and I am a scribe at The Brooklyn Eagle."

"You don't say." He slaps Walt on the back.

"Will I see you and the boys tonight at Sandy Welsh's beer cellar?"

"You can depend on it, Walt."

"Waiter! Oh, waiter! I demand to speak with the proprietor this instant!"

"I am Daniel Sweeny. What vexes you, sir? Victuals not to your liking? I'll remind you, this is a sixpenny eating house not some fancy restaurant. If you seek fine cuisine, might I suggest Delmonico's?"

"Mister Sweeny, my issue is not with the cook, but in the tabulation of the bill."

"Well, let me see if any unintentional arithmetic errors were made."

"Please do. Eight shillings is outrageous."

"Hmmm... See here. No errors were made. Clamsoup - sixpence, roast beef - shilling, extra bread - three, butter - sixpence, pickle - sixpence, pudding - sixpence, steam ales - two shillings."

"Sixpence for butter? For that price, I may as well have dined at The Astor! I am surprised there is no charge for salt and pepper."

"Sir, might I suggest a bit of temperance in your patronage. A tumbler of cool Croton is most refreshing and gratis from the hydrant."

"Your insolence is duly noted and not one bit appreciated!"

Looking over the menu, Tim can hardly wait for the food to arrive. "I've never been to an eating house before. We sit here like kings at a feast, but the poor waiter could use some help. Why is everyone so impatient with him? His face is wracked with strain, twisted with stress. Can't you see he's trying his best only to get hollered at? I wouldn't treat Pa in such a manner when he is busy cooking supper. The dogs know better than to pester and get underfoot. But where then is my cup of Croton? He brought another tray of porters but still no cup of water for me."

Following the busy footprints in the sawdust, through the wooden swinging door with the round port-hole window into the chaos of the kitchen, flames shoot up from the broiler, barking orders.

"Beefsteak and taters with vegetables, number 20! Order up!" The iron handle on the oven door clinks shut. Steam rises from the boiling pot. "Mutton, turnips, corned beef, pork and beans! Plate that order for pick-up! We need clean plates!" Tim goes over to the sink, Croton Aqueduct Co. on the pump handle.

"Where on earth did you disappear to?"

"Oh, I got myself a cup of water from the kitchen."

"Timothy, this is an eating house. The waiter serves us. There's no helping yourself."

"But he seemed very busy, Pa. I didn't want to put him out. God helps those who help themselves."

Old Elephant slaps him on the back. "How about refreshing my mug?"

Tim gets up, but Old Elephant laughs, "I spoke merely in jest!"

A hearty meal on pewter plates with two pronged forks. Another course ordered by Old Elephant and his considerable appetite.

Nathaniel plops down another round of porters.

"Time for a toast!" shouts Young Elephant.

"Let's hear from Connie," says Balky Bill.

Rising slowly to his feet, Cornelius lifts his mug up high. "Here's to Jeremiah T. O'Sullivan, as fine a fighter as I ever saw clench his fist. Thank you for letting me live to see the end of this day. To his young son, Timothy, I bestow my heartfelt wishes in your newfound indenture studying under Mr. Mathew Brady. You are one lucky lad! May you take pride in your work, heed your master, earn a decent wage, be safe in your labors, and make your mother and father proud. Take it from an old Jehu, follow your horses, Tim. They shall guide the way!"

Tim knows better than to correct Cornelius about his mother. He thinks of her up in heaven.

"Here, here!"

Pewter mugs clank and spilleth over, raised up high to reveal their glass bottoms.

CHAPTER 7 — FRIDAY, SEPT 13TH

1850

"Rise and shine, Timothy! Quick as a wick or you'll miss The Josephine! Never keep a lady in wait or she'll leave without you. And then where will you be?" His father shouts. "Thomas, make sure Rip Van Winkle gets out of that bed. I have breakfast to tend to."

"C'mon then, Tim. You've got to get up. If you miss the ferry, you'll be swimming all the way to York." With that Thomas gives his brother one last shout, "Tim-Oh-Thee!" Seeing no movement, a devious little grin breaks across his face as he opens the door and calls for reinforcements. "Here now Salty! Pepper! Rex! Come and Get Him!" The dogs jump on the bed wagging their tails burrowing under the blanket to roust the ferret out. Little Salty starts at the pillow and tunnels with his cold wet nose. Rex stands over the lumpy quilt while Pepper barks at the moving feet stirring beneath the blankets.

"I'm up. I'm up. The dogs are soaking wet!" he says as Rex shakes the morning rain from his shaggy coat.

As the dog finishes showering Tim, the musty warm smell of the wet fur of the dogs fills the room. "Well, at least you won't be needing to wash your face," says Thomas. "My, you were like a sack of potatoes when Pa tucked you into bed last night. What was it like over in York?"

Tim stretches out and leans his elbow on the pillow. "It was magical, Thomas. Pure magic. You've never seen so many ships as in New York Harbor. Then we rode on top an omnibus up Broadway. The streets are all paved, the sidewalks too. There is not much call for a carpenter over in York – all the houses are built of granite, marble or brownstone. Then we went to Barnum's and saw the Witch of Staten Island. She's an old sea hag who butchered a mother and child."

"She is not an old sea hag."

"Well, you haven't been to Barnum's have you?"

"Listen, Tim, I've seen Polly Bodine with mine own eyes, on a dare, tending to her garden outside her house on Richmond Avenue. Let me tell you, she looks nothing like a witch."

"Breakfast is ready!" their father's voice bellows. The dogs charge off in a stampede down the stairs. Sitting around the kitchen table, his father lifts the lid on the cast iron stove and puts another piece of wood on the fire, slices of ham sizzle in the skillet, potato pancakes fritter in the pan.

"Get from underfoot!" he shouts while stamping his foot. The tea kettle begins to whistle with a blast of steam.

"Pa, should I put the dogs outside?"

"No, Thomas. Leave them be, besides little Salty does not like the rain. Timothy, be sure to wear your oilskin." He cracks an egg on the side of the iron skillet and pours the tea. "Put butter to the biscuits, boys." Setting the ham and potato cakes down, he turns to the eggs. "What do you say to sunny-side eggs on this rainy morn?"

With his back turned, the boys dig-in grabbing biscuits with their hands, poking ham with their two-pronged forks. Tim puts a slab of ham in his biscuit, the butter melts as he takes a bite.

"Timothy!" his father shouts. "We haven't said Grace yet!" He slams the frying pan of eggs down on the table.

"Sorry, Pa."

"You know well the rule. I shouldn't have to repeat myself."

"Yes, Pa, Grace before meals."

"I'm no saint. Maybe I let you boys run wild, but we must give thanks."

"Yes, Pa."

"Ye boys don't know how lucky ye are to have this here food on the table…" he points to the skillet of ham.

Oh, dear God, please don't let him start lecturing about The Hunger. He'll go on and on like a never-ending sermon about The Hunger once he gets started.

"And Thomas, you had better wipe that grin off of your face, before I wipe it off for you with the back of my hand. I saw you chomping at the grub as well. Now take a moment and give thanks."

The boys bow their heads and mutter a few words before digging in. After breakfast, Jeremiah grabs Tim's coat off the hook. "Now, Timothy, early this morning I stitched a secret pocket inside of your coat here. Look closely, now. Pull this thread. There's money in case you should need it."

"What for?"

"Well, you never know… And don't be buying striped candy or any more souvenirs. This is only to be used in an emergency. Understand?"

"Yes, Pa."

"Good. Now here's fare for the ferry and spending money for the day. Keep this in your front pocket." He wraps some biscuits in a checkered napkin and stuffs it in his coat pocket. "This'll be for your midday meal."

"Say now, Pa. What day is it?" asks Thomas as he mops egg yolk from his plate with a biscuit.

His father looks at the page torn from the Farmer's Almanack nailed to the wall near the stove. September hath 30 days, reads the page. The monthly short story, The Ditch, tells the tale of poor Patrick, who was found "beam ends in the bottom of the ditch with his bottle for his pillow. It was his last drink… Paddies will be paddies."

"Why it's Friday, September 13th."

"Aye, that's a bad omen for his first day of work."

"Pay him no mind, Timothy. That's foolish talk from the Old Country... Now get your boots on before you miss the ferry."

"Aren't you coming with me, Pa?"

"No, son you must go it alone."

Walking along York Avenue, all alone in the rain. What a difference a day makes. Thursday, bright and sunny, Friday, clouds and rain. I wish Pa was here with me. Yesterday seems so very long ago. It's like it never happened, just a dream. How shall I make it on my own? I already miss Pa, Pepper, Rex, and Salty — even Thomas.

Just then he hears the approaching steam whistle of the ferry. Quick as his feet will carry him, Tim runs with all his might down York Avenue skidding on the slick wet pavers near Mooney's Stables. He falls in a heap, hands scuffed, pants torn, knees scraped.

Why must people wear shoes? The slick soles have no grip. I wouldn't have slipped in bare feet. Now look at me. How can I go to work looking like this? I shall turn back home. Pa will surely understand. Home is where I belong. I know what Pa will say, "Oh, look at you, you're soaked to the bone. You'll catch your death of cold, let's get you out of those wet clothes." Then he'll make me a cup of tea.

"Come here," said his father earlier this morning. "Let me button that oil skin coat. Now where's that new hat of yours?" Tim dons his cap with a tug to the side. His father shouts, "Thomas, come have a look at your brother."

"Well, would you look at the fine young gentleman in his fancy hat and shoes headed over to York. Before too long, he'll not be associating with the likes of us, Pa."

"Nonsense, don't listen to your fool brother." He adjusts Tim's cap and levels it off. "Just do your best."

"Yes, Pa."

"Fare thee well oh little Broadway Dandy."

"That's enough out of you, Thomas." Turning back, he whispered, "Do us proud, Tim." Then he gave me a swift whack on the back-side pushing me out the door. "Off with ya."

The ferry whistle blows again, The Josephine is calling. Hurry now, she says. Standing alone at the rail, this is the spot where Pa and I stood. No one is out on deck, they're all huddled inside. It's just a bit of the wet. Well, I've made it. Here I stand all on my own on the way to York.

At the foot of Whitehall Street, Tim looks amongst the omnibuses in the pouring rain for Old Elephant.

"Pardon me sir, have you seen Old Elephant?" he calls up to the driver.

"Old who?"

"Old Elephant. He is a Jehu on the Knickerbocker Line."

"Never heard of him."

"I speak of Cornelius Ryan, commander of the Lady Washington."

"I know him not. Hop aboard."

Tim grapples the wheel and thrusts himself up top. "Just where do you think you're going? Passengers down below."

"But Old Elephant let me sit beside him."

"Passengers down below. You'll find shelter from the rain."

Tim climbs back down the pegs and spokes of the wheel.

"Don't forget the passage. Sixpence in the trap if you please."

Inside the crowded omnibus, the dank smell of rain-soaked wool reminds him of the wet dogs back home. There is no place to sit. Limited to Twelve, reads the sign. Men standing, women sitting.

"Sit on my knee here," says a kindly old woman with pale blue eyes patting her knee. She looks like Grandma back in Kenmare with her long shawl pulled around her. The omnibus jostles along the bumpy street. Tim can't reach the straps high above and loses his balance with a stagger. "I got you, lamby pie," says she. "I won't bite, rest yourself."

Tim cautiously sits himself down. "That's a good boy." Hands holding a newspaper across from him, New York Daily Tribune, No. 2936, Friday, September 13, 1850. Price Two Cents. I can't hardly see out the windows, elbows, shoulders and hats blocking the view. Rain patters on the roof. I wish I was up top with the driver even in the rain. Oh, how I love the soothing rain. It's just a bit of the wet. People always tell me to come in from the rain before I catch my death of cold. It's only water from the heavens. The windows rattle over a bump.

A gentleman turns the page to his paper, the New York Herald. Jenny Lind Opera Glasses for sale, Victor Bishop, 25 Maiden Lane, upstairs. Jenny Lind Concert Hats – just imported from Braga, for sale by John & Robert Osborn, 111 Wall Street. One advertisement with three exclamation points catches his eye, Lind! Lind!! Lind!!! — The best Engraving of this distinguished lady may be obtained at the American Daguerreotype Galleries of the Subscribers… Meade Brothers, 233 Broadway, opposite the Park Fountain.

I wish they would open the windows steamed over and let some fresh air in. The rocking motion of the omnibus swaying back and forth on the leaf springs banded tightly together. The comfortable lap of the nice old lady, her soothing voice whispers, "There, there lamby pie." She pats his head as he drifts off to sleep.

An uneasy dream, I'm running away, but my legs have given out, they can't carry me. I fall to the ground and start pulling my body, crawling with my elbows but it's so slow dragging my heavy body. I can't feel my legs. I can't even bend my knees. Oh, no, there's a mouse in my coat pocket moving around rummaging for food. Wait, that's no mouse, that's a big wet river rat after me biscuits that Pa wrapped up for me. Now the rat is nuzzling in my pant pocket. I can feel him against me leg. Parched lips stuck together, a dry taste in his mouth.

"Sssh, now. Go back to sleep. Rest your little head." A gentle pat, fingers through his hair, scratching his scalp ever so slightly. A little breeze blows by his ear, a faint whistle, rumbling waves like a seashell to his ear. Her chest inhales and blows another breeze. "Sssh…" She draws another breath. "Sssh…"

A sharp pinch to his thigh. "Wake up now." His heavy sleepy head snaps back with a jerk. "Wake up, I said!"

Staggering to his feet disorientated. "What is this place? Where is Pa? Where is Salty? Hands clenched tight around his throbbing wrist, blocking the blood. A violent tug. He stumbles to the ground. Dragged along the pavement, "On your feet!" Crowds of people passing by. A flash of light, clap of thunder, a smash across his head, cheek stinging, ears ringing, head throbbing.

Who is this? I've seen this face somewhere before. He tugs back to wrench his wrist free. The blue eyes, not so kind now, boiling fierce, the jolly wrinkles from years and years of laughter, grimace with hate. She's winding up again. Tim ducks. She pulls him closer and wallops him repeatedly.

Muffled shouts, I can't quite hear what she's saying. A gentlemen bumps into me and gives me a harsh look. What have I done? Where am I? Where is she taking me? Her strong grasp I cannot break. Kicking her about the shins, pulling hard. Down a side-street alleyway.

"Quick now, Boys. I caught a fresh one, just off the boat." She pins him down on the ground, stomping on his chest. "Act lively now! Take his boots, Michael!"

Lifting up his ankles, tugging off his boots. "Search the bottom of his boots, Jimmy! Search his pockets." She bends over to spit in his face, "Where's the rest of it? Give it up!"

She unbuttons his coat. "Ah, here's his hiding place." She pulls the thread and takes the dollar note.

As the boots pop off and his feet break free, Tim rolls over on his belly, staggers to his feet, and runs off down the street. Bare feet on wet stones. I'm free. Rain keeps pelting. "Go, get him boys!" Keep running, don't look back.

Across the street is a massive stone building with great granite columns, police officers tugging on prisoners, some just little boys, in leg irons and hand clasps, wagons with cages, Paddy Wagons. Wait now, isn't that the Halls of Justice that Old Elephant pointed out on my Souvenir of New York. He called it The Tombs. You don't want to wind up there, he said.

Not ever.

"Stop Thief!" he hears the boys call out behind him. A gentleman steps in front of him grabbing Tim in a bear hug.

"I'm no thief, sir, please let me go. I'm the one that was robbed."

"Nonsense."

The two boys catch up to him breathing hard, one wearing his Tom Thumb cap and the other his shiny new boots. "Thank you kindly, sir," says the boy tipping his cap.

"Take this street urchin where he belongs – to The Boys Prison at The Tombs."

I shall never see New Brighton again. My half-bed across from Thomas, the candle table riddled with wax. This must be a bad dream, please let me wake up. Please let me wake up next to Thomas snoring.

"Stop fidgeting will ya! Don't worry, we're not taking you to The Tombs," says one of the boys. "We're taking you back to Nana at The Five Points."

A locomotive rumbles slowly down the tracks of Centre Street, loudly blowing its whistle – New York and Harlem Rail Road. Tim's rain-soaked wrists. I can break free and slip out of these hand shackles. Now is my chance. The train whistle blows. Sudden stop. Tug hard. Pull with all your might. Right hand free. Sidewinder to the jaw. Left hand free. Hold the nail steady. Double-tap, then drive the nail home.

Tim crosses the tracks then darts off down Leonard Street. Hands to his knees, gasping, panting. littering the ground — brown stoneware beer bottles. Peter Ballantine & Sons reads one. Croton Ale reads another.

Lifting his head, standing upright Tim looks for the two boys. Before him a small triangle park, a rickety wooden fence, pigs munching at the refuse heap... there's not a soul around. Probably sleeping off last night's celebration. The wild retreat among the rocks - the woe-begone party. A cow lifts her head and looks him straight in the eye. You're not from these parts. What are you doing here?

I am lost, hopelessly lost. I will be ever so late to work. What is this place? Tim sees a sign nailed to a tree with crude letters, Paradise Park.

I am not sure where I am or which way to go. If I stay here much longer, those boys will surely find me. Quick breaths fighting back tears. I wish Pa would come find me. Please Pa. How does that prayer go?

Please Saint Anthony please come around, I am so lost and cannot be found. Blurry tears. Stop that now. Stop sniveling. Take a deep breath. Which road should I take? Quick now. Decide. Follow your horses. Cross Street or Orange Street or...

See that street sign. What's it say now?

Anthony Street! Tim sprints with all his might muttering his little prayer in stride. "Please Saint Anthony Street, please come around, I am so lost and cannot be found."

In the distance he sees an omnibus cross the road. That must be Broadway up ahead. Fast as you can. He stops at the corner and sees a sign. "Dr. John Moffat – Life Medicines." The cantankerous rider on the Lady Washington was on his way to see Dr. Moffat. Look, there is New York Hospital, wrought iron letters on the fence read, No. 319 Broadway. Oh, it is good to be back on Broadway. Now, I must make my way to Mr. Brady's.

CHAPTER 8 — LATE

1850

"Beggar boy, Be-gone! You'll find no hand-outs here!"

"I'm no beggar, sir. I'm Timothy. I am here to see Mr. Brady."

"What is your surname?"

"O'Sullivan."

"Ohh…" he repeats flipping through the broad sheets to a heavy ledger book, "I see no appointment for an Ohh Sullivan. There must be some oversight."

"I'm not here for a sitting, sir. I am here to work."

"Work? Look at the time!" The brass pendulum swings back and forth. The clock reads quarter-past nine. "You are late! Nearly two hours late! Boys are to report at half seven sharp. You think you can waltz in to work late? And look at your sorry state! Your services are no longer required. Boys come by the bushel on Broadway. There are five dozen boys out there who would gladly fill your shoes. Oh pardon me, you haven't any shoes."

"But I was told to ask for Mr. Brady, sir."

"I repeat, your services are no longer required at this establishment. Benjamin, be a good boy and escort this wet troll back to the squalor whence he emerged."

Walking a block down Broadway, bare feet upon the wet, rainy slate, Tim passes the corner of Dey Street and stops at 187 Broadway, outside J.C. Booth's Tailoring Shop. I'll just have to take The Josephine back home to New Brighton. My services are no longer required. That's all there is to it. That's what the man told me.

What man? Pa will surely ask.

Tim stands underneath the awning, and peers into the display case at the foot of the stairs leading up to Jeremiah Gurney's establishment at 189 Broadway. Rain dripping down, pattering the canvas. He will grab me by the shirt with two hands so he can look me right in the eye.

Don't lie to me, he will say. Was it Mr. Brady you spoke with? You know what he looks like?

Yes, Pa. I didn't get his name, Pa.

Well, Aunt Maggie will not be pleased one bit. Not one bit. She went to much trouble to get you this indenture.

Tim stares at the daguerreotypes on display in their red velvet cases. "Copies of a superior daguerreotype of Jenny Lind for sale," reads the sign pointing up the stairs. I wonder how they are made.

Tim reaches his hand into his pant pocket. I haven't the money for the fare. In a panic, he reaches for his secret stitched pocket. No, Nana stole that too. How shall I ever get back home?

Well, you march yourself right back there and get that gentleman's name for to tell Aunt Maggie. She will demand it and then she will have a word with Mrs. Brady. Perhaps Mr. Brady will lend you sixpence to get back home to Salty. Promise to pay him when you see him at church.

Tim turns about face and heads back up Broadway. He notices a a sign pointing up the stairs to Martin M. Lawrence's Daguerreotype Gallery.

He stops outside Edward. Anthony's Shoppe at 205 Broadway. He looks inside the storefront display of daguerreotype materials: glass bottles marked: iodine, bromine, gold chloride, and mercury. There are copper plates, an assortment of polishing pads, and there standing on a tripod, is a wooden box with a brass cylinder. He looks at the hand pointing up to Brady's Gallery. Tim takes a deep breath and ascends the creaky carpeted stairs.

"You again? I thought I told you to vacate these premises."

"Please, what is your name sir?"

"You impudent little shirkster. I need not tell you my name."

"I must speak with Mr. Brady, directly."

"That is not possible. He is in an important meeting with Mr. Barnum."

"Well, I shall sit here and wait."

"You go right ahead. I am sure Mr. Brady will take great satisfaction in dismissing you himself — the guile in showing up late to work, not to mention your unkempt, filthy wet, slovenly appearance. The tone of your voice is truly astounding!"

Tim takes a seat on the plush sofa. He looks at the brass name plate on the closed door, Mr. Mathew B. Brady. I wonder what the B. stands for, Bartholomew perhaps. Strange how he spells Mathew with one t. Tim stares at a lithograph hanging on the hallway wall, New York from the Steeple of St. Paul's Church, Looking East, South and West.

Why, there is Mr. Brady's shoppe at the corner of Fulton Street – further down there's a furniture warehouse, Hopkins and Crow, Glass, Paints and Oils, Piano For... Strange, the lithograph just ends at the word 'for'. The artist ran out of room. Perhaps it reads, Piano for sale or Piano Forte. Piano means soft. Forte is strong.

Looking at Broadway he sees Smith's Segar Store. That's where Pa got his pouch of tobacco. Next door is Genin the Hatter at 214 Broadway then Barnum's Museum. So true to life. Look at all the omnibuses. There is a little girl holding her father's hand, stretching, breaking the grasp. Look on the rooftop, there is the Camera Obscura that Pa and I ventured into – the Dark Room. I wonder who drew this. Tim steps forward to examine the lower left corner. He leans in closer – "By J. W. Hill."

"Step away from there – do not press your pug nose to the glass."

"Sorry, sir, I was merely looking."

"You may as well take your leave. Mr. Brady's meeting with Mr. Barnum is taking longer than expected. His appointment book is rapidly filling up. Perhaps you can come back tomorrow?"

Tim hears loud voices coming from the other side of the door then a loud slam on a tabletop like Pa sometimes does to the kitchen table when he wishes to emphasize a point.

"If it's all the same to you, I will wait here."

"You are merely wasting your time."

Suddenly the ornate door handle turns with a click and the door swings open. Standing before him, a tall man with broad shoulders in a fine black coat with satin collar holds his tall stove pipe hat. The face of a friendly but tough barkeep, ready to serve, ready to smile, ready to snarl, and ready to clobber. He has a big bulbous nose, pock-marked cheeks probably from the small-pox. Isn't that the man standing beside Tom Thumb in that daguerreotype by Samuel Root. Why yes it tis. That is Mr. Barnum.

He turns around. "Brady, have you any idea how much I've invested in the Jenny Lind Enterprise: Mr. Julius Benedict, her musical director, Signor Giovanni Belletti, the baritone, the concert halls, printer's ink, advertisements, playbills, passage on The Atlantic, her servants, the suite at the Irving House. I can assure you, I have laid out not a ha'penny less than $50,000."

"Mr. Barnum, I am merely trying to schedule a sitting."

"I am her manager. She has her third concert tonight, rehearsals and dress rehearsals. She hasn't the time."

Looking up, short in stature, Brady wrinkles his nose behind his spectacles, blinking. "The public demands it, Mr. Barnum."

"Don't lecture to me about the public. I know all about the public. The public is a very strange animal. Her schedule does not permit." With a sway of his arm, stovepipe to his crown, he tips his hat and descends the staircase.

As the scene before him draws to a close, Tim stands to speak with Mr. Brady but the door quickly closes shut.

"I wouldn't do that if I were you..." he hears behind his back, knuckle poised before the door.

No, Tim thinks to himself, now would not be the opportune time to ask for sixpence. I know not to trouble Pa when he walks in the door after a hard day's work. Wait for him to pull his boots off and light his clay pipe. That's when to pester him and not a moment before. Perhaps one of the bootblacks at South Ferry will loan me the fare. His knuckle poises inches from the door. He hears his father's voice. Do us proud, Tim. Before he can stop, he hears himself knock on the door.

A soft murmur, he turns the door handle and enters.

Grabbing Tim from behind, "Mr. Brady so sorry for the rude interruption, shall I escort this miscreant to the street?"

"No, Mr. Fredricks that will not be necessary. And please close the door on your way out."

Spectacles with blue tinted glass at the tip of his nose, sitting behind his desk, holding an elaborate gold pen with a diamond tip, scratching away on a sheaf of paper, a fresh clean shaven face of about 30 years, thick wavy brown hair moist with hair tonic, as though he just dunked his head while swimming in the Kill von Kull, Mr. Brady looks up and says softly, "Take a seat, Timothy." How on earth did he know my name. "I've been expecting you."

Staring down at himself, torn pants, scraped knee, soaked to the bone, the wet smell of the dog clashing with Mr. Brady's cologne, what a sorry sight I must present. He places his hand on his knee to conceal his ripped pants.

"Mr. Brady, I would ever be so grateful if you could lend me fare for the Josephine. I shall repay you promptly."

"Whatever for?"

"Well, you see, Nana took all me money and her boys took me shoes and cap and I have no way to get home to Staten Island. You see, it is too far for me to swim."

"So, it tis." He pauses a moment and reaches into his waistcoat for his change purse and places two shillings within reach. "I am just a bit dismayed as you have decided not to pursue your apprenticeship as a daguerreotyper. There is much promise in the new art. Is there anything I can say so as to change your mind?"

"No, Mr. Brady."

"Is my establishment not to your liking? Was the staircase too steep a climb?"

"Oh no, Mr. Brady."

"Did my altercation with Mr. Barnum put you off? I rarely blaze with outbursts."

"No, Mr. Brady."

"Well then, your mind seems to be made up." He pushes the coins to the edge of the desk then lowers his head scribbling with his pen dipping in the inkwell he says half to himself. "Such a pity, I had high hopes for you."

Turning the door handle, looking down at the coins in the palm of his hand, he's given me far too much. "Mr. Brady…"

"Yes, what is it?"

"Mr. Barnum was not exact with you…"

Taking off his spectacles, "how do you mean?"

"Well, you see, you've given me too much coin. The fare is only sixpence for the ferry."

"That is quite alright, my boy. Now then, what do you mean Mr. Barnum was not exact with me?"

"Well, you see, he has the same name as my father, Jeremiah."

"Who does?"

"Jeremiah Gurney. Yes, that is how I remembered his name when we visited Barnum's yesterday and saw the stacks of daguerreotypes of Jenny Lind by Jeremiah Gurney for sale."

Brady's fist slams down on the desk. "I knew it. That scoundrel!"

"Then after I was told my services were no longer required at this establishment, I took a walk down Broadway in the direction of the ferry and saw the display case outside Mr. Gurney's at 189 Broadway. He had a sign which read 'Superior Daguerreotypes of Jenny Lind for Sale.'"

"Superior? Poor Mr. Gurney, he caved-in to Barnum's demand. I, however, shall not abide." Coming from behind his desk, he takes out a five dollar note. "Here this should be more than enough. I am but a Doubting Thomas. Bring me the likeness of Jenny Lind. I must see it with mine own eyes. Quick as your little bare feet will carry you."

"Yes, Mr. Brady."

Running to the door, he hears Mr. Brady, "And one more thing Timothy, your services are required at this establishment. Pay no mind to Mr. Fredricks, he is my trusted gatekeeper."

Running down the stairs, Mr. Fredricks hollers after him, "You won't last the day... Boys come and go at Brady's!"

Darting past the carriages and wagons crisscrossing Broadway, Tim pays the price of admission at Barnum's ascending the staircase to purchase a daguerreotype of Jenny Lind. Running with all his might, he returns to Mr. Brady's office with a knock on the door.

"Excellent work, Timothy." Taking the daguerreotype in his hand, Brady sits down in his chair to examine it closer. "The light is too harsh and her expression is strained. This was clearly a rush job. I mean no disrespect to Mr. Gurney, he is the true pioneer of the new art— the first to study under Professor Morse, the first to open a daguerreotype studio on Broadway, the first in this country, but this is clearly not his best work. I can tell Barnum was looking over his shoulder making the atmosphere tense – utterly toxic — pure poison to a proper sitting. I can do better. Sit here while I finish my demand letter to Mr. Barnum then you shall messenger it over."

Sitting in silence listening to Brady's diamond tipped pen scratch away at the paper and the soft mutterings of attempts at the written expression, he scribbles some more than crumples the paper and tosses it into his brown leather trash receptacle with a sigh of exasperation.

"How is your hand at penmanship? My eyes grow weak and my

unsteady hand cramps with the holding of this implement. Let me see you make your mark."

He reaches for a pen in the silver box, etched letters, Bard & Brothers, 101 William Street, New York. Tim holds the fine pen and carefully writes his name, Timothy H. O'Sullivan.

Brady takes a look. "Highly commendable. Such fine strokes. You shall be my scribe. Here take my chair whilst I dictate... Mr. Barnum, comma, Sir, I beg leave of communicating these few lines soliciting your attention..."

Hand to his chin, pacing the room, Brady thinks of the next sentence while Tim stares at an image of a man with a black flowing cape, his hair combed forward like a Roman statue. "Is that Julius Caesar, Mr. Brady?"

Brady turns himself round. "Oh, goodness no, Timothy that is none other than Thomas Cole, the great landscape artist who passed away two years ago. Unfortunately, the daguerreotype did not exist in Roman times, would that it did. The daguerreotype is but a recent discovery. What year were you born?"

"1840."

"Ah, you see the daguerreotype was but in its infancy at that time. The year was 1839, a golden sun-drenched October morn, when I was but a jewel case manufacturer at 189 Broadway."

"You worked for Mr. Gurney?"

"Oh yes, above J.C. Booth's. I made the cases for all the wares at Mr. Gurney's Watch and Jewelry Shoppe. You see, every precious stone, every diamond ring, every watch, and necklace needs a proper case. Proper presentation to the customer is paramount. I also made jewel cases for Tiffany and Young, and supplemented my income whilst working as a clerk at A. T. Stewart's."

"I went to the Marble Palace just yesterday."

"No, this was in the day before Mr. Stewart built his Marble Palace when his establishment was located at Chambers Street next door to Tiffany's. I also did work for Mr. Edward Anthony and Company, making surgical instrument cases and miniature jewel cases."

"You mean the shoppe downstairs?"

"Yes, the very same. Here come have a look at a sample of my work." In Brady's hand a jewel case with crushed blue velvet, brass cornered edges finely trimmed with a gold inlaid harp. He hands it to Tim.

"Such fine workmanship, Mr. Brady."

"The harp is my trademark. Push the button here."

The case magically opens like a tiny book, to the left blue velvet padding inlaid with swirling gold braided motifs, to the right a small daguerreotype with brass matte set behind glass, a stark image of a man as if etched on a silver plate.

Tim sighs with wonder.

"This is a daguerreotype, what we call the mirror with a memory," says Brady, "Do you know how they make a looking glass?"

"No."

"They coat the back pane of glass with silver, mercury, tin and copper then they paint it black. Look into the mirror with a memory, tell me what you see…"

"I see a man…"

"Not just any man, that my boy is Samuel F. B. Morse, the inventor of the telegraph."

"That's Professor Morse?" says Tim incredulously. "I somehow pictured him differently."

"Did you know the man of science is also a portrait painter? Oh yes, a most gifted artist. Well one day he was in Washington City painting a portrait of Lafayette when word arrived via horse messenger that his wife was gravely ill. When he arrived at his home in New Haven, Connecticut, his poor wife had already been long buried before he could say his proper goodbyes. From that day on he resolved to discover a more rapid means of communication. Look out my window, gaze upon the telegraph lines extending the course of Broadway clear all the way to Albany for all we know. There is talk of a transatlantic cable."

Brady walks about his office and points to a daguerreotype hanging on the wall beside Thomas Cole. "This is my dear friend William Page, a talented portraitist who encouraged me to become an artist like himself. I became extremely attached to William. He took an interest in me and gave me a bundle of his crayons to copy.

"While I had the calling and the temperament to become an artist, alas I had not the talent," he says looking down at his hands. "Unfortunately, these hands of mine would not comply much in the same way my penmanship was ill-kempt so too were my brushstrokes — in want of a graceful hand. But the sirens still beckoned to me. So, William and I set off from Albany on a steamer bound for York. We shared a studio on Chambers Street back in the day when I worked at Stewart's and honed my craft as a jewel case manufacturer at night while William studied under Professor Morse at the New York University overlooking Washington Square."

"Did Mr. Page aim to learn the telegraph and the Morse alphabet?"

"Oh, no Timothy, William studied art with Professor Morse who was painting portraits at starvation prices. Then one morning while having scones and tea, William read the paper aloud to me as he often did, the date was September 30, 1839. See here, I saved the clipping in this frame — it was the first mention I ever heard of the New Art. The New York Herald reported on the curious crowds gathered outside Chilton's, the chemist at

263 Broadway. "Oh, I can hear William now, 'Mathew, listen to this…'" dabbing his mouth with a napkin, clearing his throat. Here, allow me to read the account from the Morning Herald…

"The New Art – We saw, the other day, in Chilton's, in Broadway, a very curious specimen of the new mode, recently invented by Daguerre in Paris of taking on copper the exact resemblance of scenes and living objects, through the medium of the sun's ray's reflected in a camera obscura. The scene embraces a part of St. Paul's church, and the surrounding shrubbery and houses, with a corner of the Astor House and for aught we know, Stetson looking out a window, telling a joke about Davie Crockett."

"Oh, how William laughed at that part."

"Who is Stetson, Mr. Brady?"

"Mr. Stetson is the highly respected manager of The Astor House. He is from Boston, you know. Now getting back, the article explains the process…

'First, take a small sheet of copper-plate copper, of the dimensions of the picture to be represented – Second, let the surface of this sheet be silvered over and diluted with nitric acid.'

"Etcetera, Etcetera… I won't bore you with the full explanation, but the article goes on to explain the entire process in great detail.

"When William finished reading the article, he entreated me, 'Mathew! This is your chance to become a practitioner of the New Art. I can provide you with an introduction to Professor Morse. He is trying to supplement his meager wages by teaching a course in the daguerreotype process for a fee of $25 per pupil,' he said to me.

"I was a bit hesitant. Now, remember I was but seventeen. That was a considerable sum back in the day and I had the rent collector to contend with despite the generous assistance of William from time to time."

Mr. Brady continued his story staring into the eyes of Morse cradled in the jewel case. "So later that evening, I discussed the matter with William and he offered, no, he demanded that he pay for my education with Professor Morse. I expressed my misgivings, that I had not the aptitude to become a practitioner in the New Art.

"William dispensed these notions, 'Mathew, you are forgetting your skills as jewel case manufacturer. Do you not realize what an integral part this is to a successful daguerreotype artist?'

"Judging by my look of bewilderment, William proceeded to explain, 'Presentation is everything! Each daguerreotype needs a proper jewel case to protect it and cherish it.'

"Why, I never thought of that William."

"That is precisely why you have me, Mathew. You and your self-doubt can be your own worst enemy. I still think you had the makings of a great portraitist if you had not given up on yourself. Think of it, you and I will one day be artists. Perhaps, we can get a proper place in the country, say in Staten Island and keep our studio in York."

"That would be most agreeable."

"There is just one thing, Mathew that concerns me."

"Yes, I shall fully repay you William, with interest. I promise."

"No, Mathew, that is but a trifle. My concern is this. I shall gladly make your introduction to Professor Morse if you promise to lose that lilt."

"My lilt? Why, you've never mentioned that before."

"See there just now, your lyrical pronunciation of the word 'bah-four'. That is from the streets of Cork. Professor Morse is not partial to Catholics, even less so with Hibernians. He is an active member of the Nativist Party. Now then, where were you born Mr. Brady?"

"My father, Andrew, is from Cork, my mother, Julia, is from Cork, I am from Cork, you fully know that William."

"Oh, Mathew, you must relent. Think of the New Art."

"And so, the next day, William and I made our way to Professor Morse's rookery on Washington Square East to the Main Building of the New York University, that impressive gothic structure."

"Oh, yes I saw it yesterday when we made our way around the Square to the beginning point of Fifth Avenue then we went all the way up the Avenue to 42nd Street to see the Croton Reservoir. Mr. Brady, what is a rookery?"

"Well now, in the true sense of the word, a rook is from the crow family and a rookery is a crow's nest. Some use it to describe a hovel. But the meaning I'm after is an atelier – that is an artist's workshop or studio.

"Oh, you've never seen such a pigsty. Utter chaos, but the inner workings of a true genius's mind were on display. Dinnerware and drinking glasses, half-eaten meals, crisscrossing telegraphic wires stretched about the room, his precious electro-magnetic machine on one table, clothes strewn in a state of disarray, waistcoats and stockings dangling from the wires. On another table was one of Daguerre's cameras then there were his canvases and an easel, paints and stiffened brushes. Then staring at me on the wall was a portrait of Thomas Addis Emmet, the great Irish patriot, painted by none other than Samuel F. B. Morse. I nearly bowled over!"

"Why Mr. Brady? Did you nearly trip over a telegraph wire?"

"No, lad, have you not heard of Thomas Addis Emmet?"

"No, I can't say as I have, Mr. Brady."

"Well, look out my window onto St. Paul's churchyard down below. Do you see that marble obelisk standing thirty feet tall? You can't miss it. Well, that marble was brought here from…"

"Don't tell me. I know… from the quarries of Tuckahoe."

"How on earth did you know?"

"I learned a thing or two from Old Elephant."

"Old who? Well, never you mind. You shall learn a thing or two about Thomas Addis Emmet. That obelisk is dedicated to his memory. He was a proud member of the United Irishmen, fighting for independence much like the Sons of Liberty. His brother, Robert, was captured by the British who not only hanged him, but then beheaded him for added measure."

"Hanged then behead? But wouldn't the hanging alone have killed him, Mr. Brady?"

"Yes, indeed, it would."

"But why cut his head off? I wouldn't want that to happen to my brother despite all our fights."

"You see, Timothy, the British wished to make an example of Robert Emmet and quash the United Irishmen. He was a good friend of Theobald Wolfe Tone. You've heard of Wolfe Tone haven't you?"

"No, I have not."

"Oh my... Well, Thomas Addis Emmet escaped persecution and came to this city. He took up the practice of law and fought for the liberty of slaves taking refuge in New York. He was a good friend of Robert Fulton. You've heard of Mr. Fulton?"

"Yes, Mr. Brady, he invented the ferryboat, The Jersey."

"Thank goodness. Well, Mr. Emmet went on to become Attorney General in New York. You'll find the American eagle and Irish harp chiseled in that marble."

"So, why did his portrait bowl you over Mr. Brady?"

"Well, Morse is not too fond of the Irish, and here he is painting the portrait of none other than Thomas Addis Emmet!"

"Well, I suppose a starving artist cannot be too particular about who sits in his chair — even if it is some Irishman."

"Truer words were never spoken, Timothy!" he says with a laugh. "Now getting back to the University rookery – Morse ushered us into his laboratory."

William said, "Allow me to introduce my dear friend Mathew B. Brady, who has expressed interest in learning the New Art."

"Brady?" Morse eyed me a bit suspiciously. "Where does your family hail from? I've seen your face someplace before."

"In my stilted new accent, I replied, 'My birthplace was Warren County, New York, in the woods about Lake George. Perhaps you recognize me from your visit to Jeremiah Gurney's shoppe above Booth's haberdashery. I am a jewel case manufacturer by trade.'"

"Yes, Professor Morse," interjected William, "Mathew and I met in Saratoga before we ventured to Albany and set off to find our fame and fortune in York."

"Allow me to introduce Mr. John William Draper, professor of chemistry here at the University of the City of New York," said Morse. "John is from England although we won't hold that against him. Professor Draper has been instrumental in capturing the first portrait of a human face, that of his assistant and dear sister, Miss Dorothy Draper. He makes his home in Staten Island."

"Morse presented sample daguerreotypes for closer examination: William and I moved in closer while Morse kept repeating the word 'delineation' over and over.

'The exquisite minuteness of delineation cannot be conceived. No painting or engraving ever approached it… The impressions of interior views are Rembrandt perfected.' Morse paused a moment, 'It is one of the most beautiful discoveries of the age.'

'This one of the Unitarian Church was taken by me out the third story window on the staircase of the University,' Morse said proudly.

Holding Morse's portrait, Brady closes the daguerreotype case.

"I'll tell you something, Timothy, Samuel F. B. Morse is a man of many talents. He is the Benjamin Franklin of our generation — artist, inventor of the telegraph, pioneer of the daguerreotype, university professor, and one of the most talented hucksters I've ever seen tread upon Broadway. Oh, he could sell indulgences to the Devil."

"But the Devil could never get into heaven, Mr. Brady, even if he purchased some indulgences from Mr. Morse."

"My apologies Timothy, that was my feeble attempt at humor."

Brady continued, "In the days before photography, only a prince or a priest could afford to have their portrait painted. Now all of us can have a likeness of ourselves, of our mother and father, of our children and grandchildren. But ten years ago, this was beyond the means of the ordinary citizen.

"You know something, Timothy, I did not know who Professor Morse was when I first saw him. I had heard his name of course — he's one of the most renowned men in York, if not the world. He had made headlines demonstrating his telegraph at Castle Garden, but I had never seen his face before. This was an accepted inconvenience like being blind in the days before the camera — to hear a person's name, but not be able to see their face. We were all blind before photography. You've heard music by Frederic Chopin on the piano-forte, but do you know what he looks like? Take a look at one of the only known portraits of Chopin before he died last year. It is one my most prized possessions in my private collection."

"No, I have not heard of Chopin, Mr. Brady."

"Well, you will one day hear the Ballade for Piano No. 1 in G Minor, Opus 23. I shall see to that. What about Charles Dickens surely you've read some of his works or seen performances of Oliver Twist at the Park Theatre, but would you recognize the Great Boz if you met him on the street?"

"No, I have not read any of Charles Dickens."

"Goodness me..."

"But my father reads to us from The Sketch Book. I am fond of Rip Van Winkle."

"Now gaze upon my wall," he says pointing at the portraits in his corner office overlooking Broadway and Fulton. "This is my private collection — the ones near and dear to me. I am a great hunter and these are my most prized trophies. See if you can point out Washington Irving." Brady patiently waits while Tim stares at the various portraits on the wall.

"Oh, not fair! You've read the name plate. But are you surprised at connecting the name with the face? Washington Irving was a delicate person to handle for his picture."

Tim looks at other portraits on the wall and the corresponding name plates. "Mr. Brady, there must be some mistake. That cannot be Ichabod Crane," says Tim pointing to a portly man in military uniform, with two rows of buttons, a golden tassel hanging from his shoulder epaulet. "That's not how Ichabod looked. 'He was tall, but exceedingly lank.'" Tim can hear his father's voice reading aloud, describing Ichabod "as some scarecrow eloped from a cornfield."

"I can assure you that is indeed the real Ichabod Crane who lives on Staten Island, not the literary fancy of Mr. Irving."

"Who is that man, Mr. Brady, the one with the haunting gaze?"

"That is Edgar Allan Poe. I had great admiration for Poe, and had William Ross Wallace bring him to my studio. Poe rather shrank from coming, as if he thought it was going to cost him something. Many a poet has had that daguerreotype copied by me. I loved the men of achievement... and the women of course like Jenny Lind."

Brady checks his pocket-watch. "Where has the time gone? Let's get back to that demand letter to Mr. Barnum. We must capture Jenny Lind, and add her portrait to my gallery wall, just like that great hunter, the Deerslayer."

"The Deerlayer? Who is that, Mr. Brady?"

"Why, The Deerslayer is one of the Leatherstocking novels by Fenimore Cooper — it is the cognomen of Nathaniel Bumpo before he became known as Hawkeye."

Brady points again to his private collection of portraits.

"You see, Timothy, we are hunters you and I. Hunters of men. Look upon my gallery wall. Gaze upon all my trophies. Quiet now... We must pursue our prey, utilizing all our faculties just like the Deerlayer. Lest we come back empty handed and leave our loved ones with nothing but hunger for dinner. Feast or famine. That is the eternal struggle of a daguerreotypist on Broadway."

Brady points to his camera in the corner.

"Look there! That is my Killdeer!"

"I don't understand, Mr. Brady. What is Killdeer?"

Brady walks over to the corner.

"That is what the Deerslayer called his trusted musket... This is my Killdeer, my first camera, designed by the optician John Roach."

"Where is Fenimore Cooper? What does he look like? Where is his portrait on the wall, Mr. Brady? I don't see it."

"Mr. Cooper has eluded me these many years, he is the most sought-after subject amongst all the Broadway portrait artists. Many have tried, but all have failed. No one has captured James Fenimore Cooper, but capture him I shall... Now then, where did we leave off?"

"Mr. Barnum, Sir, I beg leave of communicating these few lines soliciting your attention..."

"Yes, yes... Let us add, 'As an artist bound by the principles of freedom of expression, I shall not abide to your conditions. On behalf of my brethren daguerreotypers, and in the interest of informing the American public, I demand full and unfettered access to Miss Jenny Lind. I can assure you, I seek no remuneration in exchange for my considerable efforts and expertise. I offer my humble services pro bono and shall provide you with daguerreotypes of Miss Lind gratis. I seek only your cooperation in this matter as a friend and colleague in the museum profession. I am respectfully your obedient servant'."

Brady looks over Tim's shoulder. "Good then, now let me read that back before I make my mark. Excellent work, Timothy. Oh, I just had an idea. At the top of the page, in your best handiwork, in large letters with flourishing strokes, write 'Declaration of Artistic Independence.' That should capture Mr. Barnum's attention, don't you think?"

"Yes, Mr. Brady."

"Now get this over to Mr. Barnum. Quick as a telegraph, Tim!"

CHAPTER 9 — THE PHOTOGRAPHY WORKSHOP

1985

Down the dank, dark steps of the Crestwood underpass, I listen to the echoes of my footsteps through the long tunnel, down deep beneath the train tracks. Up on the other side, I pass through the wrought iron fence with high pointed pikes and make my way to The Photography Workshop on this rainy day in April, 1985.

Across the street is the Crestwood Market and the shoe repair shop, inside the cobbler wears his leather apron, working early with the light on, the commuters stop at the bakery for a cup of coffee and hurry on their way to the southbound track.

Crestwood isn't a town or a village; it has no post office or zip code to call its own. It's just a train stop on the Harlem River Line — known simply as 'The Station'. This was Norman Rockwell's stop when he lived up the road, up Mill Road. He painted the Crestwood train station for the cover of the Saturday Evening Post back on November 16, 1946. Commuters stand on the platform as the train pulls into the station. A little boy in a red cap sells newspapers to the commuters rushing by.

I take shelter from the rain beneath the black and white striped awning of The Photography Workshop, at 3 Fisher Ave. On the storefront sign is a silhouette of a 4x5 view camera with the bellows extended — you can almost see the black leather ridges. I push back the hood of my poncho and look at the window display of old photographs.

There is a family portrait from the turn of the century – young girls in summer white dresses, one with a big bow in her hair. A boy stands close by wearing a stiff collar. There are three nearly identical versions of the same image.

Old Black & White Photographs Copied, reads the sign. The faded original sits next to the rich tones of a black and white copy and a chocolate-brown version. 'Sepiatone' reads the little placard.

I look over my shoulder at the four-sided clock in the center of the intersection. 7:00 am on my first day of work. I turn the doorknob and hear the buzzer beep as I break the red-eye beam monitoring the threshold of The Photography Workshop.

Standing before me is a man in his 50s with reading glasses at the tip of his nose and a cigarette clenched in his mouth. Beneath his open-collared shirt, a tuft of grey hair pokes out of his V-neck undershirt. He has beady blue Frank Sinatra eyes, a weathered grin reminiscent of John Wayne, his namesake and hero. He extends a welcoming hand.

"You can call me, Duke. Everybody calls me Duke." It was only later, much later, that I learned his first name, Armando. Armando Longobardo. "Here, give me that wet raincoat of yours. We'll hang it up to dry." He disappears through the black curtain into the back room while I look around the little shop.

There is a wide array of photo frames – 8x10s, silver-plated 5x7s, and antique-looking, pewter frames. A display case of photo gadgets captures my attention – a magnifier loupe with a tiny light, a dust blower with brush bristles, an orange felt cloth for cleaning negatives, and cans of compressed air.

Behind the counter, a display case holds box after box of Kodak film. There is a large machine next to the counter, an Ilfochrome machine for making Cibachrome prints. Over in the corner is one of those old-fashioned cameras with a leather bellows extending out like an accordion on a big sturdy tripod – a 'view camera' they call it – the same type of camera that Ansel Adams used.

Duke pokes his head from behind the curtain. "What are you doing out here? C'mon, we've got work to do."

I follow him past the black curtain. Darkroom, reads the sign on the door, Knock Before Entering. On the other side, I'm blindsided by bright fluorescent lights buzzing above mixed in with the dank smell of developer and the formaldehyde of the fixer.

This is a room not meant to be seen in the light. Like a bar at closing time when the house lights turn on signaling everyone to go home, the charming pub turns into a dilapidated dive. I look around the brightly lit darkroom at the mismatched dark oak and maple wood paneling on the wall. The floor tiles are worn down in the high traffic foot-paths – the diamond shaped patterns have all but disappeared down to the wooden floorboards.

Box upon box of photographic paper are stacked up high on the shelves – 5x7, 8x10, and 11 x14. But these are not the familiar black and yellow colors of the Kodak brand.

A box of 8x10 paper sits on the counter. There is a captivating black and white photograph of a wind-swept beach. A slat wooden fence trails off into the grassy dunes creating linear shadows in the contours of the sand. Amongst the white space of the box cover are the bold, black letters: Ilford.

"I've never heard of Ilford."

"They're an English company. We only use Ilford paper and chemicals. They make a good line of fill-em too. I'm surprised you never heard of them... they've only been around for a hundred years."

"We used Kodak paper and chemicals in our darkroom back home."

"Over here," motions Duke. "This is the fill-em closet."

"What's that again?"

Duke stares hard for a split-second. This is a man who does not mumble, who does not stutter, and who definitely does not like to repeat himself.

"I said, this is the fill-em closet."

Duke opens the doors to reveal a closet of dangling strands of film.

He pronounces the word 'film' like one of The Bowery Boys in that old black and white movie, Angels with Dirty Faces, the one with James Cagney, Pat O'Brien and Humphrey Bogart. This movie started the whole series of Dead-End Kids and Bowery Boys movies that were on Saturday afternoons. I can see Duke with a toothpick in his mouth, sitting on a stool talking to Louie who ran the luncheonette. Who was that guy who played opposite Satch – the guy with the fedora hat folded back? Terence Aloysius Mahoney – what was his nickname? Slip, yeah, yeah, that's it. Slip.

"Hey now, are you paying attention?"

Duke busies himself unhooking all the black and white film that had been hung to dry in the closet from the night before. He gingerly cradles the long strands of film in his arms and gently lays them down on the work table.

"Now, see this here number label... this is what we call a twin-check. This is so we can match the roll of film to the order envelope." He digs through a stack and finds the corresponding number. Holding out the envelope containing slots for name, address, phone – hastily jotted numbers and letters, he taps his finger at the box marked instructions.

"You see, they want a contact sheet... so we cut the fill-em into strips of six like this."

He snips the 36 exposure film into six strips of six in six quick snips. He puts the orange scissors down, puffs into a glassine envelope, and slides the negatives in.

Faded tattoos on his Popeye forearms, he reaches for his cigarette teetering like a seesaw on the ashtray – the filter side level, the ash about to collapse.

He hands off the scissors with the handle extended in my direction, as I note the small gesture, the concern for my safety.

"Now let's see how you do..."

While Duke busies himself making a pot of coffee, he comes over to check on me. He keeps a watchful eye.

"Stay between the frames. You're cutting too close to the negative. That is sacred territory," he warns. "Photographers don't appreciate you trimming their negatives. When you get to the end of a roll, never, ever leave a single frame negative. Cut so you leave two frames."

"Duke, this envelope is marked 'Proof'. What does that mean?"

"A proof sheet and a contact sheet are the same thing."

He pauses a moment sensing uncertainty.

"You know what a contact sheet is? Right?"

There is no answer, only an awkward pause.

"Don't worry if you don't know," says Duke. "I'll show you… You know what you'll be when I get through with you?"

"No, what?"

"A Darkroom Technician."

"What exactly is a Darkroom Technician?"

"That's the work we do. We develop and print black and white fill-em."

Duke takes off his reading spectacles and looks me up and down in a skeptical sort of way. "Where did George find you anyways?"

"There was an ad in the Herald-Statesman."

"I understand that." He squints his eyes like John Wayne and prods further. "But where do you come from?"

"Oh, across the tracks. I grew up in Crestwood."

"And what sort of work did you do?"

"Well, I worked at Nathan's as a dishwasher and a prep-cook, then I worked at the Sizzler Restaurant on the salad bar, then I became a broiler cook and a meat-cutter while I went to college."

"College?" He stops me like I said something wrong, or inadvertently uttered an insult or a profanity. He looked deeply offended.

I try to cushion the blow. "You see, I'm not in college anymore. Well, actually I guess I should say I flunked out. Or I dropped out, depending on how you look at it."

"Well, which is it?"

"I'm not exactly sure."

"Tell me this. Did they teach you common sense at college?"

I consider some of the courses I took in freshman year: Biology, Chemistry, and Pre-Calculus. Perhaps common sense is an elective for senior year. That would be a worthwhile course to take.

"I have yet to meet a college graduate with any common sense. They can't even gap a spark plug." As if on cue and in total agreement, the coffee pot lets out a dramatic sigh in a mist of exasperation.

"The coffee is ready… let me get you a cup."

"I don't really drink coffee."

"You will," says Duke as he hands me a mug.

Behind us, a big machine kicks on with three successive beeps.

I take another sip of coffee. "What's that thing?"

"This here is the Ilford 2001. This is considered state-of-the-art." He pats the machine the size of a dishwasher sitting in the middle of the room. He removes the cover then places a small magnet by the sensor, triggering the machine on. He places four 3½ x5 sheets of photographic paper on the silver feed tray, spaced evenly apart. Gears start grinding, cogs and sprockets gnash and grit their teeth together, the rubber rollers start turning and grab hold of the paper pulling it tight within its grasp.

Duke provides the play by play action. "Watch the paper as it works its way through the developer bath," he narrates. The paper dives deep down into the dark brown pool. It winds its way then resurfaces. "See, now it's in the stop bath." Then it works its way through the fixer then the wash cycle and finally into the heat of the dryer. Out plop four muddy grey, purple sheets of paper.

"Is the machine broken?" I ask. "Somehow, it doesn't look quite right."

Duke sighs a deep sigh, he whispers a silent prayer. God, give me strength, then he explains, "No, you see, I was merely trying to show you how this machine works with the light on. We need to have the light off and the cover on in order for it to develop prints properly... This here paper is fogged. You know what that means, right?"

"Sure, I do. I learned how to print black and white from my father in our basement back home. Fogged means the paper has been accidentally exposed to light. You can't use fogged paper to make prints. It's worthless. You should keep photographic paper in a lead box. You can only work with the safelight on."

"That's basically right," says Duke with a sense of relief. Maybe this college drop-out will catch on. Maybe, I'm not wasting my breath.

"You don't have to keep the paper in a lead box though. Ilford supplies a light-tight black bag with each box." He stops for a moment then adds, "That's how me and George started out in our basement."

Duke continues the tour of the darkroom. "Now over here, you'll find the Omega D-2 enlargers that George uses. They're equipped with Schneider lenses – the best lenses that money can buy. But you won't be using these – you'll be over here working next to me."

He walks around the Ilford machine, past the long stainless-steel sink with hoses going this way and that, to the long worktable with two enlargers next to each other. "The Durst M600 is the one you'll be using.."

He reaches up and grabs hold of a long chain with a metal film clip at the end connected to those buzzing, flickering fluorescent bulbs. "Now are you ready to learn how to make a contact sheet?"

"Sure." I say with much anticipation.

"Now let's get some work done. George will be here soon, and we need to get out on the route by 10:30."

He pauses a moment.

"Make sure the door is shut tight. You got your cup of coffee?"

Still holding the chain, Duke looks over his shoulder at me then disappears into the darkness.

CHAPTER 10 — BACK TO BARNUM'S

1850

"Where's your ticket, Boy! You can't come waltzing in here without a ticket!"

"I'm not here to see the Museum. I have a most important message for Mr. Barnum!"

"Important message for Mr. Barnum!" shouts the doorman down the entranceway.

An usher sees the boy approach, "Step right this way, messenger boy!" He extends his arm pointing down the gas-lit hallway. He shouts to his cohort way down the corridor with a wink, "Joseph! Important message for Mistah Barnum!"

"Step right this way, lad. Mr. Barnum anxiously awaits your urgent message. Right this way. Do you need a signature for verification? Mr. Barnum will gladly put his mark to your delivery book. Just the other side of the door…"

Tim pauses a moment. Something is not quite right.

"Go on then, Mr. Barnum is waiting for you."

Tim turns the door handle. A thrusting kick to the backside, he tumbles down. Wham! The door slams behind him. A dark brick wall before him drips with perspiration. He feels in the darkness turns the corner of a back-street alleyway. Deliveries Only, reads the white painted brick. Big bales of tobacco leaves are unloaded from the wagon near the loading dock of Smith's Segar Store. Tim follows the alley back to Fulton Street and makes his way back to Brady's office.

"What happened to you, Timothy?"

"I asked to speak with Mr. Barnum, the next thing I found myself in a back-alley with no way to get back in."

"You were given the runaround, my boy. They probably mistook you as a messenger serving creditor's papers to Mr. Barnum no doubt. Goodness knows he has overextended himself with all his renovations to his museum. Seek out Mr. John Greenwood, Jr., his assistant manager, then and only then, tell him you have an urgent letter for Mr. Barnum. Understand?"

"I do."

"This is a serious matter, most serious. I am relying on you Timothy. I must have Jenny Lind."

"Yes, Mr. Brady."

"Do not disappoint."

From behind the ticket window, a befuddled cashier with black arm sleeves up to the elbows of his white shirt, visor cap. "How many tickets, boy?"

"I'm not here to visit the museum. I need to speak with Mr. John Greenwood, Jr., the assistant manager."

"I am he. What can I do for you?"

"I have an important message for Mr. Barnum."

"Oh, you do? Well give it to me. I will see to it that Mr. Barnum receives it. Well, hand it over."

"No, sir, I need the favor of an immediate reply directly from Mr. Barnum. This is from Mr. Mathew B. Brady and he instructed me to seek your assistance."

"His office is straight down that hallway."

"Would you be so kind as to show me the way, Mr. Greenwood?"

"Well, all right then, but I must warn you, Mr. Barnum is a very busy man and in a most harried state."

Outside the office, a long bench seat with an assortment of callers seated in wait. Tim finds a spot next to a youth dressed in a bright red suit with gold piping. Mr. Greenwood knocks on the door just below the brass plate, P.T. Barnum, Proprietor and General Manager.

"Who is it now?" Barnum roars. The door opens, his commanding stance looms. "Oh, hello Mr. Greenwood, I am in the midst of an interview with this scribe from the New York Herald."

"There is a boy here to see you."

"A boy??" Barnum cuts him off midsentence. "You interrupt James Gordon Bennett and Phineas Taylor Barnum with some trifling boy??"

Abruptly the young musician in the bright red suit stands up, his trombone clanks to the floor. "Yes, Mr. Barnum, you see I have not received my pay. It is Friday after all."

"Pay!" cried the showman with a fine display of indignation. "We said nothing about pay. The honor of playing in my band is pay enough for a youngster like you."

"But…"

"But, you wound me deeply with your insinuations. I give you the most prominent stage on all of Broadway to display your talents to the multitudes. Think of the band leaders, concert hall promoters, the talent scouts and booking agents who pass by my corner. Why even Mr. William Niblo himself passes this way every day."

"The one who owns Niblo's Garden?"

"The very same. Who do you think gave me my start? Why Mr. Niblo of course. And out of the goodness of my own heart, I give you this platform to perform your music, free of charge, I might add. Have you any idea what it would cost to rent out a stage on Broadway at the corner of Ann Street?"

"No, I never thought about that."

"I didn't suspect you would. Mr. Greenwood, see to it that he turns in his uniform. Your services are no longer required at this establishment."

"Oh, please Mr. Barnum, please give me another chance."

"I don't know why I should. You will only trample upon my good will again. But I shall not let the likes of you douse my Drummond Light burning bright, my faith in humanity flickers still." Barnum pauses for dramatic effect. "Go then, go play your trombone on my stage free of charge. Go now, before I change my mind."

The door slams shut and Mr. Greenwood knocks again.

"Mr. Barnum, this is the boy I wished to bring to your attention."

"This?" He looks down, his voice booms from on high out of his barrel chest like a great actor upon the stage. He reaches into his pocket and puts coins into Timothy's hand. "Does my generosity to the unfortunate know no bounds?"

"Mr. Barnum this is no pauper. This is one of Brady's boys. He has an urgent message."

"What now! I just called on him this morning. Blast Brady!" He sighs a moment, looking down at the little lad. "Gentlemen, step into my office, this is no discussion for the hallway." He shuts the door.

Tim looks with wonder around Barnum's office. Over in the corner is the cast iron safe – what riches it must possess behind that brass combination dial. Barnum takes a seat at his secretary desk, with wooden shelves, tiny drawers and little cabinet doors. There on the center shelf is that portrait of Barnum and Tom Thumb by Samuel Root.

Spread out on the desktop, a ledger book, Tim looks over his shoulder. Expelled from the museum, reads the top of the page, unaccompanied female, waylaying patrons in balcony, two boys brawling, young man possessing spirits…

"Step back, boy! You're breathing on me! Over in the corner there."

Hanging on the wall is a poster. The Greatest Natural and National Curiosity in the World. Joice Heth, age 161 years, the nursemaid slave to George Washington. Next to it is a painting of a majestic building from a faraway land with Byzantine arches and white marble domes.

"Excuse me, Mr. Barnum is that the Taj Mahal?"

"Did I ask you to speak, boy? No, I don't recall doing so. But to answer your rude interruption, no, that is not the Taj Mahal, that is Iranistan, my home sweet home on the shores of Bridgeport, Connecticut. I wish I were there now with my dear wife, Charity, and our beloved children."

Barnum stops a moment before trailing further away on his tangent. "Where did Brady find you anyway? Wallowing in the mud at the Five Points? He must be desperate for help."

"No, Mr. Barnum, I come from County Richmond."

"You mean Staten Island? Why, I was there a fortnight ago. I went there to meet Jenny Lind on her transatlantic voyage. We dined at the Pavilion."

"Yes, Mr. Barnum, I live in New Brighton."

"And they teach you about such places as the Taj Mahal?"

"Oh, yes. Brother Finnerty is ever so fond of architecture."

"Your brother is an architect?"

"No, he is a Christian Brother, his father was a stone mason."

"C'mon Phineas, let's finish the interview. I have deadlines to meet."

Barnum turns his attention to the man seated in the visitor's chair, an important looking man holding a mysterious black lacquer box. On the cover is the Souvenir of New York. Someone must have dipped the lithograph in glue and pasted it to the lid. Painted in block silver letters: N.Y. Herald and below that the name, James Gordon Bennett.

Taking a small key, the gentleman opens the lid to reveal a portable writing desk on his lap — the smell of cedar, a light-weight wood, a sheaf of paper set out on the blue velvet blotter, worn down in the corner, the resting place for his right hand. He unlatches a compartment, unscrews the ink bottle, pen at the ready.

"My apologies, James, this boy aggrieves me like Brady. Now, getting back to our discussion, is it not critical to first emphasize the discover-er rather than the discover-ee?"

"How do you mean?"

"Well, as a former knight of the pen, you know I wrote articles for the Sunday press to keep the pot boiling at home."

"Yes, Phineas."

"Well, James, I have the utmost scruples, I would not deign to dictate what you should write, I merely make casual observations…"

"Go on."

"Well, if the pen were in my hand, I would first emphasize Professor Morse and his genius, then I would put the telegraph in the second paragraph. The same would hold true with Robert Fulton, he would be mentioned in the first and the Clermont in the second.

"Alas, I am but a fallen scribe unworthy of the trade. Do not listen to my ramblings. Far be it from me to influence the ink strokes of your pen, but the simple fact remains — the American public would never know the dulcet tones of the Swedish Nightingale if 'twere not for me. I am a most modest man, James, I needn't remind you. At the conclusion of Jenny Lind's September 11th Premier, remember how the crowd vociferously called for 'Barnum' and I reluctantly responded to their demand."

"I was there, Phineas. I saw it with mine own eyes though very distantly, from way up high in the rafters. Remember the choice seat you gave me. But I am concerned about the numerous accusations being levied at my paper."

"What accusations?"

"Well, there's talk of buying printer's ink — that you are purchasing all of these front page, two-column, top of the fold articles about Jenny Lind day after day after day."

"That is preposterous! A bold-face lie! These are unbought, unsolicited articles."

"It's not just the Herald, but Mr. Greeley over at the Daily Tribune has felt the sting of these charges. We are merely satisfying the public's insatiable appetite. They want to know everything about her… her comings and goings, whether she went to church, her voyage on the Steamship Atlantic commanded by Captain West and on and on…"

Barnum laughs out loud. "The high and mighty Greeley accused of graft and corruption?"

"Oh, very humorous indeed, Phineas, you pocket $5,000 net each concert, $15,000 per week… while the papers receive nothing but vituperation for their services, except, indeed, a few tickets given grudgingly, and very often to the worst part of the house."

"Pardon me, Mr. Barnum."

"What now, Boy! Can you not see I am having words with Mr. James Gordon Bennett?"

"It's no trouble, Phineas," says Bennett, "the boy must meet his deadline as do I."

"Brady perturbs me to no end, James, to no end!" He leans in closer. "All the artists in York bow to him: the literary, the landscape, the portrait, even the lowly con-artist politicians genuflect before his camera obscura. God help me if I ever stoop so low as to become involved in politics. Brady is deemed the curator of America's history.

"But where then is the genius of his Gallery of Illustrious Americans? Is it not found in my American Museum? THAT is where he found his inspiration. Brady is a mere copyist of the Great P.T. Barnum. Free Admission read his adverts! How that galls me. A thumb in my eye. Where then is my due? Who shall paint my portrait? Where are the newspaper poets clamoring to praise my efforts at preserving our history??"

A man barges into the office without knocking.

"This had better be good, Rupert. I was on a roll…"

"Mr. Barnum, some patron has made off with the club which killed Captain Cook!"

"Not again! Go up to the attic and fetch another from the relic room. Tell me, General Washington's Flag is still there!"

"In all its glory, Mr. Barnum."

"Good. Now get, before I get thee!" says Barnum with a fury.

Turning his attention back to Bennett, "Tell me this, why do the poets of the press fawn over Brady? Nathaniel Parker Willis sings his praises and

C. Edwards Lester coddles him with more tenderness than his mother! Oh, how they prate paragraph after paragraph about him. Who painted the golden hallow around his crown?"

"Not I, Phineas."

"Do you think the late, great Thomas Cole would ever admit that he passed beneath the transom to Barnum's? No, perish the thought. But he ever so proudly sat for Brady, as did Washington Irving, neither of whom would ever admit to visiting my Museum."

"I know that Phineas, but Brady sets himself apart from all the slip-shod studios popping up like weeds through the slate up and down Broadway. He has vision. He sees beyond the beyond like Hawkeye even if he is feeble-eyed behind those strange blue spectacles of his."

"I've heard the same rumors, James… Brady can no longer focus the lens to his camera and relies entirely upon his operators. He acts merely as a conductor while his journeymen strike the chords."

"Phineas, I've heard the whispers too. But remember, Beethoven could no longer hear his own symphonies. Nonetheless, Brady is still a maestro of the new art."

"A maestro! Brady is a showman just the same as me. But I know what they say about me. Old Barnum has made a half million by humbugging the public with a little boy whom he took from Bridgeport and represented to be twice his real age. How I even pulled the wool over Queen Victoria's eyes weaseling myself into Buckingham Palace for a free dinner with Tom Thumb. These are the same who attempted to deter Jenny Lind from making my engagement with me, by assuring her that I was a humbug and a showman."

"Pay no heed to such talk, Phineas."

"Yet, I was the one who discovered Jenny Lind. Now every merchant on Broadway lays claim to a piece of her. Why just look at the advertisements in your paper, James. Jenny Lind canes, Jenny Lind hats, Jenny Lind opera glasses, Jenny Lind daguerreotypes…"

Barnum pauses a moment. "Oh yes, you there, Brady's boy, come closer. I won't bite. All right then, handover the note. I shall send a reply later today."

"But Mr. Brady instructed me to wait for your answer."

"Can you not see I am engaged at present? Mr. Brady can wait."

"Mr. Brady begs the favor of your immediate response."

Exasperated, Barnum opens the letter. "Oh this is rich… Declaration of Artistic Independence. My, my, my, Brady fancies himself a Thomas Jefferson. Here is my immediate reply, boy. Take this down!"

He hands Tim a pen dipping it in the ink well.

"Yes, Mr. Barnum." Tim anxiously awaits. "I'm ready…"

"Soft Soap."

"Soft Soap?"

"Yes, tell your Mr. Brady that is the requisite qualification of a good showman — the faculty to please and flatter the public so judiciously as not to have them suspect your intention."

"Shall I write that down, Mr. Barnum?"

"Yes, this instant! Now, begone with you. I have pressing matters to attend to!" He watches Tim walk sullenly to the door. "Boy! Come here a minute. Take this five-dollar note and get yourself properly clothed. You look like somebody rolled you."

"Thank you ever so kindly, Mr. Barnum."

"Skedaddle!"

Back at Brady's office...

"Timothy, what on earth took so long? We are losing precious daylight. I expected an immediate response."

"I am sorry Mr. Brady, Mr. Barnum was in a meeting with James Gordon Bennett. This is his reply which I wrote down on your stationary."

Brady takes up the letter closely, and wiggles his nose like a rabbit beneath his blue spectacles.

"Soft soap?"

"Mr. Barnum said that was the requisite qualification of a good showman."

"Oh, I know all about soft soap. You needn't explain."

"Is soft soap like saddle soap?"

"Not quite, soft soap is what we call blarney."

"I see, Mr. Brady there was something I forgot to mention."

"Yes, Tim..."

"This morning on the omnibus one gentleman was reading the Tribune then another next to him was reading the Herald. Then Mr. Barnum discussed the advertisements with a Mr. James Gordon Bennett, the editor of the Herald."

"Yes, Tim..."

"Which reminded me about the paper this morning."

"Go on..."

"One of the advertisements mentioned the best engraving of Jenny Lind, Meade Brothers, 233 Broadway, opposite the fountain. That's where we sat with Old Elephant near the weeping willow."

Brady slams his fist on the desk. "Those upstarts from Albany! I taught those Meade boys all I know and how do they repay me? By opening their own studio two blocks up the 'Way. They do not belong on Broadway. They are not true practitioners of the new art. They churn out portraits at ridiculous rates."

"Mr. Brady, there is something else."

"Yes, Tim."

"Mr. Barnum gave me a five-dollar note to get some proper clothes."

"Oh, he did, did he? I will take you directly to Stewart's myself. We won't be accepting charity from Mr. Barnum, however good his intentions. Yes, that's it, we won't be accepting anything from Mr. Barnum. Not anymore. We will get you properly fitted at the Marble Palace then we shall go directly across Broadway to the Irving House and call upon Miss Jenny Lind. We will ride my phaeton up Broadway and give Miss Jenny a ride back to my studio. There is the proper light still, and the hope. But how frail a thing is hope. We will have this sitting, with or without Mr. Barnum's consent. Mr. Fredricks!"

"Yes, Mr. Brady?"

"Have my phaeton brought around. Immediately!"

Later that day… the descending light of the sun strains through Brady's corner office overlooking Fulton Street. Tim looks at the Thomas Addis Emmet obelisk in Saint Paul's churchyard, the shadow of a sun dial.

"This is most disconcerting. Those impenetrable crowds gathered around the Irving House, those foolish doormen. Do they not know who I am? If only I could speak directly with Miss Jenny and show her my book. Surely, she would recognize a fellow artist and consent to a sitting. If only I could get through to her."

A knock on the door. "Will there be anything else then Mr. Brady?"

"No, Mr. Fredricks. Thank you though."

"Shall I lock the door on my way out?"

"No, I shall listen for the bell. See you in the morrow."

Getting up from his desk, Brady turns his attention to the stack of parcels from Stewart's Department Store. "Let's see what we have here…" he says shifting shirt boxes, shoe boxes, and packages wrapped neatly in brown paper tied with twine. Tim feels an uneasy sense of guilt at all the fine clothes that Mr. Brady purchased for him. Against the wall, Tim notices a long row of boxes stacked three high, D'Avignon Press, 323 Broadway.

"What's in all those boxes over there, Mr. Brady?"

"Oh, those…" he says a bit wearily, "Those are my books — my unsold books haunting me."

"May I take a look at one of them?"

Brady places the large heavy volume on the desk with a thud before the boy. "The Gift Book of the Republic," reads the upper caption in gold letters. Surrounding the shimmering silhouette of George Washington is the title, "The Gallery of Illustrious Americans." Towards the bottom of the book is the Great Seal of the United States, the pyramid with the raised eye in a triangle, beams of light emanating, Latin phrases, hovering above, "The Union Now And Forever."

"This is most impressive, Mr. Brady." Tim puts his fingertips to the blue leather cover feeling the little bumps and impressions. He turns to the title page. "From Daguerreotypes by Brady – Engraved by D'Avignon."

"Actually, that is my single greatest disappointment. I should have listened to Julia, my voice of reason."

"Never have I seen such a book as this in all my life, Mr. Brady." Tim turns the thick page, then gently peels back the protective, delicate tissue leaf, and sees an image of Zachary Taylor, then John C. Calhoun, Daniel Webster, Silas Wright, Henry Clay…

Brady continues, "The lithographic stones were engraved by F. D'Avignon. They cost me $100 for the stones, the book sold for $30. John Howard Payne the author of 'Home Sweet Home' was to have written the letter express, but Lester did it."

"Who is this man with the beard, J.C. Fremont?"

"That is John C. Fremont, the Pathfinder — one of the greatest explorers this country has ever known next to Lewis and Clark. There is talk that he will one day be president."

"And this Millard Fillmore? I've heard the name somewhere before?"

"Why that is the President of these United States for goodness sake!"

"Oh, I didn't realize, Mr. Brady."

"Well, that is quite all right, my boy. You are not alone. Much as the work received glowing reviews in the press when the book was published in January of this year, most of the public could care less or so it seems for my Gallery of Illustrious Americans. Even when I reduced the price to $15 from $30, well below cost, they sit there in my office still."

"What if you sold copies to the libraries and universities, Mr. Brady?"

"That is a capital idea, Timothy." Brady closes a paper box. "What was that? I think I heard the bell."

In the studio parlor stands a gentleman hand to his whiskered chin closely studying the portraits on the gallery wall holding a brown leather portfolio case under his arm.

"I am sorry Sir, the light is fading and there will be no more sittings."

"I am not here for a portrait," he says in an unfamiliar accent.

"Oh, perhaps I could interest you in our wide array of daguerreotype cases. We have miniature cases over here."

"I vish to purchase your book, Mr. Brady."

"Really?" says Brady taken off-guard. "Are you quite sure?"

"Most definitely," says the man. "Here is my calling card."

Brady places the large volume weighing nearly five pounds on the countertop. He picks up the card. "John Carl Frederick Polycarpus von Schneidau, Daguerreotype Portraits, Stockholm, Sweden."

"Oh, so you are a kindred spirit, Mr. von Schneidau and from Sweden no less." Extending his hand, "So pleased to meet your acquaintance! The price of my book has been reduced from $30 to $15."

"In dat case, I vill take two, one for myself and one for my dear friend."

"Excellent, Mr. von Schneidau. So, what brings you to York? Are you touring our country?"

"Yes, and no… You see, I plan to open a studio of my own."

"That's wonderful. Where do plan to open it? Here on Broadway?"

"No actually, in Chicago. But for now, I am looking for temporary work as an operator while visiting the next few weeks with my friend."

"How fortuitous! One of my trusted operators, Edwin Bronk has but recently left for St. Louis."

"If you are interested, I have brought along samples of my work."

"By all means, I would be only too happy to look them over." Brady flips the pages to the portfolio. "Very fine portraiture, Mr. von Schneidau. You have the gift." He turns the pages with admiration then stops dead in his tracks. His hand begins to shake, "Hold on a minute, isn't this…" His voice quivers in shock unable to complete the sentence.

"Yes, this is an old schoolmate of mine," he pauses a moment then adds as an afterthought, "from Sweden."

"From Sweden you say?" repeats Brady almost incredulously.

"Ya, Sweden. Her name is Jenny Lind. Perhaps, you've heard of her?"

Brady raises his arms on high. "You answer my prayers!" Bursting with excitement, unable to contain his glee, "Mr. von Scheidau, I have a proposition for you. Can you secure me access to Miss Lind? I have been most unsuccessful in all my communications."

"I would be only too happy to oblige you, Mr. Brady, if you will permit me to collaborate in the sitting?"

"Most assuredly, I would be delighted to have you as my assistant. My studio is your studio. Shall we say noon tomorrow?" Brady extends his hand greeted with a grasp.

"Noon it is."

"This warms my heart, Mr. von Scheidau, ever so much. Permit me to ask a favor. Would you be so kind as to give this volume of my book to Miss Lind with my compliments?"

"I would prefer not."

"Oh, I see," says Brady with quiet disappointment.

"No, it would be best if you presented it to Miss Jenny yourself. You must join us for dinner at Delmonico's. I insist, as does my old schoolmate. She sent me to call upon you."

As the bell on the shop door rings closed, Brady says, "Come now, Timothy, it is time to close up shop. Tomorrow is another day."

CHAPTER 11 — SATURDAY MORNING

1850

Early morning, a flurry of activity, the drapes are drawn, the sunshine from Fulton Street mixes with the shadows of Broadway. The windows are cleaned with the smell of vinegar and the squeak of polishing cloths.

The birds chirp with excitement at the dawn of a new day as Mary Higbie, a young girl with braided blond hair, opens the door to the gilded cage. The singing birds flutter their wings and take flight drawing Tim's gaze to the high ceiling — ornate tin molded into cornices with pineapple shapes and intricate patterns emanating outward with the crystal chandelier at the center. The gas lamps turned down low, flicker ever so slightly.

Swooping high near the plush drapes, a little bird pauses at the very top of an oval wooden frame suspended high by a thick golden rope with tassels. Behind the glass, held in place by the brass matte, the luminous image of a young woman, dark expressive eyes, shimmering silver skin, pink tinted lips holding tight for the pose, rose blushed cheeks, pinpoint accents of gold to the locket held by a black satin necklace.

Mary places fresh sheets of the Daily Tribune down in the cage, and pours sunflower seeds in the dish. She extends her hand and finger as a perch, her somber lips give call and the singing birds answer.

"Back in the cage, my little children there is fresh cool Croton for your morning bath."

"You boy! Yes, You! Take your hands out of your pockets this instant and get to work! Saturday is our busiest day!"

Standing there awkwardly, suddenly conscious of his hands, unsure what they should do, where they should go, he retracts his hand, hiding it in the sleeve of his coat and starts buffing the marble-topped table with circular motions trying to look busy.

"See here! Just what do you think you are doing?"

Tim turns to answer.

"Stop that, before you scratch the marble surface with your buttons." Stepping from behind his ledger desk, advancing closer, he stoops down to eye level, "Why are you here, boy! Refresh my memory."

"How do you mean, Mr. Fredricks?"

"Don't answer my question with a question!"

"I am here to work, Sir."

"Doing what? Staring at the ceiling? I'll have you know, we run a tight ship at Mr. Brady's. We have 21 dedicated workers in our employ, each with a special skillset. Professor Tarbox is our chemist, Mr. Pettifog toils in the mercurial room, Luther Boswell over there is one of our top operators, Mary Higbie is our talented colorist bringing portraits to vivid likeness, while young Benjamin Bleecker there prepares the plates with ne'er the slightest imperfection. Each of us knows our function and performs it diligently to keep things running smoothly. I ask again, why are you here? What skills do you possess?"

Tim stares down at his new buckle shoes unsure of an adequate reply.

"I thought as much. Get the broom and the water can and see if you can sweep the flagstones properly. Quick now, follow me, before the foot-traffic picks up."

Growing impatient, watching each broom-stroke on the sidewalk of Broadway, Mr. Fredricks simmers while Tim dodges the foot-traffic, holding the broom waiting for pedestrians to pass by. "Sweep boy! Sweep! Put the broom to the pavers. Pay no heed to the pedestrians!"

Tim extends the broom, pushing the dirt towards the curb, tripping a little girl holding a blanket, landing on her elbows with a thump of tears and sobs. She gets up and runs away.

"That is not the way we sweep on Broadway. I am not sure where you come from, but we do things with finesse on Broadway. Firstly, we sprinkle water upon the pavers," he says grabbing the water-can, traipsing on the flagstones with a sun-shower behind him, grabbing the broom, he applies vigorous brush strokes, "See boy, like this."

Tim drifts off and looks for the girl.

"Have you been kicked by a horse, boy!"

"No, Mr. Fredricks."

"You exhibit slow motor skills both in speech and physical exertion. Are you quite sure? Tell the truth!"

"No, Mr. Fredricks."

"Well then, when I come back, I expect to see the corner of Broadway and Fulton swept clean as a dog licks his plate clear round to Gibson's Saddler Shop. Do I make myself clear?"

"Yes, Mr. Fredricks."

"Be sure to get between the hitching post, the telegraph pole and the gas lamp! We must keep our end of the bargain with Mr. Edward Anthony and keep the sidewalk swept clean as part of our rent."

"Yes, Mr. Fredricks."

"This is Broadway after all! We want her to sparkle like crystal!"

"Yes, Mr. Fredricks."

"Don't 'Yes me' boy! I'm wise to your sluggard ways – showing up late to work, in a slovenly appearance. Your feeble yes after yes does not me impress. I take note of your actions, boy! Not your, 'Yes, Mr. Fredricks'," he imitates in a taunting, high-pitched falsetto.

"I understand, Mr. Fredricks."

He thrusts the broom sideways which Tim catches in his grasp.

"Wait now, where is the display case?"

"Display case?"

"It should be at the foot of the stairs. Look thar! Tell me what you see next door."

"Warnock the Hatter, Lanphier the Tailor."

"No, see the glass case over there, Martin M. Lawrence, Daguerreotypes, 203 Broadway. The display case catches the eye of the passersby while the hand points the way up the stairs. You see, ours is a rooftop profession, we do not have the benefit of a ground level storefront, we must entice the pedestrians to climb the many steps to our gallery."

Tim stands holding the broom.

"Did you not hear me! Go up the stairs, summon Benjamin and bring down the display case."

With a stumble, the glass showcase tumbles down the stairs with Tim close behind.

"Look what you've done!"

Assorted daguerreotypes litter the stoop amongst the shards of glass.

What a mess I've made of things. What skills do I possess? I don't even know how to sweep properly. Now I've broken the showcase. Look at all this broken glass.

While Timothy sweeps with his back turned, a sleek black carriage with polished leather seats, thin spokes, pulls up to the corner.

"Oh, Timothy so good to see you on this glorious morning, what a magical evening I had last night, you'll never guess who I dined with..." says Mr. Brady holding a huge bouquet of flowers in his arms.

"Would you be so kind as to bring these flowers up to the gallery? Beauty, tranquility, and fragrance – the three essential requisites for a proper daguerreotypist's room!" He stops midsentence. "What on earth is wrong, Timothy? Your face is flushed and wrought with worry. What vexes you, boy?"

"I've ruined the display case, Mr. Brady. It slipped from my grasp and shattered to bits falling down the staircase. I am so truly sorry."

"That is quite alright. We needed to freshen up the display case. It is but a material trifle in this existence we experience together. Don't you see, Timothy?"

"But I broke it to bits, Mr. Brady."

"No, you need to step back a bit to gain perspective – to see the order of things. Take a ride upon my phaeton round to the stables then you shall put that behind you."

"But what of this mess I've made?"

"Leave it for now. Grab hold the reins, let the horses be your guide."

"That's what Old Elephant told me."

"Old who? Never mind now, grab the reins."

Trotting down Fulton Street, the high iron fence of Saint Paul's churchyard to their right, Tim sees the River, the docks and ship masts in the distance.

"Mr. Brady, why do you call this carriage a Phaeton? My father used the same term the other day at New Brighton Landing."

"This is a special type of carriage named after the son of the sun-god."

"Son of the son?"

"Look up yonder at the life-giving force."

"You mean the sun, up there. Oh yes, I see it."

"Behold, Helios, the Greek god of the sun. One day Helios let his son Phaeton take his solar chariot for a drive around the globe. But Phaeton could not control the fire breathing horses. They sensed a weaker hand at the reins and the chariot veered out of control. First the chariot went way up high and the earth grew cold. Then it swerved too close to the sun burning up all the plants and trees, the rivers and lakes, creating the Sahara Desert in Africa. Finally, Zeus, the king of all the gods, struck down that solar chariot with a lightning bolt plunging it into a river in Hades."

"Did Phaeton die?"

"Oh yes, Helios was quite upset with Zeus for killing his only son, but there was no other way. You see, Phaeton nearly set the world on fire. The ancient Greeks taught us much with their myths. Did you know that it was the ancient Greeks who first discovered the camera obscura?"

"Mr. Barnum has one on his rooftop, Mr. Brady. I went inside."

"He does? Well, that camera obscura later became the camera, the wheel that turns photography's carriage and the sun is the horse pulling us along. There are some in our profession such as Marcus Aurelius Root who decry the term photography as a misnomer and insist that we call the new art by its proper name Heliography, after Helios, the sun god."

"Is that the same Mr. Root who doggery-typed General Tom Thumb with Mr. Barnum?"

Brady winces then laughs at the pronunciation of daguerreotype. "Oh, Timothy, my how you mangled the good name of our profession. You are certainly not the first! But to answer your question, I believe it was Marcus' brother Samuel who captured that memorable portrait, though I wished that I could have put my name to the bottom and added it to my gallery wall. Such is the competition amongst my brethren daguerreotypers. We vie against each other to capture the next daguerreotype. Notice my pronunciation of daguerreotype..." as he slowly repeats the word, dragging out the double-rr... rolling it on the tip of his tongue, down in the guttural portion of his throat. "Repeat after me... daguerreotype."

"Dahggery-type."

"A bit better. You'll get it soon enough."

"Such a curious term... so difficult to say, how did it come about?"

Brady reaches into his breast coat pocket and pulls out a locket case opening it. "This Timothy, is Louis Daguerre from France, the creator of our art. T'were not for Daguerre and his marvelous discovery, I would probably still be a jewel case manufacturer. All he asked for in return was to acknowledge his discovery with the name, Daguerreotype – so there you have it. Now, do you know who captured this cherished image?"

"Why, you of course Mr. Brady."

"Sadly, no. Much as it galls me to admit this, Charles Meade of Meade Brothers and Company at 233 Broadway took this portrait overcoming the greatest of difficulties. What a feather in his cap! Taking one of the only known portraits of Daguerre! Imagine that," he repeats with his lilt, "A daguerreotype of Daguerre! First, his brother Henry tried and failed. He went all the way to France to visit Daguerre's chateau, to pay homage to the father of our art. But do you know what happened?"

Timothy shakes his head.

"Daguerre refused to sit for a portrait. He sent poor Henry on his way empty-handed all the way back to America. He has always objected to having his likeness taken. The following year, in the spring of 1848, Charles set out to accomplish what his brother could not. He sought out Madame Daguerre and entreated her good graces to sit before the camera. Then and only then did the Great Daguerre subject himself to the gaze of the lens. And very impatiently, I might add. You see, Daguerre still does not appreciate the full potential of his invention."

"How do you mean?"

"Back in 1839, when Professor Morse journeyed to France to demonstrate his telegraph, Daguerre in turn showed him his secret new discovery. But he said to Morse that portraiture of living persons was not possible, not ever, because the exposure took much too long."

"So, you are cross with the Brothers Meade?"

"No, I spoke out of turn yesterday, in the heat of the moment in my disparaging comments about them. I have the utmost respect for Henry and Charles. You see, there is a fine line between resentment and admiration. The true mark of a great portrait is wishing you were the artist who captured the pose."

Closing the case with a snap, "Now then, we must get to the studio and finish with our preparations. Come now, jump down from the Phaeton."

Walking around the corner of Fulton Street with the bouquet of flowers, he sees Mr. Fredricks with the broom in his hand. "Good morning, Mr. Fredricks. Commendable job repairing the display case."

"Thank you, Mr. Brady, Good day to you! There is a gentleman by the name of John Polycarpus von Schneidau awaiting your arrival."

"Excellent. Come up stairs, Mr. Fredericks. I have a most important announcement to make to the staff."

Clapping his hands, summoning the staff, Mr. Brady stands in the center of the grand reception room. There is a marble bust of a man with long, wavy hair, a mustache, head squarely set on his shoulders with no neck to speak of, chiseled along the base in capital letters: DAGUERRE.

"Now then, I should like to introduce a guest member to our staff, John Carl Frederick Polycarpus von Schneidau. He is a most talented operator who will add greatly to our reputation as the finest Daguerreotype Gallery on all of Broadway. Let us all extend a warm, heartfelt welcome..." There is a short burst of applause as Mr. von Schneidau takes a bow.

"Hold on a moment, is everyone here? I don't see Mr. Pettifog. Benjamin, would you be so kind as to go up to the mercurial room and tell him there is an important matter to discuss?"

In the interim, Brady walks about the reception area to the gallery, stopping at the gilded cage whistling to the little birds chirping in return, he adjusts the arrangement of flowers, gently spraying them with the spritzer bottle, he puts his gloved finger to the table top checking for dust. "Excellent," he says catching a glimpse of himself in the looking glass, he adjusts his cravat, spritzes his hair then takes out his comb.

Rushing down the stairs in a mad dash, an energetic old man with grey hair sticking up, red flushed cheeks starts shouting, "Black vomit! Black vomit! That's all I sees — Black vomit!"

"Now, now, now, Mr. Pettifog. There's no yellow fever to worry yourself over," consoles Mr. Brady. "I can assure you."

Mr. Pettifog raises his finger to his ear, flapping the cartilage like an elephant. "What's that you say Mr. Brady?" he says.

"This is the newest addition to our staff, Mr. John Polycarpus von Schneidau, who will temporarily take the place of Edwin Bronk until I can find a permanent replacement."

"Oh not another operator for me to break-in! Where has Mr. Bronk gone off to?"

"To St. Louis... Please Mr. Pettifog, try not to interrupt. I have an important announcement to make. This is a momentous occasion. Mr. von Schneidau shall assist in a sitting we shall remember for many years to come. I shall depend on each and every one of you from the buff-boys polishing the plates, to the apprentices in the coating room, to my skilled camera operators, my trusted chemist, my colorist, my portrait painter, the ticket boys, my talented jewel case manufacturers and framers..."

"Hey now! How dare you forget the mercurial room — the heart and soul of the Daguerrean beast!"

"Yes, Mr. Pettifog, you are quite right — I saved your department for last. The most honored, the most remembered part of a proper tribute is the last, but not least mention. As you all know, without Mr. Pettifog and his mercurial room there would be no daguerreotypes."

"Cut to the chase, Mr. Brady, the spirit lamps need tending to and I have a whole list of materials we need downstairs at Mr. Anthony's. There'll be a back-log of sitters out the door, down the stairs and around the corner to Gibson's Saddler Shoppe."

"Yes, Mr. Pettifog, but…"

"QUICKSILVER!"

"Yes, Mr. Pettifog?"

"Quicksilver! I am in dire needst of quicksilver! Have you lost your hearing, Mat, on top of your sight? Blind as a bat you are! Deaf as a blaster on the Hoosac Tunnel?" Suddenly, he breaks into song:

Working on the Hoosac, Blast, blast away
Working on the Hoosac, Blast our ear drums
Working on the Hoosac, Blast all to kingdom come.

In quiet mutterings, Mr. Fredricks grins while voicing his doubts, "Why do you insist on keeping this bummer on your pay muster, Mr. Brady? He is clearly afflicted with the mercury vapors these many years."

Mr. Pettifog continues singing Working on the Hoosac.

In a quiet whisper, Brady responds, "He has been my rock from my humble start. We toiled many an hour together in that mercurial room."

"He is a barnacle, Mr. Brady, dragging at your keel. You must scour him away. He will only slow you down."

Mr. Pettifog pauses before singing 'Blast, blast away', "I hear all Mistah Fredricks, quiet clearly, quite clearly."

"You run a sad ship of affairs, Mr. Brady. A sinking ship."

Brady slams his fist down on the marble-topped table, grabbing Mr. Fredricks by the cravat wrenching him down to his eye level, peering over his blue spectacles, fire in his eyes, a change in cadence to his voice coming from another time, another place. "Watch the words you choose, Mr. Fredricks. I strongly advise."

Breaking the turmoil with the swirling sound of strings, Lydia Littlejohn strikes the chords of her double-action harp, making circles with her hands, magic waves of sound, the birds chirp, and Brady releases his grasp walking over to the window looking out at Fulton Street.

"Who do we portrait now, Mr. Brady? Please not another post-mortem. The little boy in his nightshirt holding a white rose, eyes closed for all eternity. I cannot wash that image away. It is forever fixed in my memory."

"No, Mr. Pettifog, I can assure you that this sitter still breathes."

"A pity. Post-mortems hold so very still. Such cooperative sitters. No blinking eyes. No retakes. No wasted copper plates."

"Yes, Mr. Pettifog, under such sad circumstances," he says with his back still turned. He holds the curtain looking out at the steeple of St. Paul's, listening to Lydia at the harp play, Nearer my God to Thee. The morning sun grows stronger.

"Burning daylight! Mr. Brady! Burning precious daylight! We are all ears," shouts Mr. Pettifog.

Turning around, tugging down on his waist coat, he paces to the center of the room with his hands clasped together behind his back to the marble bust of Daguerre, leaning his right hand at the base.

"We will be shutting up shoppe at noon today..."

A collective gasp then successive gripes: "What? Another day without pay like yesterday?" asks George Clumpf, one of the camera operators.

"Please don't send me home, Mrs. Boswell will not be happy to see me. I will go back to polishing plates with the boys, anything you wish," says Luther Boswell.

"I saw clear skies this morning from up the rooftop. No dark clouds in the distance." George adds.

Raising his hands to quiet the grumblings, he waits for silence to continue, "This will be a private sitting requiring our undivided attention."

"Whoever shall it be, Mr. Brady?" asks a young girl stepping forward with a little curtsy.

"Why, if it isn't Mary Higbie. I am shocked to hear your little voice. So quiet and careful with your delicate brush strokes so precise..." He distracts himself removing his grey felt gloves. "If I answer your question, you must promise to keep it in the strictest confidence. You must all swear an oath not to breathe a word of what I am about to say — not to a single blessed soul."

In unison, like a congregation, they respond, "we promise, Mr. Brady."

He pauses a moment while they wait an eternity. His chest heaves to inhale, his mouth opens to breathe, his lips formulate words from somewhere mysterious inside as they project outward from his wind pipe flying magically through the air at the speed of sound past their eardrums to the three, tiny little bones in the middle ear — the hammer, the anvil, and the stirrup — collectively called ossicles then to the inner ear through the cochlea to the auditory nerve then over synapses of the cerebellum to comprehension at an instant in their mind.

"Henry Hudson! No, not Jenny Lind! Anything but Jenny Lind!"

"Lower your voice, Mr. Pettifog! Broadway is all ears!"

"I am so weary of reading about her day after day in the Tribune, and the Herald and the Sun. This is madness. Jenny Lind canes, Jenny Lind riding hats, tickets to her concerts, why even the new book The Life of Jenny Lind. I can't take it any longer... Jenny, Jenny, Jenny."

"Well, you must endure, Mr. Pettifog, I am relying on you."

"What's this about The Life of Jenny Lind?" asks Hannah Buttle.

Taking his copy out of his back pocket, Mr. Pettifog holds up the book with a lithograph image of Jenny Lind on the cover, hands folded, flowers in her hair. Another collective gasp as the staff surrounds Mr. Pettifog holding the book up high, juggling successive questions: Let me see. Can I borrow it for a bit? How much? Where can I get a copy?

"Across the 'Way at Bangs and Platt's, number 204 Broadway. G.G. Foster penned the tale; he is the author of New York by Gas Light. Cost me a shilling."

Mr. Brady claps his hands, trying to restore order. "Now then Mr. Fredricks, we will close the register book at half eleven. I want this studio to look its very best. We want her to sparkle like crystal." He pauses a moment considering the long list of tasks. "Why are you all milling about? Continue with your preparations. Remember, we have a most important sitting at noon today."

CHAPTER 12 — QUICKSILVER

1850

As the staff begins to disperse, Mr. Brady paces back and forth, "There is something I am forgetting. I am quite sure." Looking about the room he sees Timothy in the crowd looking bewildered. "Hold on a moment everyone. Just one more announcement... Timothy step forward. Seeing how most of you went home early yesterday on account of the inclement weather, I shall now make a proper introduction of our newest staff member. Everyone, this is young Tim from New Brighton, Staten Island – the same town where I now call home with my sweet bride, Julia. He is a good industrious little boy. Who will show young Tim the ropes?"

An awkward silence, even the canaries hush to listen as they sway on their little trapeze.

"QUICKSILVER!" shouts Mr. Pettifog. "Are ye not hearing my words? I am in dire needst of Quicksilver!"

"That settles it then, Timothy. You shall attend to Mr. Pettifog and assist him with his preparations. Get whatever he requires and have it put on my account with Mr. Anthony."

"This way young Tim," says Mr. Pettifog bounding up the stairs, two at a time to the third floor. "C'mon then, we haven't time to waste. Quick now! There's so much for me to show you. So little time. So little time."

The church bells at Saint Paul's chime nine times. Tim climbs to the top of the stairs pausing to catch his breath.

"Old man you are!" he says with a laugh. "You'll get used to climbing the stairs soon enough."

"I didn't know there was a third floor."

"Oh, yes and a fourth. Second floor is the gallery. Third floor is the studio. Fourth floor is but a recent addition, the Palace to the Sun. Step right this way..."

Down the hallway, he knocks on the door of the chemist's room. "Professor Tarbox, allow me to introduce Tim. Tim, this is Professor George Tarbox, our chief chemist. George and I were classmates together studying chemistry under Professor John William Draper at New York University. George knows his scruples from his drams. Scruples from his drams... twenty grains in a scruple, three scruples in a dram. Isn't that right, George?"

Dressed in his leather apron, black arm-sleeves stretched to the elbow of his white shirt, "Yes, that is quite right, Henry. Professor Draper is to my mind's eye the true inventor of photography. With his knowledge of chemistry, he solved the problem of fixing the image and took the first sun portrait ever captured of his sister Dorothy. After finishing our studies with Professor Draper, Mr. Pettifog and I pushed aside our plans of one day opening an apothecary shop and devoted ourselves to the New Art."

"Oh, I can hear my dear, departed mother now," says Mr. Pettifog in an old woman's voice, "'Whoever heard of such a thing? Throwing your life away making doggery-types instead of following your true calling,' she scolded me over and over."

"Tut, tut, Mr. Pettifog. If only your mother could see you now, she would be very proud indeed," says Professor Tarbox as he gently tries to clean a tarnished daguerreotype. "Oh bother, why was this poor daguerreotype left in direct sunlight and not in its jewel case? People are so careless. See how the image has all but turned black with tarnish."

"What is in this bottle with the skull and bones, Professor Tarbox?" asks Tim holding it in his hand.

"Put that down! That my boy is potassium cyanide which I use to restore daguerreotypes – one grain of it taken internally, would kill you in instant! Henry, remind the boy – this is not child's play!"

"What say we let Professor Tarbox get back to mixing his magic potions?"

With his mortar and pestle, Professor Tarbox grounds a powdery substance, then adds it to a clear glass beaker stirring with a crystal rod round and round and round, suspending the solution. Suddenly, an awful stench hits Tim between the eyes, he grabs his nose and gasps for breath. The two men laugh and seem not to notice the horrible smell.

"That my boy is bromine tickling your olfactory. It is named for its offensive smell. Bromos – dead odor," says the Professor.

"You see, young Tim, I much prefer calling Professor Tarbox by his more apt title — might I present our esteemed Alchemist!"

"Bite your tongue, Mr. Pettifog. Would you have me burned at the stake for practicing the Dark Art!" He startles Tim with a sinister look, grabbing him by the collar. "You won't turn me in to the constables, now then, would you?"

"No, Professor Tarbox."

"Luckily for me, this is no longer the Dark Ages," he says with a laugh. "This is the age of steamships and locomotives, telegraphs and photographs. Professors Draper, Morse, Pettifog, and myself are free to practice our precious chemistry to our hearts' content. But centuries ago one of those alchemists working in the shadows, late into the night stumbled upon something quite remarkable in the quest for the philosopher's stone..."

Professor Tarbox pauses a moment. "Come gentlemen step inside and I shall demonstrate the driving force in photography."

He shuts the door and lights the red lantern. In the ruby shadows he takes a copper plate and coats it with a substance in a tray. "This is silver chloride or what the old alchemists of the 16th Century called 'horn silver'. Watch what happens when we open the door."

Before his eyes, the silvery plate turns flat grey then dark black. "This young Tim is what propels photography – the rays of the sun blackened the horn silver. Thomas Wedgewood made a similar observation in 1802. He also noted that sunlight through a red glass had but little effect upon the silver which is why we can work under the light of the red lantern."

"Horn silver?" murmurs Mr. Pettifog. "No! No!! No!!! I am in needst of QUICKSILVER! We must make a list of much needed supplies. Somebody lend me a pen and paper before I forget."

Feverishly, he scratches away at the paper, hastily jotting down what he thinks half to himself. "Hyposulfite of soda at 50 cents a pound, gold chloride at 42 cents a bottle, and you mustn't forget the quicksilver! Quick Timothy, take this list downstairs to Mr. Anthony's establishment and get me some quicksilver! Post-haste my boy! Post-haste!" As Tim runs off, he hollers after him, "Look to the list! Don't forget mu buttercakes whatever you do! I cannot work without buttercakes."

Tim stops in his tracks. "Where shall I get the buttercakes… at Mr. Anthony's?"

"Goodness no, Timothy! Go to Buttercake Dick's. You know where that is don't you? It's on Spruce Street."

"I've never been there, Mr. Pettifog."

"That's alright lad. Let me draw you a map." He scrawls triangles, rectangles and intersecting lines on a sheet of paper. "See here, this is Chatham Row, on Nassau Street when you get to the Tribune Building on the corner, go down the cellar stairs, there you'll find Buttercake Dick's."

"Down in a cellar?"

"You can't miss it. Just follow the newsboys. Might I suggest you make this your first stop on your errand then work your way back Mr. Anthony's and get the quicksilver. Think you can find it?"

"Yes, Mr. Pettifog."

"That's a good boy, now here's two shillings, be sure to get plenty of buttercakes."

Downstairs at Edward Anthony and Co., Daguerreotype Materials, Tim walks past the display case of cameras, towards the back where the chemist's supplies are located.

Standing at the counter, he thinks back to his little adventure to Buttercake Dick's. Walking down Ann Street, past Daniel Sweeny's, past Theatre Alley, he stopped at the corner of Nassau Street – there's the Evening Mirror building and some stairs leading down into a basement, perhaps this is the place... then he sees a sign — Sandy Welsh's Beer Cellar. No, this is not the place.

Taking a left, he walks among the shadows along the dark and narrow Nassau Street. This is the street where Moses Beach and his New York Sun call home . Nearby is James Gordon Bennett's New York Herald. Up ahead Tim sees Nathaniel Currier's Lithograph Shoppe at 152 Nassau Street, stacks of lithographs wholesale at sixpence apiece then next door at 154 is Horace Greeley's New York Tribune Building.

Tim rounds the corner of Spruce Street, notices the steam from the printing presses coming up from the grates, boys huddled together, using broadsheets as blankets. Down the dank steps, crowds of newsboys sitting at tables in the cellar of Buttercake Dick's, gulping down hot coffee, smoking rank cigars..

"Will there be anything else?" says the clerk as he ever so slowly places four tiny bottles on the counter with much deliberation as if he were lifting a sledgehammer.

He must not be used to hard work, thinks Tim. T'is only a small bottle. He reads the label marked 'mercury'.

"Sir, I think a mistake has been made. Mr. Pettifog requested quicksilver, not mercury."

"There you have it, lad. Quicksilver is mercury. Now be sure to give Mr. Pettifog my best regards. Tell him Mr. Henry H. Snelling wishes him well. We hardly ever see him anymore."

"What do you mean? He's just up the stairs," asks Tim as he grabs one of the bottles but he nearly sinks to the floor at the weight in his hand, heavy as an anchor dragging him down. "Goodness!"

"Careful now," advises Mr. Snelling. "You must take great care with mercury. Yes, poor Mr. Pettifog, he rarely ventures out, not even down to our establishment. A shut-in always working away. Sad really. If you ask me, he works much too hard confined in that dark room."

Back at the studio, Tim knocks on the door with the painted letters, Mercurial Room, Professor Henry Peter Pettifog in smaller letters beneath. He hears a series of latches and locks, clicks and clinks. The door opens outward to reveal a black curtain ante-chamber, a hand draws him closer, then Mr. Pettifog's muffled voice, "Quick now. Shut the door behind you. Lock it and latch it!" he repeats, "Lock it and latch it!"

Inside the darkroom, Tim sees vague shadows by the faint haze of the red lantern. "Your eyes will soon adjust. Hand me a buttercake like a good boy. And have one for yourself. You haven't lived to 'til you've had one of Dick's buttercakes. He used to be a newsboy, you know."

Tim reaches in the paper bag and grabs hold of a heavy biscuit with a lump of butter in its belly, dripping from the edges crisp and blackened, then he takes a sumptuous bite.

Mr. Pettifog takes a look at Tim's face, "The best three cents you could ever spend."

Mr. Pettifog grabs a tiny bottle in between bites and pours out a small amount of mercury — a shimmering liquid metal globule slides slowly back and forth in the dish. "Come see my precious quicksilver. Mercury is the mysterious metal — a liquid at room temperature."

He strikes a match and lights the small brass spirit lamp beneath the cast iron fuming box – an inverted pyramid with a side slot for the thermometer. "We must get the quicksilver up to temperature." He pulls out the glass tube filled with mercury and peers through his bifocals at the incremental degrees. "Rule number one for developing a proper daguerreotype – Keep the mercury hot!"

He strikes the match to another spirit lamp and places a small kettle on top.

"Are you heating up some more quicksilver?"

"No, Timothy, I am brewing up a different potion. A magical potion, a potion that alchemist's discovered long ago…"

"You cannot fool me, Mr. Pettifog. I recognize the smell. That is coffee you're brewing."

"Right you are Timothy, but without my coffee, I cannot develop all these daguerreotypes. It's as important as my quicksilver."

Just then a hand reaches through a small window past a dark curtain and places a black plate-holder on the work desk. "The plates are piling up. We have much developing to do. The gentlemen operators expose the plates and we must turn them into fine daguerreotypes. Think of the timber business. The operators are the lumberjacks out felling trees, sending them down the river. We work at the sawmill ripping the bark, cutting the logs into planks and beams. We must develop plate after plate after plate, or else there will be a log jam."

Tim watches Mr. Pettifog pull up the dark slide to remove the exposed plate then places it face down in the fuming box. "The temperature is just right at 155 degrees. The mercury vapors are doing their work. He lifts the lid to take a peek at the exposed image. "Just a wee bit more… there she is… now a quick dip in the hyposulphite bath to wash away the light sensitive silver."

"Is it finished, Mr. Pettifog?"

"No, not nearly, Timothy, for we must gild the image." He lights another spirit lamp and pours a thin layer of gold chloride ever so slightly on the plate careful not to let a drop spill. "Take a look now. See how much richer the tone, see how the gold hardens to the silver sheen."

"Is it finished now?"

"Oh no, not just yet. We still have to wash the plate with Croton. Next, I will dry the plate with the spirit lamp."

A bit bored, Tim looks about the dark room, objects become more distinct. He sees a cot in the corner with a nightstand and washbowl. "Why is there a bed in here, Mr. Pettifog?"

"Oh, Mr. Brady is most kind to let me call this my home." He suddenly breaks into verse by John Howard Payne, "'Mid pleasures and palaces though we may roam, Be it ever so humble, there's no place like home. Oh, there's no place like home...' Now then take a look. Oh such beauty, dark raven hair, expressive eyes, deep dark pools conveying her essence. I can almost read her lips. She whispers to me..."

"What does she say?"

Transfixed, staring at the image, "What now? Words not for a boy to hear. But I will say this, that is certainly no dead fish on a silver plate!"

"Dead fish, Mr. Pettifog?"

"A dead fish is a poor portrait — eyes without life's expression staring blankly at you from the silver plate. Mr. Brady does not tolerate inferior portraits. Come now, step this way, we must take this daguerreotype to the colorist room."

Squinting his eyes in the bright sunshine room, the drapes pulled back, Tim looks past the grid of square wooden panes, up beyond the trees at the spire of Saint Paul's. He places himself before that lithograph on the wall, New York from the Steeple of St. Paul's Church by J.W. Hill and looks down at Brady's Daguerrean Gallery through the window.

Three girls sit on the work bench with their backs turned, hair pulled back, twisted tight into ropes, tied in intricate weaves and knots. The girl with auburn hair stipples the paint brush in rose madder and delicately applies it to the woman's lips with burnt sienna, she flushes the cheeks to a slight blush.

"Buff-boy, step back, your panting breath on my neck shall spoil this woman's portrait."

"Timothy, this is Hannah Buttle, our most talented colorist." She turns not around to show her face. "Seated next to her adding sparkle and glisten to the plate is Mary Higbie."

Dipping the brush in liquid gold, she precisely dots the earrings and necklace to a woman's portrait. "Hello thar, Tim," she says blinking blond eye lashes faint as the paint brush, flaxen hair, silky smooth.

"Ignore the boy and attend to your work, Mary," says Hannah.

Lydia Littlejohn mixes paint on the white fabric of the inside lid of her paint box. She turns grey pants Prussian-blue to a captain's full-length portrait, a dab of gold to the hilt of his sabre and the epaulets on his shoulder, silver to his buttons.

"This buff-boy is quite the nuisance, Mr. Pettifog," sighs Lydia, "Shouldn't he be polishing plates?"

Hannah turns her head around, alluring eyebrows, as if painted by an artist with dark, defined strokes, drawing attention to her emerald eyes. "I couldn't agree with you more, Lydia. Away with you buff-boy. It isn't polite to stare." She turns her head with a toss.

"Smitten with you she is!"

"Please Mr. Pettifog, we have considerable work to do. Shall I summon Mr. Fredricks?"

"Oh, Miss Hannah Buttle, that will not be necessary."

"Continue on your way, if you must, Mr. Pettifog. I am sure Mr. Darby would be happy to have a visitor."

"Yes then, let's continue on our way..."

After a polite tap on the door of Henry F. Darby, Portrait Painter, Tim sees before him an artist at his easel with a near-complete canvas, holding a palette, studying a daguerreotype of an elderly looking gentleman facing to the right while the painting is a mirror image looking to the left.

"Good morning Mr. Darby, I am showing Tim about the studio. This is Mr. Darby our portrait artist in residence."

"Mr. Pettifog exaggerates my title, I am no artist, not by any means, I am a mere copyist working directly from Mr. Brady's daguerreotypes."

"Is that man from the pages of Mr. Brady's book?"

"Why yes, he is, that is Mr. Henry Clay. I've been working on his portrait for some time now. He is the great compromiser — Mr. Clay and his omnibus."

"I rode on top of an omnibus with Old Elephant. Is Mr. Clay a driver on the Knickerbocker Line?"

"No, this is a different sort of omnibus, Tim. Mr. Clay is the senator from Kentucky who averted a national crisis with his omnibus bill. Oh, he loaded all sorts of legislation on this little omnibus of his, crammed them in like passengers riding on board the morning tide. He put the Fugitive Slave Act, Prohibition of the Slave Trade in Washington City, not to mention adding California and Utah to the Union.

"The bill passed last Saturday on September 7th then the Senate approved the House's omnibus bill on Monday. We've had such tumult — such uncertain times in this country since President Taylor died of cholera over the summer. Now we have Millard Fillmore of New York."

"Mildred who?" asks Mr. Pettifog bending his ear.

"Millard! I said, Mr. Pettifog, in case you hadn't noticed, Millard Fillmore has been president of our country since July 9th."

"He has? Very well then, enough of politics, Mr. Darby, Timothy shall be dulled senseless. It matters not to the likes of us."

"Listen he must. This affects each and every one of us. Look lad, there is the man who averted disunion with his omnibus — the great Senator Henry Clay. I must do him justice with my brush."

"Oh, for goodness sake, Mr. Darby, you've been dabbing at the same canvas for days on end."

"See here, Mr. Pettifog you can have your dead fish on a silver platter, but make no mistake, your sun portraits will never be viewed as true works of art. Just compare my portrait of Washington Irving with the original daguerreotype taken by Mr. Plumbe."

Mr. Darby walks over to his painting of Washington Irving hanging on the wall. "Take note of how I removed all the imperfections. Look at all the unsightly scratches and transverse grooves and then you tell me which is superior. My work or yours…"

"Well, that may very well be the case, Mr. Darby. But I can have a daguerreotype ready in ten minutes and send the sitter on their merry way. In the time you paint one portrait, the staff can have 600 daguerreotypes developed, fixed, gilded, and framed."

"That is a gross exaggeration, Mr. Pettifog! And you well know it!"

"Gentlemen, gentlemen, please lower your voices," says Mr. Brady stepping into the room. "You will upset the clientele. I can hear you out in the studio. Now then Mr. Pettifog shake hands with Mr. Darby. This is no time for dueling pistols. Remember you are kindred spirits. Shake hands. Mr. Pettifog, I suggest you return to your work in the mercurial room and let Mr. Darby attend to his portrait of Henry Clay. Timothy, stay close at my heels. Remember, this is a historic day."

CHAPTER 13 — IN THE DARKROOM

1985

In the faint orange glow of the safelight, unsure of my surroundings, I call out like a little kid, scared of the dark. "Duke, where are you?"

"Over here," he says. "The safelight is still warming up."

Dangling overhead is the Thomas Duplex Super Safelight, the best in the profession, weighing over 20 pounds, secured by thick chains to eyebolts in the ceiling. The low-pressure sodium lamp requires five minutes to reach full candle power.

"Before you know it, you'll be able to read the newspaper by that safelight."

Duke then flicks on the radio to a Big Band station, WNEW 1130-AM on the dial. William B. Williams is the DJ and his opening signature song begins to play.

It's make-believe ballroom time,
Put all your cares away,
All the bands are here,
To bring good cheer your way.

The music stops for a split second, the second verse kicks in...

It's make-believe ballroom time...
It's no time to fret,
Your dial is set for fun...

Something tells me I'm gonna like it here. This is just like the darkroom in the basement back home. Dad would pop in his favorite cassette tape, Benny Goodman Live at Carnegie Hall in 1938. Gene Krupa pounded out paradiddle-diddles on the floor tom during his drum solo in Sing Sing Sing.

We would spend hot summer nights in the cool of the basement darkroom. The old fan squeaked as it oscillated a gentle breeze. Dad's swivel chair creaked as he adjusted his Federal No. 245 Enlarger that he's had since 1940. It was made in Brooklyn – cost $29.50 – a lot of money back then. The black powder-coat spray paint on the enlarger reminded me of the SS helmet sitting on the shelf in the darkroom – a souvenir Dad brought home from the War. Over in the corner was a German Mauser rifle. The P-38 pistol and holster belt sat on the second shelf in a beat-up cardboard box along with his Bronze Star medal and two Purple Hearts.

After focusing the negative, Dad lifted the lid to the lead-lined box to pull out a glossy sheet of photographic paper. He would mutter to himself while he counted, exposing the paper underneath the white light of the enlarger. One potato, two potato, three potato… then he would hand me the 5x7 to put in the developer tray.

I had the best part of the job in our little production line – beneath the eerie glow of the red safe light, I watched the white glossy paper magically transform before my eyes in the ripple of developer waves into a photograph.

"That's good," says Dad lifting the corner of the tray, giving it a final, gentle swish, "Now, hand it off to Billy."

Bill, my younger brother, was the short stop in the production line – grasping the print with the rubber tipped prongs for a quick dip in the stop bath before a long soak in the fixer – all the while laughing and singing along to these Big Band tunes… Beat Me Daddy, 8 to the Bar.

"Cut that out, Billy!"

"OK, Daddy-oh… Beat me Daddy, 8 to the Bar!"

"Did you hear what I said?"

"Yes In-Deed!" he quotes a Tommy Dorsey song.

"Now, that's enough…"

A Glenn Miller song, Pennsylvania 6-5000 comes on, the melody bounces along, the music stops, the telephone rings, then the boys from the chorus sing out, Pennsylvania 6-5000. I wait for Bill to join in… I know he will. It is just a matter of time.

The phone rings again and Bill belts out, "Pennsylvania Six, Five, Oh! Oh! Oh!"

That is the phone number to the Hotel Pennsylvania in New York City located across the street from Penn Station.

"Now cut that out, I said!"

German weapons and German cameras were in that darkroom. Dad gave each of us an old German camera to learn how to take photographs. Bill had the Agfa 120mm camera with the fold-out leather bellows while I had Dad's pre-War Exakta 35mm.

"This is considered to be the first SLR camera ever invented," he explained. "SLR stands for Single Lens Reflex. Notice how Billy's camera has the range-finder. He uses that to set his focus, but he is not looking through the camera lens. He is only getting an approximate idea of how the picture will come out." He answered another question, "The side-ways 8 stands for infinity. Infinity is beyond the horizon… far as the eye can see… forever."

He unscrewed the lens and demonstrated how the mirror dropped down, then clicked up when the shutter was released. "That sound you hear is the reflex mechanism bringing the mirror up and down after you take a picture. This mirror lets you sneak a peek and see exactly what the camera sees."

Holding the Carl Zeiss lens, he set the aperture to f-16. "Here look inside... the aperture is like the pupil of your eye, closing tight in the bright light or opening wide as a cat's eye in the dark."

"Should I set the shutter speed to 400 with this Tri-X film, Dad?"

"No. No. No..." Again, he tried to explain the difference between film speed and shutter speed. "The shutter speed is different from the film speed. ASA stands for American Standards Association — they are the ones who set the speed of the film. Now, look at the black curtain in the camera. That is the shutter. See how it opens and closes at the blink of an eye. Think of your eyelid. It opens and closes to let light in the camera. If it's a bright sunny day, you will want a quick shutter speed of 250th, 500th, or even 1000th of a second, or you could use a very long time exposure like the time I took those pictures of Niagara Falls at night, but then you need to set the camera on a tripod."

He looks at our confused expressions.

"Don't worry about ASA for now... just set your shutter speed and f-stop to what I tell you, okay?"

Holding the Exakta, I look downward to see through the viewfinder. Everything looked backwards like looking into a mirror. This was before the development of the pentaprism. This old camera did not have a built-in light meter. Dad would read off the shutter speed and aperture settings from his Konica camera.

Dad explained the term, camera obscura — room dark. "The ancient Greeks were the ones who discovered the principles of the camera obscura way back in 400 BC. Now the word, 'camera' means room and 'obscura' means dark. When light is projected through a pinhole, an image is projected on the wall."

Looking at the inside of the Exakta, I find a miniature room painted black with a black curtain opening and closing, it's a little darkroom, a little camera obscura.

"I still don't get it, Dad. What makes photography work?"

"What do you mean?"

"How does the image stick to the film like Silly Putty?"

"Silly Putty?"

"You know, it's sort-of like PlayDough. You can flatten it to a Sunday comic strip and the image transfers to the Silly Putty."

"I see..." says Dad. "Think of the silverware tea set in the dining room. What happens to it over time?"

"Well, it turns dingy-black, then after you polish it with that pink cream the silver shines like chrome."

"That's it. Silver tarnishes because it is photo-sensitive. Silver is sensitive to light just as you are – red as a lobster in the sun if you're not careful. The rolls of film we buy are coated with silver halide – silver salts – that's what makes the image stick. Silver."

"Silver?" I repeat, almost in disbelief.

I remember hanging the prints up to dry. Dad judged our shots like we were on a fishing trip — this one's a keeper, this one's a tosser. Bill always won hands down with that Agfa. I remember that shot he took at Fort Ticonderoga — the artillery crew had just finished loading the cannon. The powerful flash-burst of black-powder from the cannon muzzle looked like a smoke ring from Dad's pipe. You can almost hear that deafening cannon blast.

This was the summer of 1977. In the autumn of that year, a TV show came on the air, James at 15, it was my favorite at the time. James had a red light bulb hanging in his darkroom as he developed prints. Then he would put on his down winter coat and go out on assignment with his SLR on the Freedom Trail in Boston taking photographs of the Old South Meeting House and the Paul Revere statue in the North End. On Halloween, in the auditorium, we all watched Johnny Tremain, a movie about an apprentice working in a silversmith shop in Boston, then it was off to the Crestwood Library to read that book by Esther Forbes, then later on, her other book, Paul Revere and The World He Lived In. Dad bought me a Vivitar Light-Meter for my 12th birthday that year.

"This is cool, Dad... What is it?"

"It's a hand-held light-meter. You set the film speed here, now you can choose from these corresponding f-stops and shutter speeds, say f-16 at 125 or f-11 at 250..."

"Alright Danny," says Duke, "Are you still with me?"

I look over his shoulder as he lifts the thick glass to the contact easel. He wipes it down with a felt orange dust cloth.

"Dust and fingerprints are our two greatest enemies."

Taking out a fresh white sheet of glossy 8x10 paper, he arranges the 35mm negatives, then closes the glass down – compressing them flat to the paper.

"Now, you'll find machine printing is less forgiving than tray printing in your darkroom back home." He sets the GraLab Timer to 4.5 seconds then pushes the button. The enlarger lamp sheds white light down on the easel. Seconds tick by, precisely by tenths counting backwards to zero.

"My Dad counted potatoes..."

"This is different. You have to be right on the money with your exposure. You will have to learn how to read the negative."

"Read the negative?"

"Yes, you will have to use your judgment."

After making another contact sheet, he takes a red grease pencil to write down the twin-check number on the back then feeds it into the processor. "Wait for the beep."

I watch as Duke sets up another contact sheet. "Now, how 'bout you give it a try."

I place the paper down and arrange the 35mm negatives, but have considerable trouble fitting all 36 exposures on the 8x10 sheet. The negatives retract like coiled springs – fidgeting and unruly, they refuse to cooperate.

"Duke, I can't get them to stay in place. They keep moving about."

"Here, let me show you," he says calmly. With an experienced hand, the negatives heed to his command at an instant. "There you go... there's nothing to it."

He feeds the 8x10 into the machine. "Now remember to wait for the beep." He hands me the finished proof sheet. "There you go. You've made your first contact sheet. We'll make a Darkroom Technician out of you yet. And just think, you're getting paid to learn. We're teaching you while you earn a paycheck. You should be the one paying us for all we're going to teach you."

"I never thought of it that way, Duke. That's a good point."

"You dropping out of college was probably the smartest decision you ever made."

Just then the buzzer beeps followed by a quick knock on the door. As it swings open, bright sunlight is briefly visible through the crack in the curtain, then it slams shut. George stands there tall with shoulder length black hair and a Paul McCartney-Hey Jude-beard.

"Morning George. Coffee is ready."

"How's he making out, Dad?" George asks his father.

"Not bad," he fibs. "Not bad at all."

George immediately sets to work. He snaps a 4x5 copy negative to shake off the dust specs then blasts it with the compressed air for good measure. He sets the negative in the holder then loads it into the Omega D2 enlarger and cranks it up and down peering through the focus-finder. This focus-finder looks like a small microscope with a mirror set at an angle so he can look directly up into the inner guts of the enlarger — up through the Schneider lens – past the refracting lenses — the convex and the concave. He stares directly into the bright light of the enlarger like staring into the sun — he adjusts the fine focus — searching for the sandy grain of the negative — the gritty silver salts of the black and white film.

Meanwhile, Duke is rattling off 3½x5 glossy prints — reading each negative by eye like a light meter, setting aperture, then exposure, beep goes the timer, then he lifts the easel, reloads a sheet of paper, repeats this procedure 36 times in rapid fire succession.

Meanwhile, I fumble with the negatives to another contact sheet then feed it through the machine. I stand by the catch-pan as two minutes tick away. Out plops a pitch-black sheet of paper.

I show the results to Duke. "You need to cut back your exposure time," he advises.

George goes to the second enlarger, the enlarger with the extended support column which he cranks high to the ceiling. He stretches his arm to focus then sets up the 16x20 easel and makes a test print. He works in rhythm with the Ilford machine – while one print is running through the machine, he is setting up the next enlargement.

On the radio, William B. Williams discusses Francis Albert Sinatra. He never calls him Frank, always Francis Albert, old Blue Eyes. Benny Goodman was the Sultan of Swing, just as Babe Ruth was the Sultan of Swat. Duke Ellington was the Duke, as was John Wayne, and the man standing beside me. Another contact sheet plops down. George picks it up and hands it to me. The paper is mottled grey, the negatives are glowing white. There are no discernible images visible.

"You need to increase your exposure," advises George. "Contact sheets must be black."

Strangers in the night, sings Francis Albert, exchanging glances.

How did I get here? I ask myself. I'm in this dark room with two strangers — Duke and George, father and son. Where did George find me, anyways?

Wondering in the night...

I think back to reading through the Help Wanted section of the paper, sitting at the kitchen table with Dad.

"There's nothing here, Dad. I can't find anything." It's hopeless, utterly hopeless... I am hopeless. I am Bartleby.

"Here let me take a look."

He puts on his glasses and snaps the broad sheet of the Herald-Statesman then folds it over. Slow and methodical, taking his time.

"Here's one for a bank teller."

"Dad, I'm not any good at counting money."

"Here's one for a dishwasher at a restaurant."

"I don't want to go back to washing dishes."

Dad quietly mutters to himself. "Doesn't like doing dishes, doesn't like counting money..."

See, I told you, there's nothing there, I say to myself. Sitting there in his horn-rimmed glasses, hair combed back neat, Dad reminds me of Benny Goodman and guys of his generation – Glenn Miller, Tommy Dorsey, even Clark Kent.

He reads out another job listing. "Darkroom Technician – Experience developing black & white. Must have car."

"I don't know, Dad."

"This is the place down at The Station where you got your photo taken for your college application. Remember?"

This guy in a black beard took my picture.

"I don't know, Dad."

"You can do this. Think of what I showed you in the basement."

Duke is on a roll cranking out prints. He joins Frank at the end of the song singing Scooby Dooby Doo, We've been together. Dooby, dooby, doo...

CHAPTER 14 — A SITTING

1850

Following Brady's brisk strides, Tim gradually loses pace and gets lost in the crowd of customers milling about the studio. Standing in the center of the room, beneath the skylight, sun rays streaming down reflect off the white ruffles of Brady's shirt sleeves, he points to an imaginary spot beside him. Tim makes his way past the long frock coats to the spot.

Mr. Brady crouches down to his eye level.

"Goodness, such a big crowd, even for a Saturday. Look about the room. Tell me what you see."

"Lots of people standing about – reminds me of Whitehall Street waiting for the ferry."

"What else do you see?"

"A little boy looks lost. He is going from person to person tugging at their sleeves."

"Go on…"

"Much confusion. That man there checking his pocket-watch looks agitated. He has someplace to be."

"Very keen observations, Timothy. Now permit me to point out the order to this chaos."

With a broad sweeping motion of his arm, he begins to make a statement, but strikes the backside to a passing woman's bustle.

"Madam, I humbly beg your pardon. I was merely trying to point out something to the boy."

"I believe you have." She glances back, chin to shoulder for a fleeting moment. He looks after her as she disappears into the crowd.

"You were saying, Mr. Brady…"

"Ah, yes, this is the main portrait studio. This is where we do our work — downstairs is the gallery and reception area. Now look to the left at the series of doors leading to workrooms. Behind that door there is the buffing room where the boys work with great care polishing the Scovill Plates. Next is the coating room where my assistants sensitize the plates with bromine and iodine. Now keep a sharp eye on the movements of the camera operator – his hands move quicker than a legerdemain picking your pocket. See how he reaches to his left through the small window with a black curtain. He has the prepared plate which he places in the camera in the blink of an eye. Look now – he moves to the right with the exposed plate and pushes it through that small window into the mercurial room."

"Yes, that's where Mr. Pettifog works."

"Right you are, Timothy. Now look to the right side of the studio at the adjoining workrooms. In the corner is the chemist's room, that's where Professor Tarbox calls home. Next door is Mr. Pettifog. Then the finished plates are brought to the colorist's room if the customer desires to have nature's colors put to their likeness. Then over there is the finishing room where the daguerreotypes are put into frames, gold lockets, or breast pins depending on their wishes. Then there is the receiving counter where the customer picks up their portrait in as little as twenty minutes. Remember, left side plate preparation, right side plate finishing."

"Yes, Mr. Brady," with a bored sigh.

"That little boy is Stephen Neb, our ticket agent, who keeps a steady flow of sitters at the ready. Admission is free to the gallery on the second floor, but no one is permitted up to the studio without a ticket. See now, he is taking his cue from Luther Boswell, one of my top operators. He gives the 'At the Ready' sign. Stephen signals back, 'group portrait, two'. The assistants bring an additional chair and head-rest from the side. While an elderly gentleman gingerly takes his seat, the assistant lowers the tripod behind a young girl and tightens the head-clamp like a vise.

"Ow! You're hurting me!" says the little girl aged about seven.

"Look thar!" says the operator. "Hold still for your grandfather."

"Stop calling him my grandfather! I told you, he is my father!" She raises her voice and stamps down her foot. "This is the third time I've corrected you. Why won't you listen to me? We will take our business next door to Mr. Lawrence's studio if you persist."

"Luther, what is all the commotion about?"

"The little girl refuses to sit still, Mr. Brady. We've wasted plate after plate. She is most uncooperative. You know how difficult children can be."

Brady steps around the camera and tripod toward the portrait chair extending his hand. "What an adorable child you have, sir," to the old man with white hair holding a walking cane.

"My name is Rensselaer Havens and this is my pride and joy, my little Katrintje."

"So, good of you to come to my studio, Katrintje. I am Mr. Mathew B. Brady, the proprietor of this establishment."

"Katrintje is the Dutch for little Katy. My name is Catherine Elizabeth. I don't like it very much. It makes me think of Marie Antoinette and all those old queens with long names. She lost her head in a guillotine. You may call me Katy."

"Katy, it tis – and you shall call me Mr. B. I insist." He crouches down to her eye level. "Now let's make this a special portrait of you and your dear father – one that you shall treasure. Tell me something, have you ever played Still as a Statue?"

"Oh, yes, I almost always win. What's more, I have never lost a staring contest."

"I don't believe you. Can you hold your gaze for say thirty seconds?"

"Oh, quite easily, I accept your challenge with relish."

He takes out his pocket-watch. "Are you ready then?"

"Not fair, take off your blue spectacles, Mr. B. Look me in the eye."

The second hand ticks slowly by. Windows to the soul. Such a confident gaze with sadness in repose. She worries about her father. She sees right through me. I am a fraud, not a true artist. Water wells up. Eye lids twitch.

"There you blinked!"

"I most certainly did not."

"Yes, you did, Mr. B. I saw it quite clearly."

"All right then, perhaps if you stood next to your father, he could brace you. Now the camera will be able to see your beautiful dress."

"That will be most agreeable, Mr. B. Will the camera see my ring?"

"Ring?"

"Yes, my gold ring. Father gave it to me at New Year's to remember him by."

"Oh, we shall make every effort to include your ring." Brady snaps his fingers and whispers a hushed aside. "Luther, recompose the frame. Now then, Katy, where do you call home?"

"We used to live on Lafayette Place, now we live on Ninth Street near University Place. It is a beautiful house and has glass sliding doors with birds of paradise sitting on palm trees painted on them. When the doors are shut tight and the lights turned up bright, we know the supper is getting ready. The lights shine so pretty through the glass panes. On the mantel piece in the library is a very old clock that my father brought from France in one of his ships. Isn't that right, Papa?"

"Yes, Katrintje."

"You must know Mr. B. that we gave up our parlor and library for two evenings to hold a fair for that dreadful famine in Ireland. All my schoolmates and our friends made things to sell. My brothers made pictures in pen and ink and sold them for fifty cents apiece. We sent the poor Irish people over three hundred dollars."

"That is remarkable, Katy, most remarkable." Brady fusses and fidgets not content with the pose. "Might I suggest your father put his arm around you – this will create an endearing embrace, don't you think, Katy?"

"Why, yes, Mr. B. I should like that very much. People won't believe he isn't my grandfather. My father is a very old gentleman. He is seventy-four and was born before the Revolutionary War… Isn't that right, Papa?"

"Yes, Katrintje."

"Perhaps if you hold your father's hand."

"Like this Mr. B?" She tucks her little hand in the clutch of her father's big paw holding tight, holding to this fleeting moment in time.

"Oh, yes, that is a precious pose. Hold tight."

"Is my ring visible Mr. B. I want to make absolutely sure. My brother Henry went last year to Eureka in California."

"Luther, please re-check the composition."

Her left hand hangs down and shows the gold ring on her fore-finger.

"Now then, Katy and Mr. Havens, this shall be a thirty second exposure. I need…"

"Mr. B. my father's father lived on Shelter Island, and had twenty slaves, and their names were: Africa, Pomp, London, Titus, Tony, Lum, Cesar, Cuff, Odet, Dido, Ziller, Hagar, Judith, and Comas."

"Now Katy, please hold still so my assistant can focus the camera."

"But my grandfather thought it was wicked to keep slaves, so he told them they could be free."

"Most fascinating, I did not realize slavery was common in New York."

"Oh yes, very much so, just like the Southern States."

"Hush now, Katrintje, let Mr. Brady attend to his work."

"But Papa, I have just one more question I have to ask Mr. B…"

"Yes, Katy, ask and I shall answer."

"Well, my friend Mary Lanagan lives on Ninth Street between Broadway and the Bowery. She is a classmate of mine at Miss McClenahan's school. She has a lot of brothers and they tease us."

"Oh, that is quite remarkable," Brady says distracted.

"No, teasing isn't remarkable. It isn't remarkable in the slightest. Mr. B. are you even listening to a word I say? Mary told me Miss Jenny Lind was coming to your studio at noon today."

"Oh, my goodness! Where did you hear such a thing?"

"As I was telling you, from Mary Lanagan on Ninth Street."

Brady drops to his knee and looks Katy in the eye. "Do you know if she told anyone else besides you?"

"Oh yes, I am quite sure. She has many friends and so many brothers. My father took my sister to hear Jenny Lind in Castle Garden. Isn't that right, Papa?" She nudges him.

"Yes, my dear Katrintje."

"When she sang, 'I Know That My Redeemer Liveth' the tears ran down his face. Right, Papa?"

"Yes, little angel."

"She sang a bird song, Mr. B. She is called the Swedish Nightingale, because she can sing just like one."

"Yes, so I've heard…"

"Mr. B. you look troubled. I hope I didn't say something wrong."

"No, child, let us compose the sitting, one more time. Now try to keep your eyes open. Think of your favorite rhyme or poem."

"How about arithmetic, Mr. B.? Sometimes our class has to stand up and do sums in our head."

"Yes, that will be fine, but don't move your lips. Now hold still."

Luther removes the brass lens cap then steps behind the camera focusing the image beneath a black fabric curtain. His head reappears and then he places the lens cap back on.

"Steady now," he says as he quickly places the black plateholder into the back of the camera. He lifts the curtain slide, then says calmly, "hold your expression." He pauses then removes the lens cap. Chests hold still, lips pursed together, eyes glaze over holding open, hands hold tight, four seconds drip slowly by, as he studies each of their expressions, watching facial muscles twitch imperceptibly at the strain of holding still.

"Twice six, less one, multiply by two, add eight, divide by three. How much? I love to do that," she says to herself. "So handsome is that Mr. B. He wears blue spectacles like Mr. Hoagland, our writing teacher. With a few flourishes of his pen, he can make a beautiful swan. One day one of the girls pulled the chair out from under him and down he went between two desks. It was a very cruel thing to do, but perhaps she did not mean to, but I am afraid that she did. Mr. B is so patient and kind, I should one day like to marry him, but I am very sure my father would not let me marry a Catholic."

"That will dew," says Luther as he covers the lens.

Brady clasps his hands together with a sense of relief. "There now, the impression on silver is thus forever etched. I am quite sure that will be a most satisfactory sitting, Katy."

"You think so, Mr. B.?"

"Most assuredly."

Her father gets up rather stiffly, leaning upon his cane. "Oh, it is good to be free from the clutches of your vise, Mr. Brady. An infernal contraption if ever there was one. How soon until we see the results?"

"In but a few moments. Why don't you and your daughter step over to the receiving area and choose a suitable frame or protective case, we have the finest morocco leather adorned with plush velvet linings."

Out of the corner of his eye, Brady notices Esther Boswell standing with her back turned, trying to look inconspicuous in the crowd. Tapping her on the shoulder, "Good to see you Mrs. Boswell, I didn't mean to startle you."

"Oh, no, Mr. Brady."

"So, what brings you to our little shoppe this fine day? Did Luther forget his lunch pail?"

"Oh, no, Mr. Brady, I just happened to be strolling down Broadway and thought I might pop in for a visit."

"I see... you didn't happen to hear anything out on your stroll now, did you?"

"No, Mr. Brady, well, nothing worth repeating. I wouldn't want to be spreading rumors."

"Heaven forbid someone should let the cat out of the bag."

Just then he hears Katy's voice. "Look Papa, our likeness is ready. Come see. Come see. You look so noble. So, distinguished — just like Old Hickory."

Mr. Havens pulls Brady to the side and slips a five dollar note into the palm of his hand. "I wish to thank you from the bottom of my heart for your adept attention to my little Katrintje. You are a true diplomat, sir. How you changed course, averted the rocky shore, and rescued the sitting."

"Please sir, I cannot accept such a kind gesture."

"I insist. You have no idea how much this sitting means to me."

Brady pauses a moment to watch the elderly man leaning on his cane holding his daughter's little hand as she helps him slowly walk away.

CHAPTER 15 — A RUSE

1850

Brady checks his pocket-watch. He summons Timothy with a finger-point. "Now, we shall continue our tour and go to the buffing room, where you shall begin your apprenticeship for the next five years or so." Suddenly he notices the large crowds milling about the studio. "My, my, we have a packed house. This is standing room only. I've never seen such crowds in all my years! Something is amiss!" Brady wades through the crowd to the top of the grand staircase looking down at the gallery on the second floor to the throng of visitors crowded shoulder to shoulder. "Oh, my, my, this will not do at all. Timothy, go down and summon Mr. Fredricks."

"We must close the gallery and studio at once before we have an Astor Place Riot on our hands."

"And turn away good, paying customers?"

"I detest the notion, just the same as you, Mr. Fredricks, but we have no choice. We must gently, ever so gently, thin out the herd."

"Yes, Mr. Brady, you are right. We don't wish to have a stampede — a Dis-Astor Place."

"Precisely."

As the crowd gradually recedes, a few stragglers are reluctant to leave. "But it says on your sign, Admission to the Gallery is Free. Why on earth should I be forced to leave?"

"We will give them a golden token to a half-price sitting."

"Well now, Mr. Brady, the studio is nearly clear of visitors except for that woman over there holding a basket of apples. She is stubborn. Refuses to leave. Must speak with the proprietor, she demands."

"All right, Mr. Fredricks, it is nearly quarter to noon. We haven't time to waste. I'll have a word with the apple lady."

Hunched over in a ratty shawl, wearing dark spectacles, and a tattered bonnet tied tight about her face, the old woman meanders about the gallery tapping her cane back and forth.

"I am sorry Madame, but there will be no more sittings today. Might I purchase a half dozen of your apples?" Brady gently touches the back of her shoulder.

"Keep your hands off me! Thief! Thief! Help an old woman!" she shouts, "Stop THIEF! STOP THIEF!"

Most alarmed, Brady jumps back with a startled look.

The old apple-woman twirls in a flourishing pirouette tossing off her cape in a brandishing flurry spinning around and around.

Mr. Fredricks and the other assistants come running to the corner of the gallery. "What on earth is the matter?"

As Mr. Brady pulls the tattered shawl from over his head, he looks in a frightened state, his hair is all out place, he gathers his bearings, gaining composure, staring at the woman before him in a light blue satin dress, white lace collar, long sleeves to her wrist, crushed blue velvet breast plate embroidered with flower motifs, her flaxen hair tied tight, grey blue eyes.

"Why if it isn't Miss Jenny Lind! Such a performance!" clapping his hands shouting, "Bravo!"

"You see Mr. Brady, people forget of my acting abilities."

Laughing at himself, "Oh my, did you give me such a fright!"

"I thought I stepped on a cat. What a squeal you made!"

"Oh, Miss Jenny, you are a comedienne as well."

"Please forgive my ruse, Mr. Brady. Wherever my carriage goes, there is a great crowd collected around it. So intense are the crowds and their fevered pitch, it is like a violent sea storm. Luckily for me, Mr. von Schneidau found this disguise for me. He purchased the bonnet and shawl from the kind woman outside Mr. Stewart's Marble Palace, the spectacles, apples, basket and all"

"Well then, we must act quickly."

"Yes, before they discover I am not really me. Unfortunately, these daguerreotypes have made my face recognizable to all. I have discovered that the crowds are not so easily outwitted, they think like a collective beast — a swarm of bees."

Jenny walks over to the window, standing to the side, carefully peering through the drapes, across the 'way she sees Barnum's Museum on the corner of Ann Street, the canvas sheet four stories tall, the size of a clipper ship mainsail ripples in the breeze suspended by ropes from the rooftop. From this vantage point, she can only see the edge of the canvas, but she knows what is painted on the other side.

She hears the hawkers shouting from down deep towards the bottom of their lungs, projecting their voices through the open air. Loud as thunder he is. Back seats two dollars! Promenade tickets one dollar! My, he has a set of lungs. I would never consent to sing outside without the proscenium to amplify and contain the sound – outside the voice just flies away from you disappearing up to the clouds. Balcony seats one dollar! The power of the human voice — quiet as a church whisper, silent as thoughts to myself, or loud enough for a crowd of five thousand to hear at Castle Garden. Why even the newspapers told of the boats anchored about the harbor who heard my voice plainly.

Brady's staff comes out of their workspaces and cubby holes, the boys from the buff room make their way downstairs, the girls from the colorist room, the men in the framing room tapping with their little hammers, they all gather about the circular red velvet couch at the center of the gallery beneath the chandelier, on tippy toes, peering over shoulders, crouching down trying to see past the waist coats to catch a glimpse of the angel from on high. Elbowing his way, pushing past the staff surrounding Miss Jenny, Mr. Pettifog bursts through, falling to his feet, bowing to her, muttering, "Miss Jenny, Miss Jenny, I can't believe my eyes, is it really you before us? I must have died and gone to heaven to see such an angel with mine own eyes… You radiate light!"

"Mademoiselle Lind allow me to introduce Professor Henry P. Pettifog, my most dutiful friend and trusted colleague."

"To your feet, kind sir, I am neither queen nor saint. I am a mere singer strutting my hour upon the stage. That is all. Nothing more, nothing less."

"You are kinder and more beneficent than any queen known to history. Please sing for us Miss Jenny. We would be ever so grateful," pleads Mr. Pettifog.

"Oh, I couldn't. Someone might hear then we would have a mad rush pounding down Mr. Brady's door." She pauses to look at the disappointed faces of Brady's staff. She goes to the piano forte. "I relent… I shall sing something softly." She plays a few notes on the piano thinking of an appropriate number. "I know just the one… This song was composed by my dear friend Julius Benedict. It is called By the Sad Sea Waves."

By the sad sea waves, I listen while they moan,
A lament o'er graves of hope and pleasure gone,
I am young, I was fair, I had once not a care,
From the rising of the morn, to the setting of the sun,
Yet I pine like a slave, by the sad sea wave.
Come again bright days of hope and pleasure gone,
Come again bright days, come again, come again,

From my care last night, by holy sleep he guiled,
In the fair dream of light, my home upon me smiled,
O how sweet the dew, Every flower that I knew,
Breathed a gentle welcome back, To the worn and weary child!
I awake in my grave by the sad sea wave,
Come again dear dream so peacefully that smiled,
Come again dear dream, come again, come again.

Looking at the misty eyes, savoring the last note of the refrain, Jenny breaks the silence. "Oh now, look what I've gone and done… I've made you all sad." She reaches in her purse. "Life is too short for sad sea waves." She pulls out a pink rubber ball and bounces it on the floor. "Who should like to play catch with me??"

Multiple shouts, "Throw it to me, Miss Jenny! To me, to me, to me! Please throw it here!"

"Oh, how I love my India-rubber ball. It eases my mind before a performance. When I peer through the curtain at all those people's faces, I simply toss my cares away with a bounce-catch. But Mr. Barnum loses his wind with the throwing and catching. 'I give it up,' he says. Then I tease him mercilessly. 'Oh, Mr. Barnum, you are too fat and lazy; you cannot stand it to play ball with me.' So, who among ye shall play catch with me?" Bouncing the ball to her side, she tosses it up way high in the air. The ball appears to float for a brief moment, breaking gravity's grasp, then it descends into the palm of her waiting hand.

"Please pick me! Please pick me, Miss Jenny!"

"You there, boy," she says to Tim standing in the shadows behind the girls. "Don't be shy. I won't hurt you, I promise. Ready now?" She tosses the ball across the room.

"One handed! What a good catch! Now throw it back to me. Very nice. Very precise. Now come closer. I won't bite you." She bends down to whisper in his ear. "You may keep that." She reaches in her purse. "See, I always keep an ample supply with me."

Mr. Pettifog steps forward holding his copy of The Life of Jenny Lind. "Would you warm an old man's heart by inscribing your book?"

"I would be delighted, Mr. Pettifog. Tell me, Mathew, have you heard of this N.P. Willis?" as she takes the fountain pen.

"Oh, yes, Nathaniel Parker Willis. He is considered to be part of New York's literary triumvirate – along with Washington Irving and Fenimore Cooper. Why do you ask?"

"Oh, just curious..."

He steps closer. "Now then, you can confide in me."

"Well, I've heard the disparaging comments repeated in hushed whispers. How I avoid gay and fashionable society, how I turn down invitations. They say, when I cease to sing and begin to converse – how did he phrase it? She has in her voice but two favorite notes... yes and no."

"You must dispense with such talk, Miss Jenny. I implore you, as one who has the felt the sting of many a vocal barb, many a time. Words, unlike weapons, wound not just once, but time and time again, as often as they echo inside the caverns of your mind. But you must not permit yourself. Under no circumstances must you listen to the naysayers. Pay no heed to the Sirens."

Her eyes well up. "You are quite right, Mathew."

Holding her hand in his, "Block it out. You are too good and kind."

She pulls out a delicate lace handkerchief from her wrist sleeve.

"Pardon me for the interruption, Mr. Brady."

"Yes, what is it, Mr. Fredericks?"

"The surly mob is gathered at the entrance. How long I can keep them at bay is anyone's guess. If they should break down the door…"

"We shall retire upstairs to the studio. Please Mademoiselle Jenny. This way if you please." Brady snaps his fingers. "Jenny this is Hannah Buttle, she will attend to your needs while Mr. von Schneidau and I make our preparations for the sitting."

Hannah escorts Miss Jenny to the ladies dressing room fitted with a luxuriant chaise lounge and a vanity table with three fold-out mirrors. On the table is a sterling silver brush, a comb with fine white ivory teeth and a hand-held beveled mirror. Jenny takes a seat on the plush comfort stool while Hannah stands behind her spritzing a mist, looking at her in the mirror.

"Such beautiful hair you have, Miss Jenny. Such delicate curls, now we must ensure that not one strand is out of place. An errant lock is easy to comb before the daguerreotype, but not after. Daguerreotypes are set in silver like chisel marks in stone. Mistakes cannot be corrected."

"Tell me about yourself, Miss Hannah Buttle."

"Oh, there's not much to tell…"

"Come now, Hannah."

"Well, I live with my mother at 84 Greene Street. She is a widow."

"So sorry to hear, Hannah. That must be tough for you. Do you like being in Mr. Brady's employ?"

"Oh, yes. There's much variety in my duties. I am a colorist by trade, but I also help the ladies prepare for their sittings, or sometimes I play the piano or tend to the customers."

"That is wonderful, Hannah. Who taught you the art of painting?"

"Well, first it was my mother, then I honed my skills as a colorist working for Mr. Nathaniel Currier at his lithography shop over on Nassau Street. So many girls worked there, we each applied only one color to the lithograph, then passed it along down the work line. Mr. Currier imported his colors from Germany that never faded in the sun. The girls called me Burnt Sienna. Mr. Currier paid us a penny-a-piece. Mr. Brady is so good to us, he pays me $5 a week.

"I'll tell you something about your Mr. Brady. You'll never guess…"

"What is it?"

"He is a fine tenor. He is. Last night he sang for me, The Girl I Left Behind. How he blushed afterwards. But such a fine voice."

A knock interrupts their conversation, Mr. Brady pokes his head in.

"Are you ready, Mademoiselle?" He looks perplexed at their laughing expressions. "What on earth is so amusing? Have I spilled some chemicals on my shirt again?"

"Sing for us, Mathew! Please for Miss Buttle."

"I'm not to your mind of thinking, Mademoiselle. I think you have me mistaken for someone else. Signor Belletti perhaps?"

"Not in the slightest, Mathew. Don't you recall your performance last evening?"

His puzzled look, "Very vaguely now... perhaps the champagne flowed too freely."

"I should say so. Toast after toast, how the crystal glasses chimed! Remember I told you the story of Mr. Barnum, the teetotaler, drinking to my health and happiness in a glass of cold water. Shall I repeat your comment?"

Brady winces covering his eyes with his hand like a visor, "I am sure you will refresh my memory."

"Blast Barnum and his Temperance Movement. Never trust a man who doesn't drink. Then you slammed your fist down on the table, oh how the crystal rattled when I told you Mr. Barnum tried to get me to sign the Teetotaler Pledge and become an advocate to his noble cause. Then you retracted your denunciations and said that you too needed to sign the pledge. You swore an oath and promised over and over first thing this morning... Shall I go on, Mathew?"

"Please no, Miss Jenny."

"Then sing for us."

"This is blackmail." He shuts the door behind him, standing with his back to the door so none might barge in. He tugs down on his black satin waistcoat.

All the dames of France are fond and free,
And Flemish lips are really willing,
Very soft the maids of Italy,
And Spanish eyes are so thrilling,

Still although I bask beneath their smile,
Their charms will fail to bind me,
And my heart falls back to Erin's Isle,
To the girl I left behind me...

"Bravo, Mathew, Bravo!" says Jenny, "You are indeed a man of many passions – art, literature, history, science, and music."

Hannah beams, "That was wonderful, Mr. Brady."

An urgent knock on the door, "Yes, Mr. Fredricks?"

"I am not sure how much longer we can keep the crowds at bay."

"Barricade the doors with the piano if you have to! We must have this sitting without further delay. Ladies are you quite finished? Then let us adjourn to the main studio."

Two operators, von Schneidau and Boswell make their preparations before the camera, adjusting the reflector providing light from the right.

Brady surveys the setting, hand at his chin in contemplation. "That plain wooden chair will not do. The proper chair is needed. I know just the one in my office which will complement the beautiful pattern of your fine embroidered dress."

Brady returns with a mahogany framed chair with ornately carved berries and leaves, the needlepoint backing features a large rosebush set against a light pink background.

"Now, Miss Jenny, if you sit ever so slightly forward, the camera will be able to see the fine needlepoint flowers to the back of the chair. That's it, just lean forward a bit more... Such fine posture you have. That's it... Hold on a minute! What are you holding in your hand, Miss Jenny?"

"Oh, nothing..." she clenches her hand trying to hide something.

"Come now, Jenny, Let me see..."

He pries her grasp open. "What's this?"

"It's just my India-rubber ball, Mathew. I can assure you no one shall notice."

His nose wrinkles, his blue spectacles move up and down.

"My concern is this..."

"It soothes me, Mathew," she says with defiance. "This is my portrait after all."

"Will this make you happy?"

"Yes, Mathew... ever so much."

"Now then Miss Jenny, your old schoolmate Mr. von Schneidau shall take the first exposure followed by my assistant Mr. Boswell." Brady stands to the side while his assistant focuses the camera. His calm presence, his reassuring voice from years of experience sets the sitter at ease.

"Oh, that was serene, Jenny, most serene. Keep the same pose, but let's avert the direction of your gaze. Now then follow me with your eyes – that's it hold that expression. Look directly at me. Now, breathe a sigh, look past the lens, and gaze into your great, great grandchildren's eyes..."

Waiting in the wings for the portrait to be finished, Brady catches the gaunt expression on Mr. Fredrick's face as Luther puts the brass cap on the lens. Addressing him in the familiar, as he rarely does, "Charles, whatever is the matter?"

The plate-holders click while Luther pulls them from the camera then pushes them through the black curtain to the mercurial room and the waiting hands of Mr. Pettifog.

"Miss Lind must appease the gathering mob at once. All of Broadway and all the Bowery is out there chanting her name in unison over and over. "Jenny! Jenny! Give us! Jenny! Jenny!"

"I know just what to do." She goes over to the windows and pulls back the drapes and throws open the sash. Leaning out the window, she tosses kisses to the cheering crowds. "Oh, my goodness, look at that man clutching to the telegraph pole, waving his arm. I hope he doesn't fall."

"Miss Jenny, please step away from the window."

"When the Atlantic docked at Canal Street, they had to fish people out of the river who were pushed off the pier by the crowds." She yells to the man, "Please sir, hold on with both hands, I beseech you."

He waves wildly having captured her attention. She tosses down a lace handkerchief.

"Please Jenny, please step away from the window. We must put together a plan to get you safely back to The Irving House."

"No, Mathew, a simple plan will not do, we need a ruse... Is there a back entrance?"

"Why yes, we have the side entrance out to Fulton Street."

"Wonderful. Have your carriage brought around to the main entrance on Broadway. Hannah, might I borrow your bonnet and cape so I can make my escape?"

"Certainly, Miss Jenny."

"I see," says Brady. "Hannah will go out the Broadway door and you will go out Fulton's way. As Shakespeare said, 'O, what a tangled web we weave, when first we practice to deceive!'"

"No, Mathew, wrong on both counts. Firstly, that oft repeated line was writ by Sir Walter Scott. Second, Hannah is not going into that mob. I will not throw that precious girl to the lions."

"No? Well if she is not going to play the decoy, who is?"

"You are."

"Me??" he says high-pitched in shock. "But I bear no resemblance to you whatsoever."

"You will in Hannah's bonnet and cape. Besides, you are the same height as me. Then I shall use Apple-Annie's bonnet, shawl and basket. I should like to explore Broadway and sit down beside the fountain at The Park. None shall be the wiser to me in these dark specs."

Just then Mr. Pettifog emerges from the mercurial room with the finished portraits, holding one in each hand. "Mr. Brady they are finished. Now show care not to put fingertips to the surface. Hold them by the edges."

"Yes, Mr. Pettifog, I know well how to hold a daguerreotype," he says exasperated. "Mademoiselle, come see your likeness. So radiant... such poise."

"Turn it away, I cannot bear to look at that horrible image."

"Come now, Jenny, take another look. You are too hard on yourself. You must see the beauty that we see."

"Oh, Mathew, you needn't use Mr. Barnum's soft soap on me."

"Please take another look. I must know in my heart that you are content with your portrait. I seek only to serve. Look at the depth of tone, the softness of light and shade..."

She takes another fleeting glimpse. "See, I told you no one would see the India-rubber ball in the palm of my hand."

Jenny puts on Hannah's bonnet and cape then approaches the window to the cheering crowd. Brady taps her on the shoulders. "Would you be so kind as to hold up the daguerreotype for the crowds to see?"

"Yes, Mr. Brady," she says crestfallen then turns around to the crowd holding the portrait up high.

Brady turns to Mr. Pettifog, "Henry, we will need 100 copies by the end of the day then an additional 200 copies by Monday."

"I shall have to work all day Sunday to meet that tall order. I'll need an assistant. How's about young Tim?"

"Just this once, Mr. Pettifog. But understand, Timothy is not to work for a prolonged time in the mercurial room."

"And why not?"

"The vapors, Mr. Pettifog."

"That's an old wives tale, Mat. Quicksilver never hurt a soul."

"That may be the case, but Tim is to work in the buff room."

Miss Jenny turns around and hands back the daguerreotype.

"The carriage has arrived, Mr. Brady."

She takes off the bonnet and puts it on his head then throws the cape around his shoulders. She tilts her head while tying the chinstrap. "Oh, you look so lovely. Now be very brave." She kisses him on the cheek and whispers in his ear, "Goodbye to you, Mr. Mathew B. Brady."

CHAPTER 16 — VIEW CAMERA

1985

Quiet afternoon at The Photography Workshop, back from the route, I man the counter while Duke works the 4x5 view camera. The bright studio lights shine on the wall against a green metal grid with black lines indicating 5x7, 8x10, and 11x14.

Duke unpacks a large manila envelope with an 8x10 portrait which looks to be from the 1940s. Thick photographic paper with a slight curl, silvery shimmering paper, a Hollywood head-shot, the woman looks as mysterious as Lauren Bacall. The silver salts have almost crystalized against the thick paper giving it the texture of the silver screen. This is an old, fiber-based print, not the modern resin coated paper we use today – coated with plastic for machine printing.

I know not to trouble Duke while he works. He has a stack of work to do. If we stopped to look at each and every photograph, we would never get any work done, well, Duke I mean. He secures the photograph to the metal grid with long magnetic strips. He puts the magnifying loupe to the back with the glass grid squares of the 4x5 view camera. He focuses the camera moving the leather bellows back and forth along its track. He takes a 4x5 film holder and locks it into place. He gently flips the slide – the silver tipped edge indicates unexposed film, the black edge indicates exposed film. He cocks the shutter and gently squeezes the cable release. He has made a 4x5 copy negative – he has taken a photograph of a photograph with a large format negative producing the best results possible.

When a customer comes in the store with a precious old photograph, a family heirloom from long ago, the first question we ask, we ask in vain, for we already know the answer. Do you have the negative? Nobody saves the negative. Negatives get lost, negatives get tossed, but the positive remains. So, Duke must make copy negatives in order to make a positive print. He does not use a 35mm camera – that negative is too tiny, too inferior to produce satisfactory results. Duke is photographing photographs – flat, two dimensional objects. The 35mm negative, the size of two postage stamps is not up to the task.

Watching Duke with the loupe to the ground glass, focusing the 4x5 view camera, I think back to that documentary I saw a few years ago in 1982. It was about Ansel Adams way up in the mountains with a pack mule. He unpacked his camera equipment. Sturdy legs to a tripod with spikes at the tip dig down in the soil. Latches unhook to a white metal trunk as he pulls out his wooden 8x10 view camera, sets it on the tripod then expands the bellows. He takes readings with his hand-held light meter. He focuses the camera beneath a dark cape, then inserts the large format negative holder. Before him is Yosemite Valley.

I admire Duke's dexterity with the view camera. He snaps the holder into place with a click. This is not a point and shoot camera. Shooting a view camera is like loading a musket – any misstep along the way causes the camera to misfire. There is a four-step process for exposing one negative. He cocks the shutter, opens the lens wide then focuses the camera. Before putting in the film holder, he remembers to set the shutter, set the aperture then turn the silver side of the film slide around to the black side.

There was that time he let me get behind the 4x5. He extended the 8x magnifying loupe in my direction. It looks like an upside-down shot glass with a black eye cup.

"Here, let's see you give it a try."

With much anticipation, I step to the back of the camera and look through the ground glass grid and I am utterly disappointed. I can't see a thing.

Duke points out the image for me – the photograph on the wall.

"I still can't see it."

"Here let me show you…"

The image is faint like looking at a movie screen when the house lights turned on – the silver screen washed to white without detail.

Duke doesn't trouble himself beneath a dark focusing cape. He has too many copy negatives to make. It would only slow him down.

View camera, I ask myself, why do they call it that? You can't view much of anything.

"Everything is upside down," I notice. "And backwards…"

"This is the same type of camera that Mathew Brady used," says Duke. "You've heard of him, haven't you?"

I think back to that time Dad came home from work. I had just watched, "They Died with Their Boots On," an old black and white movie starring Errol Flynn as General George Armstrong Custer at Little Big Horn. Every now and again this General Sheridan character appeared in the film. When Dad walked in the door, I waited for him to take off his coat and settle down. That's when I asked him about General Sheridan.

"Why he's only our great, great, grandfather," he said. "My brother, your Uncle Phil was named after him. My father was from the same county in Ireland, County Cavan. Philip H. Sheridan was a famous Union general in the Civil War. Didn't you ever hear of Sheridan's Ride? Come let me show you."

I followed him from the kitchen to the library in the den. Dad looked through the bookshelves then pulled out The American Heritage Picture

History of the Civil War and set it out on the table. He flipped past pages of battlefield maps, glorious paintings of cavalry charges, then haunting images of corpses strewn on the battlefield in stark black and white. He stops at a page with a photograph of Major General Philip H. Sheridan.

I point to the headline on the facing page, Phil Sheridan Devastates the Valley. "What's this about?"

Dad reaches for his trusty old 1938 Columbia Encyclopedia and reads aloud, "Sheridan now set about the systematic devastation of the Shenandoah, burning barns and homes, killing or driving away livestock, stripping the country side so bare that he reported to Washington that even a crow flying over the place would have to take his supplies with him... His name is anathema in Louisiana even today."

Then I was off to the Crestwood Library to take out a book about General Sheridan. On the cover was his black horse Rienzi. He was a quartermaster in the army.

It wasn't until years later that I questioned Dad about the family ties to General Sheridan. If his father came over around 1900, how could he possibly be related to General Sheridan who was born in 1831?

"You believed me?" he said. "I was just kidding. Let this be a lesson to you, you can't believe everything someone tells you... especially family legends."

"Do you know who took this photograph of General Sheridan?"

I shake my head.

"Mathew Brady." Then he proceeds to take out Mathew Brady's Illustrated History of the Civil War and tell me about the great Civil War photographer and his "What-is-it" wagon. Photo by Brady beneath photograph after photograph.

As Duke repeats his question, "You've heard of Mathew Brady, haven't you?"

"Yeah, Duke, my Dad told me all about him."

This was my favorite time of day at The Photography Workshop – back from the 100-mile route. The Chevelle and me made it through another day. We had some close calls together, sat in long traffic jams on 95 waiting at the toll booth. After hours of driving from town to town, now I'm stationary – just sitting on the wooden stool – customers come and go to drop off their rolls of film.

I go back to watching Duke make copy negatives. He unpacks an envelope then mutters loud enough for me to hear, "Oh boy, would you look at this!"

Duke is no amateur. He is a professional. He has been shooting 30-40 copy negatives a day, five days a week, year after year. He has seen his share of vintage old black and white photographs. This is no time for show and tell. This is no museum gallery. There is no time to pause and look – no time to examine the detail – no time to appreciate the photograph. We have work to do.

But Duke makes an exception, he calls out to George behind the black curtain in the darkroom who is busy getting the film ready to develop. He checks the temperature to the developer, replenishes the chemicals then arranges the canisters of 35mm film in neat domino rows of four on the counter. In the center is his trusty little can opener. In complete darkness, he will crack each canister then load the film onto stainless steel reels. Luckily, Duke catches George before he locks the darkroom door.

"George! Come take a look at this."

"What is it, Dad?"

"I think it's a tintype."

"No actually, this is a daguerreotype. This is even older than a tintype," says George with hushed amazement. He is Spock-like — never showing emotion when looking at a photograph. He maintains a detached distance. We are not here to observe photographs. We check for contrast, focus, dust specs, and density, then it is on to the next order. But he makes an exception, he takes a moment to look at this relic from the past in a crushed velvet case.

"Should I take it out of the frame, George?"

Shooting through glass, Duke is concerned about reflection from the lights and the loss of sharpness. He wants the best results possible. He often takes photos out of their frames. But this is no ordinary old black and white in a frame. This is a daguerreotype from long ago.

"No Dad, I don't want to chance it. The frame itself is often as valuable as the photograph. Have Danny hold it while you take a time exposure."

Duke turns both of the studio lamps sideways. He hands me the daguerreotype in its case to hold against the copy board – it is too cumbersome, too heavy for the magnetic strips, and too risky.

"Now hold steady while I bracket a couple of shots. And whatever you do, don't drop it."

Don't drop it, I repeat to myself, feeling the heat from the studio lamps. I have been at The Photography Workshop for six months now and have made my share of mistakes. Holding the daguerreotype in my hand, much older than me, this relic dates probably to the late 1840s, I hold my breath.

You can never replace a photograph once they are lost. That's what George told me the time the photo satchel bag was found along the road. It must have blown off the roof of my Chevy. I must have put it there for a second while I reached in my pocket for the keys. Luckily, a Good Samaritan found it lying in the road.

"This is what people run back into burning buildings for… for photographs," explained George. "People entrust us with their family photographs." There is not a hint of outrage in his voice. Not a tinge of derision at my foolish mistake. There is only a logical Spock-like explanation. "You could never replace a photograph once it's lost. Once it's gone, it's gone forever. This is not the shoe repair shop across the street or the jewelry shop next door." George put it right, photographs are more precious than diamonds.

After making two exposures at two different settings, Duke pulls the film holder out from the back of the camera.

"Hey now Danny, don't you have a drum lesson to get to?"

"Will you be OK on your own?"

"Sure," he says with a twinkle in his eye that conveys his, 'don't you worry about old Duke', expression. "Now, get going."

I grab my drumsticks and the Buddy Rich rudiment book. It is a short walk up Fisher Ave to Eastchester Music. I've walked this way many times over the years on my weekly trek to my drum lesson. Just before the playground, there is a chain link fence around this strange enclosure. High stone walls jut up from an abandoned rectangle pool with dark murky water down below. I haven't time to waste, I have an appointment to make. But on the way back, I make a mental note to take a moment, to pause and look at the historical marker to this mysterious place.

In the music store, I make my way past the instruments for sale, guitars on the rack, drum sets on the floor, amplifiers to the side, to the back studio rooms. I sit down on the drum stool, practice pad on the snare and run through some rudiments – the seven-stroke ruff, the double-stroke roll and the paradiddle.

But my mind is elsewhere – that strange mysterious place. How come I never noticed it before walking back and forth? There is a white marble block, I pause a moment to read the historic marker:

"Tuckahoe's largest and most prestigious marble commission came in the form of an order for material for the Old Custom House constructed at the corner of Wall and Nassau streets, New York City in 1830."

The old Custom House, (Federal Hall), is the building with the statue of George Washington marking the spot where he took the oath of office. Looking down at the water filled quarry, I think of that movie Breaking Away, the sons of the stone cutters swimming in an abandoned quarry. Marble from this quarry was used for the Arch at Washington Square – the place where I went to school — where I dropped-out.

Back at The Photography Workshop, the quiet afternoon lull is replaced with the five o'clock commuters getting off the train, returning from the city, stopping off to pick up their dry-cleaning next door and their film orders on their way home.

"Duke!" says one customer extending his hand like an old friend.

"Glenn!" returns Duke.

I overhear bits and pieces while waiting on other customers. Wearing a beard and a suit, holding a portfolio case, Glenn tells Duke he is looking for work in the city as an airbrush. artist. "Work is tough to come by. Everything is computers nowadays."

Near closing time, as the shop door is locked, Duke tells George about the visitor.

"Glenn used to work for us restoring old photographs," says George.

"He could work magic with that airbrush," recalls Duke.

George hangs the rolls of 35mm film in the closet then uses his two fingers as a squeegee trying to eliminate water spots.

Duke hangs the 4x5 negatives. "Glenn said everything is computers nowadays. No more need for airbrush artists."

"They say in the future, computers will replace photography. That's what the Kodak rep told me," said George. "There'll be no more need for paper and chemicals. No more need for film."

I scoff at the notion. How could you possibly take a photograph with a computer?

"No more need for fill-em?" questions Duke.

"Don't worry," George reassured us. "It's a long ways off."

CHAPTER 17 — BUFF-BOY

1850

Monday morning in the buffing room, Tim watches as Benjamin Bleecker reaches into a small wooden box with dove-tailed corners, black lettering on the side, "W.H. Scovill Company, 57 Maiden Lane, New York". On the next line he reads cursive letters, Manufactory ~ Waterbury, Connecticut. The young boy, younger than Tim, takes out a copper plate faced with silver then clips the corners and turns down the edges with the plate bender.

Tim looks about the crowded room, lit by flickering gas lights, long tables, boys busy at work, elbows moving back and forth. With a turn of the wooden vise, Benjamin secures the plate onto the polishing mount and points to it. "This is what we call Benedict's plate holder," he says. Pale and thin, wearing a black-smeared smock, hair slicked to the side, a persistent cow-lick sticking up, he stares plaintively at Tim. The little pedagogue sees distant eyes, drifting off into a daydream far away from this place. He tries to reel him in.

"Now then, Timothy, pay close attention, first we prepare the plate with this bottle of rottenstone," he says sprinkling the powder through a fine muslin cover stretched over the top. He dampens a square cloth with dilute alcohol and starts making circles, pressing two fingers to the plate.

"We must take great care in preparing the plates, Timothy…" He stops himself midsentence changing the tone of his voice from instructor to friend. "Mind if I call you, Tim? I much prefer the familiar. Timothy is too formal for me." He unbuttons his high collar and extends his hand. "And you shall call me, Ben. All right then?"

The two shake hands. He has a strong grasp for a slight boy. Rolling up the sleeves of his smock, Tim notices defined lines and contours in Ben's forearms.

He hands him a smock. "Here put this on. We wouldn't want you to soil that fancy shirt of yours." Ill-fitting, stiff with starch, Tim buttons up the canvas shirt.

"We are buff-boys after all, you and I. We have the highest responsibility at Mr. Brady's Studio. That's what Mr. Brady told me himself, those were his exact words. 'Benjamin,' he said to me one day, 'without you and your hard work, I should not have the reputation as the finest daguerreotypist on all of Broadway.' So, we must strive to take great pride in our work and think of Mr. Brady and his reputation, or else…"

"Or else?"

"Well, let's just say, Mr. Fredericks does not hesitate to call attention to the slightest imperfection he notices in the plate. We must meet with his satisfaction." Ben quickly changes the unpleasant subject. "I live on Lispenard Street. That was my grandfather's middle name, Lispenard. Anthony Lispenard Bleecker."

"I know well Anthony Street. I got lost near there."

"Yes, and there is a Bleecker Street too – all named after my grandfather. Where do you call home, Tim?"

"I live on York Avenue in New Brighton over on Staten Island."

"That's where Mr. Brady lives. So far away you travel!"

Tim watches the gyratory motion scouring the plate, following the finger-paths in the powdery sands of rottenstone go round and round.

"Lispenard," he repeats to himself. "Where do you call home?"

Back home in New Brighton earlier this Monday morning, Jeremiah snapped the paper and read aloud to his boys hunched over the breakfast table from the New York Herald dated September 16, 1850.

> Mademoiselle Jenny Lind
>
> The theme of every tongue is still Jenny Lind, her concerts, and her munificent charities. She has won all hearts. Hence, wherever her carriage goes, there is a crowd collected around it, and the people feast their eyes upon her as if she was an angel, and not a mere woman.

"See Pa, this is the India-rubber ball Miss Jenny gave to me."

"She didn't," says Thomas. "I don't believe you."

"She did."

"You mean to tell me the Swedish Nightingale plays with an India rubber ball. I never heard such a fib."

"That's enough out of you, Thomas," says Jeremiah. "Now let me finish reading the newspaper account."

Just then there is a knock on the door. "Tim, go and see who it is. Pray to God it's not Father Murphy here to pester me about not attending mass yesterday. You boys let me oversleep again. You should have woken me."

Aunt Margaret steps into the kitchen. Tim is relieved to see a beaming smile on her face, flushed with vigor from her brisk morning walk. There is no stern expression about to reprimand.

"Good morning, Jerry. Don't trouble yourself over me. I shan't be long. I merely came by to say a quick hello."

"Sit yourself down, Maggie." He sees a look of hesitation. He twists her arm. "Come on now, have a sip of tea and a buttered scone. Listen while I read from the morning paper... It's all about Jenny Lind."

"Oh, I suppose a moment's rest wouldn't hurt."

Jeremiah takes a gander at the printed page then pauses before reading aloud in his narrator voice.

> On Saturday last, as 12 o'clock, she visited Mr. Brady's magnificent daguerreotype gallery, at his earnest solicitation, in order to have her likeness taken...

Aunt Maggie interrupts the tale. "Tell us all about it, Timothy."

"Well, Miss Jenny sang a song for us, Aunt Margaret. And what's more, I have a doggery-type to remember her by. Mr. Pettifog gave it to me."

"Well, where is it? Please, get it this instant. I must see it." Tim returns with the daguerreotype. "Let me have a look see," says Maggie like a young school-girl filled with glee. She takes it into her hands. "Such poise. Look at her posture."

"May I please keep this, Timothy? I would be ever so grateful. The girls would be so impressed."

"Of course, you may, Aunt Margaret."

She gives the boy a thankful hug and takes another look. "What a fine sitting. Did you assist, Mr. Brady?"

"Oh no, Aunt Margaret, I am to be a buff-boy. Today, I shall learn how to polish the plates. I am not permitted to work in the Mercurial Room, not ever again, that's what Mr. Brady instructed me, much as I like Mr. Pettifog and assisting him in the Mercurial Room..."

"Mercurial Room? Polish the plates?" she repeats.

"C'mon then, Tim, follow me to the warming box," says Benjamin as he makes his way to a long tin box lit by a spirit lamp. He pulls out the buff-board, about four inches wide and thirty inches long. Grabbing it by the handle, it reminds Tim of the paddy-whack hanging on the wall in Brother Finnerty's classroom. 'For Incorrigible Boys' was branded with an iron into the wood then in stark grooved letters, 'Paddy Whack'. He bore a hole in the handle – there it hung by a leather shoe-string. He would point to that flat board more as a deterrent than as an implement. God forbid if he ever saw you yawn. That he would not tolerate.

"You see, Tim, we must keep the buff-board clean and dry. This is the buckskin side. Now watch me as I polish the plate to a high sheen." He sprinkles rouge on the buckskin. "This helps eliminate any imperfection."

Ben applies vigorous strokes, moving the buff-board back and forth, fast as his father with a handsaw. He does not stop. He buffs and buffs.

"Now, here's a buff-board for you to use. Clamp the plate securely like so. And buff."

"Ben, my arms grow tired. I can't buff anymore. Can I please stop?"

"Why, you have only just begun to buff, Tim. You must keep at it. Each plate takes 20 minutes at least to polish."

Arms burning, muscles begin to cramp, beads of sweat dripping from his brow, Tim gasps for air.

"C'mon now, Tim. Put your back into it!" He shouts beside him while still buffing away. "Don't give up! Keep going! That's it. That's it."

Tim tries to keep pace with Ben's long steady strokes.

"Don't worry, you'll soon grow accustomed to hard work. Keep polishing, Tim. You must take great care not to make any scratches to the plate. Mr. Fredericks will not tolerate shoddy work. Now repeat after me, Buff-Boy, Buff-Boy, put your mind elsewhere. C'mon now, Tim, repeat."

"Buff-Boy, Buff-Boy, put your mind elsewhere..."

His father continues reading aloud...

> As soon as it was known she was there, a large crowd collected around the place, which continued to increase to such a degree, that it became rather formidable to face it by the time the likeness was completed.

"That's right, Pa. All of York was outside Mr. Brady's door."

His father loses his place then picks up where he left off...

> A ruse was accordingly resorted to, and she was conducted out of the door in Fulton street, instead of Broadway; but the crowd were not to be outwitted so easily. The moment they perceived the movement, they made a rush, and one of the hard-fisted actually thrust his hand into the carriage and held it, swearing that he must see Jenny Lind. The carriage was completely surrounded, and the driver whipped the horses, when one or two persons were thrown down, but were not severely hurt.

"That's not the way it happened, Pa. That was Mr. Brady in the carriage pretending to be Miss Jenny."

"Did you not hear what the paper said?" says Thomas. "If it's in the Herald it must be so. That's what Pa always says, isn't that right?"

"Stop your squabbling you two. Not another word."

Maggie takes a final sip of tea. "Well, Jeremiah, I must be on me way or I shall be late to work."

"Here now, finish your scone. I haven't got to the end just yet."

His tone turns somber as he picks up the paper.

> Mademoiselle Lind remained in retirement all day yesterday, not having gone out even to church.

He adds dramatic emphasis to that last phrase as if he has just proven a very important point.

"Don't sound so smug, Jerry."

"What on earth do you mean? I was merely reading from the paper."

"I know what you're after. You want me to excuse you and your boys for not going to mass yesterday just the same as Jenny Lind. Well, two wrongs don't make a right. I shouldn't have to tell you that! Now, Timothy, you will escort me to the door like a gentleman. I wouldn't want to trouble your father," she says as he starts to get up from his seat. "Sit yourself, Jeremiah, sit. Don't get up on my account. I wouldn't want to inconvenience you."

In the front parlor, Aunt Margaret takes a moment to put on her bonnet as Tim opens the door. She crouches down, stooping to his eye level. He looks downcast. I know she has spoken with Mr. Fredericks. Why are you here, boy? Refresh my memory. What skills do you possess?

She waits for him to look her in the eye. "Mrs. Brady spoke ever so glowingly about you after mass yesterday. I wish you were there. Her Mathew has high hopes for you." She kisses him on the cheek. "Your mother would be so very proud of you, Timothy."

Tim closes the door and takes a passing glance at the silhouette of his mother hanging on the wall. He thinks to himself, I can't remember her face, for the life of me, nor the sound of her voice. I can only see the vague hint of a traced outline, a black void...

"Give it a rest, Tim. You've done fine work. See what you can do when you put your back into it. We'll make a buff-boy out of you yet," says Benjamin slapping him on the back.

Just then the buff-room door bursts open, standing before them is Mr. Fredericks. "Inspection time, buff-boys! Why do you stand there dallying when you should be hard at work? Show me your work!"

Over the shoulder of Mr. Fredericks, out of the corner of his eye, Tim sees a woman pass by in the hallway, her long dress dragging along.

Benjamin brings over a stack of plates while Mr. Fredericks puts on his spectacles to take a closer look. He takes up a plate, holding it an angle. "Transverse grooves!" he shouts to the rafters. "That's what I see. Transverse grooves! Who buffed this plate?"

Stepping forward, Benjamin holds out his hands.

"You should know better by now, Benjamin. We do not tolerate transverse grooves in our plates. How many times have I told you? This plate would spoil the portrait. A waste of time. A waste of effort. A waste of a Scovill plate. I shouldn't have to repeat myself. This is quite unlike you, Benjamin." He stops himself and points to Timothy standing there trying to look inconspicuous amongst the other boys in their smocks.

"You there. Yes you! What is your name again?"

"Timothy, sir. Timothy O'Sullivan."

"Ohh Sullivan, how could I forget? Step forward, Mr. Ohh Sullivan. Take a look at this Scovill plate. Lackluster!" he shouts. "This looks like your handiwork. Dull as you are!"

He picks up another plate and admires his reflection. "Now this is what I call a properly prepared Scovill plate. This is what you should aspire to... buffed bright as a looking glass."

There is a knock on the open door. Mary Higbie stands quietly there with her hands folded.

"Yes, what is it Mary!"

"Mr. Fredericks, you are wanted downstairs in the gallery."

"Well, who is it? You can tell them to wait."

"It's Mrs. Brady, sir."

"Mrs. Brady?" He breathes out a huff, heading for the door, he turns around. "Do not worry, my buff-boys, I shall return to finish the inspection… Depend upon it." The door slams shut.

"Pay him no mind," whispers Benjamin as he gathers up the plates. "Now Tim, we shall take these buffed plates to the coating room." He hands Tim a stack.

"Follow me," Benjamin narrates as they walk down the hallway, "The coating room is where the older fellows sensitize the plates — first with bromine vapors then with iodine. Perhaps a few years down the road, you and I shall graduate from the buffing room and one day work in the coating room." He pauses to look around and whispers softly, "But we must take great care to avoid working in the mercurial room. You don't want to wind up like Mr. Pettifog or Mr. Lawrence." After dispensing with the unpleasant subject, he resumes his natural cadence, "Who knows Tim? With a little luck, perhaps one day you and I shall become operators just like Angel Gabriel. Wouldn't that be grand! Imagine earning $10 per week."

Knocking on the door, he leans forward to listen. "Be sure to wait for the entry knock in answer…"

"Benjamin, I just have one question. What exactly is an operator?"

"Remember, call me Ben. An operator handles the portrait box."

"Portrait box?"

"The camera obscura, they call it."

"And who is this Angel Gabriel?"

"Gabriel Harrison is the new operator who works up on the roof-top studio. How the girls fawn over him. Hannah Buttle swoons at the mere mention of his name. Gabriel, Gabriel, Gabriel — that's all they ever talk about."

As they step inside, Tim can barely see in the darkroom overcome by that awful stench of bromine. He sees vague shapes of tall shadows moving about. On the opposite wall, he sees a window covered with red tissue paper. Rolled up sleeves, hands holding a plate up inspecting it by the red light.

"Alrighty, you two, back to the buff-room with ye, we have much, much work to do."

Outside the door, "Oh, fresh air! The smell of that room is worse than a privy," says Tim, "How do they put up with it?"

"They don't notice the smell at all, Tim. They become senseless to it."

"Ben, how long have you been a buff-boy?"

"Let's see, it will be two years this November, that's right, I started my indenture a month after my seventh birthday."

As they head down the hallway, Tim sees a woman standing in front of Mr. Brady with her back turned. She fusses with his cravat. "Now, hold still, Mathew."

"Julia, Please! I can't be bothered with appearances at the moment."

"Oh, you're incorrigible. Such the little boy, hold still now!"

"Stop doting on me, Julia, you embarrass me in front of my staff," he whispers, then addresses Tim. "Timothy, allow me to introduce my dear wife. Julia, this is young Tim."

She extends her hand, gloved in white lace. Tim looks down.

"I've heard so much about you. A pleasure to meet you. So shy, isn't he, Mathew? Mathew?" She turns her head, but he is not there. "Oh, he has run off on me... It's just as well. Timothy, come have a word with me over here on the sofa." She pats the waiting spot on the couch. "Come now. Don't be frightened. I shan't bite."

Tim sits down and looks through the scrim curtains out the studio windows at the steeple of Saint Paul's. He thinks of the lithograph in the frame outside Mr. Brady's office downstairs. "Look at me." She is too pretty, such beautiful eyes, skin like porcelain, brown hair coiled into silky curls. She takes his hand into her lap. "I should like you to know something..."

"Yes, Mrs. Brady." She is about to tell me my services are no longer required at this establishment. She has spoken with Mr. Fredericks. I'm not any good at buffing plates. First, I destroyed the display case then I spoiled the Scovill Plates with transverse grooves. Offer to repay Mr. Brady. "Is it about the transverse grooves on the Scovill Plate?"

"Oh, no Timothy, to the contrary, pay no heed to Mr. Fredericks. Let's just say he is a man of great ambitions. I suspect he shan't be with us much longer...." Her voice trails off as she thinks out loud. "That is, if I have anything to say about the matter. No, what I wished to say is that Mr. Brady sees a spark, a spark he should like to nestle with tinder in his hand like so..." She blows a gentle breeze into the cup of her white laced gloves.

"You must know, my Mathew is an excellent judge of character. He survives by his wits. He would not have lasted all these years on Broadway without them — he trusts his intuition. He says you are different. He has high hopes for you. But you must promise me this..." Placing her fingertip under his chin, she raises his gaze looking him in the eye.

"Yes, Mrs. Brady?"

"You must swear an oath to never, ever, ever, leave his shop and go elsewhere... It would only break his heart. You see, I cannot bear him a son. He is taken with you, Timothy. He sees that spark of an artist, that same spark he had in his youth with William. Promise me you shall never leave him."

"Yes, Mrs. Brady. I promise."

CHAPTER 18 — WIPEOUT

1985

Driving the Chevelle on a hot summer day along Route 287, I listen to the clickety-click of the straight-six-cylinder engine. The heat is blasting away to keep the radiator from boiling-over. I keep a cassette player beside me, not having the heart to tear apart the chrome dashboard and remove the classic, push-button AM radio. The D-batteries are giving out and REM's album Murmur begins to slow...

A letter stamped Luft-Post from a distant friend backpacking his way across Europe arrived in the mail the other day. Steve Van Vlack, Stephen Hero, I call him, was the lead singer in our band. His family, the Van Vlacks date back to the early Dutch settlers of New York back when it was called New Amsterdam. Summer is nearly over. He is bringing home his girlfriend from Denmark, Pernille Lemming. Can we pick him up at the airport?

I haven't been to school in a long time. I won't be returning this fall. There is a letter sitting on my desk — it's been there for five months, dated March 22, 1985, from the assistant dean of academic standards.

"I am offering you the option of taking an Official Leave of Absence... You will then not have to apply for readmission..." This is my ticket back to college. But I never responded. And I'm not sure why. I'm not sure where life is taking me as I drive the 100-mile route day after day. I am always headed somewhere, but I'm going nowhere... fast.

I flick down the turn signal to get in the fast lane. I check the side-view mirror. Over my shoulder, there in the remote corner of my peripheral vision, in the blind spot, is a car about to collide with the Chevelle. A blaring horn screams in my ear. Inches from the oncoming car, I hear the roar of the highway — locking brakes, screeching tires. I crank the steering wheel and skid out of control — swerving across three lanes into the breakdown lane.

Head swirling adrenaline rush.

I look over at the empty passenger seat.

"Are you trying to kill me?" I can hear Duke say.

I take a deep breath. The Rolling Stones echo in my mind, 19th Nervous Breakdown. This is where I belong – the breakdown lane. I'm not moving from this spot. I don't trust myself. I'm a menace. The cars rush past. I look around. The quick-thinking driver who prevented the crash is long gone. "C'mon, Danny," says Duke. "Get the hell off the shoulder before you get rear-ended."

Back in the darkroom, highway accident photos drop in the catch tray. The photographer takes scenes of the car crash, of skid-marks and the curve in the highway, the big oak tree. Flash photographs of a nighttime horror scene. Bodies strewn across the street. Blood in black and white. A lifeless teenager lies in a crumpled heap by a tree, another in the grass. A fence post smashed through the windshield. There is a close-up of the driver's head crushed to one side.

I can't make it go away... I put on the headphones and practice Larry's drum intro to Sunday Bloody Sunday. He plays 16th notes on the snare with a steady thump on the bass drum. He goes back and forth from the hi-hat to the snare tapping out a marching beat. "I can't believe the news today," sings Bono. "I can't close my eyes and make it go away."

My mind wanders back to a summer afternoon trimming the hedges in Grandma's backyard overgrown with maple trees in the Woodlawn section of the Bronx. Across the street is Saint Barnabas Church. This is no ordinary church. It stands like a Roman temple with the architect drawing inspiration from the original structure in Venice.

Dad set up his dentist office in the back room of Grandma's house, the house he grew up in. There are mismatched chairs in the waiting room and a big gaping hole in the plaster ceiling with the wooden slats exposed. Hanging on the wall is his diploma from Georgetown Dentistry School. He was a one-man operation. He had no receptionist or hygienist.

I sat at the dining room table eating a sandwich Grandma made – ham on rye smothered in butter. I looked at her china cabinet – antique Belleek and Waterford crystal. She sat in her favorite chair by the window – a recliner covered in an afghan that rocked back and forth while she knit. There is an old photograph of her in a summer white dress, hair up in a bun, holding a parasol. She came to the U.S. in 1901 at the age of 16.

"Grandma, did you ever want to go back?"

"Back where?"

"To Ireland."

"Goodness no, Dan." She said in her soft Cork lilt. "It was miserable there. The snow always turned to slush – it was grey and dirty. You're so lucky here to have white snow."

She leans forward in her recliner, "Now, have you given any thought to the matter we discussed?"

"A little bit, Grandma." She has a great sales pitch about the priesthood, she is about to pounce...

"Just think of it Dan, you'll have no worries about finding work, they give you a house to live in, you work Sunday but get days off during the week, and you are guaranteed a place in Heaven!"

I nod my head and wince. I wonder if my Dad had these same talks. He attended Cathedral Prep, and nearly became a priest, but he was drafted when he turned 18 and then served with the 90th Infantry Division – the Tough 'Ombres.

"Think of your Uncle Jim, he heard the calling and joined the priesthood. He became a monsignor and led Catholic Charities," she pauses a moment, and drives the nail home, "Your mother up in heaven would be so proud, Dan…"

My father walks through the door from his dentist office into the dining room. He stands at the table, flipping the pages to The New York Times and The Daily News. He reaches for his cigarette.

"Al, now sit down and eat your lunch." It was always strange for me to hear my father's name, Al, instead of Dad.

He takes a sip of his coffee. "No, I've got to get back. I have patients waiting."

"They can wait. You sit down and eat your lunch."

Dad flicks on the TV while Grandma fusses over him.

"I'm alright, don't worry about me," he says in a huff.

"Calm yourself down."

A smile comes over my face watching Dad being waited on hand and foot. Grandma treats him like a prince. Meanwhile, back at our house, he is the one taking care of us, cooking dinner for his seven children, doing the dishes.

The news at noon comes on the set – Lord Louis Mountbatten killed while on vacation in Ireland. The IRA claimed responsibility.

"Dad, isn't that the man we used to watch on public television?"

"Yes, Danny."

As we get ready to leave, I kiss Grandma Good-bye. She tucks a tightly folded twenty in the palm of my hand. "Don't breathe a word of this to your father."

After a sip from his coffee mug, Duke turns the radio dial to oldies rock-n-roll. From somewhere mysterious, deep inside the speaker, there is a sinister giggle, a pause, and then a shout, "Wipeout!"

"That's more like it," says Duke. The drums thunder away in this song without words, a surf-rock instrumental. "Peter, the drummer in George's band, played this drum solo note for note."

"No kidding. George was in a band?"

"Sure, he played guitar. I used to help load their equipment at the clubs on Yonkers Avenue."

"What's this song called again?"

"Wipeout," says Duke, "by The Surfari's."

"Wipeout," I repeat as I reach down into the catch tray to pick up some of Duke's prints. Two young women dance barefoot in the grass, naked in the night, in the pouring rain, outstretched arms trying to catch raindrops, hair drenched like a shower, beads of water glisten upon their skin.

"C'mon, Danny, it's getting late, you'd better go help George pack up the work and get out on the route."

My eyes must be deceiving me as another print plops down in the tray… they stand close together in a tight embrace.

"Danny, are you not hearing me?"

Sitting at his desk, filling out invoices, George quietly inspects the prints underneath the lamp one last time before handing them off to me for packing up. Pretty soon, I will be headed out on the 100-mile route. I try to get my mind off what might happen on the road. One time the engine over-heated, then another the brakes gave out, the pedal went all the way to the floor. Then that the driver went through a stop sign and crashed into the driver's side of the Chevelle, crushing the door, crumpling it like paper. There will be long traffic jams on 95 at the tolls…

I look around the shop. There is a color photograph of an acoustic guitar on the wall. Golden rays of the morning sun highlight the woodgrain of the guitar. It stands propped by a rocking chair — the spokes in the backrest cast shadows on the hardwood floor. A still-life study of craftsmanship — I think of the chair and the woodworker bending the oak, of the guitar-builder placing the inlaid ivory in the fretboard, of the worker down on his hands and knees setting the floor boards, and the one who built the trees with the rain, the earth, and the sun.

"Where did you get that photograph, George?"

"I took it."

"Wow, I've never seen a photograph like that. It radiates light."

George turns around from his desk. "I shot it on Kodachrome, and made the cibachrome print with that machine there, the Ilfochrome."

He points to it with a look of dismay. All this time at The Photography Workshop, I've never noticed this big elephant in the room, the large machine with a TV screen, standing dormant by the counter.

"Does it still work?"

"Yes, but it never gets much use, it just takes up space. People don't understand what a cibachrome print is. They don't appreciate how superior it is to a regular color print — that is a positive from a positive. They don't realize when they send their slide film out to have prints made that Kodak makes an inter-negative which the customer never sees, and then after they make a print, Kodak tosses the inter-negative away."

"What is an inter-negative?"

"It's a color negative from a slide, like a copy negative, but you lose a generation — you lose the sharpness and the brilliance of the original slide film." He sighs wearily, "But no one seems to care…"

"Is that your guitar?"

"Yes, a Martin."

"George, I didn't know you played guitar. My brother plays a

Rickenbacker."

"I had a Gibson Les Paul and a Fender Telecaster."

"What was the name of your band?"

"Snow," said George.

"Snow," I repeat, "Man, that's a cool name."

Snow fell as Steve and I waited in line outside the record store to buy tickets for the U2 concert at the Coliseum. Steve's glasses fogged up in the wet falling snow. We waited for hours and hours, but the concert sold out in minutes. Tickets to U2 concerts are near impossible to get. They're not your average MTV band anymore.

"I used to play drums in a band," I tell George. "But after high school, we all sort-of went our separate ways."

"Yeah, that's what happened to our band."

I think back to the audition for the talent show, we set up our equipment in the hallway outside the gym. A crowd gathered – Bill played the opening chords just like The Edge, I pounded on the floor-tom like Larry, Gregg played the bass, and Steve sang the opening line to I Will Follow. We passed the audition.

At the U2 concert on April 3, 1985, and we listened to Bono sing this song about Martin Luther King, Jr. "Early Morning, April Four, shot rings out in the Memphis sky..." A week later, I started work at The Photography Workshop.

"C'mon Danny," says George, "you'd better hit the road."

CHAPTER 19 — A TIP OF THE HAT

1850

Pen in hand, Tim carefully writes out the name and address across a large manila envelope in deliberate strokes: Mr. Henry H. Snelling, 61 Ann Street while Mr. Brady fumbles through the heap of papers on his desk.

"This is a most important delivery and Mr. Snelling must have it today. I promised him. You see, he is launching a publication devoted to the New Art. He is calling it The Photographic Art Journal and I am to be featured in the premier issue. But you must promise not to breathe a word of this, not to Mr. Pettifog, not even to Benjamin."

"Yes, Mr. Brady."

"Oh, where has it gone off to now? It was here just a minute ago… Come back, my little lost lamb!"

"What have you misplaced, Mr. Brady?"

"Help me find it, Timothy, would you please?"

"What exactly are we looking for?"

"My profile by C. Edwards Lester! I must find it!"

"There it is Mr. Brady, right under your nose."

"No, Timothy that is my portrait — the lithograph engraved by D'Avignon which shall accompany my profile."

Tim stands up to assist Mr. Brady in his search. Behind his desk, behind a pile of papers, his back to the corner office windows, Broadway and Fulton is groggily getting up. Push carts are taking their places. Street sweepers busy with their brooms. The tide is slowly coming in… one lonely omnibus comes down Broadway. Newsboys carry great big bundles of papers tied with twine, one little boy is teetering over, way to one side, trying to counter-balance his heavy load. He gets shoved by a larger boy – stiff-armed. He crosses Broadway and disappears from view.

Tim thinks back to Mr. Brady's sitting. He sat with such remarkable poise. Luther, the operator, took plate after plate with nary a complaint. But Mr. Pettifog was all in a tizzy.

"What's wrong with this one, Mat? Looks perfectly fine to me."

"I don't like my expression."

"Don't like your expression? Your eyes are open. There is no motion blur. What more could you ask for?"

"I am looking for that indefinable something which conveys my artistic vision."

"You've got terrible vision, Mat! Everyone up and down Broadway knows that!"

"I am not satisfied."

"Well, all right then. Let us waste some more Scovill Plates. Mr. Boswell, have at it! And I shall bring the quicksilver up to temperature. You are without doubt the most difficult sitter we've had in months."

"But Henry, this is most important to me."

"Why Mathew? Why are there more portraits of you than General Tom Thumb and Jenny Lind combined?"

"I can't tell you. Now, Luther, focus the camera, but not too sharply."

Mr. Pettifog turns in a huff muttering away, "'Tis all vanity!"

"Timothy, have you located it?"

"Can you tell me what it looks like?"

"It is the article written by Charles Edward Lester. At the top of the page, across the top, he scripted large letters: M.B. Brady."

"Oh, I see…"

"You've found it?"

"No, not yet." Tim says his little prayer, Please Saint Anthony, please come around. Something is lost which cannot be found."

Just then P.T. Barnum barges into Mr. Brady's office, removing his hat, placing it over his chest in as grand a gesture befitting the great actor, Junius Brutus Booth. He pauses a moment — for dramatic effect — listening for stillness — that attentive silence before beginning his soliloquy. From his years as a barker, he breathes deep, down to the depths of his diaphragm, to thrust out with all his might, projecting his voice for all to hear…

"I have lived in abject poverty, I have seen hunger on my children's faces, I dabbed the tears from Charity's cheeks, trying to quell my wife's darkest fears. I have known abundance and her bountiful blessings, I have lived in palaces… and jails. I have dined with Queen Victoria and fought over scraps with bummers on the Bowery. I have snookered the best confidence men. I am not afraid to admit that I made my living as a legerdemain and picked many a pocket. I was the man behind some of the greatest newspaper hoaxes ever orchestrated… second only to the Moon Hoax of 1835."

"Really?"

"You see, Brady, I know the inner-workings of the newspaper press. I used to write articles to keep the pot boiling at home. They need to feed their behemoth presses, just as I need to feed my elephants their insatiable appetites — day after day after day. Truth be told, I was the one who planted the story in The New York Herald about the Feejee Mermaid."

"You don't say, Mr. Barnum!"

"Yes, Brady, I may as well confess that those three communications from the South were written by myself and forwarded to friends of mine… This fact and corresponding post-marks did much to prevent suspicion of a hoax and the New York Editors thus unconsciously contributed to my arrangements for bringing the mermaid into public notice."

"You orchestrated all of that?"

"Some say I inspired Poe and his Balloon Hoax... He was rumored to have said, 'If the Great Dumb Beast,' that was his preferred term when referring to the public, 'should believe what they read in Moses Beach's New York Sun – that there are flying monkey's on the moon, they will surely believe someone crossed the Atlantic Ocean in a balloon.'"

"Most fascinating, Mr. Barnum! You should write all of this down."

"Don't use soft soap on me, Brady. I'm wise to you and your ways – one humbug to another. That is the reason for my call this morning." He thrusts out his arm pointing in accusation, demanding the truth down through his fingertip.

"Are you the one who has been planting seeds of doubt and distrust with Mademoiselle Lind?"

"Why, whatever do you mean?"

"Have you attempted to deter Jenny Lind from making my engagement with me, by assuring her that I was a humbug and a showman? Come now, Brady! Is it no coincidence that she has recently began to voice her concerns since meeting you? She even encouraged me to imbibe. 'It will do you a world of good, Mr. Barnum,' said she. Now tell the truth, I command you — one humbug to another!"

"Oh, Mr. Barnum, my how your imagination runs wild!"

Tim looks after the newsboy. He is on the east side of Fulton standing beneath the 'Dollar a Daguerreotype' sign. He is not selling many papers at that spot. He has not lightened his load.

"Boy, what on earth are you looking at?" shouts Barnum. "Your daydreaming gaze has distracted me!"

"You were saying, Mr. Barnum... One humbug to another..."

"Yes, that's it Brady. I call on you this glorious morning, one humbug to another to give you a tip of the hat. You have outwitted me, sir. For that, I must commend you. That is no mean feat. I congratulate you, Mr. Mathew B. Brady, wholeheartedly."

"I've found it, Mr. Brady. I've found it!" shouts Tim. "Here on this stack of papers by the windowsill."

"Nobody interrupts Phineas Taylor Barnum. Hold on, is this the same wet river rat I took pity on?"

"Why yes, it is, Mr. Barnum. This is young Timothy. Please allow me to repay your kindness."

"Repay me, you shall Brady, and then some... You have circumvented me, sir. While I admire your cunning, your guile, your tenacity, I will not tolerate being cheated from what is rightfully mine."

"But Mr. Barnum, Miss Jenny is not your chattel. I promised to provide you with as many daguerreotypes as you wished. And I have done so."

"So, you have. But so have all the other daguerreotypists on Broadway. I wish you would consider for a moment my investment in the Jenny Lind Enterprise. She is in my charge. I was the one who discovered her in England and brought her across the Atlantic Ocean. I was the one who put $50,000 on the table. It is time for me to recoup my investment. Now then, tell me how you propose to repay me for all the exposure I have given you?"

"Exposure, Mr. Barnum? I don't follow you."

"Come now, Brady. Pickpockets feign innocence better than that. I refer to the articles in the Herald, the crowds gathered about your gallery, the kind of exposure which money cannot buy and which cannot be repaid with mere stacks of daguerreotypes. The Meade Brothers and Mr. Gurney have provided me with more than an ample supply. I'm sure we can come to an arrangement... one humbug to another..."

"But Mr. Barnum!"

"Careful now, Brady, I hear that brogue of yours breaking through..." His voice trails off as he pauses a moment looking at Tim. "My, you've cleaned him up rather well, just as I found Little Georgie wandering the streets of Bridgeport. But send him away — this instant!"

Brady gathers up the lithograph and the papers penned by Lester. He tucks them in the portfolio folding it closed. "Now Timothy, be so good as to take these materials to Mr. Snelling's office at 61 Ann Street. Take great care with this delivery. Put this directly in his hands."

"Yes, Mr. Brady, but what if he isn't there?"

"You shall stand there and wait. Do not disappoint."

"Enough quibbling! We must come to an arrangement!"

"That will be all for now, Timothy," says Brady gently closing the door. That look in his eye — that forlorn look reminds him of Thomas about to accept his sentence for a much-deserved licking from Pa. 'Get out of here, Timmy!' He'd plead.

"Shut the blasted door!" shouts Barnum.

CHAPTER 20 — BACK TO THE FUTURE

1985

Back on the route, driving from camera store to camera store, I hit the rewind button and play back last night's scene of picking up Steve and Pernille at the airport.

"What the hell happened to the Chevelle, Dan?"

"I had an accident, Steve, and some close calls."

"She looks all beat to hell."

Back home in Crestwood, REM is on the record player in my room as Steve unpacks his duffle-bag stuffed with contraband from Europe. Wrapped in a tube sock is a bottle of Caarlsburg beer from Denmark then in another is a bottle of Tuborg. I am not sure how he got through U.S. Customs. "You can't buy these here in the States," the smuggler with John Lennon glasses explains, "American beer is all watered down." He tells tales of backpacking across Europe and staying in Youth Hostels as he digs out a bottle of Belgium beer, brewed by monks. Then he crossed the Irish Sea in a ferry to visit the Guinness Brewery. He hands me a bottle of stout while Pernille tries to teach me a few phrases in Danish. She is tall and pretty with short brown hair.

"Perfect circle of acquaintances and friends," sings Michael Stipe.

I park the Chevelle at another camera store and ponder the name George chose for his shop. All the other stores on the route have the word 'camera' in their name – Bronxville Camera, Scarsdale Camera, Hartsdale Camera, but George called his place simply — The Photography Workshop. He sold no cameras other than a few Kodaks. He had no interest in cameras. There was no glass display case with Nikons and Cannons. This was a workshop devoted to photography and photography alone.

When a customer asked his opinion about which camera was the best — the Cannon A-1 versus the Cannon AE-1 or the Nikon F2, he would shrug his shoulders. "They're all good. It's hard to say."

"C'mon George, which camera is the best?" I asked after the customer left the store. "Nikon, Minolta, Pentax, Cannon, or Konica?"

He doesn't say one way or the other.

"What about my old Exakta?"

He just shrugs.

"But George, it has a Carl Zeiss lens."

"Danny, it's just not considered that good a camera. It's certainly no

Leica."

"Leica?"

"Leica is considered to be the best 35-millimeter camera hands down. I'm surprised you've never heard of Leica. But, I'll take a Hasselblad over any 35-millimeter."

"Hassa-what?"

"Hasselblad – it's a medium format camera like the Rollei. But the best camera in the world is not going to take great photographs on its own. It's a combination of the photographer and the darkroom technician. Some people will spend thousands of dollars on a Leica, and then they will take their film to a drug store and have cheap machine prints made instead of taking it here to be developed — that I don't understand."

"But don't we make machine prints with the Ilford?"

"No, we make custom prints."

George went on to discuss the difference between a machine print and a custom black and white enlargement. I thought of watching him in the darkroom — how he would hand craft prints — burning in certain areas, dodging other sections to bring out the negative.

Driving in the Chevelle that summer of 1985, I imagine there is a flux capacitor underneath the hood, I am quite certain of this, and suddenly I am transported in time like Marty McFly, the Irish insect, in the DeLorean from 1985 to 2000 — Back to the Future.

The '67 Chevelle takes me all the way to the year 2000. I am sitting in class learning a program called Photoshop. It is a condensed down, easier to pronounce, version of George's Photography Workshop. Photoshop, I repeat, short and to the point. I think of the cost of Photoshop compared to all darkroom equipment in the back room of George's shop. He had the best equipment money could buy. The Omega enlargers and Schneider lenses cost thousands of dollars, not to mention the Ilford processor. All of these tools are contained in Photoshop accessible to most everyone.

The teacher points with a laser at the Adobe Photoshop tool bar on the projector screen. I see George's hand that he used to sculpt light – it is called the Burn Tool then I see the Dodge Tool. The average person back then could not afford the equipment, and all the supplies – the chemicals, the paper and all the time and labor involved to develop one roll of Tri-X black & white film. Photoshop puts an entire darkroom on your desktop.

Suddenly, the shop door opens and the buzzer beeps. I am back to the past, back to 1985, sitting on the wooden stool, staring out the window past the painted letters of The Photography Workshop. A photographer walks in the shop with his medium format camera. He plops his camera and rolls of 120mm film on the counter for drop-off and pick-up and calls out, "George!"

"Can I help you?"

"George!" He shouts.

Professional photographers did not want to waste time with me. I am not really a darkroom technician. I make contact sheets — that is all. They wanted George's individual attention.

I turned to Duke working the view camera for help.

"Frank, George is in the back developing film. He can't come out of the darkroom for another 45 minutes. Why don't you grab yourself a cup of coffee at the bakery across the street? Before you know it, the time will pass by like that," says Duke with a snap of his fingers.

Now, I am back to the future. I watch a documentary narrated by the son of Ansel Adams, Michael. He demonstrates how his father hand crafted that famous black and white photograph, Moonrise over Hernandez. I think of that same poster I had hanging in my room in Crestwood. This is one of the most expensive black and white photographs ever sold at auction for over $600,000. The black ink sky – classic f-64 – the artistic movement, named after an exaggerated f-stop, emphasizing depth-of-field, everything is hi-def — crystal sharp focus.

The documentary illustrates the difference between straight printing and custom printing — the reason why Ansel Adams is equally known as a landscape artist and as a darkroom technician. He brought out his work in the darkroom – he honed that negative, dodged and burned that sky. Ansel made diagrams with cryptic instructions on how he hand-crafted prints in his darkroom. His son showed a straight print from that famous negative — the sky is flat grey, not black, the moon opaque. He rode in the back seat as a little boy when his father stopped by the side of the road to take that world-famous photograph, but it is the darkroom technician that brought another dimension to that negative.

I read an article about two boxes of negatives purportedly taken by Ansel Adams purchased for $45 estimated to be worth $200 million. Adams' grandson seriously doubted whether these negatives were actually taken by his grandfather and questioned how they could be worth $200 million noting that much of the value is in the prints made by Ansel Adams, not just the negative. See, said the old darkroom technician to himself, your work did have value. It is not just the photographer exposing the negative, it is the darkroom technician making the positive.

The other day while digging through my past – my darkroom supplies – I open the lid to the storage bin – the smell of chemicals brings me back – the way old familiar smells trigger forgotten memories – I breathe in the developer, the fixer and stop bath. I find a box of Ilford paper – 250 sheets cost $84.

I dig through my storage bin of cameras. Katie, my eight-year-old daughter, looks over my shoulder – she is on summer vacation. She's having a bummer summer. I find the Exakta – the fact-checker in me wanted to verify if I held the camera at my waist. I remember looking down. The viewfinder did not have a pentaprism. This is the first SLR – technically the second SLR – this is the Exakta II. So, Katie is looking over my shoulder at this old camera, the Exakta II from 1948 – this is a primitive camera – no light-meter, no auto-exposure, no auto-advance, no auto-focus, no auto-rewind. You set the aperture, the shutter speed, and focus manually.

"Dad, where's the screen?"

I don't understand her question at first. This little girl – she's not so little. She is a tall eight-year-old with a curious mind.

"What screen?"

"Where is the little TV screen so you can see the picture you took?"

I think of her digital Kodak and the video screen on the back. She points to the back of the Exakta – there is a metal rectangle – the decorative leather has peeled off the back – it looks like the place where the TV screen should be. Such a perceptive observation for a little girl – one I could not envision asking.

I show her one of my old Kodak brownie cameras – with a push of the button, the leather bellows extends out. "This is where you put the film."

"Dad," she stops me, tapping me on the shoulder, "what is film?"

If only Duke could see her now…

In a sip from my coffee mug, I travel back to the past… George emerges from the darkroom, squinting his eyes, adjusting to the bright light. He pushes the contact sheets to the side. George doesn't waste time with them. He holds the negatives up to the storefront window with his loupe. He chooses the shot.

"This is the one," he says to Frank.

He makes the decision. This is why photographers came directly to The Photography Workshop. They valued his opinion and trusted him with their negatives. He is the one who will make the print.

Late in the day, George and Duke finish work out back, while I sit at the counter entering names and dates in the Kodak logbook. The buzzer beeps as I look up to see a distant relative standing before me.

"Why hello, Daniel, don't you recognize me? You look as though you've seen a ghost."

There before me is my mother's cousin, Adrienne Hiddleson, from the neighborhood. She removes the silk scarf from about her head – she looks hauntingly like my mother. Something tells me she is not here to drop off a roll of film.

"So how have you been? I hear you are no longer attending college."

I nod my head and prepare myself for a lecture – for being a drop-out and a disappointment. But there is an understanding look in her eyes.

"Life can be hard. You'll get back on your feet in time." She pauses a moment, "Listen, I have some old photographs that I've been meaning to get copied."

"Do you have the negative?"

"Goodness no, these were taken so long ago..."

"Well, we will need to make a copy negative and then print from that."

She removed the old photographs from her purse, "I'd like to get copies of these made."

There on the counter is a turn of the century family portrait from about 1912. She points out my grandmother, Nora Lynch, wearing a bow in her hair. "The little one here is my mother, Margaret. This is Uncle Jim, who became a priest, this is Nellie, she was the mother of your Aunt Madge and Aunt Helen. And this is Daniel. That poor boy..."

"Who was Daniel?"

"That is your namesake. His death broke Delia's heart."

"Who was Delia?"

"His mother." She points to a wedding photograph from 1893. "This is Delia, your great-grandmother, and her husband, John."

"Oh, so that's who my sister Delia was named after. Her middle name is Nora."

"Yes, after your grandmother. So how is your sister Delia doing and your brother James?"

"They're both doing well."

"So, when I can pick these up?"

"In a few days, would you like to have the prints sepiatoned?"

"Are you sure it won't ruin the original? These are dear to me."

"Not at all. Once we make the negative, we work only with the copy and never touch the original."

"Yes, okay then, that would be fine."

"It will take an extra few days. We sepiatone the prints on Saturday."

As she gets ready to leave, I ask a parting question. "So, what exactly happened to Daniel?"

She turns around briefly. "One of many tragedies in the Lynch family... a story for another time." Then the shop door closes shut.

CHAPTER 21 — ANGEL GABRIEL

1850

With a faint knock on Mr. Brady's door, Tim turns the handle to see a lank figure of a young man reclined in the visitor's chair. Feet propped on the edge of the desk, long legs extended, hands behind his head in a butterfly clasp, the white ruffles of his shirt sleeves catch the morning breeze like a bird extending its wings ready to take flight. A thick shock of brown hair purposely disheveled — carefully spritzed with hair tonic to look wild and romantic, just as his black satin cravat is loosely tied, dangling down just so... There is an auburn patch of hair just below his lower lip and just the wisp of a mustache on his upper. His eyes are closed, lips trembling, as if in silent prayer. It is October 7th.

"Mr. Brady, I delivered the package to Mr. Snelling at 61 Ann Street, just as you requested."

"Thank you kindly, Timothy, allow me to introduce Mr. Gabriel Harrison."

Gabriel's eyes pop open as he stands to attention, extending his hand down to Tim.

"So, you are to be my powder monkey? Put it there, Timothy!"

"Pleased to meet you, Mr. Harrison. You may call me, Tim."

"I much like Tiny Tim. And it's Gabriel to you."

"Take a seat, Timothy," says Mr. Brady. "You see, Gabriel is on loan to us while Mr. Lawrence recuperates at The Mountain House. He quite nearly became yet another martyr to our art."

"I don't follow you. Who is Mr. Lawrence?"

Gabriel sighs. He goes to the Fulton Street window, looks out clutching the drape.

"Mr. Martin M. Lawrence is one of the most respected Daguerreotypists on all Broadway."

"Yes, I recall now. His studio is located right next door. Is Mr. Lawrence being thrown to the lions?"

"Not quite, Timothy."

Gabriel turns around dramatically, fluttering his white sleeves.

"May I interject, Mr. Brady?"

"Please do, Gabriel."

From his tall stance, he crouches down on his hindquarters to eye-level with Tim.

"You see Tiny Tim, Mr. Lawrence has fallen victim to the mercury vapors from his endless hours toiling away in close proximity to the fuming hood. He suffers from the most acute pain and is unable to walk. His legs and arms have swollen to twice their ordinary size."

Tears well up in Timothy's eyes. "But what is to become of Mr. Pettifog? He works hour after hour in the mercurial room and never ventures out. He is a dear friend of mine. He keeps a cross over his bed — that's where he makes his home — in the mercurial room. I should hate to see him become a martyr to our art."

"Tut, tut, now," says Mr. Brady giving the boy a hug. "I can assure you, nothing shall happen to Mr. Pettifog. Not as long as I am around. He is my rock. Henry Peter Pettifog is impervious to mercury, same as the arrows bounced off Achilles."

Gabriel chimes in, "and with a few weeks respite – breathing in the cool Catskill Mountain air, Mr. Lawrence will be right as rain and then he will reopen his studio. Then you shall be free of me."

He sees a confused look.

"It's like this Tiny Tim. I need a powder monkey and you are he."

"I am no monkey."

"You misunderstand, Timothy. You are to be Gabriel's assistant on the rooftop studio – the new addition. He needs a third, fourth, and fifth right arm."

"That's right, Tiny Tim."

Suddenly, Tim walks over to Mr. Brady's desk, going directly to his chair-side. He pulls Mr. Brady closer to whisper in his ear. "Mr. Brady, tell him to stop calling me 'Tiny Tim'. I don't like it. Not in the slightest."

There is an awkward pause. Brady takes a soft breath. "It seems young Timothy has taken issue with being called 'Tiny Tim'."

Gabriel looks shocked for a moment then laughs out loud.

"Fair enough, Tiny Tim. Oops, pardon me. Now then, when I shout, 'Black powder!' You must scamper down those stairs in your silk slippers as fast your feet will carry, all the way down to the bowels of the ship to the magazine and bring me the black powder. We are on board the USS Chesapeake you and I. The HMS Shannon lies off in the distance. Can you see her, Tim? Remember the famous last words of Commodore Lawrence: DON'T GIVE UP THE SHIP!"

"Gabriel alludes to his tireless efforts in commissioning the monument to the memory of Captain James Lawrence in the cemetery of Trinity Church. He has written letter after letter to all the papers calling upon the city fathers to erect a monument to a true patriot. Gabriel formed a board of trustees with Moses Beach of the New York Sun, Horace Greeley of the Tribune, and N.P. Willis. The list goes on and on."

Gabriel explains, "There was nothing but a disordered and unseemly heap of bricks which marked the spot in Trinity Church yard where rested the remains of the gallant Commodore Lawrence."

"Who knows what would have happened to his memory if it 'twere not for Gabriel?"

"Oh, Mr. Brady, you give me far too much credit. The Lawrence Monument was a collective effort. I was always told as a boy that next to his mother, one must love his country best."

"What a remarkable story, Gabriel. You are to be commended for your efforts." Turning in his chair he continues, "You see, Timothy, ever since the visit from Jenny Lind, the steady stream of customers has not abated. With this new studio up on the rooftop, and Gabriel's help, perhaps we will be able to keep pace. But, you must keep Mr. Harrison well supplied with prepared plates, while at the same time bringing down the exposed plates to Mr. Pettifog. Do you think you are up to the task?"

"Very much so, Mr. Brady. Must I wear silk slippers?"

"Of course not, Timothy, Gabriel, spoke merely in allegory. Now you follow him while I attend to more important matters."

Up on the rooftop, Tim looks out the studio wall of windows through a surreal haze of blue-tinted glass. "Gabriel, why are the windows panes made of blue glass?"

"Mr. Brady is a firm believer in blue light and its ability to bring out the deep rich hues necessary for a superior daguerreotype."

"But the windows are so dirty and smudged over. Would you want me to clean them?"

"No, by all means, no. That is Mr. Brady's intent – 'Keep the glass dirtied over to diffuse the light,' was what he told me."

Tim watches a woman hanging laundry to dry on the line, unfurling white sheets like sails. Stretching before him, he sees flat roof after flat roof covered in black tar paper, in the far distance the blue sky of New York Harbor is punctuated by church steeples and ship masts.

While Gabriel busies himself checking the camera and plate-holder box, Tim sees a portrait on the wall of a young boy clinging around the pedestal upon which rests a bust of the immortal Washington.

"Mr. Harrison, why is this boy hugging a statue of George Washington? Most curious."

"That happens to be my son, George Washington Harrison. This is one of my descriptive daguerreotypes – where I try to tell a story with the camera."

He points to a poem in a frame hanging nearby. "You see this poem was written by my dear friend, Eliza C. Hurley, inspired by this daguerreotype of mine."

He reads a few lines aloud...

"Look up thou bright eyed boy,
Behold thy country's ornament

Which time will not destroy."

"She wrote a very fine poem about your daguerreotype. Didn't she Gabriel?"

"Yes Tim, you see I wish to do more with this camera than simply take portrait after portrait. We have not begun to fully realize the potential of this new discovery," says Gabriel pointing to the camera. "That's why I am universally known as the Poet Daguerrean. I have an unbound love and admiration for the art and a sincere desire to see it rise still higher in character and excellence."

The first customers of the day begin to appear. A woman with a young boy appears at the doorway, holding their ticket, waiting for their portrait.

"Will this hurt?" asks the boy adding, "terribly?"

"You won't feel a thing," assures Gabriel.

"That's just what the dentist said."

"Hush now," says the mother. She pulls Gabriel in closer. "You're sure that box can't see through my dress?"

"Madam, you have my word."

As the steady stream of customers file up the stairs, waiting their turn, there is a momentary lull.

"Gabriel, did you start out as a buff-boy?"

"Oh no, Tim, I started as an operator for Mr. John Plumbe in 1844. I was a favorite with his customers and contributed much to his fame and fortune, before he was beset with a series of most unfortunate circumstances."

"Where is his studio?"

"Gone now. The most lavish studio I ever saw... It was at 251 Broadway, but one day the banks seized all his assets and shuttered the doors. Mr. Plumbe was nowhere to be found. I had heard he was stricken with Gold Fever and absconded to California leaving his wife and children behind... desperate to find his pot of gold. Let this be a lesson to you Timothy – always be careful to keep the wings of ambition well-clipped.

"Also, you must take great care in choosing the studio you work for or one day you will find yourself locked out. This happened to me both as an operator and as an actor."

"You were an actor, Gabriel?"

"Oh yes, indeed. I played the part of Othello. I accepted an engagement at the Avon Theatre in Norfolk, Virginia. But no sooner did I get there when I found the new theatre was sold for a church. There I was, twenty years old in a strange city far from friends and family– a bummer begging for ha' pennies on the street corner."

"I can't picture you as bummer, Gabriel."

"There I was, wandering the streets of Norfolk with no hope of seeing my beloved mother and father again. I had no means of returning home.

Standing at the dock pelted by the rain, I heard the strains of that lament by John Howard Payne sung in the distance:

Mid pleasures and palaces though we may roam,

Be it ever so humble, there's no place like home;

"As I heard the repeated refrain, I promised myself never to take home for granted again. When I returned, I assisted my father with his printing press to support my beloved mother and our large family of sisters. In 1844, my father's printing business fell on hard times, and I turned my artistic eye upon daguerreotyping."

Throughout the day, Tim noticed a common reaction from the elderly to the very young – one of dissatisfaction – a reluctance to look at oneself. "That's not a very flattering likeness of me, is it?"

"Don't you see how distinguished you look, sir?" Gabriel would say to a gentleman. Then to a lady he would say, "My how refined and regal is your expression."

Gabriel does this time after time – applying the soft soap just so. "But I look like I saw a ghost!" complained one sitter.

"I would be more than happy to retake the sitting at your expense, Sir, but I don't see the necessity. This is one of the finest portraits I have ever taken. You remind me of Napoleon standing there."

"I do?"

"I would hate to see you waste money on another sitting."

Scampering down the stairs, weaving his way through the thicket of customers waiting in line, Tim makes his way to the mercurial room and knocks on the door.

"What now! More plates from the Poet Daguerrean himself? Oh, how I count myself fortunate to be his handmaid. Let me drop everything and attend to Angel Gabriel's plates. Do you realize he earns ten times your salary? That he does. I know well Mr. Brady's pay-muster. He allots him $10 a week. Gabriel takes precedence, so said Mr. Brady. We can't keep Angel Gabriel in wait."

"Thank you kindly, Mr. Pettifog."

"Tell him to watch the harsh shadows and mind the focal length." He sighs and tries to retract his escaped words. "On second thought, say nothing. Best not to ruffle his delicate wings – he is so very fragile. I will say this for him, he keeps the sitters moving along – taking plate after plate. I counted 45 plates to the hour. Now, I best be back to work."

As Tim makes his way over to the coating room to collect a fresh supply of Scovill plates, he knocks on the door and waits for his answer in reply. With his ear to the door, he feels a tap on his shoulder.

Startled he turns around to see Hannah Buttle there with an engaging smile and those alluring eyes. She looks so happy to see me – but I am just a buff-boy.

"Hello there, Timothy."

She's never acknowledged me before, not by name, not even by glance.

"I have a small favor to ask. I realize you must be very busy assisting Mr. Harrison, but when there is a lull, perhaps late in the afternoon, would you be so kind as to show him the way to the colorist room?"

She moves in closer. Tim feels the warmth of her breath. She extends her arm to the wall. "Tell me, what's he like?"

"I am not sure. We have only just met. He is very tall."

"Has he mentioned any interests?"

"Oh yes, Miss Buttle. He says one must love their country. He took a portrait of his son hugging a statue of George Washington. For a time, he was an actor."

Suddenly the door to the coating room opens releasing that awful stench along with a stack of Scovill plates. Tim turns around to say something more to Hannah, but she is gone.

Back on the rooftop studio, Tim sees Gabriel lift the black slide to one of the plates and looks over at him with a sense of relief. "Excellent timing, Timothy, I was down to my last plate."

"Now hold that pose just so, madam," says Gabriel calmly to an elderly woman holding a clay pipe in the corner of her mouth, hair parted in the middle, wearing a bonnet and thick eye glasses. "That will dew just fine, madam."

"How soon till it is finished?"

"Oh, in just ten minutes."

"See here," shouts a voice from the back of the line. "I must be the next in line. It is imperative!"

"Sir, you will kindly wait your turn, just as all the others."

He jostles his way forward wearing a captain's uniform tugging the arm of his ten-year-old boy.

"Get back to your place!" shouts Gabriel. "Or take your leave!"

There is a ruckus of pushing and shoving in the line. A woman is shouting at the top of her lungs. "Someone help! He pushed me to the floor! Call-out for a constable!"

Just then, Mr. Brady appears at an instant. "What on earth is all the commotion about?" He holds up his hands trying to quell the unruly mob.

"This man cut the line!"

"Yes, Mr. Brady, this is what transpired."

"Well sir, what do you have to say for yourself?"

"I am Captain Buckman of the steamship North America. I must be down at the Albany Dock in 20 minutes. Four hundred passengers depend upon me. I cannot be late!"

"All right, captain. I will make this exception. But let us take a moment to thank these good, patient people for giving up their turn."

Brady turns to the young boy dressed in a sailor's uniform with brass buttons and a nautical hat. "And who we have here?"

"This is my son, David Lear Buckman."

"Pleased to meet you, young David. Let's make this a memorable sitting. Gabriel at the ready! On my cue let's arrange this father and son portrait…"

Tim takes quiet note of how Mr. Brady has delicately defused a volatile situation like placating a cantankerous drunk. Never argue with a drunk, his father warned his sons, slamming his fist down on the table.

Tim looks at the waiting line of customers and notes all the different walks of life standing together in a row – all so different – yet much the same. All wearing different hats, but each holding onto something dearly precious for the camera to preserve. A stevedore stands tall with his oil skin hat, black and slick, broad shoulders from working on the docks – the short stub of a cigar clenched tight. He holds up the grappling hook used to unload bales of cotton from all the Southern ships.

Watching portrait after portrait, Tim remarks at how Gabriel adapts to the temperament of each sitter – he brings forth a little table so the chemist can set his scale beside his mortar and pestle. A fur trapper steps forward, his flowing beard muffles soft spoken words, hoping the camera will see his great big Jim Bowie knife tucked loosely in his belt. Standing next in line is a little girl in a pretty dress holding her china doll. A pressman wearing a leather apron has brought along some typeset holding his printer's mallet up for the camera to see.

"What a marvelous instrument you've got there," says Gabriel to a fireman in a bright red shirt, holding a great big brass bugle in his lap. Engine No. 6 in white letters on the black leather helmet.

"This is not for making music," says the fireman. "This is for calling out orders to the bucket brigade."

Running downstairs with another stack of plates, Tim knocks on Mr. Pettifog's door. "What now? Are you trying to run me into the ground? The two of you need to ease up. Here, take two cups of tea and some of these buttercakes up for you and Gabriel. And whatever you do, get him to stop. I have a log jam of plates piling up."

"Thank you kindly, Mr. Pettifog."

As Gabriel finishes the last sitting, the customer heads down the stairs in the late afternoon while Tim sets out the teacups.

Gabriel looks drained having taken so many portraits. He stretches out on the chaise lounge in the waiting area pulling over a blanket. He notices Tim staring at a portrait on the wall of three young ladies: one facing to the left, one facing center, and the other to the right.

"That is another of my descriptive daguerreotype which I titled, 'Past, Present, and Future'. Those are my dear sisters."

"I see you have a portrait of Washington Irving by Mr. Brady."

"He told you that? Are you quite sure, Tim?"

"Yes, Gabriel, I'm quite certain that's what he said."

"I can attest to lady justice holding her scales in the balance that I was the operator who captured that likeness. I manned the camera when Washington Irving sat in the chair in Mr. Plumbe's Studio at 251 Broadway. And I can tell you this, Mr. Brady was not there." He stops himself short, saying half to himself, "Remember now, you are a mere operator… It matters all for naught."

"Who is that, Gabriel?"

"That young Timothy is none other than John Howard Payne who was indeed captured by your Mr. Brady, as far as I know."

"So that's the man who wrote 'Home, Sweet Home.' Mr. Brady had hoped he would write the words to his Gallery of Illustrious Americans."

"That's what I would like to do, one day… write."

"What then?"

"The life story of John Howard Payne."

"With your camera, Gabriel?"

"No, with words. You see, I have literary aspirations. His story must be told and tell it I must."

"Don't you like being an operator, Gabriel?"

"Oh yes, very much so. This is a fine, respectable profession. But I wish to be a writer like Poe. Do you know, today is his death date – October 7th… But, taking portrait after portrait, day after day, is rather taxing work. You see, Tim this is the end result of all your training. What do you think of someday being an operator like me?"

"Well, my Pa tells me, I should thank the good Lord I am not digging a ditch like poor Paddy – now, that's hard work."

"That puts things in perspective. I must commend you, Tim," he says in between bites. "You are a faithful assistant – always at the ready. You should join forces with Mr. Lawrence when he returns – you would find him most agreeable to work for."

"But I've made a promise to Mrs. Brady."

Just then Mr. Brady appears in the studio. "Oh, there you are. I am glad you have not gone for the day. Gabriel and Timothy, I have a special request for a customer waiting downstairs. This is a situation that will require a delicate hand."

Gabriel sits up. "What does the situation entail, Mr. Brady?"

"This is a house-call, Gabriel," he pauses a moment to add. "A post-mortem. Timothy, you shall assist Gabriel."

CHAPTER 22 — POST-MORTEM

1850

Standing outside the side entrance on Fulton Street, Gabriel and Timothy busy themselves loading the camera equipment into the trunk of the phaeton.

Mr. Brady comes down the stairs holding a slip of paper in his hand looking a bit concerned. "Now, Gabriel, are you sure you're not forgetting anything? Don't hesitate to expose a few extra plates. Mr. Pettifog will not mind in the slightest. This is one sitting we cannot reschedule…"

He hands Gabriel the slip of paper – Gates residence, 112½ Elm Street. "You are familiar with Elm Street?"

"I know it very well. I reside at 191 Elm."

As they take their seat, Mr. Brady gives a kind pat to the sleek brown Hackney horse while holding the bridle. "Now, be kind to my sweet Louis Daguerre," he pronounces the name Louie. "Hold tight to the reins, and spare the whip."

"Not to worry, Mr. Brady, I am no teamster."

As they ride up Broadway beside the gate of City Hall Park, the October 7th winds swirl about the dry leaves in a circle. There are no more summer white dresses to be seen walking through the park. Tim sees an old friend, the black squirrel collecting acorns.

Gabriel leans back, "There is a bleak north-west wind and dark fleeting clouds. Autumn makes her approach with winter close at her heels."

"Gabriel, why must we make this house call?"

"Well, Tim this is a certain circumstance where it would not be practical for the sitter to visit the studio. This is a post-mortem. You understand the phrase?"

"The Brothers taught us Latin, but the context has me at a loss. What exactly is after death?"

"We shall all one day find out the answer to that eternal question…"

Gabriel turns right on the corner at Chambers Street. "That's it, my gallant Louis. Jehu could not have negotiated that turn much better!" Tim notices the back wall to City Hall painted white to match the white marble from Stockbridge, Massachusetts just like Old Elephant said.

"We are to photograph a dead person, Tim. A child."

There is a pause. Gabriel tugs hard to the left on the reins.

"Step smartly, Louis!"

The phaeton begins to make a left turn onto Elm Street, but grinds to a halt in the middle of Chambers Street. An omnibus approaches.

"Oh my Louis! Don't stop here!"

Gabriel snaps the reins again and they head up Elm Street, a narrow residential street.

"What do you think?" Tim's voice trails off for a moment... He tries once again. "Gabriel, what do you think happens to us after we die? Do you believe there is a heaven?"

There is no answer as the phaeton rumbles up Elm crossing over Reade Street.

"I'll tell you my wild notions, if you promise not to tell a soul."

Tim crosses his heart.

"Look up to the heavens and tell me what you see."

"Oh, the clouds there?"

"Those clouds are wisps of water vapor that will one day rain down on the earth, just like you and I came down from heaven as rain."

"As rain?"

"Yes, Tim. Rain... Think of yourself as a raindrop. You landed with a drop in New Brighton, then you trickled down a little stream, and worked your way across the harbor to join Mr. Brady at his little shop on Broadway."

Gabriel gives Tim a moment to ponder before proceeding.

"Then one day you shall flow down to the vast ocean, and get tossed about with the rest of us in this mighty tempest of thrashing waves, cresting higher and higher to the precipice until you shall come tumbling down, crashing into the deep swell. You shall feel the tug of the riptide, and you will struggle with all your might to resist, but remember, you are powerless to do so, these are strong currents... you will feel the pull and give in. The sea purse shall pull you down to its deepest darkest depths then after you die, you will rise to the surface and Helios, the Sun God, will shine down on you and evaporate your little droplet into vapor and take your soul back to heaven. There, you will mingle in the cloud with all the other lost souls until you rain down once again as a raindrop in the eternal return."

Tim looks up again as the sun breaks through the clouds. He turns to Gabriel as they near Leonard Street. "Have you ever done this before?"

"What? A post-mortem? Oh, yes, it is a fairly common practice."

"I don't understand the reason."

"It's like this Tim, in all that we do as daguerreotypists, we try to stay one step ahead of the grim reaper before he makes his steady but sure approach carrying his scythe. We will never stop his arrival, but we can cheat him."

"How can we cheat the grim reaper, Gabriel?"

"Ever so slightly... by preserving images and memories of persons with our silver plates."

"Somehow, it seems wrong to photograph the dead."

"That's a valid point, but I ask you this – what would you prefer, to have a lasting impression of a loved one in final repose or nothing at all? Death leaves a void — nothing but a vague memory, an intangible wisp of vapor that cannot be captured and passed down to future generations. We at least provide some modest degree of comfort in a time of true sorrow. I shall be frank with you, this shall be no easy sitting — it will be most difficult, but think of the lasting solace we shall provide, a salve to a searing heart. You see?"

"Yes, Gabriel."

"Well, here we are," he says after passing Canal Street, "112 and a half Elm Street." He ties the reins to a hitching post and lends a hand to Tim. They climb the stairs and knock on the door to the old dilapidated frame building.

"Does Mrs. Gates live here?"

"No sir; down in the basement."

Into a deep cellar basement they descended bringing along the camera equipment. The door was partly open – the dying embers in the grate gave off a faint orange glow while the small basement windows up high without a view provided meager light. On a scantily furnished couch lay the victim of the fell destroyer, marble like and cold – the mother, on her knees beside the bed leaned over her darling, her only child, with her face buried in her hands, and giving way to low heart-rending choking sobs.

In the dim light Timothy trips on the rumpled rug dropping a stack of Scovill plates disrupting the somber scene with a loud crash and thud.

"You're here," she said, as she started to her feet, "Oh! A thousand, thousand thanks!"

Gabriel scoops up the crumpled heap – clutching the back of his coat like a mother cat with a kitten. He sets him down – dusting off his shoulders.

"Madam, allow me to introduce my able, though somewhat clumsy, assistant Timothy. I am Gabriel Harrison."

"He who God protects."

"I beg your pardon…"

"Your namesake, Gabriel the Archangel."

Gabriel doesn't quite know how to respond. He gazes at her. Pale lips, though motionless, spoke despair – her dark sunken eyes told of intense suffering.

"Oh! Sir, my child Armenia is dead, and I have no likeness of her; won't you take her picture."

"Yes, madam, if you will permit us to move her towards the light."

In a whisper, out the side of his mouth, "Timothy, grab hold the other end. Take extreme care. Now lift ever so slowly when I say 'heave' – on my mark, one... two... heave."

Gently they moved the death couch to the window in order to get the best light. Tim averts his gaze, trying not to look down at the little girl, but there she lies, no more than three, with that round forehead, arms lay across her motionless heart.

After Gabriel finishes setting up the tripod and camera, he hands a white cloth to Tim. "Now hold this up to give me reflected light to subdue the shadows."

"Like this Gabriel?"

"Yes..."

"Then what transpired, Gabriel?" asks Mr. Brady sitting behind his desk. Gabriel leans back, feet propped in his usual position, arms clasped behind his head. He looks over at Timothy standing quietly there. He leans forward and barely whispers:

> "All was still, I took the cap from the camera. About two minutes had elapsed, when a bright sun ray broke through the clouds, dashed its bright beams upon the reflector, and shedding, as it were, a supernatural light.
>
> "I was startled – the mother riveted with frightful gaze, for at the same moment we beheld the muscles about the mouth of the child move, and her eyes partially open – a smile played upon her lips, a long gentle sigh heaved her bosom, and as I replaced the cap, her head fell over to one side."
>
> The mother screamed – "She lives! She lives!" and fell upon her knees by the side of the couch.
>
> "No," was my reply. "She is dead now, the web of life is broken."
>
> Gabriel continues, "The camera was doing its work as the cord that bound the gentle being to earth snapped and loosened the spirit for another and better world."
>
> "I knelt down beside the mother to offer some comfort, telling her, 'If the earth lost a flower, Heaven gained an angel.'"

Mr. Brady removes his blue spectacles and dabs his eyes with a lace handkerchief tucked in his shirt sleeve.

"So very touching, Gabriel. I must tell this sad tale to Julia. It will wrench her heart." He coughs gently into his palm. "Now, I am to understand the bereaved was satisfied with the results, no?"

"Oh, yes, very much so, Mr. Brady."

"And she reciprocated in kind with proper payment, I trust. No notes were accepted..."

"I turned in the receipt to Mr. Fredericks on my return."

"Very well, Gabriel," He pats him on the shoulder escorting him to the door with Tim close behind. "But you must promise me, you will put pen to paper and submit this tale to The Photographic Art Journal."

Gabriel raises an eyebrow.

"This is the new publication devoted to our profession currently in the works by Mr. Henry H. Snelling. He plans to release the first issue this January and he is looking for contributors. Here is his calling card. Tell him, you have my well-earned recommendation."

"Thank you ever so kindly, Mr. Brady."

"Now if you will excuse me, I have an appointment with Daniel Bixby to keep."

"You mean the proprietor of Bixby's Hotel at Park Place?"

"The very same."

"I understand his hotel is a literary oasis of sorts. Is there something I should know, Mr. Brady?"

"I am not at liberty to say."

"I can assure you, Timothy and I, will keep it in the strictest confidence."

"Gabriel, I cannot discuss the matter. I must take every precaution."

CHAPTER 23 — SEPIATONE

1985

Saturday afternoon at The Photography Workshop, there is no route going out today. George and Duke are out back.

Steve and Pernille stop in to buy some rolls of film as I try to say hello in Danish. My tongue gets all tangled. Pernille smiles at my attempt as I open the little yellow Kodak box and take the canister of film out.

Steve has that look. He is about to ask me something.

I thread the 35mm leader and make sure the sprockets are properly set in the cogs of the advance mechanism as I shut the back door of the camera. I watch the spindle turn as I cock the shutter.

"Hey Dan, what if you took us down to The City?"

"The City?" I repeat. I haven't been to The City in a long time.

"C'mon, be a good ambassador," says Steve. "Do it for Pernille."

"Okay, Steve, we'll go tomorrow. Meet me at the Station."

As it gets near closing time, Duke comes from behind the black curtain and checks the clock on the wall. "Alright, lock the door! Flip the closed sign. It is time to sepiatone."

Saturday is sepia day. I head out back. The lights are still on in the darkroom. George busies himself at the kitchen sink mixing chemicals – the water is running. Duke is unpacking the large manila envelopes and setting the photographs out on the work counter.

"Shouldn't we turn the lights off, George?"

"No, we can sepiatone with the lights on."

I am greatly disappointed to hear this. I much prefer the orange glow of the safelight. I find comfort in the dark and have nothing but disdain for the buzzing fluorescent lights flickering above. I observe George as he uncaps one bottle and mixes it with water checking the temperature. Suddenly, I am overcome with the offal sulfur stench of the outhouse. I gasp for air.

Duke laughs, "See, this is why we sepiatone with the door locked."

"How do you stand it? It's like somebody set off a stink-bomb."

"You'll get used to it. After a while, you won't even notice it."

Duke brings over the black and white copies to be sepiatoned while George explains the process. "First, we will bleach the prints in this first tray. Then we will bring the prints back with the sepiatone."

George gently places the black and white prints in the tray. One of these is a turn-of-the-century photograph of my great-grandparents. I look at the hand-written caption at the bottom, "Bridget (Delia) Mitchell and John Lynch, April 23, 1893." This is their wedding day. Delia stands in a long gown, gently resting her hand on her husband's shoulder. John sits there proud — stomach in, chest out, shoulders set straight, carnation in his lapel, watch chain dangling from his vest, and his hat upon his knee.

George lifts one corner to create a gentle ripple back and forth. Slowly the prints begin to fade away in the bleach tray… the deep blacks give way to faint outlines in this reverse development process until only the ghost of an image remains.

George suddenly gets distracted. He is a south-paw. His mind is elsewhere as he stares down at his left-hand in the running water overflowing from the tray into the stainless steel sink. "I haven't heard this song in ages."

"What song?" I look up at the radio on the shelf.

"Whiter Shade of Pale by Procol Harum," says George.

"Purple Harem?"

"No, no," says George slowly, "Procol Harum."

The music is slowly swirling overhead mixing with the tranquil sound of running water in the sink. "I'll never forget that wedding I photographed. The organist played the opening chords to this song, it filled the whole church."

The ride cymbal is chiming as the drummer pounds a slow dirge on the bottom. Gary Brooker sings the opening line. "We skipped the light fandango…"

"You were a wedding photographer, George?"

"For a time, that's the only way a photographer can make a living — it's either that or work in a portrait studio."

"I was feeling kinda seasick…"

"What about Ansel Adams?" I studied his two books, The Negative and The Print. I imagined myself one day out in the wilderness, camping out, tent set up, coffee pot on the campfire, pack-mule nearby, waiting patiently for days by my tripod for just the right cloud formation – a thunderhead. Then and only then, would I expose my 8x10 plate.

"Ansel Adams was one in a million. Listen to that Hammond B3."

"What's that?"

"That's the type of organ we had in our band, the same as Procol Harum. We used to play this song through our Leslie amps."

"I've heard of Marshall, Vox, and Fender amps, but not Leslie."

"These amplifiers created that sound – that surround sound – once you flicked that switch, the speakers started spinning around and around like a merry-go-round inside the cabinet. It was considered state-of-the-art back in the 60s, but now today, it has been replaced with all these effects pedals." He sighs a bit. "It's just not the same."

The song ends with the refrain, "Turned a whiter shade of pale." I think of myself in this darkroom all summer long, not getting out in the sun. George transfers the bleached-white photographs to the sepia bath — restoring them — magically bringing the ghosts back to life in brown and white. As the wedding photograph of Delia and John Lynch reappears in the tray, I recall further conversations with Adrienne, just as memories fade away then return at different times.

"What exactly happened to Daniel?"

"He was killed on the job like his father."

"How do you mean?"

"Your great-grandfather, John Lynch was killed working in the sewer. Delia was devastated, but she still had Danny. But then he was crushed to death in an elevator shaft — the newspaper said he was a hero. He saved the lives of two of his co-workers – but his death sent poor Delia over the edge. She was never the same."

Thirty years pass by... I replay those conversations as I look at those old photographs. 'The newspaper said he was a hero...' There must have been some newspaper article about the accident. I hear the advice from my copy-editing teacher who worked at The New York Times. "If your mother tells you she loves you, you had better check it out." I think back to my days at the Columbia Journalism Review helping Margaret Kennedy, the fact-checker. She had a dogged determination in tracking down facts.

And so, I began my search through the archives for these two laborers killed on the job – father and son, John and Daniel Lynch. I look again at the wedding date scrawled on the photograph, April 23, 1893. I discovered an article about the death of John Lynch in the New York Sun, dated August 27, 1908, with the headline, "Comrades Saw Him Drown — while they tugged to save him from sewer flood."

A chill comes over me as I read the harrowing account. "Lynch was kneeling in the trunk sewer poking away at the obstruction in the lateral drain when May and McCarthy noticed a heavy volume of water coming through the trunk sewer behind Lynch's back.

"'Get out, Jack! She's coming from the other way!' cried May, as he and McCarthy climbed up the ladder..."

A year passes by, I look at a recently discovered photograph of John Lynch that a distant cousin, Clare Higgins e-mailed to me on August 9th, 2015. "Your great-grandfather was studying to be a priest," Clare informs me. "Right before he was supposed to be ordained, he told his mother he could not go through with it. She kicked him out of the house. The entire family ostracized him. He had nowhere to go, so he emigrated to the U.S. with his brother James."

I look again at his photograph. He was a drop-out like me, but he didn't just flunk college chemistry. He had God and the Catholic Church to contend with, not to mention vows of poverty, obedience, and last but not least, celibacy. His mother never spoke to him again.

Clare tells me, his brothers talked him into going back home to Ireland — to make amends with his mother. But she refused to open the door. Had he stayed in the priesthood, he would not have married Delia, and none of us in our big extended family would be here. Then again, he would not have died in that sewer.

Clare then sent me a photograph of my grandmother that I had never seen before – Nora Lynch in her first communion dress. The date is 1908, most likely April or May – several months before the accident.

If her father second-guessed himself about the priesthood, this photograph must have helped ease that doubt. Looking at her, I am reminded of Virginia O'Hanlon listening to her father's advice, "If you see it in The Sun, it's so." Only the newspaper account she read in the N.Y. Sun wasn't about the existence of Santa Claus, it was about the death of her father.

The oldest brother, Daniel J. Lynch, was killed on the job while working in an elevator shaft on November 2, 1917. I find the article in The Sun, dated November 4, 1917 with the headline:

"Giant Gives Life to Save 2 — Strength Holds Back Lift Settling on Weaker Mates."

"Daniel J. Lynch was only 22 years old, but he was six feet tall and weighed more than 200 pounds – a muscular giant, fellow workers in the building at 43 West Fourth Street, called him... the elevator, unnoticed began to settle down into the shaft... They shouted for help and Lynch braced himself, making a bridge of his own body to protect the frailer men... The injuries that Lynch suffered caused his death yesterday at St. Vincent's Hospital."

I never knew the specifics of Daniel's accident until last year. This is the hospital where I was born. I look again at the address – 43 West Fourth Street – I passed by this building on my way to the library at New York University.

George transfers the photos to the sepia bath restoring them – bringing them back in brown and white. I wonder what tomorrow will bring going back to The City.

He sighs a dissatisfied sigh.

"What's wrong, George?"

"No matter what I do, I can never make the sepia prints look as good as the olden days. Just take a look at that original. See the luster of the chocolate brown in that print, we can never duplicate that. Not with the paper and chemicals we use today."

Suddenly, I travel Back to the Future and fast forward to the year 2000. I am sitting in Photoshop class, taking notes – the teacher points out the sepia action tool. If only George could see the ease in sepiatoning with Photoshop — no bleach, no foul-smelling chemicals… all with one mouse click.

"C'mon, Danny, let's hang the prints up to dry and head home."

CHAPTER 24 — PRECAUTION

1850

Hand upon the base of Daguerre, Brady taps his ring upon the white marble.

"Where is Mr. Pettifog? He must be present for this announcement."

"I'm right in front of you, Bat Eyes!"

"So you are." He takes a deep breath, tugs down on his waistcoat, and tries to loosen the black silk cravat about his neck. "We mustn't have a repeat of the Jenny Lind affair. Let me assure you all, this is a sitting like no other."

"Tell us who it is then?" says Mr. Pettifog on behalf of the staff.

"Unfortunately, I cannot and will not."

"And why not?"

"I must take every precaution... there is a traitor in our midst."

"That is preposterous. How dare you insinuate such malfeasance without warrant."

"Without warrant? Need I remind you of the near riot we had? When you all swore an oath not to divulge the name of Jenny Lind? Someone here amongst you is a traitor to our cause! C'mon now, step forward!"

There is a long pause. Mr. Pettifog steps forward and hangs his head.

Mr. Brady steps back, aghast. "Et tu Brutus? So it was you, Peter? You were my rock."

"No, you blasted fool! Look about you. We hold more allegiance to you than we hold to ourselves. No one breathed a word of Jenny Lind – not I, not Professor Tarbox, not the buff-boys, not the coaters, and certainly not the fair ladies in the coloring room, and certainly not Mr. Fredericks. What we all experienced with Miss Jenny is a phenomenon the likes of which we shall never see again... Surely you can understand that, Mat? It was Jenny Lind mania pure and simple. Now then, tell us who it is!"

"I cannot."

"Come now, Mat. Out with it. Tell us."

"Yes, Mr. Brady," says Mary Higbie stepping forward. "Please tell us. I shan't tell a soul. I promise."

Crouching down to her eye level, "I have every faith in you, Mary."

"Then tell us," she pleads.

"Tell us!" echoes Mr. Pettifog.

Brady turns his back on his audience like a priest facing the altar. He looks at Daguerre chiseled in white, smooth and polished. He mutters a few words to himself and turns around.

"Don't you see, this is the most sought-after subject for a sitting in the history of photography, even more so than Daguerre himself."

"But that's what you always say, Mat."

"This time I mean it in all sincerity. No one has been able to capture this subject – not Jeremiah Gurney, not Martin M. Lawrence, and certainly not the Brother's Meade. Mr. Chilton had him in his sights. He nearly had him. There the subject sat when all of a sudden he jumped from the chair and refused to sit. After that daguerreotypers were afraid of him."

"Who Mat? For God's sake tell us!"

"I cannot reveal his name. This shall be the most prized trophy hanging on my gallery wall. What if Mr. Gurney gets wind of this?"

Mr. Pettifog holds up his hand. "Stop right there, Mathew. You are merely wasting your breath. I know of whom you speak. You needn't keep us in the dark any longer. I have figured it out from that bit about Chilton. But let me tell you this, you are wrong on both accounts. There is no spy amongst us and there shall be no onslaught of onlookers breaking down the doors to see this precious subject of yours. I will shout his name from the rooftop for all of Broadway to hear, but no one will stop to listen, nor will anyone care a whim. If you don't tell them, I will…" He turns around to face the staff and takes a deep breath.

"You're bluffing, Mr. Pettifog. Whisper it in my ear. That'll be enough out of you." He puts his hand to his shoulder. "Mr. Pettifog is very astute in his observations so I must relent. The subject in question is Fenimore Cooper."

There is a collective gasp amongst the staff – jumbled reactions spew forth – "Fenimore who? I thought he already expired. Is this to be a post-mortem then?"

Brady raises his arms and tries to quiet the staff. "I can assure you, James Fenimore Cooper is very much alive. I saw him this morning at Bixby's, his hotel corner of Park Place. He came out in his morning gown."

Brady pauses to look at his captive audience.

"Oh, it was a sight to behold, standing there in his slippers and his rumpled night cap squinting his eyes in the sunlight. He asked me to excuse him till he had dismissed a caller. I told him what I had come for. Said he, 'How far from here is your gallery?' 'Only two blocks,' was my reply. He said he would be right along…

"Oh my goodness, look at the time. He should be here in half an hour. But, what a jolly mood he was in, standing there in his morning gown while all of Broadway passed him by – oblivious to whom he was. He reminded me of old Ebenezer Scrooge on Christmas morn giddy with delight. He started walking back with me towards the studio. 'Aren't you forgetting something, Mr. Cooper?'"

"That's right, my caller."

"No, I was referring to your attire, sir. Perhaps something more dignified."

He slapped me on the back, turned around, and shuffled in his slippers up Broadway. Now, we must continue with our preparations – I want the Gallery to look its best. Lydia, I should like you to set the ambiance at the harp."

"Yes, Mr. Brady."

"Hannah, see to it that fresh cut flowers are in all the vases. Mary, you will tend to the canaries. Mr. Fredericks make no appointments until after Mr. Cooper has gone. Turn paying customers away if you must. Make no exceptions. You see, it is absolutely vital that we don't upset Mr. Cooper. We must present a tranquil atmosphere — we must set the sitter at ease."

The staff begins to disperse.

"Here now! The meeting is not adjourned..." Brady shouts. "It is imperative that we do not repeat Mr. Chilton's folly. He made the mistake of speaking about the subject of irritation. Once Chilton opened his mouth and asked an impertinent question, Mr. Cooper snapped shut like a bear trap!" Brady slams his fist down for emphasis. "We must not discuss any unpleasant subjects."

"What sort of subjects Mr. Brady? So, we know what not to mention," asks Mary.

"I think it best not to say, Mary, so you don't inadvertently blurt out that which you wished to avoid."

"I couldn't disagree with you more, Mat."

"What is it now, Mr. Pettifog?"

"I'll tell you all the two words in all the English language not to be uttered in the presence of James Fenimore Cooper."

He stands there quite pleased with himself – all eyes are upon him – he can't hold back the words as they echo to the ceiling, "Thurlow Weed!"

There is a hiss in the audience.

"Thurlow Weed?" someone in the back asks.

Tim thinks this a sinister name.

"Yes, that was the name that Chilton mentioned. Mr. Cooper brought that rapscallion journalist Thurlow Weed to court for libel not once, but seven times. So, we would all do well, to hide the dailies from the sitting area. Cooper is not fond of the newspaper press."

"Thank you for your insight, Mr. Pettifog."

"Not at all, Mr. Brady."

"Places everyone, I expect Mr. Cooper at any moment."

Gabriel steps forward and quietly tries to capture the attention of Mr. Brady engaged in conversation with Mr. Fredericks.

"Yes, Gabriel..."

He bows his head. "I humbly offer my assistance in the sitting, Mr. Brady. It would be an honor."

"I will consider, but please do keep this under your hat."

"Yes, Mr. Brady."

"Knock at my office door in two minutes time so we may freely discuss the matter further."

"Yes, Mr. Brady."

"And bring along young Tim."

With a knock on the door and a turn of the knob, Tim follows close on the heels of Gabriel's footsteps. He finds Mr. Brady staring out the Fulton Street window looking at the obelisk to Thomas Addis Emmet.

"Do you know what one barrister said about Fenimore Cooper after he made his closing argument in one of his libel suits against the newspaper press – 'he was splendidly eloquent,' said he to me… 'I have heard nothing like it, not since the days of Emmet.' "

"Yes, Mr. Brady, I've heard Mr. Cooper is a most litigious person – a misanthrope of sorts."

"That is the prevailing wisdom, Gabriel, but more often than not, the prevailing wisdom can be dead wrong."

He turns around to face them checking his pocket watch. "Now then there is the matter of your request to assist in the sitting of Mr. Cooper. My concern is this, Gabriel… please take a seat… you as well Tim, a lesson to be learned.

"Now, this is the same concern I have with not just you, but with all the various operators who have worked under my employ over the years. They seem to forget whose roof they are working under, and that is an unfortunate oversight. This is the house of Brady, much like the house of Tiffany. You don't suppose Charles Tiffany cuts each diamond himself. No, he has dedicated diamond cutters for that. But rest assured, you won't find their name stamped to the jewel case. When you worked for Mr. Lawrence and prior to that Mr. Plumbe, the portraits you photographed are the work product of the studio, not the operator. Mr. Lawrence provides you with the camera, the plates, the studio, the assistants, and most important of all, the clientele."

"I understand this, Mr. Brady, from the days working at my father's print shop."

"I am not so sure you do, Gabriel. I've heard you discuss one of your descriptive daguerreotypes. What is it called now?"

"The Past, Present, and Future."

"Yes, that's it. Well, I've heard you discuss this as one of your works when that is not the case."

"But I am the one who captured the pose."

"Gabriel, you merely focused the camera and removed the lens cap.

That is all... Mr. Lawrence is the one who made it all possible. You were working under his roof at the time. It is his work product."

"I understand, Mr. Brady."

"Now, if you wish to assist in the sitting of Fenimore Cooper, I want to make doubly sure you understand that my name shall be stamped on that daguerreotype, not Martin M. Lawrence, not John Plumbe, and certainly not Gabriel Harrison. You may focus the camera, but I shall set the sitter at ease and capture the expression. You will replace the lens cap at my signal. Do I make myself crystal clear?"

"Like Waterford, Mr. Brady. This will be an honor."

"So, you have said... Very well, Gabriel, someday perhaps when you run your own studio, you shall more fully understand."

There is a knock on the door. Mary Higbie pokes her head in.

"Mister James Fenimore Cooper to see you, sir."

CHAPTER 25 — FENIMORE

1850

Legs set apart in a sturdy stance like an old captain bracing for the pitch of a rolling sea, standing all alone, staring past the gallery wall, looking off into the distance at an unseen infinite horizon just leaning on his cane still as a statue. Brady pauses a moment before making his approach, taking shelter by the coat rack observing this enigmatic figure of a man, James Fenimore Cooper. He is all alone in the gallery save for Lydia Littlejohn at the harp striking notes gentle as raindrops on the lake. Brady hears the words of William Cullen Bryant spoken shortly after taking his portrait when discussing this much sought-after subject in question who had eluded him these many years… "You must approach him gingerly. He is like the bark of the cinnamon."

"Bark of the cinnamon?" said I.

"Yes," Bryant explained, "he has a rough astringent rind without, an intense sweetness within."

Approach the bark of the cinnamon gingerly, repeats Brady to himself as he walks softly towards the stout figure standing solid.

"Mr. Cooper, so good of you to drop by…"

Dead silence – there is no response, no acknowledgement, not even the blink of an eye. Cooper stands there unflinching like a guard outside Buckingham Palace at his post.

Perhaps he did not hear me. My voice is rather soft. I never had an excess of confidence. I've always been diffident despite all my failed attempts to be more assertive and outgoing. I've always reverted back into my shell — my shy old self. He stands there, still as a white marble statue, completely oblivious to my existence. Do I err on the side of persistence or patience? Do I annoy or assert myself by repeating my introduction?

He takes a nervous breath in anxious anticipation…

The marble statue suddenly comes to life in a shocking instant. He lifts his thin cane and points to the gallery wall — covered from floor to ceiling in portraits of all shapes and sizes.

"Who captured that image?"

Brady is unsure of which portrait he is referring to… He goes to Cooper's side, eye-level with his shoulders and follows the invisible line from the tip of the cane to the portrait of Thomas Cole on the gallery wall.

"I captured that image here, Mr. Cooper, right here in this very studio, only a short time before Thomas left us."

The big burly man with broad shoulders coughs into his fist. "Why has no one shown me this before? Why was I not aware of its existence? I must possess this doggerel-type."

Brady smiles warmly at the mangled pronunciation of his good profession, but he knows better than to correct James Fenimore Cooper.

"You certainly shall, Mr. Cooper. I will see to it…" He turns around, "Timothy, summon Mr. Pettifog. We require a copy of the Thomas Cole daguerreotype post-haste — in our finest Moroccan leather case."

"Yes, Mr. Brady."

The elderly gentleman, nearly 61, turns around to look Brady in the eye. "That is most kind of you sir. I shall gladly pay you. Name your price. I pull no purse-strings, I have deep pockets not long for this world."

"Oh, Mr. Cooper I couldn't… Put your coin purse away. After all, he was your Kindred Spirit. He would want you to have his portrait."

Cooper turns back and points his cane again at Thomas Cole. "To think he devoted canvas after canvas to illustrating scenes from my novels… so selfless was he."

Brady nods in agreement, "I recall visiting his Broadway studio at the corner of Wall Street to see his depiction of Cora kneeling at the feet of Tamenund. It took my breath away…"

"Falls of the Kaaterskill…" says Cooper in soft agreement, conjuring up an image of the painting in their minds.

Brady feels an instant connection, "I often wondered if that was Uncas standing there at the second tier of the falls…"

"The vantage point mystified me – how did he achieve that perspective? His imagination soared high as the hawk circling above," says Cooper.

"His canvases are so sublime…" says Brady dreamily, "brushstrokes dabbed from the heavens."

In his peripheral vision, something out of the corner of his eye, captures Cooper's attention. His cane shakes violently as if he were holding a saber pointing to a portrait at his right in the corner, about to thrust through the silver plate past the breast bone into the very heart of Horace Greeley sitting there in a rumpled frock coat, hands folded upon his lap holding a crumpled copy of his paper, The Tribune.

"Higgle!" seethes Cooper between his clenched teeth.

"Higgle!" cries Brady almost in anguish at the sudden turn of events. He feels the good tide draining out to sea leaving him high and dry. I shall be left foundering on the rocks, just like Mr. Chilton watching Fenimore Cooper storm away.

"That's what Mr. Greeley wrote in his paper, calling it the Cooperage of The Tribune, taunting me the very next day after the jury ruled in my favor. But they reduced the settlement from $3,000 to a mere $200. 'We won't higgle a bit about the balance,' said Greeley. Then he had the sheer audacity to offer me a column in his Tribune for ten days to print word for word whatever I liked... then no doubt he would graciously give me the rope with which to hang myself. Oh, how I despise the penny press. They seek to undermine the publishing profession with their monstrous steam presses and their voracious appetites for the printed word. How can reputable publishers compete with the newspaper press churning out the latest novel from London straight off the steamship without any regard to copyright, printing it in one day, and selling it for sixpence while Harpers charges $1.00 then using all their newsboys to sell these novels as extras. They have set out to ruin all publishers."

Gabriel tiptoes into the room. "Mr. Brady, we have finished with the preparations."

"Oh, thank you Gabriel, allow me the honor of introducing you to Mr. James Fenimore Cooper. Mr. Cooper, this is my able assistant, Gabriel Harrison."

"I've heard that name somewhere before. I am quite sure of it... Enlighten an old man if you will."

"Perhaps you saw me perform the part of Othello at the National Theatre."

"No, that is not it..."

"Perhaps you have seen my letters to the press calling for a monument to Captain James Lawrence."

"That's it. So you are that same Gabriel Harrison. You have single-handedly restored my faith in the youth of America, and dare I say, to some extent, the newspaper press. If memory serves me correctly, you were successful in enlisting the help of Moses Beach from the Sun and Horace Greeley of the Tribune."

"Yes, that is correct, Mr. Cooper."

"I must inform you that I served under Captain Lawrence on board the U.S.S. Wasp."

"I had no idea, Mr. Cooper."

"I am an old sea dog through and through – taking to the inland seas of Lake Ontario and Lake Champlain."

"Mr. Cooper, may I ask what prompted you to leave the Navy and pick up the pen? You see, I too have literary aspirations."

"You do, do you? Well, I will offer neither words of encouragement nor words of warning. And I won't bore you with the story of my life, but I will say this... the year was 1820 sitting with my dear wife Susan in our parlour in Mamaroneck. I finished an English novel, laid it down on the table and told her, 'I believe I could write a better myself.' "

"Then prove it," said she. "Take no precaution, James, just forge ahead and write with abandon."

"And there you have it... She gave me the motivation and the title for

173

my first novel, Precaution."

Turning his head, "All right then, Mr. Brady, let's get down to the task at hand. You have been most patient with me."

"Right this way, Mr. Cooper."

"I trust my attire is to your liking – more appropriate than my morning gown and sleeping cap."

"Very much so… if you would oblige me in removing your white gloves."

Cooper takes a seat, leaning his arm upon a table holding the gloves in his left, the walking cane in his right as if it were a writing implement. The dark satin of his frock coat is offset by the deep blacks of his velvet collar, his cream waist coat contrasts with his white shirt.

"I must confess, Mr. Brady, this is all foreign to me. I've never had a likeness taken."

"Let me assure you, Mr. Cooper, there is nothing to it. Rest your head back a bit and let the clamp support you, and the camera shall do the rest. That's it…"

"You won't make me look the fool?"

"Oh no, Mr. Cooper, my plan is this: we shall take half-a-dozen sittings then you shall not be restricted to one pose, but have six results to choose from. Will that be agreeable?"

"That sets my mind at ease, Mr. Brady. I am so used to people trying to portray me in a bad light – not truthfully representing who I am as a person. I firmly believe in the freedom of expression. I bear no ill will to the newspaper press when they express their opinion, much as I may disagree with them. The only instance where I have taken them to task is when they distort the truth. That I will not countenance. They must adhere to the truth."

Brady gently rests his palm on the rosewood camera as if laying his hand upon the Bible before swearing an oath. "Mr. Cooper, this is a faithful, impartial witness."

"I've heard that same claim from the press. What is the term they hide behind… forgive me my age… what is it now? Don't tell me… ah, yes, objectivity! I trust your camera the same as the newspapers. I have read reviews of my History of the U.S. Navy that were pure malice with a reckless disregard for the truth — just as I have seen doggerel-types that have made proud men wince with shame at their own image – left them afraid to look at their own likeness – destroying it with a ball-peen hammer so none other may see it."

"Mr. Cooper, you have my word as a gentleman that I will not permit that to happen. You must trust me and my camera," Brady's voice trails off.

He goes to the wall and takes down the oval mirror holding it over his chest. "See here, Mr. Cooper, take a look — this is what the sun shall etch in silver upon the mirror — the mirror with a memory."

Cooper catches sight of himself in the looking glass. I look in such a harried state – the perturbed expression, one of uneasy caution, those eyes of mine darting about the room looking for a quick escape. Who is this person? That can't be me, can it? Compose yourself. This instant! He begins to recognize a familiar face, an old friend in the reflection. Then suddenly all the anxiety washes away as he breathes a sigh of relief.

"That's it, Mr. Cooper. That is the expression I was after. Fix your gaze in the mirror. Gabriel, insert the plate. Remove the cap…"

"That was quite painless, was it not?" says Brady as Gabriel replaces the cap.

"How soon till the portrait is ready?"

"Oh, in about ten minutes, let us adjourn to my office for a cup of tea, right this way if you please, while my assistant finishes the plates."

CHAPTER 26 — WASHINGTON

1850

Cooper takes a seat, hooking his cane to the armrest. There is a knock on the door as Mary enters balancing the tea service tray, setting it down, "some buttercakes compliments of Mr. Pettifog."

"Thank you kindly, Mary. Now then, Mr. Cooper, if you are not completely satisfied, I would be only too happy to…"

"Washington!" Cooper shouts. "Washington!" he repeats, crumbs at the side of his mouth.

Brady takes a sip from his tea cup, pinky daintily extended out. He turns about to look around. "George Washington? Sadly, Father Time and fifty years prevented the camera from capturing his likeness…"

"NO! Not his namesake!"

Brady looks baffled. Cooper is annoyed.

"Washington Irving! Over there on the far wall!"

"Oh yes, he is one of my most prized portraits." At that instant, Brady sees Cooper's face wince in pain and tries to recover from the unintended slight for he had heard that Cooper brooded a little over the attention extended to his brother-author. "Next to you of course, Mr. Cooper… Yours shall take a most prominent place on my gallery wall."

Cooper gets up and staggers over in his sailor-like way to the portrait of Washington Irving. Standing closer, he takes up his monocle dangling from a black felt string for closer observation.

"Mr. Irving was a most delicate person at his sitting," says Brady looking over his shoulder.

"Hmm," says Cooper in a curious way, skeptical and squinting.

Brady can hear the wheels turning. He is about to make an observation of some kind.

"Did you take this doggerel-type, Mr. Brady?"

Do not correct the pronunciation of Mr. Cooper. Every bit the prosecutor, he has learned well the ways of the law from all his years in litigation. The commanding tone of a sea captain, I feel myself sitting on the witness stand, hand upon the Bible. The furrowed brow is waiting for my response. 'Need I remind you sir that you are under oath,' he shall say to me then I hear myself stammer.

"Well, Mr. Cooper, I cannot exactly lay claim to this daguerreotype."

"Doggerel-type, you say? This, Mr. Brady, is clearly not a doggerel-type. Not in the true sense of the word."

He watches Cooper take up his monocle, shuttering his left eye, peering closer for fine examination like a captain on a quarterdeck studying the horizon with one eye through his spyglass. He waits for the verdict.

"I see no transverse grooves, no scratches, but more to the point, I see no warts on his nose."

"Warts? Whatever do you mean, sir?"

"Don't quibble with me, Mr. Brady. You know exactly what of I speak."

"Mr. Irving did not have one wart upon his nose. If he did, the camera would have captured it."

"Yes, so it seems." He takes a step closer. The monocle pops out and falls down to his chest. "But I don't see any wrinkles... no saddle-bags about the eyes... no crow's feet... Where is the delineation?"

"Delineation?"

"You realize Samuel Morse is a close confidant of mine – a member of my Bread and Cheese Club. You studied under him, no?"

"As a matter of fact, I did."

"Then why does this portrait of Washington Irving have the appearance of a charcoal sketch without the minute attention to detail of a doggerel-type?"

"Because..." Oh my, the panther has me by the jugular. I feel the tip of his canine tooth pressing down to the point of puncture, the sandpaper tongue ready to lap up my gushing blood spurting out with each pump of the heart. I really do wish I was the one who captured this image of Washington Irving. I've told so many people over the years that I've begun to believe it myself. I've embellished this story so many times, I'm not sure where the truth hides beneath this heap of lies...

"Because why, Mr. Brady? I will have at the truth!"

"Permit me to explain..."

"By all means, continue."

"You have a keen eye, Mr. Cooper. This is actually a copy of a daguerreotype. There were certain imperfections to the original that would not reproduce well so we made a copy — we photographed the daguerreotype then my artiste in residence Mr. Henry F. Darby used his oils to smooth over the imperfections while bringing forth the image of Mr. Irving who was shrouded behind the clouds and mists of a fogged daguerreotype."

"A fogged doggerel-type? Where is the original?"

"I keep it in my desk for safe-keeping."

"Show it to me, I must see the original for myself."

Brady goes over to his desk and looks through his drawers while Cooper looks out the Fulton Street window at the Steeple of St. Paul's."

"I know it is here somewhere... I am quite sure of it."

Strong sturdy stance, Cooper takes a deep breath and reaches in his breast pocket for his flask. "Fine view you have here." He turns around to see Brady fumbling through his desk. "Here take a nip to settle your nerves. I didn't intend to cause you any trouble."

Bent over to the side, "Oh, it is no trouble at all, Mr. Cooper. In fact, I'm glad you brought this subject up for discussion."

Cooper shoulder taps Brady with his flask.

"Oh, I couldn't, Mr. Cooper, but thank you kindly."

He reaches down to the bottom drawer and pulls it out revealing an assortment of daguerreotypes. "Eureka! I've hit the mother lode."

"C'mon then, I've never known an Irishman to turn down a drink. Remember what Diedrich Knickerbocker wrote, "when life hangs heavy… have a quieting draft out of Rip Van Winkle's flagon."

Holding a stack, Brady takes a swig. "Ah, thank you Mr. Cooper that slakes my thirst. Now let's see now, ah yes, here it is."

Cooper looks over his shoulder at the original daguerreotype of Washington Irving looking past the numerous scratches and transverse grooves. "It is just as you so eloquently described it… shrouded behind the clouds and mists of fog."

He takes hold of the daguerreotype walking over to the portrait hanging on the wall, holding it up for a side-by-side comparison. Squinting with the monocle, his head turns back and forth closely studying the two images. He turns about face, the monocle drops down swaying about his waist coat by its black tether.

"You still haven't answered my question…"

The old prosecutorial tone of voice returns. He has the dogged determination of a blood-hound and I am a black bear up a tree with no place to go.

"Did you take this doggerel-type, Mr. Brady?"

"Well, Mr. Cooper, it was actually Mr. John Plumbe who captured the likeness of Mr. Irving. He gave this daguerreotype to me for safekeeping…"

"So I would like to establish this matter for the record. You were not the photographer of Washington Irving. Correct?"

"Yes, that is correct. Mr. Plumbe entrusted me with his most prized daguerreotypes just after he closed up shop and set out to find his pot of gold in California leaving behind his creditors not to mention his poor wife and children."

"So he deeded the rights to his work?"

"Not in those exact words, but I remunerated him handsomely for these priceless artifacts of our national identity. You see, Mr. Plumbe was not known for his dedication to proper plate preparation which is why I tried to correct some of the defects so they would meet with my standards."

"So essentially you are like a publisher in some sense reproducing the work of an author."

"I never thought of it that way, Mr. Cooper, but I suppose I am a publishing house of sorts."

There is a knock on the door. Tim enters holding several copies. "Mr. Pettifog asked me to bring you the daguerreotypes."

"That's a good boy, now set them down on the desk for Mr. Cooper to look over."

"Great merciful Lord! Is that how old I really look? I don't recognize this cadaver... put the ha'pennies on my eyes. There must have been some mistake in preparing this plate."

"Look how distinguished you look, Mr. Cooper."

"I look absolutely ghastly — a ghost not long for this world. Well, at least this shall satisfy the demand of my publisher who has been pestering me to have my likeness taken."

He sighs, disinterested, he places his own likeness down, and takes up the Washington Irving plate.

"I must say, Brady, I much prefer the original — the intrinsic beauty inherent in a doggerel-type, or should I more properly say daguerreotype..."

Brady is thoroughly impressed with Cooper's pronunciation, but resists his proclivity to interrupt. Instead, he just listens to the old man.

"I find reassurance in the original – this is a truthful representation of Mr. Washington Irving, not some artist's flattering romantic vision intended to please the paying customer. This is the portrait of Washington I want to possess, not the artist's rendering, but the original with all the scratches and transverse grooves as you call them. This is the one I desire."

"Yes, we shall see to it at once," says Brady. "Timothy, tell Mr. Pettifog this is the copy Mr. Cooper desires."

"Savage realism, Boy! That's what you tell your Mr. Pettifog! I want the unvarnished truth! To paraphrase Patrick Henry, Give me a Daguerreotype, or Give me Death!"

"Yes, Mr. Cooper," says Tim a bit frightened.

"Here is an extra shilling as incentive for your pocket and four for Mr. Pettifog."

"Thank you, Mr. Cooper."

On his return, Tim hands him not one, but two daguerreotypes bound in the finest Moroccon leather cases.

"What's this now? Why two?"

"This one is Washington Irving and this is Thomas Cole."

"Ah yes, I nearly forgot." He pushes the button to open the case. He says in a hush, "Thomas..." His eyes well up. "This is mine to keep?"

"Yes, Mr. Cooper."

"Thomas opened my eyes. He could have remained in Europe and painted the majestic Alps, but he chose to paint our humble Catskills, making his home there, devoting his life to capturing its natural beauty and preserving it for future generations."

Brady nods in agreement. "In my humble opinion, Asher Durand should have placed you standing in the Clove next to Thomas Cole in Kindred Spirits, instead of William Cullen Bryant, with all due respect to Mr. Bryant."

"Respect? Mr. Bryant does not have my respect," says Cooper. "I cannot countenance a man afraid to speak his mind. He refused to review my work telling his editor, 'Ah sir, he is too sensitive a creature to touch. He thinks his works his own property, instead of being the property of the public to whom he has given them.' "

"Still, I firmly believe your initials should have been carved into that tree... Thomas was your Kindred Spirit – the literary and landscape artists standing there."

"That is kind of you to say, Brady, but I am of the opinion that it should have been Washington Irving, and not me, and certainly not WC carved into that tree. When I look at Falls of the Kaaterskill, I hear the words in the Postscript."

"Postscript?" asks Brady. "What Postscript are you referring to?"

"In Rip Van Winkle, sir," pipes in Tim standing quietly there. "I beg your pardon, I didn't mean to interrupt."

"Go on, boy," says Cooper amused and startled.

"That's at the very end of the story..."

"Recite it, if you can."

"Once upon a time, however, a hunter who had lost his way penetrated to the Garden Rock, where he beheld a number of gourds placed in the crotches of trees..." Tim pauses searching for the next line. "I am sorry, I've lost my way. My father tells it much better."

Cooper pats the boy on the back and continues in his commanding, narrator voice: "When a great stream gushed forth, which washed him away and swept him down precipices, where he was dashed to pieces, and the stream made its way to the Hudson and continues to flow to the present day; being the identical stream known by the name of the Kaaters-Kill."

"Well done, Mr. Cooper! If only Mr. Irving were sitting beside me to hear your recitation. He would be thoroughly impressed with your skills as an orator. Tell me, do you often consult with Mr. Irving at your Bread and Cheese Club?"

"No, unfortunately, Mr. Brady, I am an incorrigible sort... I have kept aloof from Mr. Irving for many years. I thought it best to admire his works from a distance lest I should say something that might distract the artist's brush to the canvas."

"That is most admirable."

"Regrettably," pauses Cooper, "Mr. Irving has misinterpreted this distance. For some reason, he believes that I cherish some ill-feeling toward him. Perhaps he listened to the scuttlebutt that said I evidently brooded a little over the relative amount of attention extended to him when that could not be further from the case."

"It is a pity that you two could not have a sit-down to clear up this misunderstanding, a summit – a meeting of the minds."

"Those were the exact sentiments of my publisher, George Haven Putnam. He tried for years to orchestrate this detente. Fool that I am, I begged off at each and every invitation...

"Then one day, I knocked on Mr. Putnam's door to go over the proofs to a library-edition of my best works. There was a gentleman seated in the visitor's chair with his back turned. I paid him no mind, preoccupied with all the type-setter's mistakes. I was just about to voice my concerns when suddenly Mr. Putnam said, 'Mr. Cooper, here is Mr. Irving.' Oh, how my old, tired heart leapt with joy at the mere mention of his name. I immediately extended my hand then took a chair and sat for an hour chatting about almost every topic of the day."

"That's wonderful – what did you discuss?"

"Oh, a wide range of subjects – I asked if the legend of his namesake were really true? Did George Washington really pick him up as a babe while strolling in a carriage down Broadway with his nurse? He neither affirmed nor denied, but how he smiled, twinkle in his eye. Then I commended him on his vivid description of the Escarpment and Kaaterskill Falls in Rip Van Winkle – how enchanting he made it sound – how it inspired me to write. Then I asked if he often lodged at the Mountain House. He feigned ignorance. I repeated, The Catskill Mountain House, under the management of Charles L. Beach, surely you have been there, I asked. You know the place, Mr. Brady?"

"Of course, I do, that is where Julia and I took our honeymoon before venturing to Niagara Falls."

"Well, Mr. Irving had never heard of it. So, I pressed the matter as I am sometimes want to do... Call it my proclivity to play the prosecutor. I tried yet again to refresh his memory. 'Have you not viewed The Mountain House by Sarah Cole, Thomas' sister?' He stared at me with glassy eyes as if I were speaking a foreign tongue. 'Come now, Washington, surely you have been there! This is where the odd-looking personages played at nine-pins in your tale about Rip.' "

"Then he tapped me on the arm and motioned me closer to whisper out of earshot of Mr. Putnam, 'When I wrote the story I had never been on the Catskills.' "

"Never been on the Catskills!" I shouted. Mr. Putnam's jaw dropped along with his gold pen. We looked at each other in stunned silence. Then my shock and indignation turned into a new-found respect. He painted those vivid scenes not as an eye witness, but from pure fabrication, or should I say, imagination. I laughed a hearty laugh, slapping Washington on the back. 'You must go there,' I said. 'Promise me, you will venture to the Mountain House if it's the last thing you do.' He swore a solemn oath. Then I told him, 'Be sure to stop at the Rip Van Winkle House along the Carriage Road.' "

"The Rip Van Winkle House? How could that ever be? asked the author incredulously. "Rip did not really exist."

"So say you. But once you cross the threshold of Rip's house, you will see more spurious relics than all the humbugs at Barnum's American Museum."

Tim interrupts, "You've been to Rip Van Winkle's House?"

"Yes, boy, and so should you. You must go to the Catskills before all the trees are gone — cut down by the tanneries. In short time, there will be nothing left but barren hills like Ireland. Brady, promise me you will take this boy to The Mountain House before it closes down for the winter. We must instill in our youth an appreciation for our country's natural beauty just as Thomas did…"

"Yes, Mr. Cooper, I promise – that has been my intention – to educate the boy."

"That warms my heart." He turns to Tim, "You shall never forget the view once you reach the Escarpment."

"What will I see when I get there?"

"Permit me to answer for you, Mr. Cooper — Creation," says Brady sweeping one hand around him in a circle — all creation, lad."

There is a warm smile on Cooper's face. "No finer interruption have I ever experienced in all my years. That is from The Pioneers, no? I wrote that line such a long, long time ago… back in 1826 before this age of telegraphs and photographs."

Standing rather stiffly from his chair, "well, I have taken too much of your valuable time, Mr. Brady. I thank you for your adept handing of this old salt."

"The honor was all mine, Mr. Cooper."

Brady watches James Fenimore Cooper walk slowly out of his office door, broad shoulders leaning on his thin walking cane.

"Mr. Brady…"

"Yes, Timothy."

"Mr. Cooper left behind his daguerreotype."

"Oh goodness me, Mr. Cooper! Mr. Cooper!"

Brady finds him down the hallway closely examining the painting by J.W. Hill, View from St. Paul's Steeple.

Lost in thought, he doesn't hear Brady.

"Mr. Cooper!"

Turning with a perturbed glare, "Yes, what is it?"

"You've forgotten your daguerreotype, Mr. Cooper."

"So I have indeed... me and my absentmindedness – forever at odds with each other." He opens the leather case in his hand. "What do you call this again? Wait, don't tell me. Let me rattle my mind – that's it – the mirror with a memory."

"Quite right, Mr. Cooper, the mirror with a memory."

"Well, thank you again, Mr. Brady, I must be on my way."

CHAPTER 27 — ASTOR PLACE

1985

Standing on the platform at the Crestwood station, Steve and Pernille look over a map of Manhattan as I pace back and forth. The City, I repeat. It's been a long time since I've been there. A chill passes through me at the mention – like returning to the scene of an accident. I harken back to that cold November night. In the distance, an express train approaches as Pernille peers over the edge of the platform curious to see.

"Stand back!"

The ground begins to quake as the train rumbles down the tracks, barreling full throttle, rocking back and forth.

"Look out! This is the express!"

I pull her back as the train whistle blows – thundering past in a stampeding fury – nearly pulling us into its mighty vortex of wind, momentum, and sound.

In an instant, all is calm on the platform. There is an exhilarating smile on Pernille's face.

"It's okay, Dan. I like to stand close to the edge."

I awoke that strange night — All Soul's Night — unsure of my surroundings. Where am I? This is not my bed. I lift my heavy head. This is not my down pillow. Face plastered to the page of my chemistry book. Crooked neck, I am in a wooden box of some sort. I look up to see vague shapes of bookcases and a red lit Exit sign. I begin to get my bearings... I'm in the library. I take the elevator down. The kind security guard chuckles as he unlocks the door and lets me out into the cold night air.

I walk along West Fourth Street, dark and deserted like an old black and white episode of The Twilight Zone. All alone in the night, there's not a soul around except the echoes of my own footsteps. I feel a chill as I check over my shoulder to see if someone is following me. I pass by that building at 43 West Fourth Street where Daniel Lynch was crushed to death in an elevator shaft. The accident happened on November 2nd, 1917 – All Soul's Day. The newspaper said he was a hero. Giant gives life to save two... I have a long way home. I hope to catch the last train out of Grand Central, before she shuts down for the evening.

I make my way over to Astor Place and walk down the subway stairs. Construction workers are busy working late into the night with jackhammers. They blast away at the white tile box-columns to reveal the original Doric columns hiding underneath. Clouds of white dust are swirling around. Some are down on their hands and knees chiseling away in this restoration process — chipping away at the present to get to the past. Carpenter tool bags are on the floor – white canvas with brown leather.

I am the sole commuter on the platform. I dig through my backpack and find The Courier — NYU's Fortnightly Magazine. The front-page article by Karl Kilb is all about the restoration of Astor Place. November 2nd, 1984, The Place to Be, reads the headline. I look at the blueprint for the kiosk. "The MTA's Adopt-A-Station is restoring the station to its turn-of-the-century grandeur… with the design motifs in the original 1904 landmark."

I read further down. "The station is named for John Jacob Astor, who lived in the area until his death in 1840. Astor's success in the fur trade is commemorated by the terra cotta beaver motif gracing the walls of the station." For some strange reason, I tuck this article away in a safe place for the future.

Ascending the subway stairs, I suddenly step from the dark memory of that November night into the present — a crystal blue summer day just like Dorothy did when she opened the door and crossed that threshold from the black & white world of Dustbowl Kansas. Only this wasn't the Technicolor Land of Oz, this was MTV in Living Color.

Astor Place is a carnival of music videos. Modern English is playing in the background. "I'll stop the world and melt with you," — double-accent on the snare and crash. Joe Strummer is walking down the street with his Mohawk high in the air holding hands with Madonna. Johnny Rotten and Sid Vicious follow close behind punching each other in the shoulder, singing God Save the Queen.

This is London Calling mixed in with Ferris Bueller's Day Off as we stop at Astor Place Haircuts — the Mecca for the MTV Generation. There is a line out the door and down the block as we take our place behind Joey and Dee-Dee Ramone in their motorcycle jackets, long chains dangle from the wallet to the belt. Boy George is standing there chatting with Adam Ant and A Flock of Seagulls as we wait our turn. The line moves fast as an assembly line. There are three floors with barber's chairs crammed in every nook and cranny.

"What'll you have?" asks Lou Reed. Sweet Jane is playing in the background. He points to magazine clippings of head-shots scotch-taped to the wall. Choir boy cuts, Billy Idol spiked cuts, James Dean, and Elvis.

"I want the Larry Mullen, Jr."

Lou doesn't respond. He just stares at me with his big dark eyes.

"He's the drummer in U2," I tell him.

"Listen Opie, I know who Larry is. He gets a razor cut. That's shorter than a Paris Island crew-cut. Are you sure you want to go that short?"

I haven't been to the barber in months. I think back to my days in grammar school when nobody got a haircut, when barber shops nearly went of business in the post-hippie 1970s.

"Stick your head in the desk!" shouts Sister Margaret Louise, my second-grade teacher. I had long hair in Catholic School. Dad didn't have the time to take me to the barber shop – he had seven kids to look after.

"Quick now!" says Sister. "Monsignor McNamara is making his rounds. Hurry now! Before you get expelled." He had a crew-cut and a ruler for inspections. No hippies allowed. I crouched down underneath the table and stuck my head in the cubby hole with my books.

Lou sharpens the straight-edge razor on the belt strap. Sister taught me prayers like the Act of Contrition and Saint Anthony. A few years ago, I read her obituary. Both her parents died in the Spanish Influenza epidemic. She was given up for adoption. The nuns took her in – she converted to Catholicism then joined a convent.

I look in the mirror and see my kindergarten photo – I rolled out of bed in the clothes I wore the day before and walked to school. I didn't have a mother to get me dressed for school. Don't you know it is picture day? My hair is sticking up – all out of place.

Lou holds up a mirror. "You're done."

I look like a fresh recruit.

We turn the corner and step into the Antique Boutique on Broadway, a vintage clothing store. I see a whole rack of Eisenhower jackets from World War II. Eike Jackets, the troops called them, named after General Dwight D. Eisenhower – the architect of the D-Day Normandy Invasion. Madonna wore a similar waist-cut in Desperately Seeking Susan. I see punk-rockers wear them on my walks through The Village. Suddenly, haircuts and clothes from the World War II generation looked cool.

I asked Dad if I could have his Eisenhower jacket hanging in the closet. "Sure," he said. "Try it on." I was 19, the same age he was in 1944 when he landed in Normandy. I wore it all the time.

Pernille taps me on the shoulder. She is wearing a sequined hat with a black feather – she looks like a flapper from the Roaring 20s.

We make our way over to Washington Square then head down Thompson all the way past Houston then Canal in the direction of the World Trade Center. There is a street carnival with fried dough and amusements. We take some photographs at the Brooklyn Bridge then visit South Street Seaport then head over to Battery Park to look at the Statue of Liberty in the distance.

Before we head up top, I show Pernille and Steve my favorite pastime at The World Trade Center. "Let's give her a hug."

"Who?" asks Stephen Hero.

"The World Trade Center."

This is what we did on my first trip back in 1977 with my cousin Chris and my brother Bill. The King Kong movie with Jessica Lange set at the World Trade came out – a remake of the 1933 classic with Fay Wray at the Empire State. We were wearing our 1970s era-parkas on a windy March day. "Let's go right up to her and look up," said Chris. He dared us. There were no obstructions, no set-backs, nothing but one continuous, unbroken line straight up to the heavens.

I motion Pernielle and Steve to come closer. I point down and beckon them. "Closer."

"This will totally freak you out." I warn.

We stand right at the base.

"Hold tight and look up."

We lift our chins and stare straight up at 1,368 feet of silver-colored aluminum alloy into blue infinity. The massive structure, tall as the sky, sways with the wind. Vertigo takes over. We break gravity's grasp, start falling upwards, and feel the Great World Spin.

CHAPTER 28 — NEAR GRACE

1985

Late in the afternoon, we get off the subway at Sheridan Square and walk along West Fourth stopping at a tiny record shop along the way. Down some basement stairs, I duck my head beneath a low transom to buy a beat-up album by The Beau Brummel's. Then at an old bookstore, I find A Dream Play by Strindberg. As we near Washington Square, we head down MacDougal Street passing by the Provincetown Playhouse and begin looking for a place to rest our weary legs and slake our thirst. For a fleeting moment, I hear the distant sounds of Dead Letter Office emanating from a sidewalk café.

I stop to listen. No, it can't be... This is an obscure REM album, almost never played on the radio. I look again at the record sleeve, "Being a compendium of oddities collared and B-sides compiled." I stand like a zombie on the sidewalk. People bump into me as I space out.

"Dan, what's the matter?" asks Steve.

Again, I think of Bartleby. "He had been a subordinate clerk in the Dead Letter Office. Dead letters! Does it not sound like dead men?" I am pretty sure I can hear Crazy in the distance... REM's rendition of a Pylon song.

Steve taps me on the shoulder.

"Let's stop here!" I say as we take a seat at the Red Lion on Bleecker Street.

"Dan, you need to have your first pint of Guinness."

"I've had many a bottle of Guinness, Steve."

"No Dan, Guinness on draft is much different. I'll never forget my first pint." Steve recounts his tale of crossing the Irish Sea, passengers hanging over the side seasick. "I stop in a Dublin pub. The barkeep set the glass down, so I go ahead and grab it. Then he nearly throttles my neck. 'You put that back! You'll not touch that jar, until I've finished with the pour!'" Steve pauses a moment to scratch his chin. "Now, be patient."

I watch the brown, murky stout settle. The hops and barley settle like sludge in an oozing lava lamp.

"There she goes again," plays in the background, a Velvet Underground cover by REM, as we take a seat by the open window and watch The Village walk by. I think of Bob Dylan playing at clubs like the Back Fence, of jazz musicians at the Village Vanguard, and Lou Reed, the godfather of punk, the one who wrote this song.

Steve raises his glass with a Danish toast, "Skoal!"

Our glasses clink, "Skoal!"

"Oh you should have been there, Dan," says Steve as he hoists his pint glass. "Picture us at Jones Beach. It's really crowded. We find a spot. I set out the blanket and turn around for a second."

Pernielle smiles wide holding her glass, foam on her upper lip.

"Then all of a sudden she takes her top off. Everyone at the beach is staring at us. Woa now, Pernille! You can't do that! Put your top back on. Right this second!"

Mike Mills of REM echoes the refrain, "There she goes again."

Pernielle laughs. "You Americans are so uptight. You need to relax."

Steve grabs our empty glasses to fetch another round.

She leans forward. "Dan, Steve is worried about you. He tells me you are no longer at university. You should go back." She does not call it college. She is on holiday, not vacation.

"University is free in Denmark," she tells me.

"Free?" What a concept, like Benjamin Franklin's original intent for libraries. Free to all, I think to myself. Freedom and Knowledge.

As Johnny Rotten sings Holiday in the Sun, Steve plops down the glasses. "Yeah, Dan there's no price tag mentality. No tuition pressure. No designer label degree. You can study whatever you want. I don't need some fancy Ivy League name on my diploma. I'm going to study linguistics at a state school."

If I do go back, I say to myself. I will take courses with reckless abandon in philosophy, astronomy, classical music, photography, history, and literature.

"Listen Dan, I need you to think of a place we can take Pernille before she heads back home. Someplace on a shoe-string budget, someplace where she can see this country. I mean really see…"

"Let me give it some thought."

"That's the thing, Dan. We haven't much time."

"Don't you worry, Steve. I'll think of a place."

As we head home in the direction of Astor Place, crossing Broadway near Grace Church, I stop dead in my tracks as I am wont to do… One time a skate-boarder ran over my shoe and skipped fast-forward in a fall. I extended a helping hand. "Dude, you can't be stopping on Broadway." I've been here before. I'm quite sure of it.

Another time a bike messenger, slammed into me as I abruptly stopped to gaze at Grace in the distance. He had nearly the same refrain, "Man, you just can't stop on Broadway like that." Broadway darts off at an angle to the left, leaving her center-stage for all to see. Where have I seen Grace before? Perhaps it was one of those old stereographs I looked at as a boy in the library – forever etched in my memory.

Off to the right, down East 11th Street is The Ritz, the old rock club. I think of the Irving Berlin tune from 1927 which became a number one hit in the 80s — Puttin' on The Ritz. This is where we saw The Ramones. The mosh pit was a battlefield — a Blitzkrieg Bop — a raucous rumble of punk rockers and crowd surfers. This was the Wild West – general admission – no seats to contain the rabble – a rough-n-tumble stage-diving, pogoing, stampeding herd of thundering buffalo. The floor rumbled beneath our feet. I reached down to pick someone up before he got trampled. The combined body heat of the crowd was a sauna — a sweat-drenching, blast furnace. We went to the sidelines to grab a breather and a beer.

"Hey Bill, look up there," I said pointing up to the balcony.

"Yeah, I see him that's Andy Warhol." My brother was right– you can't miss Andy – that white hair sticks out like an old lady at a Ramones show.

"No, not him," I said. "Look over there." Standing there was Pete Buck and Mike Mills – the guitarist and bass player from REM. "Let's go up and say hello."

"No Dan, we should let them be."

"Well then, what if we brought them a few beers?"

"Okay." So up to the balcony we went with a handful of Heineken's. "Hey Pete, my brother plays a Rickenbacker just like you." He probably couldn't hear a word I said over the roar of The Ramones, but he shook our hands and nodded a big thanks.

Then one summer night — a night I'll not soon forget, we saw The Replacements at The Ritz perform songs from Tim. Bob Stinson raged about the stage with his guitar —, pushing the stage divers back in the mosh pit almost protecting his younger brother Tommy on bass. In the center of this tempest, Paul Westerberg stood at the mike singing, we are the sons of no one, bastards of young. We got no war to name us. Then Bob played his guitar solo. This was his last show with The Mats.

I look again at Tim, the LP I've had since 1985. I flip it over and read the liner notes on the back. It was produced by Tommy Erdelyi. In all these years, I never realized he was the original drummer in The Ramones. Tommy Erdelyi Ramone passed away in 2014.

Thirty years blink by. I have a new favorite song that I've never heard on the radio, but I keep playing it over and over like an old 45, As Far as I Know by Paul Westerberg on the Folker album, a kindred spirit in this life of mine. Just electric guitar and a snare drumbeat... As far as I know...

Strange – I look again at the Folker album cover – the red-lit scene. I never noticed this before... Paul is quite clearly in a darkroom — standing off to the side beneath the red haze of a safelight. Perhaps he too was a darkroom technician. "That's the work we do," Duke explained to me.

Maybe I'm seeing things... perhaps I haven't been getting enough sleep. Maybe my eyes are playing tricks on me. Is Jenny Lind holding an India-rubber ball in her folded hands?

As Barnum wrote about her in his own book By Himself on page 326, "She would come and romp and run, sing and laugh like a young school-girl. 'Now, Mr. Barnum for another game of ball,' she would say half a dozen times a day, whereupon she would take an india-rubber ball, (of which she had two or three.)"

I can plainly see it in her hand just as I saw the Camera Obscura on the rooftop of Barnum's American Museum. It's there. Isn't it?

I've written about September, 1850, as if I know for a fact that is when Tim started work at Brady's Studio. This is pure conjecture on my part – pure fiction, as far as I know. I am blurring the lines between ficts and facts, between fiction and faction – between non-fiction and fiction.

Some researchers have suggested that Timothy O'Sullivan did not begin working for Mathew Brady until 1858, when he was 18. Others have put him there at the age of 16. I humbly and most respectfully disagree. People today have great difficulty comprehending child labor, but nonetheless, it existed. One need only look at 5,000+ child labor photographs taken by Lewis Hine — a little girl at a spinning mill, a young boy in a coal miner's cap. Then there are the photographs of Jacob Riis and his book How the Other Half Lives, not to mention Alice Austen of Staten Island and her photographs of the boot-blacks and newsboys.

James David Horan pointed out two important facts in his book, Mathew Brady — Historian with a Camera. In a letter of recommendation, Brady states that he had known Tim "from boyhood" which indicates a younger age than 18 or 16. He did not say young man or youth, he said "boyhood." In addition to this, I note that Brady's own nephew, Levin Handy, began work at his uncle's studio at the age of 12 in 1865. This led me to believe that Tim started work at the age of 10, as far as I know...

CHAPTER 29 — THE GALLERY WALL

1850

"Where to put Mr. Cooper?" says Brady pacing back and forth in the Gallery. "This is much like a seating chart at the banquet hall to our wedding. Who sits next to whom – that is the eternal question." He takes a seat on the long plush red leather bench seat, crossing his legs, elbow to his knee, hand to his chin staring with bewilderment at the Gallery Wall.

"Someone has to go. There's no two ways about it." All available spaces have been taken – from floor to ceiling packed tightly with portraits of every shape and size. "Who shall it be?"

Standing up high on a step ladder, Mr. Pettifog grows impatient with the long, protracted indecision. "Oh, for heaven's sake! Let's take this one down and put Mr. Cooper in its place."

"Under no circumstances, Mr. Pettifog. I'll have you know I captured that portrait of James Knox Polk only 18 days before his death on March 4th, 1849."

"It makes no matter to me – let us pack him off to that dusty corner in the supply closet."

"Need I remind you, he was the 11th President of these United States. Leave President Polk be…"

Scampering down the ladder, Mr. Pettifog moves it a few steps over. "Then how about this stern looking Bible-thumper."

"That's no preacher, Henry, that is John Quincy Adams, the sixth President taken shortly before he died of a paralytic stroke."

"Well, that explains his strained expression. How about this feeble, old woman with the blanket on her lap – toss her to the trash heap, I say or put her in the bargain bin with the other unwanted, penny-portraits."

Deeply wounded, Brady tries to compose himself saying softly, "Father, forgive him for he knows not what he says…" He tugs down on his waist coat and tries to change the argumentative tone of his voice to one of reason. "Mr. Pettifog, surely you remember this portrait of the former First Lady."

"I haven't the foggiest."

"I'll give you a hint. She is my inspiration…"

"Mat, I tell you I cannot recall. She is no doubt some vain-glorious woman. But I can't be bothered putting names to the faces. Memory only clutters my brain. If only I could forget the ones that haunt me in the night. Need I remind you of how many plates I develop each day under that fuming hood? Do not taunt me any further!"

"That is none other than Dame Dolly Madison. She is the one who rescued the portrait of George Washington from the gallery wall of the White House before the British set it on fire during the War of 1812."

"And what of it?"

"Don't you realize? She preserved our nation's history in that selfless, heroic act much like my Gallery of Illustrious Americans."

"Oh, bother! I give it up! You silly, sentimental fool!" Mr. Pettifog stomps off muttering to himself. "Wasting your breath, he didn't listen to your misgiving about that book of his, not then, not now, not ever."

Gabriel steps forward. "Mr. Brady, this is evidently hallowed ground. Might I suggest we look for a more suitable spot further to the back."

"But Mr. Cooper deserves a prominent place at the head of the table so to speak. I don't wish to banish him to the back of the room."

"I know just the place," says Mr. Pettifog returning to the fray. "Over there with the pretty ladies – that's where he will garnish the most notice. For you know as well as me that is what draws the crowds to this Gallery of yours – those radiant beauties, and certainly not those stuffed shirts. Mark my words, Mr. Cooper would rather sit between Fanny Elssler, the beautiful ballerina, and Maggie Mitchell, the actress."

"I am not so sure Fenimore would approve, Mr. Pettifog, nor would his dear wife Susan. I've put much thought into arranging my Gallery Wall. Look there is my dear friend, Charles Loring Elliott who has painted more than 700 portraits. Close by is George Peter Healy with 500 portraits to his credit. Next come the landscape artists. There is Thomas Cole, Asher Durand, Frederic Church and Albert Bierstadt having a grand old time together…"

"Henry Hudson! I give it up! No sooner do you ask for my opinion, then you dash it to pieces."

"Please forgive my unintended slight, Henry."

"I have had enough!" Mr. Pettifog stomps off muttering to himself. "Wasting your breath, you are. Did he listen to your misgivings about that foolhardy book of his – that Gallery of Illustrious Americans? Oh, no! Even that pompous word – Illustrious, I warned him not to call it that. Tis best to call it plain and simple - The Gallery of Historic Americans. But did he take your advice? Not on your life! He never listens to reason – not then, not now, not ever! The lithographic stones by D'Avignon cost $100 per stone. Says he, they are worth every penny. One hundred dollars for each stone! You are merely throwing good money after bad!"

His argument thunders away as he climbs the stairs – stomping down on each carpeted stair, making his way back to his workroom.

Brady looks up at the ceiling and waits a moment for the door to slam. He blinks in anticipation and counts two and a half. The chandelier jitters and sways slightly.

Standing over in the corner, Gabriel motions with his white ruffled shirt. "Mr. Brady, I believe I've found the most appropriate spot, right here."

Tim walks over with Mr. Brady. Gabriel crouches down to Tim's eye level and points to a portrait on the wall "Look there, Tim."

"Which one, Gabriel?" The wall is lined from floor to ceiling.

"That one – the one with dark, sullen eyes… that is Edgar A. Poe. How beautiful was his genius! How divinely sweet were the tones of his poetic harp! Here ye not his silver bells? How tenderly soft they jingle in the ear!"

Brady sighs, "But where, Gabriel?"

"Simply remove that one."

"But that is none other than Nathaniel Parker Willis who gave Poe his start at The Evening Mirror. And besides, I am not so sure Mr. Cooper would approve sharing a room at my crowded inn with Mr. Poe. They would make for strange bedfellows."

"It is just as well. I much prefer Poe."

"To whom?" asks Brady.

"Well, suffice it to say, Mr. Cooper is not my cup of tea."

Brady looks a bit perturbed. "How do you mean, not your cup of tea?"

"Well, if you must know, I think James Fenimore Cooper is a bit longwinded and tiresome. He has fallen out of favor."

"Yes, that is the same observation I have often heard. Even William Cullen Bryant said as much, but with an added caveat. You see Gabriel, no longer is the novel for the landed gentry sitting in their parlours reading at their leisure. This is the age of steamships and locomotives, telegraphs and photographs. For better or worse, people no longer have the time, nor the patience, to appreciate the wait – good things come to those who wait, I was always told, but alas, no more. They want their steamship to leave on schedule. They want their portrait this instant. T'was not so long in the age of sail that you had to wait for the wind and the tide."

Brady sees a confused look on Tim's face. Gabriel breaks the pause. "I'm not so sure I follow you. What does the tide have to do with James Fenimore Cooper?"

"How did Mr. Bryant express it to me? 'The very defects of Cooper's novels. He is long in getting at the interest of his narrative… The progress of the plot at first, like one of his own vessels of war, slowly, heavily, and even awkwardly working out of a harbor. We are impatient and weary, but when the vessel is once in the open sea, feels the free breath of heaven in her full sheets…' Mr. Cooper will take you in his ship of fancy to far and distant lands. Now then, let's find an appropriate place for Mr. Cooper."

"What was he like, Mr. Brady?"

"Well, I had great admiration for Poe, but he rather shrank from coming, as if he thought it was going to cost him something."

"And you were present at the sitting?"

"Yes, of course, I was. I had William Ross Wallace bring him to my studio."

"Oh, I was under the impression that this portrait was taken by Mr. Manchester at the Masury & Hartshorn Gallery in Providence, Rhode Island."

"Who on earth told you that?"

"I'd rather not say."

"Well, I can assure you I was the one who captured this portrait. Need I remind you that Poe worked for my dear friend N.P. Willis at the Evening Mirror over on Nassau Street. He was the one who published The Raven in February of '45. He respected Poe's wish for anonymity and used the penname Quarles. But that poem spread like a prairie fire, and its true author was soon known throughout the city... evermore." Distracted, thinking of the poem, Brady pauses a moment lost in thought.

"Come now, Gabriel. By whose authority, do you question my integrity? Out with it! You shall not bear false witness!"

"Well, if you must know, Mr. Plumbe mentioned this in passing to me one day."

"I thought as much. Mr. Plumbe was extremely envious of my portrait of Poe, even more so after Poe's untimely death in 1848, when he could no longer capture the poet. Mr. Plumbe spread false rumors. Your claim sounds preposterous. Tell me this, why would Poe travel to Providence to have his portrait taken. Answer me that!"

"For love," says Gabriel softly.

"For love?"

"Yes, unrequited love. Mr. Poe gave it to Mrs. Whitman as an expression of his love for her. After she refused to engage herself with him, he very nearly killed himself when he swallowed an ounce of laudanum."

"Nonetheless, this is the portrait I captured right here in this very studio."

"Are you quite sure?"

"Yes, Gabriel I can attest to it and so can William Ross Wallace. He wrote the Hand that Rocks the Cradle and was a dear friend of Poe. They came here after taking lunch at Sandy Welsh's basement pub on Nassau Street discussing poetry and belles lettres over glasses of Burton's Ale."

"Is that the case with the Washington Irving portrait? Taken right here in this very studio?"

Brady's agitation turns to red blistering anger as he loosens his cravat and his brogue breaks through. "You can bet your life on it, Gabriel!"

"With all due respect, I'm not so sure of the veracity of your claim, Mr. Brady. Need I remind you that I was the operator at Mr. Plumbe's Gallery when Mr. Irving came calling?"

"That's enough out of you!" Brady pounds his right fist into his left and starts to push up his shirtsleeves. "I won't be disrespected in my own house!"

Tim jumps in between Gabriel and Mr. Brady. "Please, Mr. Brady, come see, come see, I've found the perfect place for Mr. Cooper."

"What now, Timothy?"

Tim tugs on Mr. Brady's shirt cuff. "Right over here." They take a few strides down the gallery hall. "Right here, next to Thomas Cole."

Brady looks up for a moment and sighs, "No that won't do. What about William Cullen Bryant? What would he say?" Brady raises his hand to his chin. "Hmmm..." He takes down the Bryant portrait, and puts Cooper in its place beside Thomas Cole. He steps back a few paces to gain the proper perspective.

"Who the devil cares what Mr. Bryant thinks? This is my gallery after all, isn't it?" He places his hand on Tim's shoulder. "Yes, Timothy, that's a capital idea indeed. We have carved Mr. Cooper's initials into that tree of Kindred Spirits in our own little way. Haven't we?"

"Yes, Mr. Brady. I think Mr. Cooper would be pleased. Is there still time to visit the gallery at Union Square as you promised?"

Brady turns around to finish his discussion with Gabriel, but he is gone. "Where has he gone off to?"

"Who, Mr. Brady?"

"Gabriel..." Brady sighs, then takes a deep breath. "Yes, Timothy, perhaps that is just what we need — a trip to the museum, as promised." Brady holds out his arm in a broad sweeping motion, holding an imaginary brush, painting landscapes in the air. "You shall see Kindred Spirits by Asher Durand with your own eyes, Falls of the Kaaterskill by Thomas Cole, and The Mountain House by his dear sister, Sarah. I can't wait to show them to you."

On the ferry ride home to New Brighton, Tim thinks of the Voyage of Life and his trip to the museum with Mr. Brady looking at the four paintings by Thomas Cole. He hears Brady's voice describe the paintings, holding his walking cane, pointing out details, and explaining the scene.

"See here, Timothy, this first panel is titled Childhood. Take note of the guardian angel over the child's shoulder, holding the tiller, guiding the boat on the river of life. So serene... The next panel depicts youth as the boy guides the boat on his own as the angel bids him farewell, but he has his eyes fixed on a castle in the sky. Next comes manhood, note the dark and foreboding clouds, the boat is damaged in the rough waters in the great struggle to survive."

Tim interrupts, "Mr. Brady, why are Mr. Cole's paintings all horizontal and all of your portraits vertical?"

"Why indeed? That is a good question, Timothy. There are two types of artists — the portrait painter and the landscape painter. Look at the portrait over there. Do you know who that is?"

Tim shakes his head, looking at the commanding figure.

"That is none other than Robert Fulton painted by Benjamin West. Before he made his mark as an inventor with his steamship the Clermont, Mr. Fulton was an artist. He painted portraits and landscapes."

"Much like Mr. Samuel Morse?"

"Yes, just like Mr. Morse. Now to answer your question, suffice it to say that portrait painters utilize the vertical frameset while landscape painters rely on the horizontal setting. You will note that in my gallery, most if not all of my portraits are vertical."

"But why aren't there any horizontals in your studio, Mr. Brady?"

"I am not sure I understand your meaning, Tim."

"Why aren't there any landscapes like Mr. Cole's in your studio?"

Brady pauses a moment. "Such a prescient observation from one so young. Yes, Tim, you are quite right. There are no landscapes in my studio. You see, landscapes are not practical with the daguerreotype."

"But why, Mr. Brady?"

"There are certain limitations with the daguerreotype and the camera. The New Art is still in its youth. Besides, there is not much call for daguerreotypes of the countryside. That's all there is to it."

Later that night, lying in bed, unable to sleep, Tim listens to Thomas snore in the shadows of the candlelight. As the ferry approached the Kill van Kull, Mr. Brady stood at the railing and pointed out a structure in the distance.

"Can you make that out, Tim?"

"Why yes, that is Robbins Reef Lighthouse."

"Such keen eyesight, you have Tim. You don't know how lucky you are. You have a fine future ahead of you as an operator with your vision. You shall be my Hawkeye. Now then, do you think your father would object to you taking a little trip with me and my wife, Julia?"

"Where to, Mr. Brady?"

"Why to The Mountain House... I have important matters to discuss with Mr. Martin M. Lawrence who is recuperating there. Much change is on the horizon with the New Art. I need a valet to accompany me. Besides, I have certain promises to keep with Mr. Cooper."

Tim turns over on his side and kicks the blankets off. He can hear his father and Mr. Brady at the kitchen table. Pa offers him a drink and then another. There is a change to Mr. Brady — a change to his voice, he becomes loud and boisterous — laughing out loud, pounding the table, having a grand old time. Then the mood darkens. "Pay!" says Pa out loud. "You want me to pay for this trip when you are the one who owes me back pay!"

"Alright, Mr. O'Sullivan. I'll settle my account with you. If you allow Tim to go on this trip."

"But he's just a boy, I don't want him to leave home just yet."

"Don't you worry, my dear wife Julia will be there to look after the boy. I'll bring him home safe and sound. You can depend upon it. "

Tim watches the candle flicker in the dark.

"When do we leave, Mr. Brady?"

"Tomorrow, first thing in the morning from the Albany Dock. Be up bright and early, packed and ready to go."

"Yes, Mr. Brady."

A drop of wax crests over the side and trickles down the candle cooling halfway as Tim falls to sleep.

CHAPTER 30 — SIMPLE MINDS

1985

"That's it!" I jump out of the dent in the living room couch. I point to the television screen. The video by Simple Minds is playing on MTV – Jim Kerr is singing Alive and Kicking.

"What's it? What are you talking about, Dan?" says Bill.

"That's the place where we should take Pernille. Steve wants to take her someplace where she can see this country. I mean really see."

"What place?"

"North Lake."

"That's not North Lake. You're seeing things."

I look again at the video racing by – quick camera cuts – split second glimpses of the band on a plateau, standing at the edge of a cliff, by a lake, and a waterfall. I can't exactly be sure.

"Dan, that band is from Scotland. Why would they come over to America, drive all the way up to the Catskills, to some rinky-dink campground, and shoot a music video?"

I must admit my brother has a point. It does sound preposterous. The video was probably filmed in the Highlands of Scotland.

But I look again and see the place where I once stood.

"I'm telling you, Bill. That is The Escarpment."

The video was over before we knew it. This was in the day before computers and YouTube. We had no DVRs. We could not rewind or pause live television.

"Let's wait for the video to come on again and pop in a tape. They'll probably play it in the next hour or so."

So, we sat in front of the TV, waiting in vain for MTV to play Alive and Kicking again. We waited and waited... holding vigil, waiting for that video to come back on MTV. Heavy metal band after heavy metal band came on the set "playing make-up, wearing guitars" as Paul Westerberg sang on Tim. We watched MTV late into the evening like a scene from Waiting for Godot. Has it come on? No. This video wasn't in heavy rotation like their hit song from The Breakfast Club soundtrack. But finally, it did air again on MTV. Bill only grudgingly conceded that the video was filmed at North Lake.

"You may be right..." his voice trailed off. "It's hard to tell. They switch scenes so fast. I still don't get it. How did this band from Scotland find out about North Lake? It's just a campground."

We showed Steve and Pernille the Simple Minds video and readied for the trip. Dad let us borrow the camping equipment.

We loaded the gear in the trunk of the Chevelle and headed north on the New York State Thruway. As we approached the Tappan Zee Bridge, my body cringed as we passed that ominous 'Last Exit Before Bridge' sign. I had flashbacks to that day.

"Hey Bill, remember that first camping trip to North Lake — the roof-rack on the Volkswagen Rabbit and going across the Tappan Zee?"

"Yeah, don't remind me," he said with a chuckle. We could laugh about it now, but back then it wasn't funny at all.

With Bill at the wheel of the Chevelle, I turn around to tell Steve and Pernille about our Tappan Zee adventure.

This was the summer of 1979 – the summer of the gas crisis with long lines at the service stations. There was talk about the American gas guzzler becoming extinct. We hadn't been on a family vacation in a long time, not since the days of our big Chevy station wagon when Mom was alive. Now we stood in the driveway scratching our heads staring at the Dad's Volkswagen Rabbit trying to figure out where to put all the camping equipment and family members. How do we fit the tent, the sleeping bags, the duffle bags, the camp stove, the rubber raft, not to mention Delia, Bill, Jim, Dad and myself into a four-cylinder tin box? Our solution was the roof-rack. The rack was secured to the roof with four suction cups. When the roof began to buckle, I voiced my concern.

"Dad, I don't think we should put the Coleman Cooler on the roof. It's way too heavy."

So, we moved that down below into the back of the hatch-back and rearranged the packing, moving the lighter items up top – the sleeping bags, the duffle bags and the tent.

As we tied the equipment down with bungee cords and clothesline, I wished I had remembered some of those knots from the Boy Scouts – like the double half-hitch that will tighten as you pull down on the slack.

"Dad, these bungee cords are not going to hold this stuff down." I sounded like a nervous ninny.

"Danny, you worry too much." He grabbed the bungee cord and gave it a tug. "It's fine."

Bill pokes his head up at the other side of the roof. "Yeah, you worry too much," he snickered.

"C'mon then let's get ready to hit the road. I'll be back in a minute, I have to go change and get a few things," said Dad.

Delia and Bill climbed in the back – the seat was folded down for more cargo storage – they crammed themselves next to the cooler sitting Indian style with no room to stretch their legs.

"Danny, where should I sit?" said my little brother Jim, the quiet one, quieter than me. Jim never knew our mother — she died when he was barely two. One day I found him in his room standing at his chalk board giving a lesson to his stuffed animals.

"Have you ever read Thoree?" he asked.

"No, I never heard of Thoree."

"He's an author. He wrote a book about life in the woods," Jim tried to explain.

"Oh, I think you mean Henry David Thoreau. You pronounce it Thor-Ohh. What's a little kid like you reading Thoreau? You're only in the second grade."

"I want to be a teacher, Dan." He said most seriously.

I looked at my little brother, the blond hair of his cow-lick sticking up, the sad lost look in his eyes.

"Don't worry, Jim. We'll find you a seat."

He stands there holding his green plastic Bugs Bunny camera. Bugs lounges across the top of the camera, carrot in his hand. "What's up Doc?" The camera shoots 110mm film. Jim has a flash cube fixed in place, he is on assignment, ready to document, ready for our camping trip adventure to begin.

Dad comes back to the car wearing his Yankee cap and this bright green terry-cloth jacket of his. This is his I'm-on-vacation-jacket. I haven't seen him put this on in years. It barely fits around his belly. It's been a long time since we've been on a vacation.

This was the first summer Dad had been sober in a long time. He went on a downward spiral after my mother died, taking care of seven children on his own. The alcohol made him laugh out loud while watching Jackie Gleason on the Honeymooners, but other than that, he just sort of gave up on enjoying life. (I've come to realize, I am just like my father. I am an alcoholic.)

Like Rip Van Winkle, he'd awoken from a long slumber. The fog had lifted, and he began seeing things in a different light. This is when he started teaching us about photography. This is when he wanted to take us on a camping trip.

"OK, is everybody ready to go?" Dad asked, anxious as a little kid.

"We have one small problem. There's no place for Jim."

Dad and Bill open up the hatch-back. I have packed everything neatly and tightly. The Coleman stove is wedged next to the Coleman cooler. The lantern, the cook-kits, the rubber raft, the life preservers are all essential items. They look at the roof-rack packed with sleeping bags and duffle bags. They look at Jim. They look back again at the roof-rack and exchange knowing glances.

Just as I am about to protest the notion of putting Jim up on the roof-rack, Delia pipes in, "I know where to put Jim. Take one of the sleeping bags. Use that as a seat. Jim can sit on the floor in the front with Dan." That's Delia – always thinking, quick on her toes, ready with a simple solution. She is the only girl on this expedition, she is only nine, but she has more common sense than Dad, Bill, Jim, and me combined.

Jim climbs in front of me with his nose pressed close to the dashboard. Dad turns on the 4-cylinder Rabbit. She strains and sighs wearily at her heavy load.

Driving along the New York State Thruway, I begin to notice the horrified expressions in passing cars. We must have looked like modern day Okies from Yonkers. Tom Joad passed by shaking his head, chugging along in his Model T-Ford. The little Rabbit engine is beating hard. There's another ghastly expression passing us by – gaping mouths, raised eyebrows, pointing at us in ridicule.

Up ahead in the distance is the Hudson River and the Tappan Zee Bridge. Delia makes an urgent announcement from the back.

"Dad, I'm starting to see the tent bag."

"Don't you worry. It'll be fine."

"Dad! I think you had better pull over. I can see the roof-rack inching to the edge of the hatch-back."

He doesn't respond.

Delia doesn't take too kindly to being ignored. She expects, no demands, an immediate response.

"Dad! Did you not hear me!"

He tugs down on his Yankee cap, pushes his foot down on the accelerator, trying to squeeze the last drop of horsepower out of the four-cylinder. Damn the Torpedoes! Full speed ahead!

He turns to me, motions upwards with his thumb to the sunroof. The summer sun is shining down.

"Stick yer head up there and see if you can tighten the ropes."

We approach that sign – Last Exit Before Bridge.

I stand on the seat and stick my head and shoulders up through the sunroof. The wind is beating hard. I can feel Dad grab hold of my belt – he is my lifeline. The little suction cups are sliding backwards. I grab hold of the rope. Dad yanks down on my belt as we make our way to the center span of the Tappan Zee Bridge.

I hold onto the rope as we pass over the Hudson – strong gusty winds – a perfect day for sailing.

"DAD! One of the sleeping bags just blew off!" Delia screams from the back at the top of her lungs. "There goes Jim's duffle bag. The tent!"

Screeching horns, swerving cars, Dad pulls to a stop.

"Get out and get the stuff!" he screams at me. "Hurry now!"

The Tappan Zee Bridge happens to be the worst place imaginable for a breakdown to occur. There's no place to pull off to the side of the highway in an emergency.

Eighteen wheelers go barreling by, cars swerve out of the way with horns blaring. I see Jim's duffle bag. I run back down the highway – staying close to the guard rail. The Tappan Zee bounces as a heavy truck rumbles over the metal plates. I run back to the car with an armload of sleeping bags and duffle bags. I jam everything in the back.

"Don't forget the tent!"

I run back for the tent lying in the middle lane. I dart out then run to the guard rail cradling the tent in both arms. A strong wind grabs hold of the tent pushing us over the edge of the waist-high fence. I teeter over and look down at the light brown Hudson – way, way, way, down below.

I made it. I got all the stuff. I returned to the Rabbit in triumph. I stood there holding the tent like a big trophy fish I had just caught.

"What are you doing standing there? Get the hell in the car!" shouted Dad.

"Hey, Bill this is the place Dad pulled off the highway. Remember?"

"Yeah, Danny, I remember..." When we got off that god-forsaken bridge and made it to the other side, Dad got out and tied those ropes so tight that the Rabbit lunged when he tugged down.

Back on the highway, Dad breathed a sigh of relief. He flicked on the radio and that song by Hurricane Smith came on, "Oh Babe, what would you say." It sounds like an old Dixieland number with Louis Armstrong singing the lead backed by a saxophone and strumming banjo, but Hurricane is from England. He engineered many of the Beatles records and produced Pink Floyd's first few albums. The song puts Dad in a good mood.

"Danny, get me a drink."

I reach for a Dixie cup and push the pep-cock to the jerry-jug. I hand him a cool cup of iced-T.

"Hey, I'm thirsty too." And so I pour drinks for the other passengers aboard this Volkswagen Rabbit trip.

"How about a salami sandwich?"

I turn around and dig through the cooler. Pretty soon everyone else is hungry.

Dad tears through the rye bread. I hand him some cheese crackers.

"All right then, Navigator. Where to?"

"Where to?" I repeat back. I thought Dad had the plan and the itinerary all worked out. But I should have known better. He doesn't like to have a plan. He just likes to GO — the open road before him. He told us stories of driving all the way around the Gaspe Peninsula to the Bay of Fundy. He didn't like plans or reservations. 'No Vacancy' didn't mean 'no room at the inn' to him, it was a sign from God – it wasn't meant to be.

I open up the big campground guidebook with maps and charts. I have

no idea where we should go. I am not even sure where we are...
somewhere heading north on the New York State Thruway. There are so
many bewildering campgrounds to choose from.

"All right then Navigator – what's our destination?"

"How about Lake George?" I think of the picture Dad painted of his
camping trip to Lake George with Uncle Rudy after the War – taking a
swim before breakfast – bacon and eggs sizzling in frying pan on the camp
stove.

"No, we're losing daylight. It's too far away. We'll go there another time.
I'll take you to see Fort Ticonderoga when we do... For this trip, let's head
for the Catskills."

"But where Dad?"

"I dunno... just pick a place."

"Yeah, Dan. Just pick a place." I hear Delia from the back.

The campground guide comes with a handy plastic ruler complete with
grid lines and legend to the varying amenities at each campground. The
stick figures indicate whether there is swimming, hiking, tenting, or boating.
"Here's one, it has 25 campsites, a river, swimming, and pit toilets."

"No pit toilets," shouts Delia from the back.

I go back to the campground guide. I slide the ruler down the page. I
skip over the non-descript North-South Lake State Park. It is far too boring
a name. I am drawn to campgrounds with alluring titles – Whispering Pines,
Devil's Tombstone, Black Bear Campground. Then for some reason, I turn
back to North-South Lake. I read out the legend key – hiking trails, beach,
swimming, and boating.

"What about the toilets?"

"Here it is... flush toilets."

"Did somebody say flush?" I hear Bill say.

Jim starts singing his goofy song. "Oh, ah, I can't let it out. Oh, ah, I
can't let it out." It is good to see him having fun. Bill joins in. They break
into laughter singing their bladder song. 23 Miles to Next Rest Stop.

We finally arrived at the entrance to North Lake late in the evening. The
ranger shines a flashlight and walks out over to the car. "Sorry folks, there
are no more campsites available."

We didn't know where to go... so much for trusting our vacation to the
whim of fate.

But the ranger holds out a glimmer of hope. "You come back
tomorrow, I'm sure a campsite will open up."

The next morning, after a night in a motel, we returned to the little
ranger outpost. We held our breath. The ranger put the campground map
before us. He circled numbers at the edge of the lake.

"What do these circles mean?" Dad asked a bit confused.

"These are open sites."

"Right by the lake?"

"Yep, right by the lake. Pick any site, set up camp, then come back here and register."

"See Danny, what did I tell you? You don't need a plan. You just GO."

We all piled back in the Rabbit and drove down the long campground road.

"Smell that mountain air," said Dad.

The tall pine trees, we all took a deep breath. Just then a large buck crossed the road, graceful and distinguished. Dad ground the Rabbit to a halt. The deer looked at us inquisitively for a moment... for a fleeting moment then he disappeared into the woods without a sound.

We pulled into our campsite – our very own lakeside campsite. We set up the tent, unloaded the gear, put the foot-pump to the rubber raft and paddled like explorers around North and South Lake. At sunset, we climbed the boulder to enjoy our million-dollar view for only $7.50 a night – nature's beauty – free to all – or damn close to it.

The next morning, I woke early and soon discovered that we had been robbed. Robbed of everything. Like Sherlock Holmes at a crime scene, I looked at the little paw prints - muddy little hands on the green metal Coleman cooler, dexterous enough to turn the locking latch. Rocky Raccoon ate everything – the salami, the butter, the hot dogs, the milk, the bacon. He even cracked open each and every egg. The little bandit left nothing but eggshells and melted ice for these dumb city slickers.

Dad just chuckled at the scene. Then all of a sudden, he saw something out of the corner of his eye. He grabbed his Konica camera and knelt down to take a picture of Jim waking up in the tent with the red kerosene lantern hanging close by. It was good to see Dad using his camera again, capturing a moment, enjoying life.

CHAPTER 31 — THE ALBANY DOCK

1850

"Julia, don't dote on the boy, I assure you he will be quite alright riding with the coachman. Won't you Timothy?"

"Oh yes, Mrs. Brady, I prefer to ride up top."

As Julia takes her seat in the hackney cab, Tim clambers up top.

"Where to sir?"

"The Albany Dock, my good man, and be in good haste."

"Certainly, sir," he says with a tip of his stove pipe hat.

The driver snaps the long line of his whip as if he were casting a fishing rod and reeling it back with a smart snap just between the horse's ears.

"My what a fine horse you have there. What type is he?"

"That is a hackney horse, my boy. Allow me to introduce myself, the name is Thursty McQuill. And you are?"

"Timothy O'Sullivan."

"Put it there, Timothy." He holds out his palm for a handshake.

As the hackney cab rumbles along West Street, Tim looks at this bustling thoroughfare along the waterfront. It is twice as wide as Broadway. To the left are the docks and all the ships, teeming with activity as the longshoremen busy themselves unloading big bales of cotton at Pier 7 – The Southern Freight Line – Savannah and Charleston. There is a long line of wagons at the Knickerbocker Ice Company. Tim sees a hay wagon, tall as a mountain, pulled by four horses. Passengers gather their luggage and steam trunks at Pier 9 – The Dispatch Line for Philadelphia. Next, he sees a sign for the Fall River Line at Pier 11 – Boston – Bristol and Providence. "Music by Splendid Bands and Orchestras. Most Attractive Route in the Country."

"How soon til we arrive at the Albany Dock?"

"Not before long, Tim. The Albany Dock is at Pier 15. That is for all the fashionable people bound to their resorts at Niagara Falls and Saratoga Springs. So where are you headed then?"

"To the Catskill Mountain House."

"How grand. We'll have you there in a half-dime's time."

"How long is that, Mr. McQuill?"

"Be sure to call me, Thursty. That's what all the fellas call me. Now then, a half-dime is a nickel, or should I say, five minutes."

Tim sees a high brick wall extending all the way down the block far as the eye can see. "What's that?"

"That is the Manhattan Gas Company which illuminates this great metropolis of 515,000 people. There are 230 miles of cast iron pipe running throughout this city. More than 1,500 men work behind those walls feeding the behemoth furnaces with 100,000 tons of coal and 60,000 bushels of lime to manufacture 1,000 million cubic feet of gas."

Tim looks up to see tall chimneys belching out smoke.

"My older brother James works behind them walls. He fancies himself a philosopher. He can talk for hours and hours about gas if you let him. As he is fond of telling me, 'a wonderful study is gas. The whole world is gas! Mankind is made of gas. From gas we come, unto gas we must return.' And to punctuate his point, he lets rip loose some noxious noise from the depths of his bowels," says Mr. McQuill with a chuckle.

An awful smell captures Tim's attention, he looks to his left at the docks. This is not the smell of horse manure. He buries his nose in the cradle of his elbow trying to escape that awful smell of death and decay. He looks over to see a barge tied at the dock with great heaps of bloated carcasses — dead horses, dead cows, and dead pigs. Piled one on top of the other, white bellies look like balloons about to burst their intestines. He sees workers off-load a carriage onto the barge.

"What is that over there, Thursty?"

"The offal boat, Tim. All the animal dead of the City are taken out into the harbor."

Tim looks away.

As the hackney pulls into Pier 15, Tim looks at the big painted letters on the wall, Albany Dock. In smaller letters are other destinations: Utica, Buffalo, and Rochester. Then on the other side of the pier, are far-away places: Ohio, Chicago, Detroit. Up above looms two black cast iron smoke stacks. Deckhands busy themselves loading wooden crates and barrels onto a ship. No sooner does Tim climb down, then he sees Mr. and Mrs. Brady surrounded by gentlemen in frock coats and top hats offering assistance.

"Take your luggage, kind sir? I would only be too happy to oblige."

"Be wary of these runners," says Thursty in a hushed tone to Mr. Brady while accepting his fare. "They will promise you the moon and the stars if you let them. Listen to that lungpower. They would blush the efforts of the barkers at the Battery." He unloads a great big steam trunk.

"Come one, come all for a splendid ride on the Hendrick Hudson - a floating palace with luxurious state rooms."

"What about the bursting boilers?" asks an elderly woman holding a walking cane with her brood milling about. "I am worried about my grandchildren. I have read about all those steamboat tragedies in The Sun. The General Jackson burst her boilers."

"I can assure you, Madam, our steamboats have no boilers."

"No boilers, you say?"

"Yes, Madam. Not one blessed boiler to worry your pretty little head about."

As a stevedore pushes a steam trunk along the dock, Tim hears a calliope in the distance. He runs over to the crowd gathered about as the organ pipes blast the steam whistle notes to Yankee Doodle Dandy. At the last blast, he looks around, but cannot find Mr. and Mrs. Brady. He runs along the dock.

The calliope strikes up another tune. Tim listens to the pistons. My country tis of thee, sweet land of liberty, of thee I sing. Suddenly, he sees Mrs. Brady's parasol walking next to Mr. Brady's wide brimmed straw hat. She is a bit taller than her husband. Off he runs to catch up to them.

"Mr. Brady wouldn't it be nice to ride on The Armenia? She has a calliope that plays these wonderful tunes."

"Yes, so I've heard. There are so many riverboats to choose from. We have booked passage on The North America."

Mrs. Brady grabs Tim by the hand. "No more running off, young man. Hold dear to me. What would we say to your father if you disappeared at the Albany Dock?"

As they walk further out the pier, they arrive at The North America. "Take a look at her, Timothy," says Mr. Brady, pointing with his walking cane. "She is over 400 feet in length — a magnificent floating hotel. Wait until you see our luxurious state room."

As the porters bring their steam trunks to their room, Mr. Brady demonstrates the pocket doors and shows Tim his side room. While Mrs. Brady inspects the room, Mr. Brady checks his appearance in the mirror, as Tim takes a seat on the sofa and becomes restless.

"Mr. Brady, may I go explore the ship?"

"Yes, of course, Timothy, off you go."

"Hold on one moment, Mathew. I don't wish Timothy to go scampering off like a lost lamb. You must escort him."

"But Julia, I wished to retire with you at the loveseat by the window and gaze at the Palisades in all their grandeur."

"There'll be none of that, Mathew. You look after the boy while I settle our affairs for a restful journey. Besides, you just might enjoy yourself, exploring the ship with Timothy." She gives him a peck on the check. "I will have the steward bring refreshments on your return, my mighty explorers."

"Alright Julia, if you insist."

Tim grabs Mr. Brady by the shirt-cuff. "Come now, Mr. Brady. Let's explore the ship."

"Timothy, this is too exasperating. We've been to the stern. We've been to and fro, here and there. We are searching aimlessly. Now then, let me be the leader."

Mr. Brady takes a turn by the dining room then heads up the stairs to the observation deck.

"Where are we going, Mr. Brady?"

"To the top, my boy."

Tim looks over the side of the observation deck at the flurry of activity on the pier as the roustabouts load stacks of wood on their shoulders and haul it up the gangway. There is a rap on the deck with a cane as Tim looks up to see Mr. Brady trying to capture his attention.

"Come, Timothy, this way to the wheelhouse!"

Mr. Brady sees a chain blocking access to the staircase with a sign swaying back and forth - CREW ONLY - No Admittance. Mr. Brady unhooks the chain and proceeds up the stairs. Tim hesitates.

"But the sign says, 'No Admittance,' Mr. Brady."

"Where's your sense of adventure, Timothy! C'mon then! What's the worst that could happen? Do you think we'll be thrown overboard?"

"No, Mr. Brady."

"Then c'mon then!"

They ascend the black wrought iron stairs to find the white wainscot door flung wide open. The Captain leans out the window shouting orders with a short, brass megaphone to the roustabouts down on the dock.

"I want 25 cords of wood!"

"But Captain Buckman, the requisition calls for 18 cords. That's more than enough!"

"Not on my watch! You load 25 cords of wood in the hold, or I'll come down there and load it me-self!"

The roustabout looks up at the captain and follows his gaze to the riverboat across the pier, The Champlain.

"Aye, so it's The Champlain you're after!"

"Button your lip!"

"Aye, Captain!"

"AND, Break the backs of your men! I'll have 25 cords or I'll have your head!"

"Aye, aye, Captain!"

"Dump it down the chute! Faster now! I have a schedule to keep!"

Unable to sit still, the Captain turns around in his swivel chair and removes the plug from the communication tube going all the way down to the engine room. He blows his tin whistle.

"Now here this! Now here this!" He blows the whistle again. "Johnny are you there??" He puts his ear to the tube. "Don't make me come down there, Johnny! I'm warning ya!" The Captain roils around in his chair growing impatient about to head down the stairs to the engine room.

"What now!" He sees Brady and Tim for the first time. "Who gave you permission to set foot on my bridge!"

"We merely came for a visit, sir. There is no need for such an outburst."

"Get out of my wheel house, before I toss you out!"

"Please Captain, you must compose yourself. Think of the boy."

"Hold on a damn minute, you're Brady of Broadway aren't you? Forgive an old drunken sailor will you? I didn't recognize you with your hat."

"It's no trouble at all, Captain. I can assure you, the matter is forgotten."

"Oh my, you did a fine job doggery-typing myself and my boy. Oh how, it warmed the cockles of my dear wife's heart. Now what do I owe for the pleasure of your visit?"

"My young apprentice, Timothy, is curious as to the inner workings of your steamship, and would ever-so be grateful for a tour."

"I would only be too happy to oblige, but at present I must stand watch at the helm as we are about to cast off."

He notices a look of disappointment in Tim's eyes. "I'll tell you what, I will have my son, David show you the ropes... DAVID!" He shouts out the window. The young boy, no more than 10, comes scampering up the stairs dressed in a dark, navy pea coat and a nautical hat like his father.

"Yes, Papa."

"Front and center!"

"Yes, Papa."

"Captain to you, don't forget!"

"Yes, Captain Buckman."

"Mr. Brady allow me to introduce my son, David Lear Buckman."

"The pleasure is all mine," says Brady. "Yes, I fondly recall meeting your son at my studio. What a fine lad! You should be proud, Captain Buckman. This is my apprentice, Timothy O'Sullivan." There is an awkward pause. "Timothy, shake hands with young Mr. Buckman."

Tim extends his hand, "I prefer if you call me Tim."

"Put it there, Tim."

Captain Buckman turns in his chair. "Now David, I want you to take Mr. Brady and Tim on the grand tour. Show them the works — the observation deck, the paddlewheels, and the engine room."

"Yes, Papa."

"Remember now, Captain."

"Yes, Captain." He says with a little salute.

"Now then Mr. Brady, be sure to return to the bridge after your little tour and I will let young Tim man the helm. I might even regale you with a few legends about our mystical Hudson."

"What a kind and gracious gesture. We gladly accept, Captain."

The Captain turns back to his son. "Now, David be mindful of those stokers! Don't get in their way!"

"Aye, aye Captain."

"We had best let my father attend to his work," says David as he escorts Mr. Brady and Tim out of the wheelhouse, "Right this way, sirs."

Captain Buckman leans out the window shouting orders through his brass megaphone.

"Deckhands, prepare to cast off!"

The gangplanks are taken in and the mooring lines released.

"Cast off bowline!"

"Bow line away!"

He shouts into the communication tube. "Engine room, reverse one quarter!" The steamship back-peddles in a frothy, swirling fury. The captain pulls down on the cord, blasting the steam whistle in one long drawn-out warning to one and all as The North America pulls away from the Albany Dock.

CHAPTER 32 — UP THE RIVER

1850

As the steamship back-peddles and positions herself to begin the journey up the North River, David points over the railing at the various ships still moored to the Albany Dock. Tim listens to the steamship breathe — puffing along like a leviathan through its two smoke-stacks — taking alternate breaths – one after the other – spraying gentle droplets of boiling water like a whale through its spout. Tim walks over to the railing to look over the side as the waves splash against the hull. The ship glides swiftly against the current — up the river.

David takes a spot next to Tim. "Going up river is quite a miraculous achievement when you think of it. If you've ever tried rowing a boat up river, fighting the current with all your might – paddling in place – barely staying stationary, you're lucky to move forward at all. It's a losing battle."

"My what a fine vantage point, David."

"Yes, Mr. Brady. You'll note some of the other river boats. There is the Hendrick Hudson, she is 400 feet in length. Further down the pier is the Rip Van Winkle and there is The Champlain trying to keep pace with us. No less than seven steamboats leave for Albany on any given day. Robert Fulton was the first to steam up the Hudson to Albany on August 17th, 1807 in The Cleremont. The boat was 130 feet long with paddlewheels at the side."

"What a knowledgeable boy you are."

"Thank you kindly, Mr. Brady. Yes, Mr. Fulton made the 150-mile journey in 32 hours — near equal to five miles per hour. Now remember, this was all up river. The wind was ahead so no advantage could be derived from sails. The Cleremont fought against the river current with the first steamship engine fitted with paddlewheels."

"And Mr. Fulton suffered much scorn and ridicule did he not, David?"

"Oh yes, Mr. Brady, Father had me read Mr. Fulton's own account. He referred to the dull and endless repetition of 'The Fulton Folly.' Then he made a sad comment, "Never did a single encouraging remark, a bright hope or a warm wish cross my path."

"If only Mr. Fulton were here standing on this deck to gaze out on all these grand steamships at the Albany Dock."

"I believe he is Mr. Brady... In 1817, ten years after the first steamship voyage to Albany, the travel time was reduced to 18 hours. Then in 1836, it was further reduced to 10 hours. In 1849, the Alida and the Hendrick

Hudson had a great race from New York to Albany. The Alida won the race in 7 hours and 55 minutes at near 20 miles per hour."

"How fascinating!"

"Commodore Vanderbilt owns nearly 50 steamboats including this one. Look yonder at The Champlain as she tries to beat us up the river. She's called a four-piper on account of her four smokestacks. She has four boilers and two engines. The bookies must be busy taking bets from the passengers. See how they wave at us, happy as can be. My how they love a good race, especially when their ship wins. Now, if you step this way sirs, we will continue with our tour."

He takes them midship to these huge circular wooden structures which protect the paddle-wheels from debris on the river such as logs and icebergs in the winter.

"Gentleman, these paddle-boxes shield the passengers from the splashing of the enormous paddle wheels which are 35 feet in diameter."

Tim takes a look through an open slat in the paddle-box. He sees the paddle-wheels, turning and thrashing the water with their massive flanks of wood secured with wrought iron bolts.

"Is this a stern-wheeler or a side-wheeler?"

"Actually Tim, The North America is a twin-wheeler with side-wheels on either side. You'll find, most riverboats on the Hudson are side-wheelers. Stern-wheelers are found mainly on the Mississippi and the Missouri Rivers. My father much prefers the side-wheelers and says they are faster with their two engines and more maneuverable than the sternwheelers."

David pauses a moment. "Don't breathe a word of this to Captain Buckman, but I would rather see a stern-wheeler in action. There are no enclosures needed as the whole ship offers protection, so you can see the paddle-wheels turn in all their glory. It is a sight to behold... Follow me this way."

Through the great dining room with an army of attentive waiters, past the dance hall and an orchestra tuning up, the reception area with its grand piano, past opulent lounges with red carpets, down the stairs, past the busy kitchen, there is a cast iron door with painted letters - Engine Room - No Admittance. David turns the heavy door handle and opens the door to the stairwell, leading down to the bowels of the ship.

"Now mind your step..."

There is a blast of heat as Tim feels his face begin to bake. Instant sweat pours down his face as they step down the cast iron stairs, hearing each clank of their footsteps. The red glow of the furnaces light the engine room as the workers stoke each of the twin engines with wood. The teams work furiously in competition with each other heaving stacks and stacks of wood into the mouths of the breathing beasts.

"David! What brings you down here?" shouts the chief engineer with a bandana tied about his neck. "No passengers allowed! You should know better than that!"

"Captain's orders, Johnny. I'm giving these gentlemen a tour."

"Aye, aye," says the engineer turning back to his work.

"Now, Mr. Brady over here are the starboard and larboard engines. Each of these engines has four boilers." David shouts louder so Mr. Brady and Tim can hear. "These boilers are enormous. They are 36 feet long and 12 feet in diameter. If you stood them up on their end, they would be four stories high. My father took me over to the Novelty Iron Works in Brooklyn to see the construction of a marine engine."

Brady is mesmerized by this scene from Dante's Inferno.

"BOY! Stand back!" shouts the chief engineer. "Careful now, before they toss you into the furnace!" He slaps Tim on the back and hoists him up by his belt — swaying him back and forth with his mighty arms.

"Please sir, put me down! Don't toss me into the furnace!"

Mr. Brady steps forward.

The engineer sets Tim down. "Let that be a lesson to you. Next time, heed the warning. Stay away from this place. Take a look around you. Hell is no place to visit. There is no escape! Only feed the angry beast! Listen to her breathe! Right boys! Those twin engines are furious with hunger! Are they not?"

"Aye, aye, chief!"

"Feed the beast, boys!"

David grabs hold of Tim's hand. "Come this way gentlemen, and I will show how the steam engine works. Further back... see that pipe over there. The steam generated in the boilers is conveyed to the engine by the steam pipe which takes it to the cylinder over there. The cylinder is the heart and soul of the engine. The steam generated in the boiler is at first quiescent and inert. Its mighty power is expended by the lifting and bringing down of the enormous pistons within the cylinder."

Tim marvels at the movement of the piston rods, tall as telegraph poles, moving the lever up and down like a giant teeter-totter, turning the crankshaft.

"Look there, Tim. That piston rod rises with the force of 100 tons. It could lift a block of granite four feet square and 80 feet high. That's how powerful it is."

David points up near the top of the engine room, nearly two stories high. "There is the connecting rod which rises to the crank shaft. Thus, the force exerted by the steam in the cylinders is finally expended in turning the great paddle-wheels."

Just then the tin whistle pierces through the noisy engine room.

"Now hear this! Now hear this!" Captain Buckman's distant voice echoes through the communication tube. "Status report! Johnny on the spot!"

The chief engineer walks over to the tube.

"Johnny here, Captain. The boilers are fired up and ready to go at 20 pounds of steam!"

"Double-down, Johnny. Give me 40 pounds of steam or give me death!"

"Is that a direct order, Captain? Repeat back!"

"You heard me loud and clear, Johnny. 40 pounds! I have a score to settle with The Champlain and a wager to win! I'll give you a ten percent cut and ten more to split with the stokers. Are you in?"

"Aye, aye Captain. Over and out."

The chief engineer turns around.

"All right boys. You heard the captain's orders. Break your backs, now! We have a race to win. Fire her up!"

He goes over to the pressure gauges then turns directly to his visitors. "You had best return to your cabins and say your prayers. When these boilers burst, we'll all be headed to a watery grave just like The Swallow. Mark me words, just like The Swallow!"

"Come gentlemen, follow me this way."

As they close the engine room door, the cool refreshing breeze brings welcome relief as they make their way up the stairs to the observation deck.

"Tell me, David," says Mr. Brady. "Is there any cause for concern?"

"Oh no, Mr. Brady. The toll of dead on the Hudson is comparatively small when the years and number of passengers transported are taken into consideration."

"But what of the bursting boilers?"

"Oh, there are many tales told in the pilot houses and engine rooms. Captains are given to speeding their boats and the passengers generally become as much interested in these contests as the captains themselves."

"But what about The Swallow?"

"That is a story for my father to tell… This way back to the wheelhouse."

Lost in thought, looking at the Palisades pass by, Tim feels a tap on his shoulder.

"C'mon Tim, Mr. Brady has beat us up to the wheel house."

One hand on the spoke of the immense helm, five feet in diameter, Captain Buckman stands still as a statue, staring straight out the picture window at the broad majestic Hudson before him. Mr. Brady stands quietly in the background.

"Helmsman, take the wheel!"

"Aye, aye, Captain!"

He turns to his visitors.

"The Hudson is a treacherous river to navigate in a fog. Last year, The

Empire ran into a schooner at Newburgh Bay — 24 lives were lost. In all my years with this old boat, I've made 1,162 trips and carried over 172,000 passengers, but I've never lost a ship or a life, though I did lose a smokestack in a squall going through the Highlands."

Captain Buckman reaches for his pocket watch to check the time. "There are shoals and rocks for the pilots to avoid. Many a boat has gone aground on the bar below Albany and remained a prisoner there for hours. The General Jackson exploded her boilers near Grassy Point and several passengers were killed. Commodore Vanderbilt's brother Jacob was captain at the time."

The Captain looks over his shoulder to see Mr. Brady and the two boys. "Now, David enlighten our guests. What is this broad expanse of water called?"

Tim pipes in, "The North River."

"No, lad."

"The Hudson River?"

"No Tim," says David. "This is the Tappan Sea, or Zee, as the Dutch call it. The river is three and a half miles wide at this point."

"Don't forget to tell them the tale of the Flying Dutchman."

"Yes, Papa. I mean, yes, Captain. Some say the Tappan Sea is haunted by the ghost of the Flying Dutchman. Washington Irving wrote about this legend — the story of Rambout Van Dam, the roistering Dutchman of Spitting Devil."

He points larboard. "One night, Rambout rowed his boat all the way across the Tappan Sea to attend a quilting frolic at Kakiat on the western shore. He danced and drank until after midnight then he got back in his boat to return home. He was warned not to go — t'was the verge of Sunday morn. He pulled off nevertheless, swearing an oath he would not land until he reached Spitting Devil, or as the Dutch call it, Spuyten Duyvil. But, Rambout was never seen again. Some say in the quiet twilight of a summer eve when the sea is as still as a sheet of glass you can hear the sound of Rambout rowing his boat — pulling on his oars — for he is the Flying Dutchman of the Tappan Sea doomed to ply between Kakiat and Spitting Devil until the day of judgment."

Mr. Brady claps his hands, "Bravo, David! A story well told."

"Not by me, Mr. Brady, but by Mr. Irving."

The captain points to the starboard side, "Over there on the eastern shore is Sunnyside, the homestead of Washington Irving. David lend Mr. Brady my spyglass." The captain points straight ahead out the open window breathing a deep sigh. "What a journey of mysterious enchantment that first trip of the Half Moon up the Hudson must have been."

"Where?" says Tim scanning the horizon with the spyglass. "I don't see a half moon anywhere."

"No, Tim. My father was referring to Henry Hudson's ship, the Half Moon, the first ship to sail up this river in 1609."

"Why is he sometimes called Henry and other times Hendrick?"

The captain raises his hand in a stop command.

"Let me answer for you, David. You see Tim, Henry Hudson was an Englishman commanding a Dutch ship, the Half Moon, flying under the Dutch flag. No doubt you've seen the Hendrick Hudson riverboat. The ship-owners thought the name Henrick offered a more picturesque rendering of the name, instead of plain old Henry."

He sees Tim's gaze start to wander.

"Now then, what was Henry Hudson searching for as he ventured up the river?"

"Gold?"

"Not far off the mark. We all hope to find our pot of gold. But Henry Hudson thought he was going to find China on his journey up the river."

"China?"

"Yes, as incredulous as it may sound, Henry Hudson devoted his life to the quest for the fabled Northwest Passage — the shortcut to India, the Orient, and all the riches they possess."

"Did he ever find this short cut to China?"

"Sadly no, Tim. In the spring of 1610, Henry was still seeking the Northwest Passage all the way up near the Artic Circle at Hudson Bay when his crew mutinied."

"Whatever happened to Henry Hudson?"

"The mutineers put Henry, his son, and seven loyal crew members into a small boat and set them adrift. They were never heard of again."

There is a lull as the fate of Henry Hudson fades from conversation.

"Look over there, Timothy. Just past Hook Mountain, train the eyeglass on those rocky cliffs and tell me what you see."

"Aye, aye, Captain," says Tim as he scans the western shore. In a notch between the high cliffs is a steep incline with railroad tracks heading straight up to the summit. There are steamboats at the pier with workers loading blocks of ice onto barges.

"What is it, Captain?"

"That there is Slaughter's Landing, one of the ice stations used by The Knickerbocker Ice Company. Rockland Lake is up at the top. During the winter, the workers saw blocks of ice from the lake and send them barreling down the sluiceway for storage in the ice-house. It is a sight to see. More than thirty thousand tons of ice are shipped from that depot. That's how the ice barons accumulate all their wealth with frozen water — more valuable than gold!"

"What's that up ahead, Captain Buckman?"

Tim points to a flotilla of about 80 canal boats lashed together.

"That's what they call a floating town, Tim, one of the most picturesque sights on the Hudson," says the Captain. "All the canal boats from the Erie Canal are making their way down river to York. Notice how slowly the tug boat is pulling them. The movement is hardly discernible."

Tim looks at the half-mile procession of canal boats. A red flannel shirt flutters in the breeze, dancing close to a woman's snowy white under-linen. A boy runs over the deck chasing after his dog, leaping from one rooftop to the next. An elderly gentleman takes a nap in his hammock swaying back and forth. Tim notices flower boxes at the cabin windows with bright-hued geraniums. Further along, he hears the lively music of a concertina and a guitar player tapping his foot on the rooftop.

"Why are there so many boats and what are they carrying and where did they come from?"

"Hold on there a minute, one question at a time… These canalers come mainly from the Erie Canal carrying all sorts of goods such as grain, lumber, and ice bound for the docks of York. It takes about a week for one of these floating towns to make the trip down river, while one of our riverboats could make the same journey in eight hours. But slow as they may go, these floating towns helped make New York into the largest city in this country."

"How do you mean?"

"Timothy, don't you see? There are nearly 1,000 miles of canals in this state. The Champlain Canal connects the Hudson with Lake Champlain and then further to the north, the Saint Lawrence River. Then of course there is that 361-mile wonder of the world, completed in 1825 with much back-breaking work, which connects the Hudson River to the Great Lakes. You know what of I speak? Don't ya, Tim?"

"The Erie Canal."

"A smart lad he is," says the Captain. "This vast system of waterways helped make New York the undisputed Empire State. And do you know who made this steamship possible?"

Tim thinks of the street where Mr. Brady's shop is located, the deckhand on the Josephine, that portrait by Benjamin West hanging in the art gallery, and the little tour with David Lear Buckman.

"Robert Fulton."

"That's a good lad. Robert Fulton was a true visionary. I read his biography written by his friend Cadwallader Colden in 1817. Do you know he invented a boat which can go underwater? He at first called it a plunging boat, then later a submarine. For four hours, he stayed underwater if you can believe it, with air stored in a copper globe. He christened his underwater ship the Nautilus and outfitted her with torpedoes — exploding underwater bombs. If it were not for Robert Fulton, I would not be standing on the bridge of this steamship. Now then, Timothy, what say you grab hold of the helm? Don't worry, I'll be right here."

Tim steps up to the immense steering wheel. He grabs hold of one of the pegs.

"Hold fast, Timothy!"

Tim feels all the world at his command.

"That's it! You've got it. Now steer straight ahead. Keep your eye on that spit of land — that's Teller's Point. Don't lose sight of her. I'll be back in a jiffy. Helmsman, keep an eye on this greenhorn!"

"Aye, aye, Captain."

"You're doing just fine, Tim," says David. "Up ahead is Croton Point. And do you know what is further inland from there?"

"No, I can't think right now, David."

"Why, that would be the Croton Reservoir bringing cool refreshing water to York." He taps Tim on the shoulder and points. "Now, over on the starboard side is Sing Sing Prison."

Tim looks over to see the high granite walls of the state penitentiary. He thinks back to the Tombs – you don't want to wind up there. Not ever.

Captain Buckman makes his return.

"How'd he make out, David?"

"Not bad, Captain. Not bad at all."

"Before you know it boys, we'll be leaving the Tappan Sea behind us, then we'll begin our journey through The Highlands."

David yanks on his father's coat.

"Papa! Look larboard! The Champlain is gaining on us!"

"Not on my watch, Davey!"

As the captain regains the helm, Tim looks over his shoulder as Sing Sing fades farther from view as they continue their long journey up the river.

CHAPTER 33 — THE HIGHLANDS

1850

"Dunder!" shouts Captain Buckman.

Tim looks over to see The Champlain with its four smokestacks puffing mightily as the paddle-wheels churn the ship at near 20 knots. Passengers out on deck wave their hands and flutter their handkerchiefs as the riverboats race up Haverstraw Bay.

"Papa! She's getting closer!"

"Dunder!" shouts The Captain louder. "High Tor, god of thunder, I beseech you. Up high in the heavens, look down on me, mere mortal that I am. Give me the strength to conquer my foe!"

The Captain sees the worried look on his son's face as he looks over his shoulder at the other ship.

"Don't worry, Davey." He pats his son on the back. "I've had my eye on Captain Pug-Nose Houghton all the while." He grabs his brass megaphone, takes a deep breath, and shouts with all his might. "Pug-Nose, now hear this! I know all your tricks. We'll take you down by the end of Haverstraw Bay — at Dunderberg — I will and vow! Nobody beats Captain Buckman!"

The Champlain pulls closer, within ramming distance and blasts her steam-whistle. The crowds on deck cheer loudly as the ships get closer.

Suddenly, The Champlain alters course to avoid hitting a schooner tacking on the leeward wind.

"Sunday sailors be damned to Hell!" The Captain tugs down on the steam-whistle as he turns the wheel to avoid a collision. "Pleasure boats have no purpose and no direction — cruising aimlessly about, or rotting idle at the dock most the time. They have no business being in my way, and on my river!"

"The Champlain is besting us, Papa!"

"Don't give up the ship, Davey! I have her in my sights. We shall not be thwarted." The Captain pipes his tin-whistle down the brass communication tube. "Engine room! Respond now!"

"Johnny here, Captain!"

"I need more power. The Champlain is passing us. Give me 60 pounds of steam!"

"No can do, Captain. The safety valves will not allow."

"Plug the steam gauges and weigh-down the safety valves if you must. I need all engines, full-steam ahead!"

There is dead silence on the other end.

"Engine room, acknowledge!"

There is no answer as the Captain puts his ear to the tube.

"Johnny, I gave you a direct order!" He listens for a second. "I'll report you to The Commodore!"

"Captain, the boilers are over-heated! What if the wood work were to catch fire? The hull would burn like a tinderbox."

"Full steam ahead!"

"Aye, aye Captain. Full steam ahead."

"See now, Davey. The Champlain is lagging. We'll beat her to the end of Haverstraw Bay. By thunder, we will. I don't care if we have to toss the deck chairs and the state room furniture into the furnace. We cannot, and will not accept defeat."

The Captain points to Stony Point Light. "Look there, boys. There is the fog bell. Do you know what Mad Anthony Wayne told General Washington before the Battle of Stony Point?"

The boys wait wide-eyed for his answer.

"General, I'll storm hell if you only plan it!"

Tim listens to Captain Buckman tell the tale of the midnight raid of on the British fort on July 16, 1779.

"General Washington ordered a bayonet charge. No loaded muskets were allowed. Remember, this was a surprise attack. You see, he did not want any muskets going off. That night, General Wayne led the charge. He received a head wound from a musket ball, but recovered. The next day he sent a message to Washington. 'Dear General: The fort and garrison, with Colonel Johnston are ours. Our officers and men behaved like men who are determined to be free.'"

The Captain points ahead. "There she is gentlemen, Dunderberg Mountain and the entrance to the grand gorges of The Highlands."

Tim sighs with wonder at the mountains in the distance. The faint purples and forest greens, are offset by the sky blues and white wisps of cirrus clouds in the background. The sunshine adds accents to the mountain scene and sparkles the deep blue river with windy whitecaps and sailboats crisscrossing the bay.

"Isn't it wonderful, Mr. Brady?"

"Yes, being on the bridge and watching the Captain in action is quite an adventure."

"No, I was referring to those mountains. I've never seen anything like it in all my life. They're so massive, reaching high into the sky. The sailboats and steamships in the distance look so small in comparison. Look at all those trees covering the mountains. There must be one hundred thousand trees. They look like splinters, but I know each and every one of them to be very tall."

"Timothy, it is indeed a sight to behold. It's as if Thomas Cole painted this scene before our eyes. Just take it all in… savor this sight and try to remember it for always."

"Yes, Mr. Brady."

"Papa, tell Mr. Brady and Tim about that great race where they tossed all the ship's furniture into the boiler."

"Oh, that was a hotly contested race a few years ago between The Cornelius Vanderbilt and The Oregon on June 1, 1847. The two of them raced down-river, neck and neck, the whole way. The ships rammed at one point, damaging the wheel house of The Vanderbilt. On the final stretch, The Oregon's coal gave out. The crew in the engine room thought the race was lost. But the captain ordered all hands to grab every deck chair, and bench they could find, and toss them into the furnace. Next, they took furniture from the state rooms and anything else that would burn to keep up the steam. The Oregon finished the race at The Battery nigh 1,200 feet ahead of The Vanderbilt. That's how close a race it was — just barely three ship lengths."

"The Oregon travelled 70 miles in 3 hours and 15 minutes, isn't that right, Papa? Near 21 miles per hour."

"Yes, Davey. That's right. The Oregon won the race and took home the whole kitty – the $1,000 wager not to mention all the side-bets. But in the end, she lost much more than that."

"How so Captain?" asks Mr. Brady.

"Consider all the shipwright repairs to The Oregon, not to mention all the lost revenue while she was out of commission in dry dock without paying customers. Short-sighted is all. Look ahead now, Bear Mountain."

Just then the communication tube echoes with a distant voice.

"Engine room to bridge!"

"Captain here."

"Permission to reduce pressure!"

"Permission denied!"

"But Captain, the boilers are super-heated. The rivets on the boiler will not hold much longer."

"Blast your insubordinance! Full-steam ahead!"

There is silence on the other end.

"Engine room, acknowledge!"

"Aye, Captain, full-steam ahead!"

"Now as we round Anthony's Nose, you'll see Sugarloaf Mountain in the distance. Tim gazes up at the steep cliff coming from on high right down to the rocky shore.

"Over on the larboard side is Lady Cliff. Take the spy glass and gander at Buttermilk Falls. See how the stream comes rushing down the rocks in cascades and foaming rapids like a broad sheet of milk. That's why the

Dutch skippers suggested its name."

The captain slaps Tim on the back – startling him as he holds the spyglass.

"There is Constitution Island in the distance. That is the spot where the Continental Army set the chains across the river to prevent the British Navy from sailing up the river. Before long, we'll be approaching West Point. You've heard of West Point, haven't you Timothy?"

"Yes of course, Captain, that's where the sun sets."

The Captain laughs a hearty laugh. "David, be a good lad and enlighten young Tim."

"Timothy, West Point is the site of the United States Military Academy. This is where all the young cadets study military tactics for a career in the U.S. Army and then perhaps one day become a brigadier general. The cadets sometimes fire their cannons to us in a salute. See that mountain over there?"

"Yes."

"That is called the Old Cro' Nest. She is 1,418 feet tall. Over there is Captain Kidd's Plug Cliff."

Tim looks up at the sheer cliff of this mountain, jutting straight from the shore of the Hudson straight up high into the heavens.

"They say Captain Kidd, the noted pirate, buried immense sums of money and treasures somewhere in The Highlands."

"Papa, there is a sloop tacking on the starboard bow."

"Don't you worry, Davey. I have the right of way. They must yield to me. Now, then take a look at the mighty Storm King at 1,800 feet. Since the time of the Dutch, that was known as Boter Berg, or Butter Mountain, since it resembled a slab of butter on the dish."

Mr. Brady steps forward. "My dear friend Nathaniel Parker Willis would be most pleased you referred to that mountain by its new name."

"Yes, Mr. Brady you are quite right. Tell us the full story."

"Well, one day I visited N.P. Willis at Idlewild, his artist retreat overlooking the Hudson at Newburgh Bay. We gazed out his back veranda at Boter Berg. 'Mathew,' he said to me, 'Does that edifice not deserve a more fitting name than Butter Mountain?'"

"Yes, Nathaniel, I believe it does."

"So, Mr. Willis thought on the matter and then appealed to the good public for a more poetic title and the more fitting name, Storm King."

"Then there is Storm King."

"Papa! That sloop is sure to cross our path!"

"Henry Hudson!" shouts the Captain as he tugs down to blast a warning. He looks to his left. "Fulton's Folly be damned to Hell! The Champlain will not heed! I cannot steer clear. Don't lower your sails! They're just young boys. You're a sitting duck sure to be crushed! Do I ram

Pug-Nose or trample that sloop to bits with my mighty paddle wheels?"

The Captain throws up his hands and shouts into the communication tube.

"Engine room! Situation critical! Respond back!"

"Johnny, here Captain!"

"All engines stop!"

"By whose order?"

"This is Captain Buckman! I repeat, this is Captain Buckman!"

"But what about the race and the wager, Captain?"

"Damn The Champlain and the wager. ALL ENGINES STOP!"

"Aye, aye, Captain."

"Reverse engines one quarter."

"Engines reversed one quarter, Captain."

"Reduce pressure. Engage safety valves. Set pressure to 25 pounds."

"Aye, Captain. 25 pounds."

As the steamship reduces speed at Newburgh Bay and steers clear of the foundering sloop trying to reset sail, The Champlain forges ahead into the distance past Polly Pell Island.

David walks over to his father at the helm and tugs on his coat.

"Papa, shouldn't we try to beat The Champlain?"

"No, Davey. Polly Pell is a bad omen. There are hob-goblins on that island lurking about."

Tim looks over at the island. "I don't see any hob-goblins."

"Hush now!" shouts the Captain. "The Heer of Dunderberg shall thrash us with his mighty winds and treacherous waters just like The Storm-Ship."

"What Storm-Ship?"

"By Washington Irving, The Flying Dutchman was lost in a brutal storm just south of Polly Pell Island. She was condemned to sail the Hudson for all eternity. Their cries for help can still be heard during violent storms."

"Papa, what about Captain Lawrence's famous last words, 'Don't Give up the Ship.' We can still win."

"No son, we have lost all momentum. If the good Captain Lawrence were standing here, I'm sure he'd tell me. 'Don't scuttle the ship!' You see Davey, I have 400 passengers to consider. Don't you worry, we'll get to the town of Catskill in good time. You can depend on it. But the grand old racing contests on the Hudson will soon be coming to an end."

"What are you talking about, Papa?"

"Down at the tavern the other night, I heard talk of the proposed Steamship Inspection Bill. There has been much public outcry to ban all racing of riverboats on the Hudson."

"But why, Papa? The races add excitement among the passengers and crew. Everybody loves to watch a race."

"Need I remind you of The Swallow?"

"Please Captain, tell about The Swallow," says Mr. Brady.

"Oh, I would be glad to tell you. Now, The Swallow was as fine a steamship as I've ever seen. In the fall of 1836, she had a memorable race with The Rochester. Starting from Jersey City, the boats were within short distance of each other all the way up the river with the tide against them. The Rochester finished the race to Albany in 8 hours and 57 minutes and The Swallow pulled in just five minutes behind her rival in 9 hours and 2 minutes."

"Tell them about the race in 1845, Papa."

"Yes, Davey. I was getting to that. Just give me a moment... I was setting the stage for these two old rivals." He goes over to his log book over on the chart table. He flips through some pages and finds a lithograph. He brings it over to show Mr. Brady and Tim. "This is an artist's rendering of that night."

Tim peers over Mr. Brady's shoulder to look at the lithograph - The Wreck of The Swallow in black and white – a nighttime scene of a sinking ship – nearly submerged – the keel broken – her back broken – the keel split in two – the stern sticking straight up. Numerous rowboats surround the ship, a plume of smoke rises from the sunken engine room.

"It was April 7, 1845, in a snow squall with three to four hundred passengers on board when The Swallow met with disaster near Athens. She ran upon a little rocky island and sank in a few minutes. The captain claimed that no racing was involved, while the passengers said otherwise. There was little doubt she was racing with The Express and The Rochester. The crews of both ships rendered what assistance was in their power. Still, the number of lives lost proved to be about 15."

"Papa, tell them what you did afterwards."

"I purchased the old wreck of The Swallow and hauled the material seven miles inland and built a fine two-story house on the Albany Post Road in the town of Valatia. Fittingly enough, I called it The Swallow House."

"What a remarkable story, Captain. I cannot thank you enough for your hospitality. This has been a memorable experience — one I shall cherish. Please accept this as a mere token in appreciation for your kindness."

"Oh, I couldn't accept such a generous offering."

"Please, I insist. We have taken up too much of your valuable time. Now we must bid adieu and retire to our state room."

"Timothy, shake hands with David and thank him for the tour of the ship."

Back at the stateroom...

Sitting at the table with white table linen, watching the river go by, Tim eats a lunch buffet set out by the steward at the direction of Julia. He listens vaguely as Mr. Brady discusses the vast tracts of lands owned by the Dutch patroons such as the Van Rennseleaer and Bronck families.

"The patroons were landlords in the true sense of the word, Timothy. Lords of the land, much like the English landlords back home in Ireland, charging rack-rent to these poor peasant farmers who did not own the land they toiled upon year after year. This led to the Anti-Rent Wars."

"Timothy, you look all glassy-eyed," says Julia. "You poor thing, you must be exhausted. We still have a long way to go. Let me tuck you into bed."

Tim feels the warmth of the blankets as Julia soothes him to sleep. "There you go... rest your eyes. I'll open the window so you can listen to the paddlewheels and watch the river go by..." She gives him a peck on the cheek as he drifts off to sleep.

Tim listens to the great ship breathe. The gentle giant puffs away as she makes her way up the river. He thinks of those poor stokers down in the engine room toiling away, feeding the beast. He feels the heat and tries to run away before they grab hold of him, but his legs won't run as he gets tossed into the blazing fires of the furnace.

Suddenly, he feels a soft breeze on his cheek and a hand through his hair. "C'mon now sleepy-head. Time to wake up. You've been asleep for hours and hours," says Julia with a whisper to his ear.

"We're pulling into the town docks at Catskill... Look out the window, Timothy. Can you see it? There in the distance that speck of white up on the cliff? For miles and miles, we can see The Mountain House — 3,000 feet above the River, like a bit of snow left on the mountain."

CHAPTER 34 — STAGE-COACH ROAD

1850

Through the open plain, the stage-coach rumbles along the dusty road as the sun beats down with the high heat of an Indian summer day.

"How are you fairing there, young gentleman sir?"

"Just fine, Mr. Vedder and please call me, Tim."

"Are you sure you don't wish to ride with the passengers down below? The seats are plush and you'll escape the blaze of the sun."

Tim takes off his black hat and mops his brow, fanning himself with the wide brim. "I much prefer this vantage point."

"Suit yourself."

"How much longer, Mr. Vedder?"

"Oh, we have not even reached Horse Shoe Turn. We have a good two hours still left to climb."

"Two hours? Are you quite sure? How long has it been?"

"By my reckoning, we left the docks two hours ago. This 12-mile journey to the summit takes four hours. Now we've already climbed about 700 feet since leaving the shore. On the last stretch, we will climb another 1,550 feet from the base to the top."

Tim looks at the four strong horses with their steaming flanks and listens to their hard breathing as they slowly pull their heavy burden.

"Mr. Vedder shouldn't we stop and give the horses some water?"

"Good heavens no! That would surely kill them. Their stomachs would twist into knots then they would keel over and die. But don't you worry, we'll give the horses a rest at the halfway point, just after Dead Ox Hill."

Tim thinks of the poor belabored ox keeling over and wonders about those four hardworking horses struggling away.

"Mr. Vedder, do you think they're happy?"

"You mean the horses there?"

"Wouldn't they rather be running free through the fields?"

"Those are Shire horses, Tim. They are used to hard work. They come from a long line of logging horses, hauling hemlock to the tanneries. I take better care of those than I do myself. Believe me, they're happy in their work. Just look at them, proud and strong, giving it their all."

Suddenly, there is a crackle of light and the distant rumble of thunder as it echoes across the valley. Tim startles in his seat and looks up at the dark grey clouds swirling in a tempest.

"Don't worry my boy. It's just Hendrick Hudson playing at nine pins."

Tim moves underneath the outstretched arm of the coachman, finding shelter in the craw of his arm pit from a loud thundering boom.

"Remember what I said, Tim. It's just the crew of the Half Moon tossing the bowling ball, knocking down the nine pins. That is all… Do you know there is a bowling alley up top at the Mountain House?"

"There is?"

"Oh yes. And a billiard's table too. You'll have a grand time. My boss, Mr. Charles L. Beach, runs The Mountain House. He makes all his money with this here stage coach line so he can take care of his pride and joy."

Big droplets of water start plopping down, pelting Tim's hat, one after the other giving way to a rain-soaking torrent. Steam rises from the dusty road as the deep ruts fill with water.

"Now, you're sure you don't want to ride down below?"

"Yes, I'm sure Mr. Vedder. It's just a bit of the wet."

"You're a stubborn, lad. I'll give you that."

There is a chill in the air as Tim finds warmth next to the driver.

"Look there, Tim. Up ahead is the Horse Shoe Turn and there at the base of the cliff is the Rip Van Winkle House."

"It looks like a shanty to me."

"See that boulder over there? That is the site of Rip's 20-year slumber."

Tim looks over at the huge boulder and wonders how it got there.

"Yes, and what's more, they found the bones of Rip's old dog right beside."

"You mean Wolf, his dog?"

"The very same."

As they draw closer, Tim sees other stage coaches stopped at the side of the road with passengers milling about.

The driver pulls the coach to a stop setting the iron slippers to brake the wagon wheels. He climbs down and unlatches the door.

"Everyone out! We've reached the halfway point. We need to give horse and rider a well-earned rest. You'll find some refreshments and victuals at Rip's Tavern. Be sure to take a tour of his humble abode, the likes of which you'll never see again. We depart for the summit in three quarters of an hour."

Finding shelter under the front porch of the tavern, Mrs. Brady comes rushing over. "Timothy, look at you. You're soaked to the bone. Let's get you out of that wet coat before you catch your death of cold. Mathew, fetch a coat from the steam trunk."

"But Julia, the driver strapped them down."

"Mathew, this instant."

She buttons Tim up in a dry coat. "Not another word. You'll ride with us in the compartment. Is that understood?"

"Yes, Mrs. Brady."

"Now then what do you say to a hearty meal? You must be famished. Let's venture inside the Rip Van Winkle Tavern. Mathew, find us a nice table over there by the fireplace. Then order us a nice hot pot of tea."

Tim sees a sign over the doorway towards the back. "This way to the Rip Van Winkle Museum."

As they take a seat Brady notices a sign hanging on the wall over the barkeep. "When life hangs heavy, have a quieting draught out of Rip Van Winkle's flagon."

"Good evening folks and welcome to Rip's Roadside Tavern. The name is Peter Vanderdonk. Now, what can I get you on this thunderous eve?"

"My dear wife Julia will have a cup of tea, for the lad, a cup of cider, and I will have a tankard of your house ale."

"Coming right up sir."

Mathew takes a quieting drink from the pewter mug with a glass bottom as Julia sips her cup of tea.

"Might I suggest the cook's special – the shepherd's pie?"

"Yes, Mathew, I should like that very much."

"Now, then for an extra two shillings, you are entitled to take a tour of Rip Van Winkle's humble abode, which I highly recommend."

"Yes, I suppose that will be fine."

"Just follow the red velvet ropes, your supper will be ready on your return."

Past the Rip Van Winkle Museum sign, they follow the crowd to the back kitchen. Standing against the brick wall of the open hearth, Tim sees a rusty, old musket with the worm-eaten, wooden stock. "Rip's Old Firelock – Do Not Touch!"

"Mr. Brady, imagine that musket sitting next to Rip during his 20-year slumber. Look there are his galligaskins and his hob-nail boots. I never knew what galligaskins were until now." Tim sees the loose-fitting breeches with suspenders inlaid with mountain flower motifs.

"Yes, Timothy now lower your voice a tad, so as not to disturb the other onlookers."

They go up the dark narrow staircase with crooked, high steps.

"Look at that Mr. Brady. There is the very chair used by Dame Van Winkle."

"Yes, Timothy I can well read the sign."

"What does that word 'termagant' mean?"

"Yes, Mathew," says Julia, arm in arm, smiling widely. "I would just love to hear your explanation."

"Well if you must know, a termagant is a… How should I put this?"

"Go on, Mathew. We're listening…"

"Well, from what I understand, Rip was a hen-pecked husband. Dame Van Winkle often scolded him and his dog Wolf for their indolent ways. He did not look after the farm. His wife often said, he would rather starve on a penny than work for a pound."

"So, what exactly is a termagant, Mr. Brady?"

"A termagant is a quarrelsome, scolding woman – a shrew. Quite unlike you, my dearest."

"Oh Mathew, you needn't have said that."

"But I mean it in all sincerity. I am reminded of what Washington Irving wrote in his story, The Wife. 'There is in every true woman's heart a spark of heavenly fire which lies dormant in the broad daylight of prosperity, but which kindles up, and beams and blazes in the dark hour of adversity.' That describes you, Julia."

"Oh, Mathew, you're using Mr. Barnum's soft-soap on me."

"Look over there, Mr. Brady. There is Rip's bed." Tim looks inside the bedroom to see long drapes hanging from the four-poster bed. He reads the sign. "This is where Dame Van Winkle gave poor Rip many a curtain lecture."

"Mr. Brady, what is a curtain lecture?"

Julia smiles with the other patrons at the strained expression on Brady's face as he hesitates a moment to wipe his brow with his handkerchief. "Yes, Mathew, tell us all about a curtain lecture…"

"Well you see, Timothy, a curtain lecture is a private reprimand given to a husband by his wife behind the bed curtains."

"Much like a scolding?"

"Yes, Timothy."

"Does Mrs. Brady often give you a curtain lecture?" A laugh comes from back in the line.

"We're waiting, Mathew…"

"Look there, Timothy. There is the bowling ball and the nine pins that Rip played with the crew of the Half Moon."

"Are you quite sure, Mr. Brady?"

"Yes, indeed. That what the sign says, doesn't it? Now then, let's head back to our table. Our supper must be near ready."

After a hearty dinner, riding in the back of the stage coach, Tim is jostled about, rocking back and forth. Trying not to fall asleep, fighting the swaying motion. Mrs. Brady offers him a comfy spot close to her. Ever since that first day on Friday the 13th, Tim has avoided riding in the cramped omni-bus, preferring to take a brisk walk up Broadway. The coach jolts and rattles with a bang of its iron rimmed wheels against a boulder.

"Here rest your head," says Mrs. Brady. "Don't worry, I shan't bite." Drifting off, he thinks back to the Albany Dock and this long day's journey into night. Oh, how I wish Mr. Brady accepted the kind offer of the waiter. 'Rooms are available upstairs at the inn folks. After breakfast, you can take the morning stage.' But Mr. Brady begged off. "I think not. There is daylight still." The incline up the mountain road grows steeper and steeper, as Tim leans further back. He feels the horses lose their traction as the carriage slips backwards.

The driver sets the brake, pushing the iron slipper tight to the wagon wheel. "Everyone out!"

"What's the meaning of this? We haven't reached the summit."

"Everyone out! I mean everyone! The horses are exhausted. We must all walk the last leg of the journey. A bit of exercise will do us all good."

As they trudge up the mountain road, the driver shouts out. "Everyone look up! There at the bend in the road."

In the twilight, the white birch tree trunks direct their gaze up past the shadows of the deep dark forest to the foreboding wall of the escarpment then higher still to the top of the cliff to the gleaming white Mountain House with its thirteen Corinthian columns.

"Look there, Timothy. Do you see what I see?"

"Yes, Mr. Brady. It looks just like that painting by Sarah Cole."

"I see the Parthenon, my boy. There is the Acropolis in Athens — a city up high on a plateau — the birthplace of democracy. For not only did the ancient Greeks give us the camera obscura, but that wonderful word – democracy — government by the people. Those columns represent the thirteen original colonies."

"Come hither, my fanciful fool!" says Julia. "Have you forgotten me? The both of you, on either side. And lend me a hand."

In the failing light, the three of them walk arm in arm up the mountain road with the other passengers following the coachman's lantern.

CHAPTER 35 — THE ESCARPMENT

1985

"Bill, remember our first camping trip to North Lake in 1979. We never did see The Escarpment on that trip."

How can you go camping to Yosemite and not see El Capitan or Half Dome? We did. It was right behind us all the time when we were swimming at North Lake. Somehow, we missed it… it's like we camped at the rim and never saw the Grand Canyon. It wasn't until four years later on our second trip to North Lake that we stumbled upon The Escarpment in 1983, quite by accident.

"Bill, remember I couldn't get the week off from work to go camping with you guys." I was working at Nathan's Famous at the time.

"That's okay, Danny, I'll come back and get you."

"Really, Dad? That's a long way for you to go… all the way back and forth to the Catskills."

"It's no trouble at all. It's only a tank of gas. I want you to be there."

Just as he promised, Dad came back to get me in his old Chevy Nova. I woke the next morning unsure of my surroundings. I stared up at the canvas roof of the pop-up camper. I remembered how I got here, the car ride with Dad in the Nova. Now, we have the pop-up camper with us. The five of us weren't crammed in a tent. We had mattresses. Dad didn't wake up with a stiff back. When the rain poured down, we didn't have to worry about the tent filling up with water like a bathtub leaving us soaked to the bone in our sleeping bags. We were high and dry, off the ground beneath the canvas shelter of our pop-up camper.

I pulled back the curtain to see Dad in the kitchen busy making one of his great big breakfasts on top of his cast iron skillet. He cooked up pancakes, bacon and eggs, corned beef hash, kielbasa, home fries. Then afterwards we were sitting around the kitchen table reading the comics, getting underfoot as Dad tried to clean-up and do the dishes.

"How about you kids go swimming?"

"It's too early Dad. We just ate breakfast."

"Why don't you take the kids for a ride in the raft?"

We went down to the lake to find our inflatable orange rowboat tied with a rope around a tree – collapsed and lifeless. Somebody popped it with a knife. Back to the camper we go and report back to Dad. Sitting dejected around the table, how 'bout we play some poker? Dad busies himself heating dishwater on the camp stove.

"No, it's a beautiful day – why don't you look at the campground map and take the kids on a hike or something?"

"We already did that Dad. We took the hiking trail around the lake."

"Well, how about you go on another hike. Go out and explore a new trail. Just GO."

I could read between the lines. Take a long walk off a short pier. Get from underfoot! He was about to say.

There on the kitchen table was the campground map with the loop roads and numbered campsites, and a walking path around the lake. Then at the bottom of the map was this strange cryptic term —Escarpment.

"Hey, Dad what does 'Escarpment' mean?"

"Well, let's see… An Escarpment is a steep cliff or precipice – why don't you go see?"

So, we filled up our canteens, grabbed our cameras, and off we went. We neared the beach area to North Lake – there was this lot in the back, some power lines leading downhill. We could see wide expanse in the distance – but the trees hindered our view – off to the right was a dirt road leading up the hill.

Up we trudged the steep road, rounding the bend there was the remnants to a basement from long ago. Further up the road was a plateau, a tree-less field of high grass. In the distance was wide-open sky – calling you to come closer, beckoning you... Bill, Delia, and Jim took off like greyhounds at the track. They bolted — running towards the expanse of sky — they had the jump on me. They didn't heed my commands to wait. They tore through the fields – canteens clanging at their side.

In the distance, I could see the edge of a cliff — the wide-open sky. At any moment, I expected to see Julie Andrews twirling around singing, "The hills are alive with the sound of music." Bill and Delia headed full stride to the edge of the cliff with Jim close behind. Stop! You guys! Stop! They went headstrong for the cliff then leaped in the air and disappeared off the precipice. Jim followed close behind leaping off the cliff! What will I tell Dad?

As I got to the edge, I could see them falling off the face of the earth, but the cliff had a second landing – a wide open step with Bill, Delia and Jim looking up at me with hide-and-seek grins. So, this is what The Escarpment is! A plateau looking out at all the world from on high! The views were as far as the eye could see. The wind was blowing all around.

Then we looked down at the chisel marks – from long, long ago – some chiseled their full names. The dates went back in time – 1950, 1930, 1910, 1880, 1860. Over at the edge of the field was a historical marker. We ran to it. Against a blue metal canvas with gold letters, the New York State historical marker indicated that this is the place where the Catskill Mountain

House once stood – where dignitaries such as Ulysses S. Grant and General Sherman vacationed. I read the last paragraph:

"As modern highways and high speed transportation superseded the steamboat, stage coach and railway connections, the great mountain resorts lost their clientele and fell into decay. Only the commanding view of this historic resort remains."

I envision what The Catskill Mountain House must have looked like with its "13 Corinthian columns of gleaming white." I think of that movie I saw with Christopher Reeve and Jane Seymour – Somewhere in Time set in the Gilded Age of grand hotels. It was a special movie to me somehow. I find the composition I wrote about this film on October 12, 1981.

Teresa Wright, the actress who played opposite Gary Cooper in Pride of the Yankees, had a small part. She was in that movie The Search for Bridey Murphy. Christopher Reeve's character traveled back in time not like Marty McFly in the DeLorean, or H.G. Wells in a Time Machine, but by lying down on a bed almost like Edgar Casey...

We headed back to the campsite – anxious to tell Dad all about our great discovery – The Escarpment. The mighty explorers returned from their expedition back to base camp breathless with excitement and wonder.

"Dad, you will never believe what we discovered. You've got to come see!"

"It can wait 'til morning. I've got to go out and get some groceries."

"But Dad, you've got to come see."

"Don't worry, I'm sure it will still be there in the morning."

The next morning, we headed out – Dad brought along his Konica camera. It was a beautiful spectacular day – crisp with dramatic clouds rolling by – we were up in heaven looking down below at the valley. We could see how the clouds cast a shadow on the little towns with church steeples.

We showed Dad the historical marker then to the right was a trail leading up the hill. We took a break beneath the canopy of the forest then continued on our way, hiking along the Escarpment Trail.

The next day we took a turn on the campground road, there was a sign leading us down a dirt road. We followed it passing by an old abandoned caboose and parked the car in a small parking lot. We followed the trail along a tranquil mountain stream — jumping from boulder to boulder... following the stream to a pool at the very edge of the precipice — to the edge of Kaaterskill Falls — water rushing over, leaping off the cliff, plunging 180 feet down below, then cascading another 80 feet in a second waterfall.

We looked over the edge.

"Stand BACK!" warns Dad.

As we took photographs and admired the old chisel marks in the rocks,

Dad scratched his head and looked around.

"Wait a second... I think I was here when I was a little kid back in the 1930s. In fact, I'm sure of it. There was a railing at the edge." Then he points to the trees up on the hill. "And there was this enormous hotel over there." Nothing but trees remained.

Later that night as we sat around the campfire, poking the embers with our sticks, Dad told us how he was wounded in the War.

Maybe it was the camp shovel that sparked some memories. I bought it at an army surplus store and thought it would be a good tool to put out a campfire. Dad grabbed ahold of that little shovel like a long-lost friend. He shook hands with it, unsnapped the canvas cover, extended the flip shovel, and tightened the turn screw into place.

"This is what we called an entrenching tool in the Army," he said. "This is what saved my life, many a time."

I wasn't sure what he was talking about. How could a little shovel like that save his life?

"When the Germans zeroed in on us with the 88s and mortars, we had to dig fast and dig deep."

Or maybe it was that little can opener. No bigger than a razor blade, this little can opener folded out and was very good at opening a tin can.

"This is what we used to open C-Rations," he recalled. "We had to travel light in the infantry. I kept a spoon in my spats along with this little can opener. You couldn't eat if you lost this."

"So, did they send you home after you got wounded?"

I pictured Hawkeye Pierce at some M*A*S*H unit telling Dad how he had a million-dollar wound. This was your ticket home, soldier.

"No, they sent me back to the front."

Then he told us how he was wounded a second time and sent back to the front again. He was one of the lucky ones. He came home alive. Looking back at the photographs, I came to realize that this was the last camping trip we ever took with Dad. I am glad he drove all the way back home to pick me up. Thanks, Dad.

CHAPTER 36 — THE MOUNTAIN HOUSE

1850

Before dawn sleeping by the open window, a brisk breeze bristles Tim's cheek. He nestles his head in the soft eider down pillow and stretches his legs searching for his foot warmers: Salty, Rex, and Pepper. Where can they be? Must be outside or sleeping with Pa. He rubs his eyes and lifts his heavy head. I must get ready for work or I shall miss The Josephine.

Looking about the shadows of his bedroom, his eyes come into focus. There is a massive Corinthian column standing outside his window. How did that get there? He jumps out of bed to examine the intricate carvings and flower motifs. Just beyond, in the faint morning light, he can see planet Earth way, way, down below as if he were floating on a cloud. That must be it, I've died and gone to heaven. Perhaps the stokers tossed me into the furnace, or maybe the boilers burst and we sank to a watery grave. Tim gazes out the third story window. I can't believe my eyes. We're higher than the trees, higher than the clouds, high as the hawk soaring above.

There is a knock on the door.

"Timothy, quickly now. Out of your nightshirt. Put on something presentable."

"Yes, Mr. Brady."

"Hurry, we don't want to miss the sunrise."

Out on the veranda, far from the gathering crowd, they find a quiet spot over at the railing. Beneath a blanket, Julia nuzzles her head on her husband's shoulder.

Looking down at the Hudson River Valley, from near 3,000 feet, the sun rises, blazing orange in the misty mountain light.

"Isn't it glorious, Mathew? It's as if we are witnessing the dawn of creation."

"Yes Julia, the view is so sublime…"

She takes his hand, squeezing it, watching the sun inch up higher and higher over the horizon.

He sighs in exultation, "For a fleeting moment, I imagined the two of us as a god and goddess atop Mount Olympus."

Over breakfast in the dining room, Tim mops his plate with pumpernickel bread. He cleans the eggs and bits of bacon from his blue Staffordshire plate, revealing a painted scene of the Mountain House on the cliff with a stage coach rumbling along the road.

He looks out the dining room window as the morning sun shines down on the church steeples and tiny towns. He marvels at the vantage point. From this high altitude, he can see how the clouds cast a shadow on a corn field below while the farm house burns white hot and the barn blazes red in the sunlight. He thinks to himself, I've never seen the world from this high in the sky. I've never seen the sunrise before that I can remember. Not from sleepy Staten Island. I've never been this far away from home... Glimmering in the distance, running like a thin sliver of quicksilver on the Scovill plate is the Hudson River.

"Look, Mr. Brady! You can see one of the steamboats going up the river."

"Yes, Timothy."

He goes back to mopping his plate.

"Mr. Brady, might we view the sunrise tomorrow?"

"Of course, I'll be sure to wake you. One never tires of seeing the morning miracle happen before our very eyes."

"Might we set up your camera to capture the sun?"

"Oh, Timothy," sighs Mr. Brady. "It just wouldn't be practical."

"But didn't Professor Draper portrait the moon? That's what Mr. Tarbox told me."

"What a wonderful idea, Mathew!" says Julia.

Brady dabs the linen to the corner of his mouth.

"Timothy, you are quite correct. Professor Draper used the telescope from the rooftop of New York University to capture that moonscape." He turns to his wife. "Would that I could, Julia. But I neglected to bring my camera as I have pressing business matters to discuss with Mr. Lawrence."

"Might I be excused, Mr. Brady?"

"Don't wander off too far, Timothy. And stay away from the edge of the cliff. Promise me!"

"Yes, Mrs. Brady."

"Be back before noon. After luncheon, Mathew promises to take us out on the lake in the rowboat."

"Yes, Mrs. Brady…"

"Isn't that right, Mathew?"

"Yes, Julia, though I hoped it to be just the two of us."

Tim dashes off, running the length of the grand piazza, past the thirteen massive Corinthian columns, down the grand staircase to the windswept cliff. He follows the walking trail along the edge of the escarpment with its breathtaking views. Up ahead he sees a sign, 'This way to Artist Rock.' Running and skipping along the trail as it leads out to a point, Tim slows down as he sees a woman sitting on a bench with a parasol on her shoulder. He sees her holding a sketch book and a charcoal rod in her hand etching lines and impressions to the page. Tim looks over her shoulder to see the Mountain House at the cliff's edge.

"What do you think?"

"Very fine indeed, Miss."

"Here, take a seat beside me and I will show you some other views." She turns the page. "This is one from the summit of North Mountain. Oh, what a strenuous hike, but the rewards were well worth the struggle."

Tim sees both lakes, North and South, and the Mountain House. She turns a few more pages. Tim sighs with wonder at the views of Kaaterskill Falls as the gushing water plummets off one precipice then tumbles off a second.

Tim thanks the artist with the sketch book before scampering off down the trail stopping at Lookout Rock and Sunset Point. Along the way he notices other people sitting down with a knee propped up as an easel for their sketch book. He thinks back to the riverboat ride, people out on deck sketching a sailboat. He is reminded of Washington Irving's collection of stories, he titled it The Sketch Book.

Tim walks around to the rear entrance of the Mountain House with the circular drive and sees all the arriving stage coaches. He makes his way past the servant's quarters, the baker's oven, and the meat cellar. Beyond the stables, he sees a curious wagon over by the barn. He runs past the garden and the chicken coop to take a closer look. Is that the word 'daguerreotype' I see? No, it can't be.

Tim runs over to this black painted wagon with gold lettering. Daguerreotype Saloon ~ Professor Levi L. Hill ~ Daguerreotype Artist Extraordinaire. Westkill, New York. Portraits ready while you wait. He knocks on the door.

"What can I do for you young man? Interested in having your likeness taken? Allow me to introduce myself, I am Professor Levi Hill at your service. I would be only too happy to schedule a sitting."

"No thank you professor, I am not here for a sitting. But I would greatly appreciate a tour of your travelling daguerreotype studio."

"Why, whatever for?"

"You see, Mr. Hill, I am a buff-boy at a doggorro-type gallery on Broadway."

"So, you're a run-a-way then? Looking for work. Well, I can tell you straight away, you've come to the wrong place. I make it a rule. Never to hire run-a-ways."

"No, sir you misunderstand. I needn't any work. I was curious as to the inner workings of your studio."

"But, I have paying customers to consider."

"Professor Hill, I would be glad to pay the admission fee."

"Well, why didn't you say so from the start. I would be only too happy to help one of my brethren daguerreotypers. Two bits if you please. Step inside my boy."

Tim looks up to see a beautiful skylight illuminate the gallery. Before him, there is a camera and the portrait chair with headrest. Over in the corner is a gilded bird cage with canaries chirping.

"This wagon is 28 feet long and 11 feet wide. It was constructed at a cost of $1,200. You will find this is as fine a portrait studio as any on Broadway."

Tim notices the red velvet wall paper and the portraits hanging on the wall. "This is very impressive, Professor Hill. Where is the mercurial room?"

"That is in the back with my living quarters."

"Shouldn't you be concerned about the vapors, Professor?"

"No, my boy. The vapors are what saved my life and gave me a renewed sense of purpose. There I was, a reverend at the Baptist Church in Westkill suffering from an acute case of bronchitis which prevented me from preaching. So forlorn was I, resigned to my fate. Then one day, quite by accident while visiting a daguerreotypist's shop, I found that the fumes of bromine and chlorine were so beneficial that I took up the practice of the New Art."

Tim gazes again at the gallery wall. He sees only portraits. "Tell me Professor, do you ever take landscapes with your camera?"

"Why, whatever for? What a foolish enterprise that would be!"

"To capture the mountains or say, Kaaterskill Falls."

"Those would merely be wasted plates, my boy. We cater to paying customers. We don't go chasing after some silly muse."

"But have you ever attempted a landscape with your camera, Professor?"

"Now that you mention it, you see that is the subject of a book I am currently working on… producing landscapes with natural colors."

"What is the title of your book?"

"The working title is The Magic Buff. You see this is all hush-hush until I've finished with my experiments. But I have developed a method for daguerreotyping in the colors of nature. Imagine seeing blue, red, violet and orange on one plate. I call my new process the Hillo-type."

"That sounds remarkable, Professor Hill. Do you have any of these plates with all of nature's colors?"

"No, unfortunately these experiments are much too fragile to display at the moment. But be sure to keep a watchful eye for my new book. It is due out in the next few months for a moderate price."

"Yes, Professor, The Magic Buff. Thank you kindly for your time."

Tim races across the circular drive to the front of the Mountain House anxious to tell Mr. Brady all about the travelling studio wagon. But as he gets near the veranda, he sees Mr. Brady talking to a man stretched out on a lounge chair bundled with blankets. He slows his pace to a tip-toe so as not to disturb their conversation.

"Martin, I beseech you. Please, do not to return to the mercurial room."

"Not to worry Mathew, I will be right as rain in another week or so."

"No, Martin. You will only become yet another martyr to our art. This is why you must come with me to visit the Crystal Palace in London. Just think of it, we shall take the grand tour of the Continent. This will give you the proper time to recuperate."

"I am not so sure of the relevance, Mathew. Why London? Why now?"

"Martin, need I remind you of the World's Fair of 1851? There is much change on the horizon. We must see the English process in person with our own eyes."

"Yes, Mathew, I will give the matter some consideration." He turns his attention to Tim, waiting in the wings. "Now then, who do we have here?"

"Martin, allow me to introduce my able assistant, Timothy H. O'Sullivan. Tim shake hands with Mr. Martin M. Lawrence."

Tim sees the kind expression of a man about 42 with a clean-shaven face except for a tuft of fur, like a lion's main, following the jawline just beneath his chin, from one ear to the other.

"Forgive my condition, Timothy. I cannot shake hands due to their swollen state. The pain is too severe to the touch. A simple nod will do. That's a fine lad. Now, are you learning much under Mr. Brady?"

"Oh yes, Mr. Brady is a fine teacher. Sir, how is your health?"

"Thank you for asking, Timothy. I'm doing as well as can be expected. My doctor expects I shall make a full recovery from the mercury vapors. Now then, Mathew, tell me the urgent news you wished to discuss."

"There is a new publication devoted to our art coming out soon."

"So, I've heard... The Daguerreian Journal by Samuel Dwight Humphrey. The first issue is due to appear in a few short weeks on the first of November from what I've been told."

"No, Martin. There is yet another publication. You remember Mr. Henry H. Snelling?"

"Yes, of course. He works at Edward Anthony's establishment."

"Well, he is to be the editor of this new publication called, The Photographic Art Journal."

"You don't say!"

"And what's more, I am to be profiled in the premier issue."

"How wonderful! That is indeed good news, Mathew."

"You're not disappointed, Martin?"

"No, of course not, Mathew. We are brothers, you and I, next door neighbors. Let there be no strife between us, we are devotees of the same art, and worship at the same shrine. I have no use for envy or jealousy."

"Well, thank you for saying that Martin. Now, here's the best news of all. Mr. Snelling should like to profile you in the second issue of The

Photographic Art Journal."

"That would be an honor."

"Mr. Snelling will need a portrait of yourself which will then be engraved for publication." Mr. Brady pauses a moment as Tim wanders off to toss stones over the edge of the cliff. "There is also another matter I should like to discuss…"

"Yes, Mathew?"

"Well, Mr. Snelling has planned out the next few issues. He told me of his intention to profile Gabriel in the March issue."

"But he is mere operator, not a proprietor like you or I."

"Those were my exact sentiments, Martin. But you see, Mr. Snelling is quite taken with Gabriel."

"Really?"

"Yes, Henry is very impressed with Gabriel's literary contributions to his publication. And, Gabriel has taken to calling himself the Daguerrean Poet with his descriptive daguerreotypes."

"You have some other misgivings about Gabriel, don't you Mathew? I can see it in your eyes. Come now, tell me."

"In my estimation, Martin, Gabriel does not possess the necessary qualities of a reliable operator. I've seen it happen time and time again. He is too strong-willed to lead the life of an operator."

"You mean an indentured servant. Don't you, Mathew? Remember, there was a time, when you and I were told we had too much ambition. I appreciate your concerns, but I shall retain Gabriel as my chief operator."

"Martin, mark my words, he is insubordinate. You would do well to heed my warning, before you find him opening his own studio right on Broadway, stealing away our clientele."

"Not to worry, Mathew. I made Gabriel sign a non-compete clause with his apprentice papers. He is only permitted to open a studio across the East River in Brooklyn. Besides, if I am to travel to the Continent as you suggest, I will need Gabriel to run my studio."

Timothy returns to the veranda.

"Which continent, Mr. Lawrence? South America?"

Mr. Lawrence laughs. "No, Timothy, I was speaking of the European Continent." His laugh turns into an uncontrollable cough. He hacks repeatedly and kicks the blankets off. Tim sees his swollen feet and ankles. It is almost too painful to look at.

Mr. Brady pours him a cool glass of water.

"Haven't you told the boy about our planned trip to the Crystal Palace to see the English process?"

"Not in so many words, Martin."

"Mathew, you must tell him about the new process."

"I was waiting for a more suitable time."

"There is no time like the present. But for now, gentlemen, I will kindly take my leave as I need my rest. Mathew, thank you sincerely for bringing these important developments to my attention. We will further discuss this trip to the Continent."

"Yes, of course, Martin."

As they walk away, strolling along the grand piazza. Tim tugs on Brady's sleeve.

"Mr. Brady, you must come see the travelling daguerreotype wagon. It is quite a sight to see. Professor Hill says he can take landscapes in nature's full color."

"But, color daguerreotypes are not possible."

"That's what he said, Mr. Brady."

"Oh, you must have misheard him, Timothy. He must have meant hand-tinted with color by his artists."

"Mr. Brady, you would be most impressed with his travelling wagon."

"Tim, I've seen the tinker's wagon many times before. They pull into town, unhitch their team of horses, set-up shop, portrait all the town-folk, and then off they go, on their merry way down the road to the next town."

"But Mr. Brady, wouldn't it be grand to have a studio wagon? We could take Mr. Pettifog with us on our travels through the countryside making daguerreotypes all along the way..."

Brady stops to lean on one of the Corinthian columns.

"Timothy, we are at a critical point. There is much change happening on the horizon. And we must be there when it happens."

Tim gazes out past the edge of the escarpment, past the Hudson River Valley for miles and miles to the Berkshire Mountains in the distance.

"What sort of change, Mr. Brady?"

"There is a battle raging."

"Where, Mr. Brady?"

"Across the Atlantic between France and England."

"What war are you referring to, Mr. Brady?"

"The war over photography. The French process versus the English process. We must choose our allies carefully and know our enemy. You see, we've been working with the daguerreotype process for these last ten years. But there have been rumblings about the superiority of this new process developed by Mr. Fox and Mr. Talbot. That is why we need to travel to the Crystal Palace to see the Great Exhibition in London."

"Will I be going to London?"

"No, Timothy. I shall need you to remain at the studio. But I will be going with my trusted colleagues such as Mr. Lawrence, James Gordon Bennett, the editor of the Herald, William Page and my dear wife Julia."

"When do you leave, Mr. Brady?"

"Not until the spring. But we must make our preparations now."

Mr. Brady checks his pocket-watch as a cool autumn breeze rustles across the valley. He places his hand on Tim's shoulder.

"Take a long last look before we head home, Timothy. This mid-October eve is the last night of the season for The Catskill Mountain House. They will be shuttering its doors and windows for the long winter ahead. Now, it is near dinner time. Let's find Julia. She must be wondering where we are."

CHAPTER 37 — NOVEMBER

1985

Way up high on scaffolding, three stories off the ground, I dip the brush in a can of pilgrim blue paint, and apply it to the hay-loft doors of the old barn behind our house. I had heard that a century ago our old garage was a fire house. The hay-loft was up on the third floor. A rotted beam of wood jutted out. I could see the spot where the rope and pulley used to be so they could hoist the hay up through the swinging doors. The horse stalls were on the ground floor and the living quarters for the firemen were down on the second.

Dad shouts up the scaffolding, "C'mon Danny, knock off! It's getting dark! Dinner is just about ready."

"Alright, Dad. We'll be down in a few."

Bill is spotting me as I nail a few two-by-fours to the roof as a make-shift ladder so I can crawl up and paint the side of dormer.

"Dad's right, we should knock off. It's getting dark."

"Don't worry, Bill. I'm used to working in the dark. I'm a darkroom technician, remember? Besides, we're just about done."

I grab the can of paint and climb up the steep roof. This has been a month-long restoration project. My younger brother was now a college drop-out like me. I feel as though I've set a bad example. He works for the Yonkers Animal Shelter, driving around town, rescuing lost dogs without a home.

Down below, parked in the driveway is our 1967 Buick Skylark Sports Coupe. She was lime green. We took her to Earl Schieb for a jet-black paint job. "I'll paint any car, any make, any model for $99," said Earl on TV. She looked like the Batmobile with her black-leather bucket seats and chrome shift on the floor.

Years later in 2018, I watched a TV show called Supernatural with Bill — about two brothers driving around in a black '67 Chevy chasing demons and ghosts.

"Bill, that's the same car we had – the '67 Buick."

"No, Danny – that's a Chevy Impala. But it's a GM just the same. Ours was way cooler if you ask me. Remember, ours was a 2-door sports coupe with black leather bucket seats."

"Yeah, Bill. I remember."

I think of the letter I mailed months ago to NYU on August 22, 1985 — asking for another chance to return to college. I wrote it after our camping

Tim

trip to The Escarpment. But days and weeks and then months went by with no response. It must have gotten lost in the mail or circular filed under another college drop-out.

Suddenly, the two-by-four kicks out from under me and I go sliding down the roof, barreling to the edge of the precipice. Bill breaks my fall and grabs me before I go tumbling over the side. Holding me by the shoulders, hanging over the edge, we watch that big can of paint fall in slow motion, banging against the scaffolding and the side of the barn, dumping paint all over the walls and windows. The can lands with a clang on the concrete driveway. That could have been me.

I look down below at the mess I made. Pilgrim blue paint dripping from the walls and scaffolding all over the driveway and spatters on the '67 Buick. I think again of Tim on the turntable. "God, what a mess, on the ladder of success. When you take one step and miss the whole first rung."

I should have responded to that letter from NYU on March 22, 1985. This was my ticket back to college. But I waited too long to respond – six months too long. I have only myself to blame. I'm just another college drop-out. There's this lyric line on the last song of Tim – "Opportunity knocks once, then the door slams shut."

"Don't worry, Danny. We'll just hose this mess down and put on a second coat tomorrow. You're just damn lucky, you didn't go splat!!"

I look at my brother. We laugh at our predicament.

A few nights ago, on Halloween, we hung out in the black '67 Buick having a few beers.

We listened to Tim, to this breezy song called Swingin' Party. Paul Westerberg sings a line, "Quitting school and going to work and never going fishing."

I take a sip of my beer, then turn to my brother all-serious like.

"Bill, I'm not sure what to do with my life."

He takes a swig, "Me neither, Danny."

Paul joins in, "If being afraid is a crime, we hang side by side."

The next day we set up the scaffolding on the patio to trim back the branches from the house. The November breeze rustles through the brown leaves of the old oak tree looming over us. It reminded me of that scene in that old movie Arsenic and Old Lace — that autumn wind. As I took the timber saw to another branch, I heard Dad from way down below.

"Danny!"

"Yeah, Dad! I know it's getting dark. I'll be down in a few."

"Danny!" he shouts again.

"Yeah, Dad! What is it?"

"You got a letter from NYU!"

Down that scaffolding, I went scampering down, skipping rungs, jumping down from one landing to the next.

245

I ripped open that letter dated October 31, 1985.

Dear Mr. Sheridan:

I am happy to tell you on behalf of the Committee on Academic Standards that your request for a leave of absence for the Fall, 1985 semester has been approved.

I couldn't believe my eyes. I thought the letter got lost. I never thought they would respond. This is my ticket back. Then I gulped. The odds are against me. Most drop-outs never return. If they do, they often drop-out again. I push all these notions to the wayside. I am not going to let this second chance pass me by. I filled out the leave of absence form and mailed it the next day.

I received a follow-up letter the day before Thanksgiving.

Dear Mr. Sheridan:

Thank you for your letter informing me of your plans to return to New York University in the Spring, 1986 semester. I am glad to hear you look forward to returning.

I think back to the time when Dad took me to The City to see New York University for the first time. He showed me which subway to take to Astor Place on my daily commute to school.

"We'll make a strap-holder out of you yet!"

All the subways were covered in graffiti.

"Dad, what's a strap-holder?"

"A subway rider, Danny."

Dad bought a couple of hot-dogs as we had lunch by the Garibaldi statue at Washington Square. I opened up my guidebook – A Walking Tour of New York University. I looked at Main Building before us. "The site of NYU's original Gothic building. John W. Draper, a pioneer in photography and Samuel F.B. Morse, inventor of the telegraph, served as members of the faculty."

While flipping through the college brochure, I envisioned being a student in E.L. Doctorow's writing class. I was much taken with his book, Ragtime. James Cagney came out of retirement to appear in this film. Both the book and the film had a strong impact on me, much like Johnny Tremain.

Brother Meade took us on a class trip to the New Rochelle Public Library to listen to E.L. Doctorow discuss his book, Ragtime. A question came out from the back of the audience. How did you think of Ragtime? Where did it come from?

Then Mr. Doctorow said words to the effect, "I was at my house staring at the wall, wondering about the wall, what it was made of – the heavy plaster and the wooden slats. Then I started seeing through the wall to the old newspapers, then I started flipping pages back…"

"What are you, out of your flipping mind?" said my oldest sister, Elaine.

"A writer? You will lead a miserable life and starve to death! Have you any idea what it's like to go hungry! NO! Absolutely, NOT! You are going to be a dentist like your father and that's all there is to it. End of discussion!"

"Danny, you don't have to be a dentist like me. Georgetown closed down their school of dentistry."

"Okay, Dad."

He tells me about returning to Manhattan College as a freshman after three years in The War. "These upper-classmen expected me to wear a little beanie on my head and carry their books around to class. No, I won't be doing any of that. I was in the infantry. Now, what do you want to study?"

"I'm not sure, Dad. I like writing and photography. Maybe I can be a photojournalist who writes articles and takes photographs for National Geographic."

He pounds the table with his fist.

"Good! You go back to college! But you finish. Get that degree. Understand!"

"Yeah, Dad. I understand."

George sighed a deep sigh when I told him of my plans to return to college. It is not logical. Why should I pay to study photography when I am being paid to learn at The Photography Workshop?

Duke throws up his hands.

"Didn't I teach you anything? Why do you want to go off and do something foolish like go back to college? Where's your common sense?"

Duke takes a puff from his cigarette.

"You'll be back. Mark my words, you'll be back."

CHAPTER 38 — EVACUATION DAY

1850

Running an errand for Mr. Brady, Tim tugs down on his cap on this cold, blustery November day. Walking down Ann Street, he buttons up the brass anchors to his dark navy-blue pea coat. A squirrel with an acorn in its cheek dodges to the left, then to the right, before scampering up a tree. Tim reaches deep into his pockets to keep his hands warm and finds his money pouch with the little bit of wages he's squirreled away. He takes a turn at the corner. A strong gusty wind pushes back as he makes his way among the shadows to the printer's office at 101 Nassau Street. The little bell rings as Tim shuts the shop door.

"What can I do for you today?" asks an elderly man with a printer's apron and blackened hands.

"Hello, Mr. Dorr, I'm here to pick up the latest issue of The Daguuerreian Journal for Mr. Brady."

"Take a look around, Timothy, and see if you can locate it. I'm a bit short-staffed today."

Tim walks over to the far counter and looks amongst the stacks of issues. There on cover is the engraved likeness of Daguerre from the portrait captured by the Meade Brothers. He looks at the date: November 1, 1850. Just below that, S.D. Humphrey, Editor and Publisher. He flips through the issue to page 15. "The first number of the Daguerreian Journal is now before the public. Our bark is launched, the sails unfurled, and we are on the broad sea of journalism…"

Lost in thought, Tim turns to the advertisements page and sees an ad for Scovill's Manufacturing Co. at 57 Maiden Lane. That's my next stop after the printer. I must be sure to get some more plates for Mr. Pettifog.

Tim finds the second issue of The Daguerreian Journal dated November 15, 1850. He takes a moment to read the article, Daguerreotyping in New York. "There is probably no city in the United States, where the Daguerreian Art is more highly appreciated, and successfully practiced than in New York… We find 71 rooms in this city devoted solely to this art; independent of the many stores and manufactories engaged in making and selling the materials. In these rooms there are in all 127 operators… also 11 ladies and 46 boys."

"Any luck in finding the most recent issue, Timothy?"

"I will take a couple of these issues back to Mr. Brady."

"The price is two-bits per issue."

Taking a left, Tim meanders down Maiden Lane passing by that candy store. He thinks back to the time he bought some butterscotch bits wrapped in wax paper and a box of fudge.

"Wasted your wages again!"

Pa pounded the kitchen table with his fist. "We needed that money for necessities! What did I tell you? Necessities come first!"

Then his father got that curious look in his eye. "Alright, hand it over. Let's see what you got." Jeremiah rummaged through the paper bag and grabbed a chunk of fudge.

"What's all the commotion about?" Thomas asked on his way downstairs. "C'mon Pa! Share some of that. Don't hog all the fudge!"

After purchasing a box of Scovill plates, Tim opens the door to Hadfield's Fireworks Depot at 47 Maiden Lane. Pa will surely understand if I buy some jossticks and crackers. It's Evacuation Day after all. The fellas need some fireworks to celebrate this important date – November 25th – the day the British finally left New York. The last shot of the Revolutionary War was fired by a British ship as it passed the Staten Island shore. I will tell him it's our patriotic duty to help celebrate this important date.

"Miss, what are these over here, the torpedoes? How do they go off? Where do you light the fuse?"

"There is no fuse. Here, let me show you." Taking a puff from her clay pipe, she grabs a handful and throws them with all her might – tossing them on the floor exploding all about Tim's buckle-shoes. Dancing around much to his delight, Tim asks the price.

"Sixpence a box."

"Here's a shilling, miss. I'll take two, thank you."

Holding the red paper box filled with fireworks, Tim passes by Strasburger & Nuhn, Fancy Goods and Toys at 65 Maiden Lane. He crosses the street to Althof's & Co. Toy Store on the corner of Liberty Street. He catches sight of something in the storefront window amongst the porcelain dolls, tin soldiers, pop-guns and wooden sabers. Sitting there in a blue velvet display case is a pocket knife.

The shop-keep demonstrates the pocket knife with all its components. "You see my boy, it has two knifes, a sawblade, a gimlet, and a corkscrew. It's like having a carpenter's tool box in your pocket."

"My it's very impressive. How much sir?"

"The price is three shillings, if you please."

Back at Brady's shop, "Timothy, what took you so long?"

"First, I went at the printer's office to get the latest issue just like you asked, then I went to get some Scovill plates for Mr. Pettifog."

"Where are the galleys?"

"The galleys?"

"Yes, Timothy!" Brady pounds his desk. "You were supposed to go to

Mr. Snelling's office at 61 Ann Street to get the galleys to The Photographic Art Journal. Or have you forgotten? What have you got there?"

"Some fireworks for the fellas. You see it's Evacuation Day, Mr. Brady."

"Yes, Timothy, I well know what day it tis. But, I thought I could rely on you as a dependable messenger boy. Bring me those galleys from Mr. Snelling's office."

"Yes, Mr. Brady. I have just one question. What exactly are galleys?"

"The galleys are the typesetter's proofs for Mr. Snelling's publication. Now then, bring them to me, as fast as your little feet can fly. Do not disappoint, Timothy."

"Yes, Mr. Brady."

Just as he is about to run off, Mr. Brady hollers out. "One more thing, Timothy!" He hands him a dollar note. "Here take this and bring back all the fireworks you please."

"Thank you kindly, Mr. Brady!"

Later in the day, Tim curls up at the window seat in Mr. Brady's office overlooking Broadway, and flips through the pages to the premier issue of The Photographic Art Journal. Beneath the banner, H. H. Snelling, Editor, there is an image of Daguerre etched on an ornate silver platter with Lady Liberty sitting to his right, bare-breasted draped in the Stars & Stripes. To the left is a camera on a tripod and a sitting chair with head clamp. Tim notices a fuming hood as he turns the page.

He is startled to see a life-like engraving of Mr. Brady right before his eyes. Tim marvels at detail on the printed page: Mr. Brady's spectacles, his cravat pin, and expression.

Tim reads through an article. Researches on Light — "And God said, Let there be light, and there was light." He skims through another article, The Difficulties of the Art, "The plate is frequently covered with little black specks, the silver is sometimes so thin the copper shows through."

Then he finds the article about Mr. Brady written by Charles Edwards Lester. "He became extremely attached to Mr. William Page, the celebrated painter. After preparing his plate, he stepped aside to wait in silence for Nature to do her work... In the early part of 1845, he formed the project of collecting all the portraits of distinguished individuals..." Tim reads further about the Gallery of Illustrious Americans, "the most magnificent publication ever brought out in this country."

Mr. Brady turns around in his chair. "What do you think of the issue, Timothy?"

"It is very fine indeed, Mr. Brady. I especially like your engraving. But shouldn't the year at the top of the page be 1851?"

"That is but a trifle, my boy. I am sure Mr. Snelling will correct this."

"Do you hear that, Mr. Brady?"

They both listen closely.

"No, I don't hear anything out of the ordinary other than the clop of horseshoe and the blab of pave on Broadway."

"There it is again." Suddenly, they hear the muffled sound of drums in the distance getting closer and closer.

"What do you think it is, Mr. Brady?"

"I believe that is the sound of a marching band. Remember now, it is Evacuation Day. Let's go up to the rooftop for a better view."

"Look at all the soldiers coming down Broadway, Mr. Brady."

"Yes, Timothy, it is an impressive sight. Look there is the Seventh New York Militia. Sometimes they are called the silk stocking regiment as they are all blue bloods. They were the ones called out to quell the Astor Place Riot."

"Look at that regiment with the golden harp on their flag."

"Yes, Timothy, that is the 9th Regiment – the first Irish regiment."

"Look at that Mr. Brady, a whole regiment of Colonial soldiers with a fife and drum corps. That appears to be General Washington on a white stallion."

"Yes, Timothy, they are recreating Washington's victory march down Broadway to The Battery in 1783."

"Look at all the people carrying torches to light the 'Way!"

"Yes, it's most impressive. Well, as it's getting near dark, we may as well close up shop so all the staff may enjoy the festivities."

Down on the street level, the lamplighters are out, lighting the wicks. The sidewalks are packed with crowds of people.

"Come with me, Timothy, I think it's best if we walk together down to the ferry at Whitehall Street. I'll leave my phaeton at the stables. Horse and carriage are not practical in a crowd as thick as this."

In the distance, they hear the artillery at The Battery fire a thunderous volley echoing throughout the city streets, shaking the ground beneath their feet.

Suddenly, the nighttime sky is illuminated with rockets streaming like comets cascading high towards the heavens, trying with all their might to break gravity's grasp, then there is that momentary pause, the acquiescence at the apex, then the heart bursting explosion, when the rocket explodes and comes crashing back down to earth.

As they get near The Battery, they see an effigy of King George the Third high on a horse, just like the one at Bowling Green. The crowd pulls hard on the ropes to topple this symbol of tyranny and set it ablaze.

The bonfires at The Battery are burning high as the treetops as the crowd gathers around the greased flagpole with the Union Jack flying.

The bugler sounds the alarm.

The Liberty Boys gather around the flagstaff.

"Who among ye shall defend Lady Liberty? Who shall tear down that blasted Union Jack and put the Stars and Stripes in its rightful place? Come, heed the call!"

The drum corps drags out a double-stroke roll. A Liberty Boy steps forward. He grabs the pole and sets the cleats to his hob-nail boots. He goes charging up the pole as the bugler blasts the call. Just as he nears the top, he loses all momentum and goes plummeting down the pole in a heap to the bottom.

The crowd lets out a collective sigh.

The call goes out again. "Who here shall defend Lady Liberty? Who shall protect her with all your might! With your very life! Who shall heed the call?"

Another Liberty Boy steps forward clutching the Stars and Stripes in his teeth. He digs his cleats into the flagpole and waits for the bugle call.

The drum roll begins...

"Do you think this one will make it to the top, Mr. Brady?"

"The Liberty Boys tore down the Union Jack in 1783 for General Washington. They'll do it again today. Mark my words, Timothy. Now then, let's be sure to get aboard The Josephine. For it is too far a swim to Staten Island, is it not?"

"Yes, Mr. Brady."

Standing at the stern on the ferry ride home, Tim and Mr. Brady watch the bonfires and fireworks celebrations of Evacuation Day, looking at the isle of Manhattan as they pull away.

"I still don't understand, Mr. Brady. Why must you travel to England? I wish you would stay in York."

"I need to better understand this new process, this new term..."

"What term?"

"The photograph."

"What exactly is a photograph?"

"From my understanding, this new English process, the photograph, involves a glass negative, and a positive printed on paper coated with albumen. There would be no more need for silver plates. You see, photographs are produced on paper."

"Paper? Are you quite sure, Mr. Brady? But, paper does not last as long as a silver plate."

"Yes, Tim. Many in our profession laugh at the notion that paper photographs can ever equal the Daguerreotype."

"No more buffing the plates? What about Mr. Pettifog?"

"Don't you worry, Tim. I shall take good care of Mr. Pettifog. I can assure you, the Daguerreotype will be around for many years to come."

The two of them watch the fireworks explode, bursting high above New York Harbor as Castle Garden fades into the distance.

Staring at the wake, "Long after we've gone, Timothy, our

daguerreotypes shall remain."

"The mirror with a memory."

"Right you are, Tim. The mirror with a memory."

Tim

THE END

POSTSCRIPT

Those camping trips to The Escarpment have stayed with me all these years. I returned there again in 1995 after another epiphany of sorts – quite similar to the one I had in 1985. I grudgingly went out on a romantic date with Terri, my future wife, to the Museum of Fine Arts in Boston. She worked as graphic artist at a weekly newspaper while I worked in the darkroom developing black & white. I recall dragging my feet and throwing a temper tantrum every step of the way. I made quite a scene. She bought me a double-cheeseburger to shut me up, I recall. Once inside, going from room to room, I stopped dead in my tracks.

"I've been there, Terri!"

"Where? What are you talking about?"

"There!" I pointed to this glorious painting of the Catskill Mountain House, gleaming white nestled in the forest at the edge of The Escarpment. I had never seen an actual image of the Mountain House before.

"I must take you there! You must see this place."

"What place?"

"The Escarpment!"

And so, we packed our camping equipment in the back of Bill's van, strapped the canoe to the roof, and headed west from Boston to the Catskills. It was mid-September. We got a lake-side campsite, the perfect spot for our canoe and the perfect setting to read The Deerslayer. You see, I got on this James Fenimore Cooper kick after seeing Last of the Mohicans with Daniel Day Lewis in 1992. I was determined to finish the Leather-stocking Series despite the advice from Mark Twain. I remember picking up The Pioneers in a bookstore and shouting out, "I'll be damned!" There on the Penguin Classics cover was a painting of Kaaterskill Falls by Thomas Cole, the founder of the Hudson River School. A chill ran down my spine when I got to Chapter XXVI:

"You know the Catskills, lad for you must have seen them on your left, as you followed the river up from York…" said Natty Bumpo.

"What see you when you get there?" asked Edwards.

"Creation," said Natty, dropping the end of his rod into the water, and sweeping one hand around him in a circle: "all creation, lad."

James Fenimore Cooper
The Pioneers, Chapter XXVI

We stopped at the old general store to get some camping supplies. This little outpost had everything imaginable stocked on the shelves and hanging from the rafters. I recall stopping here in my youth, looking at the hunting knives, the muskets, the powder horns, even kits for making lead musket balls. The wide floorboards creaked as I explored the narrow aisles. On one shelf, I saw an image of a Corinthian column on the spine of a book — The Catskill Mountain House by Roland Van Zandt. Then I pointed out to Bill to an old black and white photograph hanging on the wall in a dusty old wooden frame with an oval matte. There was an image of The Escarpment from a century ago with train tracks on trestle bridges leading straight up The Escarpment.

I asked the burly man behind the counter about the old photograph.

"That is a picture of the Otis Elevating Railroad."

Back at the campsite, I read aloud passages from Roland Van Zandt's book. He too quoted that memorable scene from The Pioneers. Holding up the book like some kindergarten teacher, I showed Terri and Bill the paintings, photographs, and maps of the Catskill Mountain House, The Escarpment, Kaaterskill Falls and the old carriage road. This was the destination for 19th Century artists and writers. I turned the page to Kindred Spirits, the painting by Asher Durand of Thomas Cole and William Cullen Bryant.

During the Gilded Age, the Otis Elevated Railway would whisk guests up to The Mountain House. Dad was right – there was a grand hotel at the Falls. It was called Laurel House. I showed them the haunting black and white photographs Roland Van Zandt took in 1961 of the gutted remains of the Mountain House – one the Corinthian Columns toppled over. Then it was burned to the ground on January 25th, 1963.

The next day Bill returned to the campsite with food and supplies. He reached in the back of his van and handed me that old photograph in the dusty wooden frame. A gift. I took it out of the frame the other day. The caption underneath the oval matte reads, "Otis Elevating R.R. Catskill Mts. N.Y. Copyright 1892, Loeffler, Tompkinsville, S.I." It hangs on my wall to this day.

I think back to the question Bill asked me back in 1985. Why would Simple Minds come over to America to some rinky-dink campground to shoot a music video?

My brother was right. North Lake is just a campground. But a century and a half ago, The Escarpment was our nation's Yellowstone and provided inspiration to such writers as James Fenimore Cooper and Washington Irving. It was here that landscape artist Thomas Cole founded the Hudson River School and attempted to provide this fledgling country with a national identity. Cole's paintings were to the Catskills what William H. Jackson's photographs were to Yellowstone, and Ansel Adams, Yosemite. They sparked an interest in the region and turned it into a destination. Sadly, however, Cole's paintings did not help protect the area in the way that Jackson's photographs helped establish Yellowstone as our first national park in the 1870's. Instead, the Catskill Escarpment region was privately owned. It became overdeveloped with grand hotels and exploited by the nearby tanneries. Today, this national treasure is just your average campground. Yet at one time, The Escarpment inspired a generation.

Over the years, I began to appreciate Washington Irving even more. Like revisiting The Escarpment, I revisited The Sketch Book. He sounds much like myself. "My whole course of life," I observed, "has been desultory (having no set plan, haphazard), and I am unfitted for any... task, or any stipulated labor."

Then he echoed my wish, "I longed to wander over the scenes of renowned achievement — to tread, as it were, in the footsteps of antiquity... to escape, in short, from the commonplace realities of the present and lose myself among the shadowy grandeurs of the past."

I began to see things differently than I did in my youth. I re-read his Postscript describing this "region full of fable." I searched out the paintings of Thomas Cole. He devoted his life to this mysterious place. He was the Stephen Spielberg of his generation. He painted scenes from Last of the Mohicans with The Escarpment as his backdrop. Look closely at his painting of the Falls of the Kaaterskill, is that little speck the Manitou or Uncas standing on a rock? He was indeed a Kindred Spirit.

I look at Thomas Cole's "The Course of Empire" which depicts the rise and fall of the Roman Empire in five panels: The Savage, The Pastoral, The Consummation of Empire, Destruction, and finally Desolation. The Corinthian column stands there with overgrown weeds climbing up its base. I contrast it with the photographs that Roland Van Zandt took of the Mountain House in 1961 of the Corinthian columns teetering over on the verge of collapse. If only Thomas Cole could see what has become of The Escarpment – its own rise and fall – how it has been restored to The Savage.

I have not returned to The Escarpment since 1995, in over twenty years. But I am there in spirit chasing after Delia, Jim, and Bill across that wide-open plateau to the very edge of the precipice. I am reminded of that exchange between Edwards and Natty:

"The recollection of the sight has warmed your blood, old man. How many years is it since you saw the place?"

The hunter made no reply.

James Fenimore Cooper
The Pioneers, Chapter XXVI

END NOTES

viii – Epigraph: Cooper, James Fenimore. *The Deerslayer.* New York: Signet Classic, The Penguin Group, 1963, Chapter VIII, pg. 129.

x – Foreword: O'Sullivan and Ansel Adams: Professor Silver. *The History of Photography.* Lecture course attended by the author: New York University, Spring, 1989.

x – O'Sullivan and Ansel Adams: Newhall, Beaumont and Newhall, Nancy. *T.H. O'Sullivan Photographer.* "An Appreciation" by Ansel Adams, Rochester, New York: The George Eastman House, 1966.

x – Samuel Morse and Dr. John William Draper: Newhall, Beaumont. *The Daguerreotype in America.* New York: Dover Publications, Third Edition, 1976, pp. 23-24.

x – Morse and Draper: Newhall, Beaumont. *The History of Photography.* New York: The Museum of Modern Art, Fifth Edition, 1988, p. 28.

x – Morse and Draper: Root, Marcus Aurelius. *The Camera and The Pencil, or The Heliographic Art,* Philadelphia: J.B. Lippincott & Co. 1864, pp. 339-345.

- Letter in reply from J.W. Draper, p. 341. About this time, I became acquainted with Professor Morse and we subsequently had a building on the top of the New York University in which we took many portraits.

* This was the first portrait taken from life.

- Letter from Professor Morse, Poughkeepsie, Feb. 10th, 1855, p. 344.

- Invited by Daguerre to see his results in private… his process was then secret. My letter… to my brothers, the editors of the New York Observer, about the first week in March, 1839. The first experiment, crowned with any success, was a view of the Unitarian Church, from the window on the staircase from the third story of the New York University… It was in September, 1839, p. 345.

x – "There were few clues, only his name, a four-line obituary…": Horan, James D. *Timothy O'Sullivan – America's Forgotten Photographer, The Life and Work of the Brilliant Photographer Whose Camera Recorded The American Scene From The Battlefields Of The Civil War to The Frontiers Of The West.* New York: Bonanza Books, A division of Crown Publishers, Inc., 1966, p. xi.

Chapter 1 – Staten Island

1 – Staten Island Map: New York Public Library, Digital Gallery, F.W. Beers, Atlas of Staten Island, Richmond County, Official Records and Surveys, 1874.

1 – "Saint Peter's Church": Morris, Ira K. *Morris's Memorial History of*

Staten Island Volume II, New York: Published by The Author, West New Brighton, Staten Island, 1900, p. 322.

1 – "Pavilion Hotel": Matteo, Thomas W. *Then and Now – Staten Island*, New York: Arcadia Publishing, 2006, p. 47.

1 – Pavilion Hotel photo - New York Public Library, Digital Gallery.

1 – "September 11, 1850": Barnum, P.T. *The Life of P.T. Barnum*. Written by Himself. New York: Redfield, 110 & 112 Nassau Street, 1855, p. 312. "Jenny Lind's first concert was fixed to come off at Castle Garden on Wednesday Evening September 11."

From the author: A sincere thanks to Google Books for making my research possible "as part of a project to make the world's books discoverable online."

1 – "Castle Garden": King, Moses. *King's Handbook of New York City*. Edited & Published by Moses King, Boston: 1892, pp. 535-36

1 – Jenny Lind Concert, September 11, 1850. *King's Handbook*, p. 536. Genin the Hatter – buying the first choice seat for $225. "Castle Garden's history as a theatre ended in May, 1855, and the building was turned into a depot for the reception of immigrants. A fire on May 23, 1870, destroyed the interior, but the walls remain intact."

2 – Barnum, *The Life of*, pp. 313-14 – Castle Garden – divided into 4 compartments – designated by a lamp of a peculiar color. The tickets were printed in corresponding colors.

2 - Pavilion Hotel Menu - New York Public Library Digital Gallery

2 – Menu - Van Zandt, Roland. *The Catskill Mountain House – America's Grandest Hotel*. New York: Black Dome Press, 1991, p. 342.

2 – "spuds… nothing else." Scally, Robert James. *The History of Ireland*. Lecture course attended by the author: New York University, Spring, 1989.

2 - Scally, Robert James. *The End of Hidden Ireland – Rebellion, Famine, & Emigration*. New York: Oxford University Press, 1995.

2 - Miller, Kerby A. *Emigrants and Exiles — Ireland and the Irish Exodus to North America*. New York: Oxford University Press, 1985.

3 - Morris, Ira K. *Morris's Memorial History of Staten Island Volume II*, Published by The Author, West New Brighton, Staten Island, 1900, p. 322.

St. Peter's Church, New Brighton – "the Rev. Patrick Murphy who served from March 1847 to Feb 11, 1848 when he died of yellow fever and was interred under the altar of St. Peter's Church. He was immediately succeeded by his brother the Rev. Mark Murphy."

4 - Quarantine Station, New York Public Library Digital Gallery, View of the quarantine grounds and buildings at Staten Island, N.Y. (1856).

5 - Garibaldi at the Pavilion. Tyrell, Henry. *Garibaldi in New York*, The Century Illustrated Monthly Magazine, Volume 74, May to October, 1907, pp. 174-175.

5 - Havens, Catherine Elizabeth. *Diary of a Little Girl in Old New York*,

New York: Henry Collins Brown, 1920, p. 38. "To hear Jenny Lind in Castle Garden when she sang… Coming Thro' the Rye."

5 – 6, "cottages… back home." Scally, *The History of Ireland*. NYU, 1989.

7 - How do you keep the boy on the farm once he's seen Paris?

Scally, *The History of Ireland*. NYU, 1989. Lecture course attended by the author: New York University, Spring, 1989.

9 - Sands Sarsaparilla - *Barnum's Guidebook*, 1850, p. 2.

10 – "the woe-begone party" Irving, Washington. *The Sketch Book of Geoffrey Crayon, Gent. — Rip Van Winkle*. New York: Signet Classic, New American Library, 1961, p. 45.

Chapter 2 – Fulton's Ferry

11 – Fulton's Ferry - Letter written by Robert Fulton in 1812, Morrison, John H. *History of American Steam Navigation*, W.F. Sametz & Co., Inc. 1903, pp. 518-522.

11 - New Brighton Landing – Trow, John F. *Trow's New York City Directory*, John F. Trow Publisher, 50 Greene St., 1861.

11 – The Josephine – Horan, James D. *Timothy O'Sullivan*, p. 22. "One can picture the country boy as he hurried off the Josephine, the Staten Island ferry boat, up Broadway to Fulton Street."

11 – Ferry Boat Images - New York Public Library Digital Gallery, Robert N. Dennis collection of stereoscopic views.

11 - Cudahy, Brian J. *Over and Back – The History of Ferryboats in New York Harbor*, Fordham University, 1990, pp. 20-28, p. 69.

11 - Renwick, James. *American Biography – David Rittenhouse & Robert Fulton*, Harper & Brothers, 1902, p. 184.

11 – Baxter, Raymond J. and Adams, Arthur G. *Railroad Ferries of the Hudson and Stories of a Deckhand*, Fordham University Press, 1999, pp. 20-27.

11 – Percheron – Weyn, Suzanne. *Snowflake*, Illustrated by Jacqueline Rogers, Cartwheel Books, Scholastic Inc., 2006.

12 – water buckets – Fulton's Floating Bridge. Letter written by Fulton, Morrison, *History of American Steam Navigation*, pp. 518-522.

12 - Quarantine Station, New York Public Library Digital Gallery, View of the quarantine grounds and buildings at Staten Island, N.Y. (1856).

12 - Savannah Route – *Trow's New York City Directory*, 1861.

13 – "Over to York" - Barnum, The Life of, p. 22. "I looked upon him as a great man for he had been to "York"."

14 - Hadfield's - *Trow's New York City Directory*, 1861.

14 – Torpedoes - Barnum, The Life of, p. 24.

Chapter 3 – The Omnibus

15 – The Omnibuses, Foster, George G. *New York In Slices*, by An Experienced Carver, the Original Slices Published in the N.Y. Tribune,

W.F. Burgess, 22 Ann Street, 1849, pp. 63-66.

15 - Knickerbocker Stage Co. - *Trow's NYC Directory,* 1861, p. 40.

15 - McCabe, James D. *Lights and Shadows of New York Life,* National Publishing Co., 1879, pp. 216-219.

15 - Lady Washington - Jenkins, Stephen. *The Greatest Street in the World — The Story of Broadway,* G.P. Putnam's Sons, 1911, pp. 145-146.

15 - Bootblacks, New York Public Library Digital Gallery, Alice Austen photographer, Staten Island.

15 — Bootblacks - McCabe, James Dabney. *The Secrets of the Great City,* A Work Descriptive of the Virtues and Vices, the Mysteries, Miseries and Crimes of New York City, National Publishing Co., 1868, p. 264.

15 - The Stranger's Handbook - New York Public Library.

15 - Souvenir of New York - New York Public Library Digital Gallery.

16 — "Ye can ride up top with me." McCabe, *Lights,* pp. 216-219.

17 — "The North River" - Baxter, *Railroad Ferries,* p. 5.

17 — "Sixpence trap" - Foster, G. G. *New York by Gaslight — Here and There a Streak of Sunshine,* 1850, p. 126.

17 — "The Dry Dock District" - Haswell, Charles Haynes. *Reminiscences of New York by an Octogenarian (1816-1860),* Harper & Brothers Publishers, New York, 1896, p. 439. "The volume of ship-building in this city, 39,918 tons... employing 2300 workmen."

17 - Haswell, *Reminiscences,* pp. 459-460 — "the shipyard of Wm. H. Brown, foot of 12th Street, East River... The Arctic 3500 tons — length of 295 feet, water wheels 35 feet in diameter."

18 - New York Steam Brewery, *Trow's New York City Directory,* 1861.

18 - Cholera — five thousand perished. Haswell, *Reminiscences,* p. 456. "New York suffered a severe visitation of cholera which appeared first in the Five Points on May 14 and spread rapidly. The public school buildings were turned into hospitals and in them alone 1,021 deaths occurred; the total mortality from the disease in this year being about 5,000."

18 - Croton Water Celebration - Haswell, *Reminiscences,* pp. 391-392.

19 — Bowling Green — Jenkins, *Greatest Street,* pp. 44-46.

19 - No. 1 Broadway - Jenkins, *Greatest Street,* pp. 44-46.

19 - No. 1 Broadway - *Hand Book of New York City,* Norton, 1859, p. 22.

20 - Johnny Pump - New York City's first fire hydrant was installed in 1808, www.firehydrant.org.

20 - Bowling Green Fence — Haswell, *Reminiscences,* pp. 11-12. "The Iron Railing around Bowling Green was imported from England 1771. It is standing at this time 1895."

20 - Bowling Green Fence — Haswell, *Reminiscences,* p. 546. "An equestrian statue of George III was erected... upon the Declaration of Independence pulled down... molded into bullets. The rails were surmounted with figure heads of the Royal Family."

20 – Litchfield - Jenkins, *Greatest Street*, pp. 21-23.

21 - Belgian Blocks - Haswell, *Reminiscences*, p. 273.

21 - Two-Shilling Operators - Newhall, Beaumont. *The Daguerreotype in America*, Dover Publications, 1976, p. 63.

22 - sixpence fare - McCabe, *Lights and Shadows,* pp. 216-219.

22 - Bunker's Mansion - Jenkins, *Greatest Street*, pp. 50-51. "where Washington lived as President. The great man strolling down Broadway for a breath of sea air from the Battery… asked him to bless the bairn who had been named after him…Washington patted the boy on the head… the youngster who was Washington Irving."

22 - Knickerbocker Stage Co., *Trow's New York City Directory*, 1861, p. 40.

23 - Trinity Church - Norton, *Hand Book of New York City*, 1859, pp. 6-7. "The highest point to which visitors ascend is 250 feet from the ground, and is reached by 308 steps. Suitable resting places are provided… As is very proper, a charge of one shilling is made for admission to the spire."

23 – bootblacks - Alice Austen, photographer Staten Island.

24 – Custom House - Norton, *Hand Book of New York City*, 1859, p. 7. The building at 28 Wall Street, known today as Federal Hall.

Author's Note: I kept finding references "to marble from the quarries of Westchester." See page 22 of *Hand Book of New York City*, Stewart's Marble Palace, the same Stewart who sent a ship to Ireland in relief of the famine. "The light cream marble is from the quarries of Westchester." Was it from the same quarry I used to pass by on Fisher Avenue in Tuckahoe on my way to drum lessons? The Tuckahoe Marble Monument. Tuckahoe's largest and most prestigious marble commission came in the form of an order for material for the old Custom House, constructed at the corner of Wall and Nassau Streets NYC in 1830… it is recognized as one of America's outstanding Greek Revival buildings."

24 - Kipp & Brown - Haswell, *Reminiscences*, p. 234.

24 – Old Elephant – Whitman, Walt, *My Passion for Ferries, Broadway Sights, Omnibus Jaunts and Drivers, Specimen Days & Collect,* London, 1887.

Author's Note: After researching and writing this chapter, I eerily stumbled upon Walt Whitman's *Omnibus Jaunts and Drivers.* I then incorporated Old Elephant as a nickname for Cornelius in tribute to Walt. "Yes, I knew all the drivers then, Broadway Jack, Dressmaker, Balky Bill, George Storms, Old Elephant, his brother Young Elephant (who came afterward,) Tippy, Pop Rice, Big Frank, Yellow Joe, Pete Callahan, Patsey Dee, and dozens more; for there were hundreds."

24 - Daniel Sweeny's – Reference to David Sweeney's House of Refreshment. *Valentine's Manual of Old New York,* 1921 Edition, p. 244. Did David Sweeney's really exist? Fact-Check: *Doggett's Directory*, 1845, p. 352. Yes, but it was Daniel Sweeny's at 11 Ann Street.

25 - Benefit Concert for Kipp and Brown - Haswell, *Reminiscences*, p. 442.

25 - Maiden Lane, Toy District - *Trow's NYC Directory*, 1861, p. 64.

Chapter 4 – Broadway & Fulton

27 - 187 Broadway, J.C. Booth - *Doggett's Directory*, 1845, p. 12.

27 - 189 Broadway, Jeremiah Gurney - *Doggett's Directory*, 1845, p. 155.

28 – Broad-way by Augustus Köllner, New York Public Library.

28 – *The View from St. Paul's Chapel, 1849* – from the drawing of J.W. Hill, New York Public Library Digital Gallery. See also:

Horan, James D. *Timothy O'Sullivan – America's Forgotten Photographer*, Bonanza Books, A division of Crown Publishers, Inc., 1966, p. 11.

Jenkins, Stephen. *The Greatest Street in the World — The Story of Broadway*, G.P. Putnam's Sons, 1911, p. 81.

28 - *View from the American Museum* – showing Brady's gallery at 205 Broadway, Woodcut by an unidentified artist, 1847-1851. The New York Historical Society, New York City. See also:

Panzer, Mary. *Mathew Brady and the Image of History*, with an essay by Jeana K. Foley, Smithsonian Institution Press for the National Portrait Gallery, Washington and London, 1997, p. 11.

28 - The Ice Wagon - *The View from St. Paul's Chapel*, J.W. Hill, NYPL.

28 - Knickerbocker Ice Co. - *Doggett's Directory*, 1849, p. 236.

28 - Knickerbocker Ice Co. – "Cool Waters, and the Lure of Danger," by Peter Applebome, *The New York Times*, July 1, 2009. "The quarry was once one of dozens near the industrial-era Hudson, in a town that made bricks, and where the old Knickerbocker Ice Company before the age of refrigeration sent 45,000 tons of ice each winter down the river to New York City."

28 - Smith's Segar, Genin the Hatter - *View St. Paul's*, J.W. Hill, NYPL.

28-29 - The cacophony of Barnum's Band - Foster, G.G., *New York by Gas-Light*, Byron. Dewitt & Davneport, N.Y., 1850, p. 7. "From the balcony of the third-story windows a cascade of horrent harmony, issuing from an E-flat bugle and three mismatched trombones, is tumbling down upon the up-turned faces."

29 – Barnum's Band - *Writing New York – A Literary Anthology*, edited by Phillip Lopate, Washington Square Press, 1998, pp. 74-90, *Open Air Musings in the City*, Nathaniel Parker Willis, p. 76. "Half past three... the band who have just commenced playing in the Museum balcony... Tune, 'Ole Dan Tucker'."

29 - Barnum's American Museum - Broad-way, Drawn from nature by Augustus Köllner; lith. by Deroy, 1850, NYPL.

29 - Barnum's American Museum "Broadway entrance." One of the few extant photographs of the exterior of Barnum's Museum. Source: London Stereoscopic Company, 1858 - Meserve-Kunhardt Collection, The Lost Museum, City University New York.

29 - Jenny Lind – nightingale poised on her hand, Barnum's Panorama of Humbug No. 1, William Schaus, c. 1850, The Library of Congress.

29 - Chatham Row - Park Row was previously called Chatham Street and later nicknamed Newspaper Row. Broadway Map1850.

29 - "Walk up ladies…" Barnum's Panorama, The Library of Congress.

29 - Bowery Boy - Nicolino Calyo, c. 1847, New-York Historical Society. The Lost Museum. "This 1847 watercolor depicted the young men who habituated New York's working-class entertainment area, the Bowery. They wore the fashionable long sideburns that gave them the nickname "soaplocks." Around them, posters advertised some of the Bowery attractions the "B'hoys" attended after their workday ended."

30 – Flagstones - Walkway - *Broad-way* by Augustus Köllner, NYPL.

30 – City Hall Park - Bachmann, John, Engraver (ca. 1850), NYPL.

30 - View from City Hall Park, *Hand Book of New York City,* 1859, p. 26.

30 – Dr. Moffat - *Doggett's Directory,* 1845, pp. 257-258.

31 – Quote from Mike Tyson: "Every fighter has a plan until they get punched in the mouth."

31 - Daniel Sweeny's *Doggett's Directory,* 1845, p. 352.

32 - Put up at the Astor – McCabe, *Lights and Shadows,* pp. 304-305. The hotels – the Astor House one of the oldest built of Quincy granite occupies an entire block on Broadway from Vesey to Barclay Streets – built by John Jacob Astor – 1831 – Charles A. Stetson. "Put up at the Astor."

32 – Astor House - *Hand Book of New York City,* 1859, p. 24. The Astor House – massive structure of Quincy Granite – 340 rooms – restaurant in the rotunda.

32 – Astor House - Haswell, *Reminiscences,* pp. 315-316. The Astor House – the wonder of the time. Interior of the quadrangle containing the bar, lunch counters was then a garden affording a pleasant view from the windows of the interior rooms.

32 - Dickens at The Astor House - Haswell, *Reminiscences,* pp. 382-383.

32 – Astor House interior – Jenkins, *Greatest Street,* pp. 138-139. The Astor House – Completed and opened in 1836 – marvel of that age… its interior quadrangle… laid out as a garden with fountain. Guests – Andrew Jackson, Houston, Webster, Clay, Lincoln, Irving, Hawthorne, Dickens, Macready, Rachel, and Jenny Lind.

32 – Astor House interior – Jenkins, *Greatest Street,* p. 142. Astor House became the resort of many a literary man. Numerous omnibuses, you could walk from Barnum's to the Battery on their roofs.

32 – John Jacob Astor – Parton, James. "John Jacob Astor," Harper's New Monthly Magazine, Harper & Brothers, NY, Feb. 1865, pp. 308-323.

Author's Notes: February 27, 2012: Last night, working on the end of Chapter 4 – Astor House – I found Walt Whitman's description of John Jacob Astor then I found an article in Harper's New Monthly about John

Jacob born in Waldorf, Germany - the Waldorf Astoria Hotel…. Further research into Astor Place my subway stop while commuting to NYU. The Astor Place Riot occurred on May 10, 1849, at the now demolished Astor Opera House – at least 25 dead, more than 120 injured. Disaster Place – a play upon Astor Place.

32 - Ermine Cap - Whitman, "Broadway Sights," *Specimen Days and Collect,* "I once saw (it must have been about 1832, of a sharp, bright January day) a bent, feeble but stout-built very old man, bearded, swathed in rich furs, with a great ermine cap on his head (ermine – weasel)… The old man, the subject of so much attention, I can almost see now. It was John Jacob Astor."

33 - Images of Brady's Gallery

Brady's National Gallery of Daguerreotypes 205-207 Broadway, Wood Engraving by J. Brown, 1850, The New-York Historical Society, NYPL. This is the same image used on p. 56 of *Mathew Brady and the Image of History,* by Mary Panzer, 1997.

View from the American Museum, showing Brady's gallery at 205 Broadway, Woodcut by an unidentified artist, 1847-1851. The New-York Historical Society. This is the same image used on p.11 of *Mathew Brady and the Image of History,* by Mary Panzer, 1997.

34 - Liberty Pole, City Hall Park - *Valentine's Manual of Old New York,* Henry Collins Brown, 1921, p. 90.

35 – City Hall – Stockbridge, Mass. *Hand Book of NYC,* 1859, p. 3.

35 – Stewart's Marble Palace - Haswell, *Reminiscences,* p. 419. Alex T. Stewart, Broadway and Chambers – his extensive store.

35 – Stewart – Horan, James D. *Mathew Brady – Historian with a Camera,* Crown Publishers, New York, 1955, p. 6.

See also - Plate 57 – Alexander T. Stewart "the merchant prince who gave Brady a job as a clerk when he first came to New York. This wet plate was made about 1856. By Brady or assistant."

35 – Stewart's Marble Palace *Hand Book of New York City,* 1859, p. 22.

Research Notes March 6th, 2012: Then I was amazed to discover that the Marble Palace still stands at 280 Broadway – declared a National Historic Landmark in 1965, clad in Tuckahoe marble.

35 - Richest merchant - Jenkins, *Greatest Street,* pp. 159-161. A. T. Stewart, Second only to Astor – richest merchant in the world.

35 - Jenny Lind at the Irving House - *Struggles and Triumphs or, Sixty Years' Recollections of P.T. Barnum,* Written by Himself, Courier Company Printers, Buffalo, 1889, pp. 104-106.

36 – Stewart – ship to Ireland - Haswell, *Reminiscences,* p. 432. "In this month much activity was shown in the relief of the Irish sufferers from famine. Alexander T. Stewart chartered and furnished a ship loaded with provisions for the relief of the suffering people."

36 – Apple Annie - *Valentine's Manual of Old New York,* Henry Collins Brown, 1921, p. 101. "A.T. Stewart – friendly interest in the old apple woman that plied her trade in front of his store and whom he would not permit to be disturbed."

36 – Apple Annie - character in *Lady for a Day*, 1933, a movie directed by Frank Capra, story by Damon Runyon.

Chapter 5 – Barnum's American Museum

37 – Meade Brothers - N.Y. Herald Sept. 14, 1850. Jenny Lind Advertisements. Lind! Lind!! Lind!!! – the best engraving of this distinguished lady may be obtained at the American Daguerreotype Galleries… Meade Brothers, 233 Broadway, opposite the Park Fountain. The Lost Museum, City University of New York.

38 – Astor House interior – Jenkins, *Greatest Street*, pp. 138-139. The Astor House – Completed and opened in 1836 – marvel of that age… its interior quadrangle… laid out as a garden with fountain.

38 - Barnum's American Museum "Broadway entrance." One of the few extant photographs of the exterior of Barnum's Museum. Source: London Stereoscopic Company, 1858 - Meserve-Kunhardt Collection, The Lost Museum, City University New York.

38 - The View from St. Paul's Chapel, 1849 – J.W. Hill, NYPL.

38 - The hawkers beckon… Titania the Queen of the Fairies - *Barnum's Guidebook*, 1850, p. 6. The Lost Museum, City University New York.

38 - The Feejee Mermaid - Barnum, P.T. *The Life of P.T. Barnum*. Written by Himself. New York, 1855, pp. 229-234. See p. 236, woodcut of the three bare-breasted mermaids. See p. 234 woodcut "a correct likeness of the Fejee Mermaid – reduced in size from Sunday Herald." NOTE: Barnum spells the word Fejee not Feejee.

38 - The club - killed Captain Cook - Barnum, P.T. *The Life of,* p. 228.

39 - The Napoleon of his profession - *Barnum's Guidebook*, 1850, p. 1. The Lost Museum, City University New York.

39 – Early American Currency - Research Notes: Sept 5, 2012: I am yet again trying to sort out Early American Currency. I have consolidated some of my research notes herewith:

39 –*Valentine's Manual of Old New York,* 1916, p. 50. "Old Time Money – Another curious thing is that we continued the use of sterling money – pounds, shillings and pence – long after the Revolution. It is also noted in old-theatre prices "admission 12½ c".

Valentine's Manual of Old New York, 1921, p. 244. D. Sweeney's Menu. I was curious about these abbreviations. (s. for shilling d. sixpence.)

1 Dollar = 8 Shillings, 12.5 cents x 8 = 100 cents.

The Spanish Dollar – Piece of Eight – cut into 8 pie-sliced bits.

Each eighth dollar was worth One Bit or 12.5 cents.

Two Bits – 12 ½ cents x 2 = Quarter or 25 cents.

Sixpence – 6 ¼ cents – two sixpence = one shilling or 12 ½ cents.

39 - Haswell, *Reminiscences*, p. 540. "fares for the various stage lines 6¼ cents – later the disappearance of the sixpence (6.25 cents)."

39 – Foster, *New York by Gaslight*, 1850, p. 126. "omnibus drivers... cracks his fiery whip... the driver's six-pence trap."

39 – Twain, Mark. *The Adventures of Tom Sawyer*, The American Publishing Co., 1884, Chapter IV. "Mary gave him a brand new 'Barlow' knife worth twelve and a half cents."

39 - *Barnum's American Museum Illustrated Guidebook*, 1850, p. 1. The Lost Museum, City University New York. Price 12½ cents.

39 – Havens, Catherine Elizabeth. *Diary of a Little Girl in Old New York*, New York: Henry Collins Brown, 1920, pp. 60-61. "Sometimes my mother gives us a shilling – ice cream – we can get half a plate for sixpence. There is another ice cream saloon at the corner of Broadway and Waverly Place called Thompson's." (Brady's Gallery was located above).

39 – image of half-cent coin, dated 1834.

40 - Entrance of Barnum's Museum, *Barnum's Guidebook*, 1850, p. 2. SEE Virtual Tour of Barnum's Museum at the Lost Museum Website. http://www.lostmuseum.cuny.edu

40 - Copies of a Superior Daguerreotype of Jenny Lind for Sale, Gurney's Advertisement in *Humphrey's Journal*, January 1851. This image is on p. 20 of *Mathew Brady*, by James D. Horan, 1955.

40 - American Flag - *Barnum's Guidebook*, 1850, p. 21.

41 - General Tom Thumb's clothes - *Barnum's Guidebook*, 1850, p. 5.

41 - Daguerreotype of Barnum and General Tom Thumb - Half-plate daguerreotype of Phineas Taylor Barnum & Charles Sherwood Stratton, National Portrait Gallery, Washington, Smithsonian Institution. Taken by Samuel Root, the brother of Marcus Aurelius Root, c. 1850.

41 – Tom Trouble - notorious pirate. *Barnum's Guidebook*, 1850, p. 21.

41 - The Feejee Mermaid - Barnum, P.T. *The Life of P.T. Barnum.* Written by Himself. New York, 1855, pp. 229-234. See p. 236, woodcut of the three bare-breasted mermaids. See p. 234 woodcut "a correct likeness of the Fejee Mermaid – reduced in size from Sunday Herald."

41 - Cosmoramic Room. *Barnum's Guidebook*, 1850, p. 28.

41 - Niagara Falls - *The Life of P.T. Barnum*, by Himself, 1855, p. 228.

42 - The Witch of Staten Island - Rasenberger, Jim. City Lore: 'The Witch of Staten Island' *The New York Times*, October 29, 2000.

42 - The Witch of Staten Island - Havens, *Diary of a Little Girl*, pp. 54-55. "We have been down to Staten Island to one of my sisters... We always ask him to take us past Polly Bodine's house. She set fire to a house and burned up ever so many people, and I guess she was hung for it, because there is a wax figure of her in Barnum's Museum."

42 – Barnum's Lecture Room, Temperance Archive, SEE Virtual Tour of Barnum's Museum at http://www.lostmuseum.cuny.edu.

42 – *The Bottle* by George Cruikshank

42 – *The Drunkard* by William H. Smith

43 - Rooftop garden – ice cream. *The Life of P.T. Barnum*, 1855, p. 228.

43 - Drummond Light - *Barnum's Guidebook,* 1850, p. 29.

43 - Camera Obscura 38 - *The View from St. Paul's Chapel*, 1849 from the drawing of J.W. Hill, New York Public Library Digital Gallery. This is the same image James David Horan used on p. 11 of *Timothy O'Sullivan, America's Forgotten Photographer*, and by Stephen Jenkins on p. 81 of *The Greatest Street in the World — The Story of Broadway*.

Author's Note: September 5, 2011. I am still astounded at The Camera Obscura atop Barnum's Museum as seen in *The View from St. Paul's Chapel, 1849.* I was curious what was on the rooftop – I zoomed in closer and closer then made out the words – Camera Obscura. I studied this image again under full magnification.

Page 43 - Brady's Rooftop - View from St. Paul's Chapel, 1849, NYPL.

Chapter 6 – The Eating House

44 – Smith's Segar Store, Genin the Hatter, *The View from St. Paul's Chapel, 1849,* from the drawing of J.W. Hill, New York Public Library Digital Gallery.

44 – Genin, John N., Hatter, 214 Broadway, *Doggett's,* 1849, p. 164.

44 – Genin - *King's Handbook*, p. 536. "(Genin, the hatter) made a business reputation, which lasted for many years."

45 – Daniel Sweeny's – *Valentine's Manual of Old New York,* 1921, p. 244. David Sweeney was a restaurant keeper at 11 Ann Street in the early 1850s. Did David Sweeney's really exist? Fact-Check: Yes, but it was Daniel Sweeny's *Doggett's Directory*, 1845, p. 352.

45 – Walk right in, Sir. - *New York In Slices*, by An Experienced Carver, (handwritten annotation) George G. Foster, Being the Original Slices Published in the N.Y. Tribune, W.F. Burgess, 22 Ann Street, 1849. "The Eating Houses", pp. 66-72. *Writing New York – A Literary Anthology*, edited by Phillip Lopate, Washington Square Press, 1998, Pages 119-126, *The Eating Houses* by George G. Foster.

45 - Laid out like the floor of a church - Foster, *New York in Slices*, p. 68.

45 - Sawdust on the floor. Author's interview with Geoffrey Bartholomew, barkeep at McSorley's Old Ale House, 15 East 7th Street, NYC. The Fall, 1987. Bartholomew, Geoffrey, *The McSorley Poems,* Charlton St. Press, N.Y., 2001. Bartholomew, *The McSorley Poems, Volume II,* Charlton St. Press, N.Y., 2012.

46 - Oh Wayyy-terrr – Foster, *NY in Slices*, "The Eating Houses", p. 66.

46 - *Valentine's Manual,* 1921, p. 244. Sweeny's menu is given herewith:

46 - Fire at Kelsey's Alley - New-York Daily Tribune Vol. X, NO. 2934, Wednesday, September 11, 1850.

46 - poets of the press. Foster, *New York in Slices*, p. 68.

47 - knights of the pen. *Valentine's Manual*, 1921, p. 82. Poe entered into employment of N.P. Willis — Evening Mirror — office at the corner of Ann and Nassau Streets — famous beer cellar known as Sandy Welsh's — resort at noon hour of all newspapermen and knights of the pen.

47 — Horace Greeley - Ziegleman, Jane. *97 Orchard - An Edible History of Five Immigrant Families in One New York Tenement*, Harper Collins, New York, 2010, p. 72. "One of his (Sweeny's) customers was Horace Greeley."

47 - Hundred gun salute, Railroad accident sawmill, Jenny Lind canes. New-York Daily Tribune Vol. X, NO. 2934, Wednesday, September 11, 1850. New-York Daily Tribune Vol. X, NO. 2935, Thursday, September 12, 1850.

47 — Walter and Old Elephant — Whitman, Walt, *My Passion for Ferries, Broadway Sights, Omnibus Jaunts and Drivers, Specimen Days & Collect*, London, 1887. A tribute to Walt. "Yes, I knew all the drivers then, Broadway Jack, Dressmaker, Balky Bill, George Storms, Old Elephant, his brother Young Elephant (who came afterward,) Tippy, Pop Rice, Big Frank, Yellow Joe, Pete Callahan, Patsey Dee, and dozens more."

48 - Gratis from the hydrant - Foster, *New York in Slices*, p. 69.

49 — Barnum's Drummond Light — Foster, G.G. *New York by Gas-Light*, Tribune Buildings, N.Y., 1850, p. 7. Barnum's Drummond Light, sending a vivid, ghastly glare for a mile up the street, and pushing the shadows of the omnibuses well-nigh to Niblo's.

Chapter 7 – Friday, Sept. 13th

50 - Polly Bodine's house on Richmond Avenue - Rasenberger, Jim. City Lore: 'The Witch of Staten Island' *The New York Times*, October 29, 2000.

50 - The Witch of Staten Island - Havens, *Diary of a Little Girl*, pp. 54-55. "We have been down to Staten Island to one of my sisters… We always ask him to take us past Polly Bodine's house. She set fire to a house and burned up ever so many people, and I guess she was hung for it, because there is a wax figure of her in Barnum's Museum."

51 — The Hunger - Scally, Robert James. *The History of Ireland.* Lecture course attended by the author: New York University, Spring, 1989.

51 - Scally, Robert James. *The End of Hidden Ireland – Rebellion, Famine, & Emigration.* New York: Oxford University Press, 1995.

51 - Miller, Kerby A. *Emigrants and Exiles — Ireland and the Irish Exodus to North America.* New York: Oxford University Press, 1985.

52 - Farmer's Almanack, September, 1850, p. 23. September Hath 30 Days. The Ditch – Alas, poor Patrick!... Paddies will be Paddies.

53 - Broadway Dandy - *Fresh Leaves from the Diary of a Broadway Dandy,*

Edited by John D. Vose, Esq., Bunnel & Price, 121 Fulton St., NY, 1852.

53 - Limited to Twelve - "The Omnibuses," Foster, *NY in Slices*, p. 64.

53 - New-York Daily Tribune Vol. X, NO. 2936, Friday, Sept. 13, 1850.

53 - Jenny Lind Advertisements New York Herald, September 1850. The Lost Museum, City University New York.

55 - The Tombs – Halls of Justice - New York Public Library.

55 - New York and Harlem Railroad – 1847 Map – Lower Manhattan.

56 - Ballantine and Croton Ale -*Trow's New York City Directory*, 1861.

56 – The Five Points – Stereo view - New York Public Library.

56 - Anthony Street, Map of Broadway - *Doggett's*, 1845, pp. 257-258.

56 - Dr. John Moffat – *Doggett's Directory*, 1845, pp. 257-258.

56 - New York Hospital – *Hand Book of NYC*, Norton, 1859, p. 29.

Chapter 8 – Late

57 - *View from the American Museum* – showing Brady's gallery at 205 Broadway, Woodcut by an unidentified artist, 1847-1851. The New York Historical Society, New York City. See also:

Panzer, Mary. *Mathew Brady and the Image of History*, with an essay by Jeana K. Foley, Smithsonian Institution Press for the National Portrait Gallery, Washington and London, 1997, p. 11.

57 - 187 Broadway, J.C. Booth - *Doggett's Directory*, 1845, p. 12.

57 - 189 Broadway, Jeremiah Gurney - *Doggett's Directory*, 1845, p. 155.

57 - 187 Broadway, Mathew B. Brady (spelled with two t's) - jewel case manf. 187 B'way and 169 Fulton, h. 63 Barclay. *Doggett's*, 1845, p. 48.

58 - Copies of a Superior Daguerreotype of Jenny Lind for Sale - Gurney's Advertisement in *Humphrey's Journal*, January 1851.

Horan, James D. *Mathew Brady – Historian with a Camera*, Crown Publishers, Inc. New York, 1955, p. 20.

58 - Daguerreotype Materials – Isenburg, Matthew R. *The Making of a Daguerreotype*, The Collection of Matthew R. Isenburg, Hadlyme CT, 2001.

See also: The Daguerreian Society - http://www.daguerre.org

58 – *The View from St. Paul's Chapel, 1849* – from the drawing of J.W. Hill, New York Public Library Digital Gallery. See also:

Horan, James D. *Timothy O'Sullivan – America's Forgotten Photographer*, Bonanza Books, A division of Crown Publishers, Inc., 1966, p. 11.

Jenkins, Stephen. *The Greatest Street in the World — The Story of Broadway*, G.P. Putnam's Sons, 1911, p. 81.

59 – Description of Barnum - Daguerreotype of Barnum and General Tom Thumb - Half-plate daguerreotype of Phineas Taylor Barnum & Charles Sherwood Stratton, National Portrait Gallery, Washington, Smithsonian Institution. Taken by Samuel Root, the brother of Marcus Aurelius Root, c. 1850.

59 - Jenny Lind – the public - *The Life of P.T. Barnum*, Written by

Himself, Redfield, New York, 1855, pp. 296-297.

p. 296 - In October, 1849, I first conceived the idea of bringing Jenny Lind to this country. The public is a very strange animal.

p. 297 – I can afford to lose fifty thousand dollars in such an enterprise as bringing to this country, in the zenith of her life and celebrity, the greatest musical wonder in the world.

60 – Mr. Fredericks – Charles DeForest Fredericks.

Newhall, Beaumont. *The Daguerreotype in America*, New York, Dover Publications, 1975, p. 66. Gurney in 1853 his famous pupil Charles DeForest Fredericks, p. 144. See Biography: Born 1823.

Panzer, Mary. *Mathew Brady and the Image of History*, p. 41.

Ryder, James F. *Voigtländer and I – In Pursuit of Shadow Catching, A Story of Fifty-Two Years' Companionship with a Camera*, The Cleveland Publishing Co. 1902, pp. 112-114. I think Brady stands at the head... His name is synonymous with photography. Fredericks too is prominent... Gurney is also... Bogardus, Plum, Lawrence, Root Brothers... Meade Brothers.

Werge, John. *The Evolution of Photography – Personal Reminiscences Extending Over 40 Years*, London: Piper & Carter, 1890, p. 72. Largest Gallery – Messrs. Frederick & Co... Mr. Brady – the corner of Tenth Street, nearly opposite Grace Church.

60 – Description of Mathew B. Brady –

Lester, C. Edwards. "M.B. Brady and the Photographic Art," *The Photographic Art-Journal*, H.H. Snelling, editor, W.B. Smith, publisher, 61 Ann Street, New York, January, 1851, p. 36.

"M.B. Phrenological Character and Biography," American Phrenological Journal (New York) Vol. 27, No. 5 (May 1858) pp. 65-67.

Reprints of the Phrenological article can be found:

Panzer, Mary. *Mathew Brady and the Image of History*, pp. 214-217

60 – Diamond tipped pen – Bard & Brothers, manufacturers of diamond pointed gold pens - *Doggett's Directory*, 1849, p. 37.

61 - Copies of a Superior Daguerreotype of Jenny Lind for Sale - Gurney's Advertisement in *Humphrey's Journal*, January 1851.

Horan, James D. *Mathew Brady – Historian with a Camera*, Crown Publishers, Inc. New York, 1955, p. 20.

61- Mr. Barnum was not exact with you.

Townsend, George Alfred ("Gath"). "Still Taking Pictures - Brady, the Grand Old Man of American Photography," *The World* (New York) April 12, 1891, p. 26.

Reprints of the Townsend Interview can be found:

Panzer, Mary. *Mathew Brady and the Image of History*, Smithsonian Institution Press for the National Portrait Gallery, Washington and London, 1997, pp. 222-225.

The Daguerreian Society - http://www.daguerre.org

"Yes, Mr. Barnum had her in charge and was not exact with me about having her sit. I found, however, an old schoolmate of hers in Sweden who lived in Chicago, and he got me the sitting."

62 – Brady's handwriting - Horan, James D. *Mathew Brady – Historian with a Camera*, Crown Publishers, Inc. New York, 1955, p. xiv.

"I thought it was unusual Brady had not kept a diary, but I was amazed to discover there did not exist among his records a single letter, a note or a receipt bill in his own handwriting."

62 - Sir, I beg leave of communicating these few lines... See reproduction of Mathew B. Brady's letter to Southworth, a rare sample of Brady's handwriting. - Horan, James D. *Timothy O'Sullivan – America's Forgotten Photographer*, Bonanza Books, A division of Crown Publishers, Inc., 1966, p. 9.

62 - When I was but a jewel case manufacturer - Mathew B. Brady (spelled with two t's) - jewel case manf. 187 B'way and 169 Fulton, h. 63 Barclay. *Doggett's Directory*, 1845, p. 48.

Horan, James D. *Mathew Brady – Historian with a Camera*, Crown Publishers, Inc. New York, 1955, p. 9.

Excerpts from Doggett's New York City Directory, 1843-44 and 1844-45, showing Brady listings. Courtesy New York Historical Society.

62 - Working as a clerk at Stewart's – Horan, *Timothy O'Sullivan*, p. 8.

Panzer, *Mathew Brady*, p. XV.

63 - Mirror with a Memory and Samuel F. B. Morse

Professor Silver. *The History of Photography*. Lecture course attended by the author: New York University, Spring, 1989.

Newhall, Beaumont. *The History of Photography*, by The Museum of Modern Art: New York. Little, Brown and Co.: Boston. 1988, pp. 27-28.

63 – William Page - Lester, C. Edwards. "M.B. Brady and the Photographic Art," *The Photographic Art-Journal*, 1851, p. 36.

63 – William... gave me a bundle of his crayons to copy.

Townsend, "Still Taking Pictures - Brady, the Grand Old Man of American Photography," *The World* (New York) April 12, 1891, p. 26.

Reprints of the Townsend Interview can be found:

Panzer, Mary. *Mathew Brady and the Image of History*, Smithsonian Institution Press for the National Portrait Gallery, Washington and London, 1997, pp. 222-225.

The Daguerreian Society - http://www.daguerre.org

64 - "We shared a studio on Chambers Street..."

Horan, James D. *Timothy O'Sullivan – America's Forgotten Photographer*, Bonanza Books, A division of Crown Publishers, Inc., 1966, p. 8.

64 – William studied under Prof. Morse. Townsend, "Still Taking Pictures - Brady," *The World* (New York) April 12, 1891, p. 26.

"Now Page became a pupil of Prof. Morse in New York city, who was then painting portraits at starvation prices in the University rookery on Washington square."

64 – The N.Y. Morning Herald - The New Art - Horan, James D. *Mathew Brady – Historian with a Camera*, Crown Publishers, Inc. New York, 1955, p. 5.

Fig. 5. "One of the first news stories about photography ever published. From the New York *Morning Herald*, September 30, 1839."

64 – Mr. Stetson - *Hand Book of New York City*, Norton, 1859, p. 24.

Charles A. Stetson – "a prince among hotel managers".

65 - "Brady's birthplace is still uncertain…"

Horan, James D. *Timothy O'Sullivan – America's Forgotten Photographer*, Bonanza Books, A division of Crown Publishers, Inc., 1966, p. 8.

Horan, James D. *Mathew Brady – Historian with a Camera*, Crown Publishers, Inc. New York, 1955, p. 4.

66 - Description of Morse's rookery…

Horan, James D. *Mathew Brady – Historian with a Camera*, p. 9.

Townsend, "Still Taking Pictures - Brady, the Grand Old Man of American Photography," *The World* (New York) April 12, 1891, p. 26.

66 – SEE: Portrait of Thomas Addis Emmet by Samuel F. B. Morse.

66 - Obelisk to the memory of Thomas Addis Emmet –

The Archives of Irish America at NYU has adopted as its logo a carving on the Thomas Addis Emmet obelisk in the graveyard of St. Paul's Chapel on Broadway at Fulton Street in New York City. The combination of the American eagle with the Irish harp was the earliest iconography used by the Irish in America to represent themselves. Emmet (1764–1827) was a member of the United Irishmen who emigrated to New York City in 1804, where he quickly became one of the state's outstanding attorneys.

67 - My birthplace was Warren County

- Townsend, "Still Taking Pictures - Brady, the Grand Old Man of American Photography," *The World* (New York) April 12, 1891, p. 26.

67 – John William Draper and Professor Morse

Professor Silver. *The History of Photography.* Lecture course attended by the author: New York University, Spring, 1989.

Newhall, Beaumont. *The History of Photography*, by The Museum of Modern Art: New York. Little, Brown and Co.: Boston. 1988, pp. 27-28.

Townsend, "Still Taking Pictures - Brady, the Grand Old Man of American Photography," *The World* (New York) April 12, 1891, p. 26. "Prof. John W. Draper counseled me."

67 - John William Draper and Professor Morse

Root, Marcus Aurelius. *The Camera and The Pencil, or The Heliographic Art*, Philadelphia: J.B. Lippincott & Co. 1864, pp. 339-345.

- Letter in reply from J.W. Draper, p. 341. About this time, I became acquainted with Professor Morse and we subsequently had a building on the top of the New York University in which we took many portraits. *

This was the first portrait taken from life.

- Letter from Professor Morse, Poughkeepsie, Feb. 10th, 1855, p. 344.

- Invited by Daguerre to see his results in private… his process was then secret. My letter… to my brothers, the editors of the New York Observer, about the first week in March, 1839. The first experiment, crowned with any success, was a view of the Unitarian Church, from the window on the staircase from the third story of the New York University… It was in September, 1839, p. 345.

67 – Jeremiah Gurney – (the same first name as Tim's father.)

The Memoirs of Jeremiah Gurney - The New-York Historical Society. http://jeremiahgurney.blogspot.com/

Author's Note: July 15, 2012 - a most spectacular discovery – quite by accident – curious about Jeremiah Gurney again… when what should my wandering eye should find – The Memoirs of Jeremiah Gurney. Remarkable! This blog is posted by Thomas E. McCarty. "Dear Reader… the journal was recently discovered, found buried under a pile of Gurney materials gifted to the New York Historical Society by the photographer's great-great grandniece, Miss Elizabeth May Possons."

The blog includes the very same 187 Broadway J.C. Booth image that I found in Doggett's Directory 1845. The one I describe at the beginning of Chapter 4. Most Peculiar!

Author's Note: July 16, 2012 - I am still dumb with amazement at the writings of Gurney – what vivid descriptions he gives – "the little silver bell that hung on the door." The visit from Morse that would change his life. This is from the perspective of an 83-year-old man – "my bones are aching with age that only moments earlier were those of a young man's."

67 – The exquisite minuteness of delineation cannot be conceived.

Morse's Letter to the New York *Observer,* April 20, 1839.

Horan, James D. *Timothy O'Sullivan – America's Forgotten Photographer,* Bonanza Books, A division of Crown Publishers, Inc., 1966, p. 7.

Reprints of this article can also be found:

The Daguerreian Society - http://www.daguerre.org

67 - View of the Unitarian Church - Horan, James D. *Timothy O'Sullivan – America's Forgotten Photographer*, p. 7.

67 – He (Morse) could sell indulgences to the Devil.

Priests sold indulgences in lieu of atoning for sins in penance. The abuse of this practice led in part to the protestant reformation.

68 - only a prince or a priest could afford to have their portrait painted.

The Photographic Art Journal – March, 1851, p. 137.

"It (photography) has brought one of the great luxuries and embellishments of life, within the reach of everybody. The time was, when no man but a prince or a priest could own a Bible; now the blessed Word of God may lie upon the table of the poorest laborer. Once artists confined their labors to opulent patrons, and no man could be expected to transmit to his children his own picture, unless by incurring a large expense, now the poorest man can have the portraits of his children taken."

68 - Washington Irving

Townsend, "Still Taking Pictures - Brady, the Grand Old Man of American Photography," *The World* (New York) April 12, 1891, p. 26.

68 – See 1848 daguerreotype portrait of Ichabod Crane – Library of Congress.

69 - "I had great admiration for Poe, and had William Ross Wallace bring him to my studio. Poe rather shrank from coming, as if he thought it was going to cost him something. Many a poet has had that daguerreotype copied by me. I loved the men of achievement..."

Townsend, "Still Taking Pictures - Brady, the Grand Old Man of American Photography," *The World* (New York) April 12, 1891, p. 26.

69 – Killdeer - Cooper, James Fenimore. *The Deerslayer.* New York: Signet Classic, The Penguin Group, 1963.

Chapter 9 – The Photography Workshop

71 – Memoirs of working at The Photography Workshop in 1985.

71 - Crestwood Train Station - Norman Rockwell took up his paint brush and painted the Crestwood Train Station for the cover of the Saturday Evening Post on November 16, 1946.

Chapter 10 – Back to Barnum's

84 – John Greenwood, Jr. - *Barnum – The Yankee Showman and Prince of Humbugs,* Written by Himself, Piper, Stephenson and Spence, London: 1855, p. 165. "Mr. John Greenwood, Jr. who has already been six or seven years in my employ."

84 – John Greenwood - *Doggett's Directory,* 1849, p. 175. Listed as a cashier on Broadway, Corner of Ann – location of Barnum's Museum.

84 – Ad for Barnum's Museum - N.Y. Tribune - February 27, 1849.

85 – James Gordon Bennett – editor of N.Y. Herald

Horan, James D. *Mathew Brady – Historian with a Camera,* Crown Publishers, Inc. New York, 1955, p. 18. Brady sailed for London in July 1851 – traveled with James Gordon Bennett.

Panzer, Mary. *Mathew Brady and the Image of History,* Smithsonian Institution Press, Washington and London, 1997, p. 110. Daguerreotype of James Gordon Bennett circa 1851, Library of Congress.

King's Handbook of New York City. Edited & Published by Moses King, Boston: 1892, p. 569. The Herald founded in 1835 by James Gordon Bennett.

85 – We said nothing about pay. Jenkins, Stephen. *The Greatest Street in the World,* G.P. Putnam's Sons, 1911, p. 198. "Pay!" cried the showman

with a fine display of indignation. "We said nothing about pay. The honor of playing in my band is pay enough for a youngster like you."

- This same story is recounted by Haswell, Charles Haynes. *Reminiscences of New York by an Octogenarian*, Harper & Brothers, New York, 1896, p. 219.

- "Pay!" said Barnum, "I pay you! Nothing of the sort."

86 – Barnum's Office – desk – safe – See Virtual Tour of the American Museum, The Lost Museum, City University of New York, http://www.lostmuseum.cuny.edu/barnum.html

86 – Barnum's ledger book - The Lost Museum, CUNY.

86 - Joice Heth - Barnum, P.T. *The Life of P.T. Barnum*. Written by Himself. New York, 1855, pp. 148-159.

86 - Joice Heth poster - The Lost Museum, CUNY.

87 - Iranistan - Barnum, P.T. *The Life of*, pp. 401-404.

87 - Jenny Lind at (Staten Island). Barnum, P.T. *The Life of*, pp. 306-307.

87 – description of portable writing desk – based on the author's antique collectible from his mother with Machinery Hall on the cover from the World's Columbian Exposition in Chicago 1893.

87 - I wrote articles- Barnum, P.T. *The Life of*, p. 215.

88 – I reluctantly responded. Barnum, P.T. *The Life of*, p. 314.

88 – unbought, unsolicited. Barnum, P.T. *The Life of*, p. 316. Unbought, unsolicited article which appeared in the New York Herald of September 10, 1850 (the day before the fixed concert given by Miss Lind in the United States:) Note the colon closed parentheses smile by Mr. Barnum. Is he winking at the reader in print just like people do today with a smiley face in an e-mail? I am not calling you an idiot :-).

88 – Horace Greeley – editor of N.Y. Tribune

McCabe, James D. *Lights and Shadows of New York Life*, National Publishing Co., 1879, pp. 225-231 vivid profile of Horace Greeley.

Panzer, Mary. *Mathew Brady*, 1997, p. 51 and book cover image of Horace Greeley holding a newspaper on his lap. Daguerreotype by Brady.

88 - "(Barnum) pockets $5,000 net each concert, $15,000 per week… while the papers receive nothing but vituperation." The Lost Museum, City University of New York. Barnum, Jenny Lind, and the Press, New York Herald, October 7, 1850

89 – the club which killed Captain Cook Barnum, P.T. *The Life of*, p. 228.

89 – Nathaniel Parker Willis – Panzer, Mary. *Mathew Brady*, 1997, p. 31.

89 – Charles Edwards Lester – Panzer, Mary. *Mathew Brady*, 1997, p. 32.

89 – Rumors about Brady's failing eyesight.

Horan, James D. *Mathew Brady*, Crown Publishers, Inc. New York, 1955, p. 18. Page 18 – the most famous photographer in America could no longer operate a camera because of his eyes.

Condition of Brady's eyesight broke into print in 1851 in an article in the Photographic Art Journal, Volume 1, 1851, p 136. "Mr. Brady is not operating himself. A failing eyesight precluding the possibility of his using the camera with any certainty. But he is an excellent artist, nevertheless… gathers about him the finest talent to be found."

89 - (Barnum) has made a half million by humbugging the public with a little boy whom he took from Bridgeport. Barnum, P.T. *The Life of*, p. 376.

90 - I was a humbug and a showman. Barnum, P.T. *The Life of*, p. 299.

90 - Jenny Lind Advertisements - New York Herald, September 1850. The Lost Museum, City University of New York.

New York Herald, September 1850

90 – soft soap - the faculty to please and flatter the public so judiciously as not to have them suspect your intention. Barnum, P.T. *The Life of*, p. 286.

91 - Meade Brothers - N.Y. Herald Sept. 14, 1850. Jenny Lind Advertisements. Lind! Lind!! Lind!!! – The Lost Museum, CUNY.

91- Meade Brothers - *Photographic Art-Journal*, H.H. Snelling, editor, W.B. Smith, publisher, 61 Ann Street, New York, May, 1852, pp. 293-294.

92 - Brady's Gallery of Illustrious Americans

Horan, James D. *Mathew Brady – Historian with a Camera*, Crown Publishers, Inc. New York, 1955, p. 14. See Source Notes 40-41.

Copy is in the New York Public Library – extremely rare, Weighs five pounds, etched in gold, Sold for $30, Released in 1850, F.D'Avignon's Press at 323 Broadway, Brady paid $100 for each lithographic stone, Critical success but a financial failure.

92 - Brady's Gallery of Illustrious Americans

Townsend, George Alfred ("Gath"). "Still Taking Pictures - Brady, the Grand Old Man of American Photography," *The World* (New York) April 12, 1891, p. 26.

Reprints of the Townsend Interview can be found:

Panzer, Mary. *Mathew Brady and the Image of History*, Smithsonian Institution Press for the National Portrait Gallery, Washington and London, 1997, pp. 222-225.

The Daguerreian Society - http://www.daguerre.org

"The lithographic stones were engraved by F. Davignon. They cost me $100 for the stones, the book sold for $30."

93 - John Carl Frederick Polycarp von Schneidau

Newhall, Beaumont. *The Daguerreotype in America*, New York, Dover Publications, 1975, p. 59. "Polycarp von Schneidau, the Swede who was the first to make a daguerreotype of Jenny Lind in Brady's gallery, opened in Chicago and became famous for his memorable portrait of Lincoln."

93 – Jenny Lind and von Schneidau

Townsend, "Still Taking Pictures - Brady" *The World* (New York) April 12, 1891, p. 26. "Jenny Lind?" "Yes, Mr. Barnum had her in charge and was not exact with me about having her sit. I found, however, an old schoolmate of hers in Sweden who lived in Chicago, and he got me the sitting. In those days a photographer ran his career upon the celebrities who came to him."

Is Polycarp von Schneidau the "he" that Brady is referring to?

94 – Noon tomorrow (Saturday, September 14, 1850).

The Lost Museum – City University of New York

Mademoiselle Jenny Lind, New York Herald, September 16, 1850

"This newspaper account details the public and commercial frenzy surrounding every movement by the singer Jenny Lind during her stay in New York City. Lind sat for a daguerreotype portrait (located in this archive) by the famed photographer Mathew Brady, whose studio was located on Broadway a few doors away from the American Museum."

FINAL NOTE:

To see complete listing of End Notes to Chapters 11 – 38,
please visit: www.timothyhosullivan.com

I plan to collect all my research notes over the years into a book titled:
Tim Journal – A Fact-Checkers guide to Writing Tim
Please visit: www.timjournal.com

I also plan to write and publish: Tim - Book II – The Pathfinder
For updates, please visit: www.danielsheridan.com

Tim

ABOUT THE AUTHOR

Daniel A. Sheridan was born in New York City in 1965. He grew up in a little town called Crestwood, in Yonkers, N.Y., and worked as a darkroom technician at The Photography Workshop while studying photojournalism and the history of photography at New York University. In 1990, he moved to Boston with his brother Bill to play drums in a band called The Immigrants. He worked as a darkroom technician developing black & white film until the age of digital cameras and pixels, and later was the editor and photographer at Low-RANGE® magazine.

Made in the USA
Las Vegas, NV
05 July 2023

74258425R00173